LUCILLA

HEADSTRONG, TEMPESTUOUS DAUGHTER OF THE EMPEROR TIBERIUS

LUCILLA

A PRINCESS FORCED INTO A LOVELESS MARRIAGE WITH THE KING OF THE ARMENIANS

LUCILLA

THE HUMAN SACRIFICE OFFERED UP TO SAVE HER BROTHER'S KINGDOM

LUCILLA

THE CATALYST IN THE CONFLICT BETWEEN THE TWO MIGHTIEST CIVILIZATIONS OF EARLY CHRISTIAN TIMES

The Fall of the Roman Empire is a towering novel of the surging conflicts, the immortal loves and the rending hatreds that engraved themselves onto the great cornerstone of History.

SAMUEL BRONSTON'S

THE FALL OF
THE ROMAN EMPIRE

by Harry Whittington

AN ORIGINAL GOLD MEDAL NOVEL

GOLD MEDAL BOOKS

FAWCETT PUBLICATIONS, INC., GREENWICH, CONN.
MEMBER OF AMERICAN BOOK PUBLISHERS COUNCIL, INC.

THE FALL OF
THE ROMAN EMPIRE

BOOK ONE

I

FROM THE HIGH GROUND where the four men stood they could see below them in the pink flush of false dawn the entire sleeping Roman encampment. In fading darkness, precise and measured movements of horse and foot pickets at the gates, and sentinels walking guard on earth mounds just inside the deep ditch entirely enclosing the *castra*, gave the silence and stillness a vaguely disturbing unreality.

Marcus closed his eyes tightly a moment, drawing the back of his hand across them. Perhaps it was his own inner sense of mortal weariness—he had been seventeen years at war and was just ending his eighth winter campaign against the Quadi and Marcomanni, drawn north to the Danube, far from Rome and warm Latium plains—but he was always cold and the very sight of the inexhaustible engineering feats of his soldiers made him more tired than ever. Down there, dimly seen through fog mists drifting across the marshes from the river, the camp was an area of perfect geometric design, as was every Roman encampment whether thrown up for a night-stop or laid down as base of a long siege. Four gates on exact compass points, north, east, south and west, the *via principalis* bisecting the camp in a straight line from north gate to south, the praetorium set in its center, quaestorium behind it, troops quartered on both sides, and the tents of the *praefecti* and *tribuni* in ordered rows before it, between the *via principalis* and the east gate. His men drew the terrible energy for these tasks, these forced marches with full packs, the erecting of precise encampments at the end of every march and sometimes after distant battles—they got such energy from some well no longer open to him.

I'm tired, he thought, tired until the fact of living asks more than I can give any longer. He leaned slightly, without meaning to, against Timonides who stood immediately behind him, almost gray in the wan light but braced strong, and while supporting his emperor, pretending he was able to hold himself erect. Good Timonides, Marcus thought, slender, gray, forty, a slave, my friend and counsellor and my silent support, alone privy to the terrible, final secret that has to be kept from the army and the world as long as possible. Good Timonides.

Before them, the blind man at the altar spoke suddenly, or perhaps only grunted as he slit the sacrificial dove with honed knife from craw to tail, its abdomen falling open, blood spurting. The bird fluttered once, its body rent apart under blind Cleander's bloody hands.

Marcus winced watching the big hands digging into the pigeon's abdomen, entrails red and gray, spilling out around those probing fingers. A tall, slender man, simply dressed in girdled tunic, strapped sandals, modestly groomed with no distinguishing marks in dress or ornament to name him Emperor; even the paludamentum, official imperial military cloak of the general, was worn against the cold and not as symbol of authority. He no longer trusted these old rites of augury, though he was scrupulous in his observance of the official Roman ceremonies and sacrifices. Stoicism had guided his personal life since he'd embraced the philosophy when he was a boy twelve years old. But Stoicism didn't exclude the practice of ordinary religious rites, even encouraged it, and as dictator, he paid the same lip service to the official religion that his people did, though he knew the state religion no longer had any practical influence upon the living. However, the augurs, along with the auspices, had believed since antiquity that the interpretation of omens, prophecy of coming events, and advice from the gods could be determined through the sacrificial *hostia* killed on these altars, and he consulted augury even when he'd lost all faith in its value.

Cleander was pretentiously aware of the awful significance of this moment and in his white robes moved unhurriedly, letting the silence stretch and deepen.

Cleander was a handsome man in his early forties, temples gray-struck, eyes empty, colorless. At Cleander's side hovered the huge, hulking Lentulus who guided the blind man and acted as his eyes.

Lentulus whispered into Cleander's ear, but none of the other three men spoke.

Marcus stared at the slain bird, feeling a spasm of sickness, a kind of omen-reading of his own. Marcus Aurelius was emperor, soldier, but first of all he was a contemplative, meditative philosopher. He could not deny seeing some terrible symbolism in the flayed belly of the dove, a symbol, a portent, so violent that he pushed it from his mind, shivering.

Strangely, Cleander found nothing fearful in the bird's entrails. His voice was cheerful, if portentous, "My lord Caesar, the omens are good—"

Aurelius nodded, not because he believed the blind augur, but because it did not matter what Cleander said. The sacrifice was over and he had paid his homage to another custom that had been part of Roman civilization for twelve centuries.

He straightened, feeling Timonides' gentle fingers at his elbow when Cleander and Lentulus bowed, the huge guide leading the blind man away in the lifting dawn.

Aurelius acknowledged salutes of the departing men without really moving his eyes from the encampment below, taking shape as daylight filtered away night mists and ground fog.

Surely a thing of precise beauty, from measured depth of trenches, to protective walls and palisades thrown up from those ditches, soldiers' quarters, drifting breakfast fires. There was a first stirring of life as the encampment came awake, men rousing in ordered quiet and discipline, further testimony to the fantastic energies and organization of Rome.

Marcus Aurelius pulled his stricken gaze from the slain dove to the orange oval of the sun slanted on the horizon. He sighed deeply, as if relieved that another night had ended, and he was still around, walking on the earth.

His voice was low, touched with the meditative irony that was part of him by now. "When I was a child, Timonides, I had a secret terror. Sometimes when I'm tired like this, I think I'm still a child, and the old childish fear is still with me. One of the childish things I didn't put away when I donned the *toga virilis,* eh, Timonides?"

"You have nothing to fear—in this world, or the next, Caesar," said the quiet voice of the Greek from close behind him.

"Haven't I? As a child I used to be afraid the time would come when the night wouldn't end—and we would live out our lives like phantoms in total darkness. . . . It was a small fear then."

Timonides stirred uneasily. "And yet, my lord Caesar, the sun always rises—and will always rise."

Marcus could not shake the mood of depression, even when he taunted himself with ironic laughter. "Because a thing has happened many times, Timonides, does not mean it must happen again. May there not be a day when the sun does not rise?"

Timonides did not speak, watching Aurelius with concern in his eyes. Those eyes had seen the glories of Greece, the wisdom of Plato, Aristotle, as well as misery and suffering and terror. He wasn't unlike thousands of other Greek slaves of greater learning, intellect than their Roman masters, but he had long ago put aside anything except admiration and devoted love for the great and good man beside him on this quiet hill.

Aurelius sighed. "It's been said that more people die at this moment of dawn than at any other time—when night is about to give way to day."

He stood, head tilted as if listening to something Timonides could not fathom, as if hearing it and drawn by it.

"Hear it, Timonides? The night whispers, 'Come away with me. . . . Sleep. . . . Sleep forever. . . . What does this new day have for you? What will you see in it that you haven't seen a hundred times before?"

Timonides stirred, troubled. He spoke anxiously, as if wheedling with Marcus to look forward with him. "The new day has life, warmth, color, people."

Marcus Aurelius didn't answer and Timonides let his voice fade away.

No one else saw how tired and ill Caesar was because he would not let them see, but he couldn't hide it from his closest friend, his slave. Timonides watched Marcus apprehensively, then turned and stared at the sun as if willing it higher into the sky, redder, hotter, brighter.

He lifted his arm, pointing.

"My lord Caesar, the sun," he said.

"Yes," Marcus said without inflection. "The sun. Another sun."

Timonides shivered, telling himself it was caused by the last of the night chill. The camp was roused, sounds coming up to them as if from the throat of a mindless monster.

Below the hill the river stretched, dark and wide, filled with rocks and shadows. Timonides saw Marcus was concentrating on something in the pink-hazed distance, and the Greek squinted, following the direction of Caesar's gaze.

He saw a tiny figure on horseback racing along a narrow roadway toward them.

Timonides glanced quickly at Aurelius' gray face, and found him smiling faintly, as if he recognized the rider at that impossible distance. Timonides stood motionless in the shadows waiting beside Caesar, and knew Aurelius didn't really know the man on that distant road, he only hoped he did.

The sun was beginning to lose its first flush from the effort of scaling the walls of the earth and was starting its yellowish climb across the sky as the encampment came into Livius' sight, ahead.

The young officer put his heels into his horse's flanks, rousing him to full gallop, vibration and thunder of clopping hooves rising from the thick surface of the spacious Roman road, lance straight and boulder solid, like everything his people constructed, built to endure—a fine highway through unbelievable wilderness.

He felt the bite of wind, heard the first distant sounds of the Roman *castra* on the leveled field ahead, sprawling and huge, like a city erected to last longer than the forest it was hacked from. His head tilted, a wind-roughened, roughly handsome face, a tribune in his late twenties who had spent the last eleven years of life in open fields of battle. Even though he was road-weary, exhausted by the long night ride, his face showed pride at the sight of the camp of the Northern Army. His army. His horse was lathered, but he booted him again, urging him toward the *porta praetoria,* the east gate of the encampment.

Sentinels sprang to life and horse pickets alerted as Livius thundered into view.

Livius pulled up, horse quivering, shouted a question. A sentinel in tunic, sagum, tufted metal helmet, and thick sandals, lifted his arm, pointing toward the hill where a temporary altar had been erected.

Livius nodded, pulled his horse around, set the animal in a gallop up the rocky slope.

Near the crest of the hill, the exhausted horse faltered.

Livius swung from the saddle, tethered the animal and strode the rest of the way upward on foot.

Climbing, Livius glanced across his shoulder. Blood pounded in his veins and his heart raced. Pride. Power. That was what he saw laid out below him. Up here he could see why no forces on earth could stand against those legions.

"Livius—"

Livius swung around, suddenly tired. It had been a long, endless night.

Timonides came hurriedly downslope toward him. Livius scanned the Greek's face as if trying to read there some news of Caesar's condition. Timonides was sensitive to every fiber of his master's being, and his face was incapable of dissembling, and there had been whispers about Caesar's health. The gods knew there had been whispers.

Timonides never changed. It seemed to Livius that he looked as he had the first time he ever saw him, years ago at a summer home of Marcus Aurelius Antoninus, outside Rome. How long ago that had been—another world—and only Timonides looked the same.

Livius showed his deep pleasure and affection in his breathless voice and laughter. "Timonides—"

They held each other's shoulders a moment in warm silence. Timonides' eyes were suspiciously red-rimmed, but Livius smiled, reminding himself that Timonides cried at pantomimes. He glanced past the Greek anxiously. "How is Caesar?"

Timonides hesitated and his dark face clouded. "We must remember, my dear Livius, our emperor has been at the wars for seventeen years, and—"

"Yes, I have!" Marcus' voice cut across Timonides', silencing him. "There is a joke among the soldiers about Timonides—"

Livius and Timonides turned as the emperor came slowly downslope to them. Timonides' face was sheepish.

Aurelius hesitated, standing a moment in shadows, as if reluctant to let the young tribune see the secrets that must be revealed in his tired face.

Half-concealed in shadow, Aurelius smiled gently and peered at Livius as if trying to be sure the young officer was well and healthy. His agonized eyes softened, his tired face glowed with warmth and love for the man who had been like his own son.

Aurelius said, taunting Timonides but watching Livius' face, "The soldiers say, 'Ask Timonides what day it is and he will lecture you on the history of the calendar!'"

Livius laughed and strode forward to Aurelius. The emperor pulled him close, embracing him as a father would his son after a long absence.

Livius anxiously studied Caesar's face, trying to hide his concern beneath a twisted smile.

"You *are* well, my lord Caesar?" He held the smile, but scrutinized the tired face more closely. He sighed because he was somewhat reassured. After all, no man standing on his feet could be as ill as whispers and rumors had Caesar. He gestured behind him toward the encampment on the plain. "It seemed to me every governor, every king in the whole empire is down there in that camp today."

Aurelius nodded, confirming it. "I asked them to come here. Consuls, princes, kings, governors, all the leaders of Rome."

Livius frowned, waiting for some word of explanation, but none came. Instead, the emperor seemed to dismiss these leaders from his thoughts and instead stared at the young tribune with a deep, brooding concentration.

His voice showed a terrible inner exhaustion that frightened Livius, made him tense, made him forget his own saddle-weariness, reject it as unworthy beside the fatigue of his Caesar.

"I have asked my son to come, too."

Livius' face showed his pleasure.

"I'll be glad to see Commodus again, Caesar."

Aurelius' voice showed traces of gentle irony. "Yes. Your great friend Commodus." He sighed as if trailing his thoughts on some bitter tangent, then shrugged and spoke quickly. "Tell me about your trip, Livius. Where have you been? What have you learned?"

"I've been—as you asked—everywhere where Rome is, my lord Caesar. And places where Rome has not yet reached." He exhaled heavily, thinking. "I learned one thing I first knew the day I met you. You're a wise man, and you truly can smell danger ahead of time."

Aurelius seemed to falter. Timonides stepped close behind him. Aurelius waved his hand tiredly, "Go on, Livius."

"I learned that the danger is as you said, greater than I thought—than any of the rest of us believed. In the East the

Persians are growing in strength. They wait for us to show just one moment of weakness. In the North the Germanic tribes seem worse because they have no—no civilization. They live like animals, the Herminones, the Herudi, Suevi, the Vandals,—like animals. Animals poised to pounce on our jugular." He scowled and gestured toward the enemy encampment far below them. "There are the Marcomanni on our frontiers. They don't even know what they want, except to kill and pillage. They kill every living thing because that's all they know. What they can't eat, they burn. And no one knows how many of these tribes there are beyond the Danube and the Oder. It is like a nightmare where you kill them, and you keep killing them, and there are always new ones leaping to take their place, always less human, more like animals than the ones you've killed."

Aurelius shrugged his knee-length cloak higher on his left shoulder, a movement to conceal the faint shudder that passed through him. He spoke softly, "We *are* in danger, Livius. . . . I wanted you to see—for yourself. . . . It was important to me that you believe that danger."

Livius straightened. His voice was eager, assured, because no matter what he saw, he had grown up reading of the legends of Roman strength and invincibility, spreading, conquering, civilizing the whole world, even when it was against their will. "We have never been stronger—"

"Isn't that always the moment of greatest danger?"

Livius' strong young voice came up heavy and confident from his thick chest, resonant in the morning stillness. "We can gather the largest army Rome has ever known. And quickly. We have always had a theoretic strength of six thousand men in every legion, let us fill them out, all of them, quickly. We can crush these barbarians before they move any deeper inside our lands. Then we must turn East and smash out at the Persians before they build any more strength and wealth, or make new allies—"

Aurelius cut him short with a weary movement of his hand.

He spoke gently. "That is an old lesson you learned, Livius. The story of Rome. Nine hundred years of glory. Nine hundred years of war. War—and then more war." His voice lifted slightly as Livius started to protest. "We are now in the tenth century of Rome's existence, Livius." His voice sagged, and his eyes shadowed, for that fleeting moment revealing the depth of his old fears. "Is this all we have learned in a thousand years of growing and building? Must we smash every man who raises his hand against us, or believes in some credo that we hold in error? Listen to me, Livius, you are a soldier and you are young and you were suckled on the milk of Rome's strength and power, but can't you see something else? Can't you see we can't go on like this?"

"Must we not protect ourselves?"

"Protect ourselves. Impose our will on others. Crush them under our heel—and protect ourselves. That is the history of our past, Livius. Is it to be our future? Can't we change?"

"We are in grave danger, my lord Caesar."

"Yes. But, Livius, might not part of that danger come from our own suspicion of others, our hatred of anyone we do not know, our refusal to understand them, or to try to live in peace with them?"

"In peace—with the barbarian?"

"Yes. Even with him, Livius. We must find new ways—peaceful ways—before the empire is bled white. We must make allies of those you call barbarians. It is not only for them, Livius, but for us. One truth I've learned: no nation can survive if it dares keep more than a hundredth part of its people under arms or on public charity. Think, Livius, of Rome—a million people, half of them slaves, most of the rest on public charity. An army, swollen, spread across the face of the earth, and must be enlarged. . . . It is not news to you that I hate war, detest it as a disgrace and calamity of human nature, but to defend my country, I—have taken up arms—"

"Eight terrible winters in this terrible north country," Timonides said.

Aurelius gave his slave a brief glance, a wry smile.

He spoke, watching Livius tiredly, sadly. "Until we can learn peaceful ways, I must fight them. . . ." He shook his head, smiling crookedly, and corrected himself. "You must fight them. I am tired, Livius. Too tired. I called you back to take command of your beloved Northern Army."

Livius felt the crawling tingling hackles of pride and heated excitement course through him.

Aurelius stared downslope toward the road leading into the *porta praetoria*, the main gate at the encampment. Sounds thundered upward and the sun sparkled brilliantly on ban-

ners and insignia of chariots roaring along the great highway.

Aurelius stretched out his arm, pointing toward the color
and loud pageantry below them.

He spoke softly. "Look. There it is, Livius, your Roman
empire—alive before you."

Roman leaders from every partition of the empire were
gathering at Vindobona for council with Caesar. Governors,
princes, kings, consuls, their aides, guards, followers, trumpeters, and convoys assembled alongside their fantastically
emblazoned chariots.

As the sun soared, the procession formed along the heat-
struck highway.

Metal-rimmed wheels ignited sparks, striking rocks as
chariots jockeyed into place, the light bodies bouncing. Only
the shafts, axles and bases of these chariots had any weight
or solidity. The carriages themselves were made increasingly
lighter, flimsier for greater speed behind racing Gallic horses
or swift Arabian steeds. They offered little protection for
driver or passenger and were suicide carts at high speeds.

Brightly clad drivers tightened reins about their waists,
holding the gaily plumed horses under control as magistrates
in finest silks were helped aboard. Each nation or province
represented offered exotic dress, design and insignia, their
banners flicking pinwheels of color in the wind.

Escorts assembled beside each dignitary in his carriage,
and mounted, scarlet-clad lictors charged in ahead of every
colorful unit. These lictors were Roman officers whose ordinary duty was apprehension and punishment of criminals,
but on state days such as these, a lictor's duty was to bear
the fasces—the bundle of rods secured around an axe with
its blade projecting and borne before Roman magistrates as
a badge of authority—as insignia of his office.

On these state occasions, a lictor's duty was to attend the
chief magistrate when he appeared in public, to clear the
way for him and to cause due respect to be paid to him.
This, the scarlet clad young officers did now, riding at full
gallop into the *porta praetoria*, proclaiming in unison the
name of their convoyed dignitary:

"Helvius Pertinax. Governor of Britannia!"

Pertinax was a dignified, impassive man, a former senator
who would return to the senate, old in the ways of ceremony.

He stood rigid, profile straight, coin sharp as his chariot raced past.

The next group of lictors, shouting as one voice, galloped forward: "Ulpius Marcellus, Governor of Syria!" and in a second chariot in his party: "Virgilianus, Proconsul of Egypt."

The lictors accompanying the Egyptian proconsul had blades showing in their fasces because this meeting was held outside Rome. Within Rome's walls, a consul was prohibited from displaying the axe blade in his symbolic fasces.

Virgilianus was a heavy-set, powerful, grizzled man in late middle age. His eyes were fixed on a vague distance and his mind seemed elsewhere in this thunder of dust and confusion.

More lictors raced forward in perfect lines, in unison, calling: "Getulus, King of Mauritania! Costobacus, King of Roxolani! Guntheris, King of the Frisians!"

One following another in a dazzling, opulent procession of emblazoned chariots: the Roman governors of the two Dacias, Greece, Cilicia, Judea, Arabia, Africa, Numidia. Behind them, more exotic with the strange dyes and hues of the orient, with their odd eastern retinues, came kings of Petra, Tyras, Olbia, Onne. Following rode the local magistrates from the four provinces of Gaul: Belgica, Aquitania, Narbonensis, Lugdunensis. All moved forward, a seething mass of nobility and entourages until the whole encampment became a boiling mass of loud excitement and clash of color, above it all a bright hazing of dust, glinting like gems in the sun.

There was a sudden hush, followed by a loud stir and then a craning forward by even the most sophisticated when the Armenian escort reached the main gate. In that blaze of unbridled color and lavish display, the entourage of the King of Armenia stood out dazzlingly, breathlessly ornate with oriental pomp unmatched anywhere else.

It was like a pageant unto itself, as if there were no other parades gathered ahead of it or behind it: a procession of Armenian spearmen, swordsmen, archers, all mounted, galloped full speed through the gate. Behind them with a terrible dignity and cold silence came the Armenian palace guard, moving as one man, one sound.

Following the palace guard, twenty-four Roman lictors, bearing the imperial insignia to proclaim the presence of a member of the imperial family, called aloud as one great chant: "Sohamus, King of Armenia!"

A statically charged thrill of excitement rolled out a carpet of awed silence as Sohamus rode into sight. His royal chariot was bejeweled, blindingly flashing, catching every lance of light as it moved. Youthful, dark, he stood erect, aloof and regal. A handsome man, he was made more striking by his oriental dignity.

The silence stretched out, following Sohamus as he moved into the encampment.

At the gate, twenty-four lictors thundered forward, shouting: "Lucilla, daughter of the emperor Marcus Aurelius!"

Heads pivoted, swinging back to catch sight of the legendary loveliness.

Her beauty was the kind that made men ache to behold it, the fire and excitement from her mother, with a depth of character and inner self-respect Faustina had never known in her unhappy life. Lucilla had inherited her father's gentle sense of dignity. She stood proud and regal in her ivory chariot which bore the laurels of the imperial family.

Lucilla's dark radiance was enhanced by the wisdom and intelligence glowing in almond-slanted eyes. One almost felt, looking at her, that he saw her not only as the daughter of an emperor, but of a philosopher.

Furthermore, not a soldier or a magistrate beholding her failed to see she wore both her overpowering beauty and great rank with a simple and natural grace. Even held aloof from them, she was untouchable, yet not unreachable, for she was unaffected and easy, making no effort to prove she was the daughter of an emperor. Her soft smile showed she saw no reason for proving anything.

Only the most sensitive man could see the deep well of unhappiness inside her, the faint shadows across her eyes, the barest look of bleakness in her smile, an old memory that never set her free.

Few saw this—the whole world professed to see her mother in her—the faithless Faustina. And the gossips waited for that moment when they would be proved right, the night when Lucilla, like Faustina, would take her first of innumerable lovers to quench the deep, tormented feelings of sensual need she must have inherited in her mother's blood and from the milk of her mother's breasts.

The Roman world stared at Lucilla's unbelievable beauty,

and doubted her purity, and whispered behind their hands of Faustina—taken in *flagrante delicto*—in its precise and literal meaning: in the very act, while the crime is blazing! The mother would live again in the daughter, and they waited, breathless, drooling, expectant.

From the altar ledge above the encampment, Aurelius, Livius and Timonides watched Lucilla's ivory chariot bound through the gate into the *castra*.

Aurelius' eyes forgot their pain, softened. He whispered her name.

Livius heard the whisper, did not pull his gaze from the ornamented chariot, the slender form within it, but he heard with a strange exultancy the pride and devotion in the very manner Aurelius spoke his daughter's name. Only a father can put quite that inflection in his voice when he speaks of his daughter; it is different from a lover's whisper, more than a lover, unbelieving, awed, full of memories, full of hope, with all the tenderness and love that only a father can know or express—more than a lover, different.

"Lucilla." Livius straightened, aware that he, too, had spoken her name, and put more in the one word than he would care to have known. Almost as if drawn downslope, he took a step forward but Timonides touched his arm, stopping him with a smile.

Timonides spoke in a low tone. "Later."

Unwillingly, Livius halted.

Beside him, Aurelius pulled his gaze away from Lucilla, glanced at Livius. Realizing that the young tribune was anxious to return downslope, that his gaze returned involuntarily to the lovely black-haired girl in the ivory chariot, Caesar, too, touched Livius' arm, restraining him. "Wait, Livius, stay at my side. I haven't told you yet—not all of it —not the real reason why I called you back to me." He sighed, and a shadow moved across his tired eyes. "A great destiny awaits you, Livius. A great destiny."

II

THE ASSEMBLAGE fell silent when Aurelius walked slowly from the shadows at the upper area of the praetorium. For some moments he stood before them, paludamentum draped across his left shoulder, his gaze moving over them in a way that was almost paternal, with love and deep understanding for even the most obstreperous among them.

When there was scarcely a sound along the intersecting camp streets, Aurelius began to speak, quietly, but with the training of an orator that carried his voice easily to the most distant auditor.

"Governors, consuls, princes. You have come from the deserts of Egypt and the mountains of Armenia, from the forests of Gaul and the prairies of Spain. You do not resemble each other, nor do you wear the same clothes, nor do you sing the same songs, nor worship the same gods. Yet like a mighty tree which has green leaves and black roots, you are a part of the great one-ness which is the Roman empire. Look about you! See for yourselves the greatness of our empire!"

A profound reaction of undeniable thrill spread through the assemblage. The upturned faces moved again to the lone man on the rostrum before them, expectantly waiting.

Before Aurelius began to speak, Livius moved through the crowd, the rows of chariots, the staffs and pennants, the soldiers and entourages, seeking Lucilla.

As Aurelius paused, Livius found her. She stood alone in her ivory chariot, full mouth parted, eyes fixed in rapt attention upon her father before and above her.

Something unexplained, unexplainable, caused Lucilla to glance around, her gaze striking at once against Livius'.

For a moment their eyes clung to each other, as if in embrace, and everyone else, everything else was blotted out for them.

Livius found himself filled suddenly with old memories, with hurt and pleasure in them, the days when Lucilla was a young girl, that summer when she was twelve. He still re-

20

called the sense of dizziness that his love for her caused him. He had felt that same quality of confusion and faintness only once before, standing alone, unbalanced on the very brink of the Tarpeian Rock.

And now he felt himself losing his balance again. He felt himself tottering, ready to plunge helplessly, falling into the depths of those slanted eyes, lost, forever lost, and only there able to find himself.

The silence deepened and the emperor's voice struck across it, authority and power in its quiet depth:

"Two centuries ago the Gauls were our fiercest enemies. Now they have become our most faithful friends. Now in the whole world there are left only two small frontiers which are still hostile to us."

He raised his right arm, pointing toward the enemy encampment in the distance.

"One here to the North, marked by this battlefield which separates us from those barbarians from beyond the Danube, known as the Marcomanni. The other frontier is in the East, where Persia rules. Only on these borders do our trenches, walls, palisades, forts remain. Only here is hatred. They come to us with blood and fire." A shadow crossed his face, sadness showed in the quality of his lowered tone. "We must answer with our swords.

"But these are not the frontiers Rome wants! Rome needs and wants—*human frontiers*.

"Governors, princes, consuls." He moved his saddened gaze across them. "We have had to fight long wars. We know the burden on you in taxes, the tribute in men for our auxiliaries. The burden has been great, but we come now to the end of that long road."

He paused, hearing the puzzled gasp as if from one man. These leaders were hearing something they couldn't even believe.

His voice rose suddenly. "Golden centuries of peace await us—lie ahead of us. My dream—" he gestured before him, swinging his arm as if in benediction across their upturned heads. "There—within our reach—the *Pax Romana*. The Roman peace our forefathers dreamed about! Well, it can come true! In your own lifetime! Wherever you live or whatever your skin or the clothes you cover yourselves with— when the peace comes, it will bring to you the greatest franchise on this earth today—the supreme right of Roman citizenship."

There was no applause, no movement, only a profound hush as the chief magistrates stood incredulous, stunned at the Caesar's radical proposals.

His voice took new vigor, lashing at them, trying to awaken them to their new opportunity and new responsibilities.

"No longer provinces or colonies. Do you understand? But Rome. Rome everywhere. A family of equal nations."

The hush lasted the space of one half a breath and then a thunderous roar of acclaim washed across the assemblage like a cloudburst inundating a dry riverbed. Above all else this equality was desired in the least provinces, but it was a dream nobody hoped to see come true, or even expected to hear publicly discussed by the lord Caesar himself.

Lucilla, under the static rage of excitement, pulled her gaze from Livius and stared upward at her father. Her upslanted eyes shone with love and pride as she listened.

Suddenly Lucilla's smile died, and her face went gray. Sensitive to every change in her father, she saw him stagger up there on that rostrum at the very moment the acclaim was at crest. He looked as if some unseen fist had struck him in the chest and he wavered under the impact. His handsome face tightened, his anguished eyes closed against the unbearable agony and tension in his chest.

She swallowed back the cry, and the ache in her throat. Her father was not only the greatest emperor, he was a soldier. She felt almost no one else saw the way he was agonized. He stepped backward into shadows, remained there as the cheers and applause rose and ebbed in waves.

When he emerged from the shadows, his fine face was pale, but there was no trace of the onset of sudden agony.

The roar of the crowd rose. Aurelius lifted his arms and spoke above the roaring as the sound abated: "May the gods hasten that day of peace!"

Lucilla saw her father was desperately tired, with a fatigue that overwhelmed him, made it almost impossible for him to speak at all, and she understood how true it was that he had given his life for their country—this great, good man.

Aurelius spoke with difficulty, "I—have called you together here—there is an important decision—we must make together—soon—"

Too exhausted to continue, he straightened, standing tall

and alone for a moment with the blazing sun and the gazes
of the Roman world relentlessly upon him. Then he stepped
back, gesturing to show that his discourse was ended.

He did not remain on the rostrum another moment. As
the assemblage realized that he was gone, it roused itself
from stunned silence, once more breaking into earth-rattling
cries of acclaim.

Timonides moved quickly to Caesar's side, touched his
arm in a hidden gesture that supported the tired dictator,
made it possible for him to remain erect another few moments. At that instant, Livius shoved his way through the
crowd to the emperor's side.

Aurelius whispered to Timonides, "Help me—into my
quarters."

Timonides nodded, supporting the emperor with his hand
under his arm, unseen by the crowd. Aurelius paused, looking at Livius with a smile. "Don't look like that, Livius.
You'll cause a panic. Don't stand staring. And find Lucilla
for me."

Livius smiled, nodding. Aurelius spoke urgently, his hand
pressing against his chest under concealing folds of the
paludamentum, "Bring her to me."

Leaning heavily on Timonides, Aurelius moved away toward his quarters inside the praetorium.

Livius watched him for one moment, the sound of cheering multitudes washing across him. A sudden excitement
built, taking over inside him. He moved into the crowd,
pushing his way through in a crooked path that led straight
toward the place where he had last seen Lucilla.

He heard uneasy whispers rocking ahead of him in the
mob, and the assemblage quieted slowly, waiting, held im-
mobile by respect for their emperor and also by fears for
which they had no name.

Lucilla stepped from her chariot, at once excited at seeing
Livius Gaius Metellus again after such a long lonely time,
and troubled by the gray agony she read in her father's
stricken face. She pushed her way through the assemblage,
going toward the rostrum and the praetorium beyond.

She moved quickly, almost as if dancing to some unheard
music, lithely slicing a way for herself through the elated,
incredulous gathering. Whispers battered against her: the
emperor's abruptly terminating his address; his promise of

Roman citizenship for all. A dream coming true. Romans, all. All Romans. Citizens.

Dignitaries who saw Lucilla approach, stepped quickly aside, bowing with deep respect, making a path for the incredibly lovely daughter of the good emperor, the greatest of all. For all the years of Marcus' rule the good of the Roman people was the paramount concern of Roman government—a fact true of no other moment in the unbelievable era of one thousand years of rulers. Their devotion for the Caesar included his daughter.

Suddenly, from the sun-catching, color drenched, bejeweled chariot of the Armenian ruler, Sohamus leaped down.

He forgot to be a solemn oriental dignitary. He was a young man, and he smiled, his eyes growing drunk on Lucilla. He stepped directly and deliberately in her path.

Lucilla was forced to stop. She controlled her impatience only with an effort. Her father was a mild man who leashed his passions, lived on reason, but in moments like these, she saw how much like Faustina she was, this fiery temper. She bit her lip, her eyes clouding.

She forced herself to be most patient because of this abrupt and hateful memory of her mother.

Sohamus bowed, greeting her with elaborate oriental *salaam*. "My lady—"

"My lord King Sohamus." Lucilla forced her pleasantest smile. "You must forgive me. Although you've chosen to stop me publicly like this, surely you will understand that I have only just arrived. I haven't yet seen my father. Please, Sohamus, would you consider it a great insult to your national pride if we talked—later—some other time?"

He spoke as pleasantly, his white teeth glittering in his dark face as his smile matched hers. His black eyes moved over her body. "As a king—I would consider it an act of war." He bowed. "But with you, it's not a matter of national pride—I am a man—and as a man, I'd be deeply disappointed."

Lucilla felt that hated temper flare, and as her father would have counseled her, forced herself to speak mildly, resigned, even if no longer able to go on smiling. "Let us talk then." She stood slightly straighter, as if reminding him she was acting only as a member of Rome's imperial family. "Rome cannot afford to offend an oriental king—"

"Oh, stop, Lucilla. Must you be a princess and I a king?"

"What else?"

"—And Armenia is not really oriental." He stiffened slightly.

"And yet it isn't really Roman, is it, Sohamus? Of course, it is because you are so undecided that you are so important to us."

Sohamus lowered his voice, spoke softly, holding her gaze. "It would be so simple to make its king decide, Lucilla." He was a young boy again now, unable to conceal his eagerness. "You know that's why I've come to Rome so often—"

"Didn't my brother always entertain you?" Lucilla said, refusing to be led any further into this conversation. "The Prince Commodus is very good at entertaining visiting—"

"Gladiators do not interest me much," Sohamus said. His voice lifted, quickening as he saw she'd bowed, ready to move past him. "So that there can be no mistaking my intentions, Lucilla, I've brought gifts. Not for your father. Not this time. But for you. And so the whole world will know how I feel, I present them to you. Now. Openly."

Lucilla caught her breath.

Before she could move, Sohamus turned slightly, gestured.

Two dazzlingly beautiful young Armenian slave girls, translucent gowns in fragile folds along their ebony bodies, ornamented with gold and jewels, stepped forward.

Lucilla scrutinized the lovely young slave girls politely, neither accepting nor rejecting the young king's gift.

She smiled in a twisted way, and spoke drily. "I think the whole world will wonder," she gestured toward the lovely girls, "with Armenia so rich in beauty—why you come to Rome so often."

Sohamus spoke in a low tone. "Lucilla. It's not easy for a king—to make gestures—in public—like this."

Lucilla bit her lip, troubled. "I know—I know."

She felt the eyes of the world leaders trained on them, the probing gazes, the leers, the curious, the knowing who knew nothing, and then with a sense of relief saw Livius hurrying towards her.

Deeply relieved, she touched the young king's hand, and spoke gently. "I am deeply grateful for your gift. . . . Now . . . will you forgive me?"

She saw the flash of rage in Sohamus' black eyes, but she had a temper of her own and she turned away. Protocol and ceremony and consideration—both human and of state—could no longer restrain her impatience.

She stood, her shoulder to the young oriental king, as Livius came through the crowd to her.

Sohamus followed the direction of her gaze. Blood flooded up across his dark cheeks. He immediately perceived the meaning of the way Livius fixed his eyes on Lucilla.

Sohamus' mouth pulled. This was not so bad. Perhaps every young man in the empire secretly coveted the Caesar's daughter. What was bad was the way Lucilla was looking at the young tribune. An under-officer in her father's army!

Sohamus clenched his fists, standing straight. The rage boiling inside him did not show in his face. These two! Were they completely unaware of what was in their faces? Or were they unaware of what was happening around them?

Sohamus inclined his head in the slightest gesture toward the young tribune. His voice was touched with enough bitterness to recall Livius to the urgent world of protocol. "Be well, Livius Gaius Metellus."

Livius turned reluctantly, bowed. "May the gods grant you health, my lord King Sohamus."

Now Livius raised his head and his eyes clashed against the black stare of the young king.

Livius felt his heart sink. In that instant he understood what Sohamus wanted him to know—the way the king of Armenia loved the daughter of the Roman emperor. This was not so bad. Perhaps the leader of every province hoped to improve his own position with Rome by an alliance with the emperor's daughter, at the same moment marrying the loveliest girl in civilization. But what was bad was the fact of Rome's shaky alliance with Armenia, and the way the Persians wooed that country daily. A marriage would end all doubt about Armenian allegiance.

Livius stood a moment, staring at Sohamus, more tired than he had ever been before. It was as if he faced some impossible task, obstacles too great for him, and found himself without strength to move forward at all.

Sohamus watched him with an amused twist to his mouth, as if he had tasted a lemon, as if he could read his thoughts.

Livius bowed again to Sohamus. Sohamus smiled and made a slight *salaam* of acknowledgment and dismissal. Lucilla laid her hand on Livius' arm and they moved away toward the praetorium.

For a moment, Sohamus did not move, stood surrounded by his two radiantly beautiful slaves, his lavish retinue, looking after them, not like a king at all, but like a sad young man.

They were encased in a vacuum of static excitement, as if removed from the mob around them, unaware, untouched, passing through it. They walked, shoulders touching, looking at each other. It had been a long time and there was so much to make up between them.

"You are lovelier than ever," he said.

She laughed. "And so are you."

He let his gaze touch her left hand on which she wore a ring with a blue stone.

"You still wear that old ring I gave you?"

Her laugh had music in it. "It's become so much a part of me, I have forgotten I was wearing it . . . or that a very long time ago it was you who gave it to me."

As they walked close together in the overwhelming dust and confusion of the mob, she held her hand up, staring at the blue stone setting, thinking over what she had just said.

"No—not really forgotten. I know when you went off to war—you were seventeen and you thought of me as a girl and not a woman. . . . But—I thought of you differently." Her manner changed quickly. "I learned from my father a long time ago that the hardest thing in life is to tell a lie. It is so much easier to tell the truth and to say exactly what you think . . . which is what I do. Many people find me difficult. . . . Did you think of me, Livius?"

He spoke carefully. "Until I saw you this morning I would have said no, I did not think of you often. Now and then before a battle—only seeing you now, I realize you were always with me."

"You came—sometimes to Rome—"

"Yes. Rarely."

"Why didn't you ever—try to see me?"

He shook his head. "Try? I tried. You always seemed surrounded by a thousand young men—any one much better suited to you. They could quote from the Latin poets by the hour."

He sighed ruefully. "All I can quote is a few rough lines

from Julius Caesar. . . . Then, suddenly after your mother's death, you were seldom seen."

He sensed her going rigid, the way her cheeks went white. He studied her face, troubled. "And there was even a rumor that you thought about withdrawing from life—all life—of becoming a Vestal Virgin."

She nodded, her face grave. "Yes—I once thought of that."

He winced, feeling the terrible loss her dedicating her life to the gods and the temples would have been; as a soldier, unable to understand how she could even have considered it.

They walked in this taut silence toward the praetorium.

"You have—given that thought up now?" he said.

"Yes."

"And now?"

"I want to live."

"And to marry?"

"I have been waiting. . . . And you?"

"I, too, was waiting."

For a moment they walked forward, their eyes on each other. Livius glanced up, almost surprised to find them at the entrance of the emperor's quarters. The praetorium was an imposing building, even in this wilderness stronghold. It was another example of the Roman's stubborn will to build, nothing too much trouble, nothing too costly in time, dinarii, or man power. The general's tent—the praetorium—was always the first point set by the surveyors who laid out these precise encampments. It marked the exact middle of the camp and stood at the junction of the two main thoroughfares that crossed from north to south and from east to west. Even in a hastily erected *castra,* the praetorium was much more than a mere tent, and in a standing camp such as this near the Danube, it was a substantial edifice. It would remain standing long after the campaign ended here. In fact, these standing fortresses, linked by the incomparable lines of Roman military roads, were like cities in a supply line set twenty miles apart because this was the usual length of a day's march for the legions. Besides lavish quarters for the general, the praetorium stored the standards and the treasury of the Northern Army. A part of it was set aside for religious uses, especially for the taking of auspices. It also contained quarters with hot baths for the young aristocrats who accompanied the general on his campaign to gain firsthand knowledge of combat and battlefield engineering and supply.

As Livius and Lucilla approached the praetorium entrance, the freshly scrubbed, smartly clad young guards snapped to attention, made way for them.

Lucilla saw the blind Cleander standing near the entrance of the building. She shivered, disliking the handsome, empty-eyed man without reason. He was scrupulously clean, faintly elegant, and yet the hulking brute forever at his arm made him somehow sinister.

She saw Lentulus lean close and whisper something into Cleander's ear, Lentulus' fat-socketed eyes fixed on her. When Lentulus saw that Lucilla was watching him, he straightened guiltily, glancing around with a bland air of great innocence. The feeling of dislike deepened into fear and Lucilla touched Livius' arm, hurrying with him past the guards.

In his purple-draped quarters, Marcus Aurelius lay motionless on his cot, eyes closed. Behind him, chained to his perch, Aquila the eagle was motionless, brooding, seeming to stand guard like a watchdog over the emperor.

With his eyes closed, it seemed to Marcus that the sounds from the streets came through the walls, engulfing him. He tried to shut out the noise, needing to think, needing quiet and rest—the very things denied him so that now they seemed like old memories without much reality.

His mind drifted away from this time and this place to his own youth. Titus Antoninus Pius, lover of religion, justice and peace, his adoptive father, the father of Faustina. Pius had ruled well, and though he had two sons of his own, he preferred the welfare of Rome to the interests of his own family, named Marcus Aurelius Antoninus to succeed him. Marcus revered the character and memory of his benefactor, loved him as a parent, regulated his own administration by the example and maxims of Pius, so that history would have to say that their united reigns—his own and his adoptive father's—were the only period of Roman history in which the happiness of a people was the sole object of government.

"I have tried," Aurelius whispered, lips barely moving. "Father, I have tried. Pius, I have tried."

Whatever he was today, it was—besides his own rigid study of the Stoics—due to the patient lectures, the midnight teachings of a tiring Pius. Memory of Pius made him an honest Caesar, following Stoicism made him a mild and patient man. The Stoics taught him to submit his body to his mind, his passion to his reason, to consider virtue as the only good, vice as the only evil, all things external as things indifferent.

He supposed now that Stoicism had come along at the very moment when thoughtful men among the Romans, and the more intellectual Greeks, were ready for it. It evolved as the aged Greek city-states were disintegrating, old political landmarks were dying or dead, and men felt the terrible need for security. Security. What better place to seek security than in abstention from worldly affairs and in isolation from the vicissitudes of fortune. So the Stoics spoke of resignation. Pantheists, they conceived the universe as an organic whole, permeated by life and mind throughout. Happiness came from living in accordance with universal law and in accepting one's fate without complaint. Man had to guard against the ups and downs of emotional life, indeed he had to suppress any and all emotions, even compassion. He had to live the stern life of duty and reason.

This he had done, being sterner and severer with himself than he would permit himself to be with anyone else, and in later years even found himself becoming more and more indulgent to the imperfections of others.

There were so many ironies in his existence. Just as well that he appreciated irony as the supreme comedy of this life. As a Stoic he should have retreated from confusion, yet he was thrown into the midst of every tumult. Even his Meditations had to be composed in the roar and thunder of army camps.

Another terrible irony was that of his attempt to suppress emotion, when his life was lived in a storm of emotions. He hated war, had spent seventeen years in the midst of it. His own wife had made marriage a mockery and he closed his eyes to it as long as the world would let him, and when they would no longer, he forced them to deify her name, accept her as a goddess of purity, forgiving her all hurt.

He opened his eyes, let his gaze touch on the bust of Faustina near his cot. He winced. The Roman world had laughed at him because for years he alone appeared ignorant of Faustina's faithlessness.

He shook his head. He had longed to live out his life

in solitude, had only few moments of quiet, lived on tensions, war, hatreds, rebellions, betrayals. He was tired, he was too tired, and it could not go on much longer, this comedy of irony.

He went tense, feeling chilled, not because he was afraid of death, but because he thought of what was ahead, what must happen in the years after his death.

In a Jewish manuscript he'd read, he had found counsel against looking back to the good days, a better time, for this was error, vanity, folly. The times past were not better.

But he could not believe this.

There was so much that was wrong in this modern world, like a sickness.

His mouth twisted. This business of Christianity, the young Hebrew from Galilee, teaching that the meek would inherit the earth, that there was one god—something like the unseen, bodiless spirit worshipped by the Romans in antiquity. These people, teaching forgiveness, yet themselves in every case the most unforgiving, self-righteous and intolerant sect he'd ever encountered. During the whole course of his reign, he had despised them, simpering, secretive, talking of the irresistible spread of their religion, as if it were something that traveled through the air and on smoke. This was the greatest irony of all. As sovereign he had punished these people, as a philosopher he despised them, because they called themselves enemies of Rome and Roman imperialism —yet the ironic fact was that only the good and endless Roman roads across the face of the earth made the spread of Christianity easy and quick, indeed, possible at all. Without those smooth roads, the sect would have been confined to one place, and in one place would have died.

But his only real fear of the Christians was the spread of their philosophy of weakness, of passiveness in a world already grown old and tired and sick.

The gods knew they needed less of this weakness of men, this increase of public charity, the state taking over lives of men from cradle to grave.

History showed that the old virtues of *continentia*—self-restraint, *constantia*—steadfastness and *virtus*—manliness made Rome great. All of these virtues were now lacking in Roman men.

One had only to look back to the good old days of the virtue of simple living and hard work, the legend of Cin-

cinnatus: called back to head the Roman State, he was found at his plow, and he left his plow, served his country again, and returned to his plow.

And now citizens left work to slaves who outnumbered them, and lived on charity. They lived in apathy because they no longer had to depend on their own efforts and energies to survive. Apathy. The gods deliver any nation from apathy.

The terrible burden of taxes was made more impossible by battles in far places, and yet the fear of the unknown neighbor made the Roman quake and shout for bigger armies, and more taxes to support a war machine. To the Roman mind, the barbarian was any man they didn't know or understand, and they told themselves these vandals would destroy the earth with fire—unless Rome smashed them first.

At home, the weaknesses showed even more glaringly. Selfishness had replaced old love of country. Divorce increased alarmingly.

There was a greater danger for which he could see no solution, and this was the ever-growing strength of the Praetorian Guards inside Rome. Here was a symptom and cause of Roman ills. These Guards, instituted by Augustus to control uprisings, rebellion, were kept outside Roman city walls until brought inside the city by Tiberius. Now they had a power that was awesome, and numbers that steadily increased.

Marcus rolled his head on his pillow, sweated, and chilled at the same moment. What was the answer? Where would he find the answers in the little time left to him?

III

"FATHER—"

Aurelius opened his eyes, startled, his heart pounding erratically. Above him, his eagle stirred on its perch.

He stared upward, saw Lucilla's face anxious and frightened over him. He spoke softly, moving his gaze across her lovely cheeks, upslanted eyes, full mouth. "Lucilla." The old awe and wonder that this fabled beauty was his daughter filled him. "How is it possible that I fathered something as lovely as you?"

Lucilla smiled, adoring him no less now than she had as a child of three, six, ten—all the years of her life. Her voice was gentle, "Father, you have only to breathe upon a thing to make it beautiful."

Livius moved forward into the tired Caesar's line of vision. The young tribune stood close beside Lucilla, watching Aurelius' face, seeing the troubled frown.

The emperor's voice was puzzled, gentle, and he continued to study Lucilla's face. "And yet . . . there is Commodus . . ." He reached out, took both her hands, holding them as if to protect her from the hurt in what he had to say: "How hard it is to leave this life!"

Lucilla cried out, leaning against Livius. She felt the young soldier tremble. "No! No, don't say that. You have a long life ahead of you." She tried to smile, gave it up, cried in anguish, "Father!"

Aurelius held her hands gently as he had when she was a little girl and he was teaching her. "Death is the order of things, Lucilla. It must be accepted."

Lucilla, eyes brimmed with tears, shook her head. Her father was a Stoic, resigned to the designs of providence, but she was not, and the young often blame the gods for misfortunes while the older accept more of the blame to themselves. "No—I cannot—I will not—"

"Is there a choice?" Aurelius cut her off in that gentle tone. He gave them both a tired, wry smile. "Soon this trickle of blood, these few bones, this foolish net woven of nerves and arteries will be no more."

Struggling, Aurelius moved on the bed. The eagle gave a sharp cry and fluttered strong wings. Aurelius glanced at the bird and sat up on the side of the cot. Lucilla fell to her knees before him, clinging to him.

Aurelius moved his hands slowly on her rich hair. "But it is not for tomorrow." His gentle voice deepened and his manner abruptly changed. "And yet—I can't rid myself of a sense of doom. I try to tell myself that these are the sickly phantoms rising from my wracked body, and yet there is this dreadful feeling that no matter what we do, all I have lived for—all I have fought for—will be destroyed." He held his left hand against Lucilla's face, reached out impulsively toward Livius, begging them in their youth and strength for aid. "Help me!"

Lucilla said, "Oh, Father! Can you doubt we'd give our lives if you asked it—?"

"No." His voice was sharp. "You both must live! I—must do all I can to leave the empire strong. . . . I must sacrifice all else." He sat for a long breath, staring at the flooring. Lucilla stirred, worriedly, searching his face, finding it bleak but determined. "All else—even the love of my son."

Lucilla straightened. "What about Commodus?"

Livius was staring at Caesar's face. For a moment both men heard something—a faint sound like mice in a wall from beyond the closed door. Both held their breath, waiting, but the sound was not repeated.

Aurelius sighed. "I—I've made my decision. . . . Commodus cannot be my heir."

Livius and Lucilla were stunned, and neither spoke.

Aurelius tilted his head, voice firm. "For five years Commodus has been in a position of power—yet he's shown an interest only in gladiators and games." When neither Livius nor Lucilla spoke, he glanced up, challengingly. "You both grew up with him. When was he happier than when I permitted him to go and *live* in a gladiator school on the Caelian? Can you say to me that he is the man to whom we can entrust the empire in this fateful moment?"

He moved his head, staring up at Livius. Livius spoke with violence. "Commodus is my dearest friend. Do not ask me, my lord Caesar."

"We are not speaking here of friendship. We are speaking of the future of the empire."

Livius remained silent, standing tall, face gray.

Aurelius continued to stare into the young soldier's battle-roughened face. "Commodus must not be emperor."

"He is your son," Livius whispered.

"I wish you to be my heir, Livius."

Livius winced, feeling as if the flooring had been snatched away from beneath him. He wanted to reach out for support, but there was none. There was only this great, good man, watching his face intently; only Lucilla on her knees, silent, scarcely breathing, and somewhere in unfathomable distance movement and confusion on the *castra* plains. "He is your son," Livius whispered again.

Aurelius spoke with the impatience of the mortally ill and fatigued. "Don't pretend it's news to you, Livius, that for almost two hundred years we've had the precedent of an emperor's putting aside family considerations in order to choose the best man to succeed him. Pius himself was named emperor with the understanding that he should adopt me—he a man of fifty, and I a boy of seventeen. He made me his heir, as I now wish to make you my heir."

There was such silence in the room, Aurelius waiting with tension and impatience because he was frightened by his own weakness, and the two young people too stunned to speak, the sounds from the encampment streets, remote, distant; then again Livius and the emperor heard the scraping sounds mice might make in the inner wall.

Livius turned on his heel toward the door to investigate, but the sound died at once, and he exhaled heavily, turning back.

Lucilla straightened, shaken and unsteady, her cheeks flushed, her gaze moving from her father to the young soldier.

Aurelius spoke coldly, yet with great affection. "Well, Livius?"

Livius drew the back of his hand across his mouth. "You said yourself, Caesar, it needs someone who can change, who will find new ways. I am a soldier. I do not know new ways."

"You have the heart for it, Livius," Marcus said. "That will let you change."

Livius shook his head, his voice harsh. "I am a soldier, Caesar. Since my seventeenth year. I know only the ways of war. I will not know how to make allies out of barbarians." His sharp impatience clashed against the emperor's. "And the rest—"

"Speak openly, Livius. Do you refuse because of Commodus?"

Livius sighed, still overwhelmed. "I cannot imagine a life without the friendship of Commodus. Nor can I see how he can remain my friend if I—take his rightful place."

"It is not his rightful place."

"He is your son."

"It is not his rightful place. It is not for him to demand, nor for you to suggest. The decision is mine." He waited, but Livius remained rigidly silent. "It is not Commodus' rightful place, Livius. The emperor Hadrian named Antoninus Pius, who was not of his blood line. Four emperors before me named as heirs, not their closest kin, but he who had the most merit. That is why our empire has remained strong. I have given my life—my blood to this great empire. My personal fortune to the public treasury. My existence to its wars and to the glory of its expansion. I am a man who could have been happy with his beloved family—" he reached out his arm toward Lucilla, "a man who could have studied and written and meditated in a garden retreat, and instead I have fought for Rome—victories dearly bought after exhausting resistance that has depleted my armies and myself. And I know that Rome must change unless she is to be destroyed. I know I must leave as my heir the strongest man I can find. You love Commodus as your friend. He is my son. I love Commodus, too, but that is only a feeling."

None of them spoke. Aurelius stirred, glancing about the shadowed room moodily.

"I must not consider feelings. Before I go, I must set my house—this empire—in order. I will ask any sacrifice. From everyone. From you, Livius. Even from my own daughter."

Livius breathed in deeply, going tense with the foreboding of terrible wrong. He glanced at Lucilla, saw color had seeped from her cheeks.

Again Aurelius took his daughter's hands as he had when she was a child and he was leading her safely and wisely into some unknown place—whether of the world, the mind, or the heart.

He studied her face, speaking gently. "It can be no secret to you, Lucilla, that the King of Armenia has long sought your hand in marriage. . . . Always and always before, I—have not wanted you so far from me. . . . Only now, with the threat from Persia growing, we can no longer refuse him. We must make alliances in the East—" He let his voice trail off, staring at her almost pleadingly.

Lucilla's face was rigid, gray. She swallowed hard. "Father, whatever you think is good—" her voice broke, "I will do."

She did not glance toward Livius because she could not without crying out her protests, but she knew the grayness of his cheeks matched her own.

Instead she kept her gaze fixed on her father's. He seemed to be saying so much with his stricken eyes, begging her to

understand it all without words, but she could think only
of her deep hurt at this moment.

Her father's hands tightened on hers, and because her fingers were like ice, his voice was troubled. "I know—"

None of them spoke for some moments. At last, Livius
was able to speak without emotion, voice flat, and his face
expressionless. "My lord Caesar, you—did not expect me to
make this decision—quickly?"

Aurelius released Lucilla's hands. He sighed and glanced
up at the tall young officer. "I had hoped—perhaps foolishly
—that you would feel yourself ready—"

"But I do not—"

Aurelius lifted his hand, thinking he was tired, time was
running out, that Livius loved him, trusted his judgment, paid
him complete loyalty. He said, "Then take time, Livius."

Livius nodded, staring at Lucilla. She stood white, and
motionless, careful only to avoid his eyes at all costs.
After a moment Livius bowed quickly, turned and strode
from the room.

It was in the hottest blaze of the mid-morning sun that
Livius paused outside the praetorium, glancing about, hardly
knowing where he was. All the brilliant pageantry remained
in the crowded streets, but he saw none of it. He stood a
moment, not really seeing anything around him.

Near the praetorium entrance two men were talking together, and when they saw Livius, they disengaged themselves from other dignitaries surrounding them. They strode
together to where Livius stood. For some moments they
waited expectantly, smiling at his bemusement, the way he
looked straight at them without recognizing them, or seeing
them at all.

At the burst of laughter from the heavy-set, middle-aged
man, Livius shook himself, becoming suddenly aware of
them. "Virgilianus! Marcellus! I didn't even see you."

Ulpius Marcellus, Governor of Syria, was only a few years
older than Livius. His handsome face was pulled in a smile
that did not quite hide his anxiety. "You seem a man with
much on his mind."

Livius was still distracted. "Nor do you seem the open,
carefree soldier I once knew, Marcellus."

The youthful governor's face twisted with a rueful smile.
"All I had to worry about in those days was whether I'd

come out of the next battle alive. I envy you, Livius, sol-diers like you, with nothing more than that on your mind. Now, I have all Syria to worry about."

There was an awkward silence. Livius was still deeply engrossed in his own thoughts. These were his great and good friends from old war campaigns, though Virgilianus was much older. At the moment, however, he could not be friend-ly, and his silent preoccupation gave them no opening.

Marcellus glanced toward the praetorium entrance, thinking about the whispers that burned through the *castra* since Cae-sar's abrupt end to his address to the consuls. He spoke solemnly. "May the gods spare our Caesar to us. We in the East know how much he is needed now."

Virgilianus glanced about uneasily. "Marcellus has been in Syria as its governor, and I have been proconsul in Egypt We have not seen each other since we were last in Rome —yet, we both have felt it, Livius. . . . Unless those changes Caesar promised come soon—we will not last long in the East."

Livius spoke with sudden sharp anger. "We've lasted for centuries. We'll be there centuries more."

He paused when the sound of a galloping horse broke through all other sounds around them in the camp. An en-voy in sweated tunic raced through the main gate, shouting, "Prince Commodus! The Prince Commodus has been sighted!"

Talk and whispers surged about the three men.

Virgilianus glanced after the sweated envoy who shouted through the camp, and spoke with an old soldier's cold hon-esty, "May the gods spare Aurelius."

Livius glanced past the two old friends toward the em-peror's quarters inside the praetorium. He abruptly made his decision and with a gesture, strode away from Marcellus and Virgilianus.

The two men stood, mouths parted, staring moodily after him.

Livius moved faster, pushing his way through the mob, running toward his chariot.

Lucilla stood at a window of her father's quarters inside the praetorium. Aurelius, still sitting bowed on the side of his cot, glanced up at her when the sound of the shouting envoys came in to him.

Lucilla said softly across her shoulder, "Prince Commodus has been sighted."

Aurelius nodded and sank back on the cot. He watched his daughter at the window, thinking about her, his son, the young soldier who had just left these rooms, the loss that showed in Lucilla's face, his own age and weariness, and his memories of all of them when they were only children.

He heard yells, galloping horses, chariots racing away.

Lucilla said, "Livius has gone out to meet him."

She heard the faint sound as her father caught his breath. She turned, left the window, walked slowly back to Aurelius.

He said, no doubting in his tone, "I am right in choosing Livius."

Lucilla nodded, standing straighter. Only one thing troubled her and she spoke about it in the direct honest way that was part of her. "Why did he hesitate? *I* would not—"

"If you—if only you had been my son." His smile was wistful.. He moved his gaze over her with love in it. "And yet I wouldn't have you other than you are. . . . Forgive me, Lucilla. I delayed—I had hoped that the gods would be kind to us—and that you would not have to make a marriage without love."

Lucilla stood straight, regal, an emperor's daughter, though inside she controlled herself only with great effort. "My marriage to Sohamus is important—"

"Yes. Yes." He exhaled, eyes clouding, voice moody. "What greater proof could Rome give of her good faith to the East? And no sense trying to fool ourselves—that proof is needed."

Her face was gray, but her voice remained steady, without inflection. "Then you know that I will kill whatever feeling I may have had—"

"Yes." His voice broke across hers because he did not want to hear her put in words something he understood even better than she. He could not hide that he was deeply troubled—because age and death had brought him to the place where he would ask such a sacrifice of her, and because she could assent to it. "Once, I would have been proud if my daughter had answered thus . . . now—now I don't know. . . . If I could live my life over—I think I would have pondered more on the human heart, the emotions, feelings, those strange, perplexing guests who come uninvited to live with us, and who sometimes take control." He sighed heavily. "And I would have pondered on love."

Now it was his daughter who displayed the strength and courage he knew to be failing him. Her voice had a deep weariness in it. "Love," she said. It sounded almost as if she hated the sound of the word: a word of weakness, of vacuity, for clowns and children. "Let us speak the truth, Father, about love. . . . What did love bring you?"

He winced, turning away from her and glancing at the classic beauty in the bust of Faustina. He had loved her. The world laughed at him because he loved her. Yet he understood her weaknesses, her drives, compulsions, her loneliness. He was so much away at battle, so deeply enmeshed in the government. You couldn't explain these things to a cynically watching world, nor to a proud and injured daughter. Time. Time only could heal the kind of hurt Faustina had left as legacy to Lucilla.

He turned back, finding his daughter's face gray, eyes intense. She spoke in a barbed whisper. "She was my mother—" she jerked her head toward the bust that was so like her, and yet at the same moment, so completely unlike her. "And one should not speak evil of the dead." With sudden passion, she moved away from the bust as a contaminated thing. "I hate her. I hate her."

She stood staring at the bust of Faustina with revulsion in her almond-shaped eyes.

Watching her, Aurelius felt pity and sorrow—for Lucilla because she was so filled with hatred. He remembered something he'd written long ago for his Meditations: how much more you often suffer from your anger and grief than from those very things for which you are angry and grieved. But he did not say this to his daughter.

She twisted suddenly, sat beside him on the cot, moved closer to him, resting her head on his shoulder.

He said, deeply disturbed, "You must not hate her . . . it only hurts you, your hatred. . . . She—could not love me— you see—so she had to look for love elsewhere—"

"Yet you had her declared a goddess! You built shrines to her." Her voice rose. "She betrayed you. You—the best— the greatest of men!"

He put his arm about her, thinking again how easy it was to brush away the years and think of her as his baby in his arms, and his need to protect her from all harm. He said softly, "Betrayed. . . . That's such a harsh word. You must know that when Cleander came to me with documents he said would prove—her betrayals—I had them burned." He drew her closer. "What is the truth? I had moments—of great happiness—great beauty—with her."

Lucilla's voice had that deep weariness and buried rages. "Moments! If that is love—then I think I will have a better life without it!"

He closed his hand on hers, clinging to her. "I'm afraid for you, Lucilla. . . . I feel such a gift for life within you—only—learn pity—learn compassion." He moved her hand close against his cheek. "Above all—for yourself—you will need them."

Lucilla knelt beside his cot, close to him, silent tears brimming her eyes, spilling across her cheeks. She pressed her face against him, clinging to him, feeling as if she were losing everything on earth that made her life worthwhile, as if he were going away from her even while she clung to him, with her arms about him.

IV

COMMODUS LAID THE leather lashes across the sweated rumps of his horses. The lightweight chariot bounced precariously on the wrinkled plain below the Roman army encampment. Behind him raced other chariots of his party, but none was able to keep pace with him.

He glanced behind his shoulder, laughing, feeling the good hot sting of wind—like lashes laid on with reeds in a steam bath, and affording him the same sensual thrill. No wonder none of the other chariots could keep up with him. All the drivers were too cautious, too much in love with life to risk everything for the terrible excitement of swaying, bounding, racing across rough, unknown ground. Those others kept lines secured about their waists, and knives in their teeth ready to slash loose the fetter of lines at the first hint of trouble. Commodus' lines trailed loose on the cart flooring, and his knife was in his girdle, out of reach and out of mind.

The chariot struck a boulder and whipped along precariously on one wheel. The frightened animals, lathered and trembling, faltered. Commodus yelled with exultation and laid the leather to them.

He felt the surge of power as the fine animals lunged forward, the chariot leveling out, leaving the slowing party deeper in the distance behind him.

In his early twenties, Commodus had a strong, powerful body, made supple and quick by long training with the gladiators. There was no trace of weakness in his muscle-corded shoulders, his deep chest or the golden columns of his long legs, beaded with sweat along the hard sinews. He had a fine head, with black cropped curls, high forehead and fiery black eyes that showed laughter when other men showed fear. The faintest sign of weakness was about his mouth: it was sensual, as if all the strength were a lie and the twist of the mouth was the only truth revealed.

He glanced once more behind him without slowing his horses. The other chariots seemed to be slipping away as if blown on the wind, and in the far distance, in a half-run, was a company of gladiators. His father would hate the sight of them this far from the arenas of Rome, but they were his friends, athletes he admired. Boring enough to come so far from his pleasures, impossible without some kind of entertainment.

Then, sounds of galloping horses, rattle of chariot and spark of metal rims against rocks thundered downwind to Commodus.

His black eyes lighted with pleasure when he saw Livius racing a chariot directly toward him at breakneck speed.

Commodus' mouth twisted. He tightened his grip on the lines, held the horses on a course that led directly toward Livius. Only at the last possible second did the carts veer suddenly apart, the two men yelling, heavy voices thundering through the scream of the wind, rattle of metal, pound of hooves.

"Gaius Livius!" Commodus yelled. "Warrior! Voyager! I've missed you!"

The chariots were almost alongside each other. Livius shouted, "Commodus! Commodus! Most Roman of them all! Are you well?"

As the two chariots swept past each other, Commodus raged in reply, laughing, "When was I ever unwell?"

In seconds the chariots were far past each other and both drivers pulled them around in wild, careening turns, turning again until both carts, side by side, were racing toward the encampment entrance.

Commodus gripped the lines, yelling: "I have much to tell you!"

Livius winced, his face changing, even in the swaying chariot. "And I—you!"

From behind them the other chariots approached, making an impressive entourage for the young prince. Among the youthful drivers of carts, Livius recognized Didius Julianus, Claudius Albinus, Pescennius Niger. Livius knew that Marcus Aurelius in an effort to save Commodus from the excesses of these young aristocrats, had, after his great patience was exhausted, exiled some of them to the provinces. When Commodus came into some power, he had his young friends returned to Rome. Livius scowled, because the presence of these spoiled, unbridled men would displease the ill emperor. But he said nothing about it. He had known and loved Commodus since they used to gamble "heads or ships" with *as* or dinarii, when they were children. Nothing enraged Commodus more than to be told his actions would displease his father.

Commodus seemed to read his thoughts. He shouted, indicating his friends. "I brought Julianus, Claudius and Niger from Rome. We'll liven the place up."

Livius nodded without speaking. With some pleasure, he saw that Marcus Aurelius was standing outside the praetorium entrance awaiting the arrival of Prince Commodus. With the emperor was Lucilla on one side, Timonides on the other. Behind them Sohamus, King of Armenia stood, and near him the blind Cleander and Lentulus.

All along the streets of the encampment, the legions stood at attention. There was a sense of expectancy among the parties of all the visiting dignitaries.

Livius slowed his chariot, seeing that Claudius, Niger and Didius Julianus had pulled away in their chariots, and were not approaching the emperor with Commodus. He sighed. They were fools, but not entirely without reason.

Commodus rolled to a stop near the praetorium entrance, bright dust clouding across him and bystanders. He sprang lightly from the chariot, moved directly, with eyes for no one else, to Aurelius.

Aurelius put out his arms and as Commodus came near, embraced him. Livius stepped from his chariot, approached them, standing at a small distance, watching uneasily.

Embracing Commodus, Aurelius whispered in low tones but with deep intensity. "Commodus. My son. My son." His voice lowered. "Where were you so long? What delayed you?"

Commodus broke from his father's embrace, studied his father's face with suspicion. Livius had seen this same thing happen when Commodus was a child, bridling at the first hint of question. The black eyes flashed, but Commodus answered easily, "It is not easy to travel fast with a company of gladiators on foot."

There were audible gasps, a moment of fragile tension. Aurelius did not speak, but Livius, looking up, found the emperor's eyes on him, holding on him.

Livius turned away.

Aurelius sighed. "It is not gladiators Rome needs now."

Commodus straightened, his face flushed, anger pulling his mouth awry. He formed a hasty answer, caught himself. He spoke coldly, "I've made a long voyage, Father."

"Then we'll speak another time," Aurelius said.

One more moment Aurelius stood gazing at his splendidly handsome son, then he turned and moved through the praetorium entrance followed by Timonides, Cleander and Lentulus.

Commodus, still standing tall and taut with the inner rages his father had always been able to stir in him with the mildest word of reproof, stared after the emperor, then pulled his gaze around to Lucilla, looking her over mockingly.

He spoke in savage, but subdued irony. "Not yet retired to become a Vestal Virgin?"

"Much too dangerous with you running loose in Rome," Lucilla answered. She gave her brother one quick survey, turned away. Her gaze softened faintly, touching on Livius, then she hurried after her father.

Livius and Commodus watched her go through the guarded doorway. Commodus exhaled, gazing upward as if asking the gods to spare him from such afflictions. "Female philosophers!"

Livius did not speak, and Commodus' spoiled mouth pulled into a bitter smile. He shook his head. "There's got to be wine somewhere around, Livius. I'm thirsty. Come on."

Striding alongside Livius, Commodus told himself he was sorry he had come. He glanced about, sweated and thirsty, at the pageantry, pomp, these regal lords and consuls standing around like beggars with hats in hand awaiting crumbs from his father. Dust everywhere, not enough wine to wash it out of his mouth and eyes. Perhaps if he poured it in his ears. Why had he come? He and his father had nothing to say to each other. They never had had. Whatever they had to say to each other could have been said by letter, and he could have remained in Rome.

He shrugged his tunic up on his shoulders. He and his father were strangers, barely polite to each other. And no sense blaming him. It wasn't his fault. Like every other Roman father, Aurelius had been too busy for him, even before he succeeded Antoninus Pius as emperor. His father liked to blame the ills of Rome on the breakdown of the urban family, the transfer of the father's duty to the mother which he said cut at the root of family life, accounted for decline of Roman character. It was not his fault his father was too busy for him, left his earliest education and training in the hands of his mother.

His mouth pulled. She had been a woman without a strong will and he had her twisted about his finger. He did what pleased him, and it pleased him little to attend classes under those intellectual Greek slaves. His father wrote his Meditations in Greek, forever cautioned him that a truly literate man must master Greek as well as Latin.

What a laugh that was. At sixteen he had made the "grand tour" through Greece and Asia Minor. He got everything he wanted without speaking one word of Greek. It was easy. Dinarii was the answer.

No sense even thinking about it. He and his father saw eye to toe on everything, they always had. The most laughable disagreement of all came when Aurelius decided to outlaw *hoplomachia*—gladiatorial combat—in favor of the mimic fights called *lusio* in which everything was staged and there was no death. On this matter, Aurelius had lost resoundingly, refuted by the people themselves.

He strode faster now, as if running away from something. He saw with pleasure that two tribunes, Victorinus and Polybus, had fallen in step behind Livius and that on his own side had come Julianus, Claudius, Niger and Verulus.

He clapped Verulus on the shoulder. Verulus was a

handsome, aging gladiator who was Commodus' favorite teacher. They were much alike in build and manner, and Commodus supposed this was because they spent so much time together in the arenas in training. Verulus knew every trick of the *murmillones*—the armed gladiator, and the *retiarii*—the stalker carrying net and trident. He had to know all the tricks, the simple fact of his still being alive proved this. He held back nothing in teaching Commodus.

The two groups of men lined up, facing each other. Livius presented his friends, the tribunes Polybus and Victorinus. He said with pride, "We've fought three wars together."

Commodus gave the two officers brief nods, looking them over. "Here is Verulus, greatest gladiator of Rome. Survivor of a hundred combats." He lowered his voice challengingly. "He has brought his company of gladiators to battle."

There was a brief, taut silence of disbelief from the three professional soldiers. Polybus said, "Gladiators? To fight— as soldiers?"

Commodus fixed his black eyes on him, and spoke aggressively. "Why not?"

Verulus stood straighter, sucking in his belly. "We'll teach your legionnaires how to kill."

None of the officers answered the gladiator, but they stared at him coldly. Commodus took a wineskin from Julianus, pressed out a long drink. Then he thrust it toward Livius who took it and drank.

Carrying the wineskin, Commodus caught Livius' arm and led him away from the others. In silence, the two tribunes regarded the three young aristocrats and the rugged Verulus facing them warily.

Julianus spoke at last, with mock solicitude. "Our Caesar —Marcus Aurelius does not look well." He drank from a flagon of wine.

Polybus took a drink. "Dying men never do," he said. He took another drink, then found the shock in the faces of the young aristocrats. "What's the matter? You knew Caesar was dying. What else could have pulled you and your kind—" he gestured with contempt, "from the city of Rome?"

The three aristocrats flushed, their faces admitting they'd heard the rumors, or else they never would have dared approach Aurelius at such close range. They did not speak, but Verulus laughed loudly. "We came because we heard there was blood to be spilled."

Soldiers and gladiator glared at each other in cold contempt.

Verulus' voice rose. "Are you soldiers? Then you make your living killing—the same as gladiators." He looked the officers over with scorn and turned his thick, scarred back on them.

Polybus handed Victorinus the wineskin. Victorinus took a long, calming drink.

Commodus glanced over his shoulder, sensing the tension between his party and that of the soldiers. He laughed, pleased. More excitement than this place had seen in months, probably.

He turned his head, studying Livius intently as Livius drank from the flagon of wine. He was aware the atmosphere of tension had stretched with him and Livius even when they walked away from the others. They brought their own charged static with them in the heat.

Livius finished drinking, glanced over the wineskin and saw the way Commodus was studying him openly.

Livius wiped his mouth, handed over the skin to Commodus who took it without moving his gaze from Livius' face.

"You've changed, Livius," Commodus said after a moment. "You're—not the same. What is it about you?" He circled him, like a stalker in the gladiator ring, studying him sardonically. "You have Father's look. My god, another philosopher." With mock anxiety, he said, "Have you begun to think, Livius?"

Slightly on edge, Livius said, "There's much for a Roman to think about these days, Commodus."

Commodus laughed, but did not speak and they moved past the praetorium to the *quaestorium* behind it where was housed the quarters of the paymaster, and the prisoners' pit.

Walking, Commodus glanced idly into the pit at the barbarian prisoners. Among them were blonde, blue-eyed women and children, the Marcomanni. All about them war loot was piled high, arms, shields, helmets.

Commodus moved on, then slowed, looking intently at two young blonde girls chained to stakes in the pit. Something about the debased position of the two women, bound and helpless, struck at Commodus, and he felt a quickening inside him. He seldom got enjoyment from ordinary pleasures any more, but when his object was helpless, or full of hatred, or fear, or rage, like the wild beasts in the arenas, ah, then this was something else.

One of the girls straightened against the stake, standing as tall as she could. Her blue eyes were glacier-chilled, fixed on Commodus and Livius outside the barrier.

The girl tilted her head, crying out defiantly, straight at them, but not speaking to them at all. "Oh, great god Wotan! God of the warriors. . . . Today we have nothing to offer you." She spat toward the prince and the tribune. "Tomorrow—your altar will be decorated with Roman heads!"

She pointed directly toward Commodus and Livius. Commodus watched her, licking his mouth with anticipation.

"What are they like—these barbarian women?" he said.

"I don't know," Livius said.

Commodus laughed, not believing him. "Shall we find out?" He took a drink from the wineskin, extending it, laughing, toward the two young girls.

When Livius hesitated, Commodus spoke irritably, "What's the matter? Have you lost your taste for that, too?"

Livius turned slightly, glancing back toward the praetorium in the sweated heat. A bitter shadow crossed his face. He took the wineskin from Commodus, drank deeply. He flung the wineskin from him, emptied.

Commodus smiled approvingly.

The two barbarian girls stood straight against the stake, staring up at them, eyes burning.

Commodus shouted: "Guard!"

A guard came running, his sandals battering the hard ground.

Commodus pointed to the two women. "Bring them to us."

The guard hesitated.

Commodus jerked his head around. "Well?"

"One of them, Highness, is—a princess."

"A barbarian princess!" Commodus laughed. "So much better. Which one?"

The guard indicated the girl who had shouted defiantly. "The Princess Xenia, Highness. The other is her hand-maid, Tauna."

"Fine." Commodus nodded. "Bring them to my quarters. Now."

There was a silence in Commodus' quarters that had nothing to do with noise. The sound of laughter, the tones of voices, the clatter of dinnerware did nothing against the din of silence. It seemed to Livius this terrible quiet was concentrated in him, the noises in the room did not touch him, and were absorbed in the static silence.

He glanced toward Commodus, lounging at the table, eating and drinking heartily. If there was silence or tension, he saw that Commodus was unaware of it.

The table before them was loaded with food such as Livius had not seen since his last state banquet, and wine by the flagonfuls.

At the foot of the table, neither of them touching the rich foodstuffs, the two blonde girl prisoners crouched, more like animals than women.

Tauna was disheveled, her animal-skin garment falling from her shoulders across her breasts. Her long blonde hair was matted, reminding Livius of the mane of a wild horse he had seen once, imprisoned, burr-clogged.

The Princess Xenia was something else again. While Tauna was uneasy, troubled by the oil-lamp lights, the rich texture of the furnishings, the quantity and odors of strange foods, twisting, watching with awed fascination every move that was made, Xenia seemed as if in catatonic trance.

Xenia's blue eyes were dull, vacant, fixed on thoughts inside herself. Wild as she was, she had more imagination than Tauna. She knew why she had been brought here, and she gazed with deep loathing upon Commodus because she was intelligent enough to see cruelty was the kind of passion that excited him, and he would get the most sensual pleasure from debasing *her* since she was barbarian royalty.

Her long blonde hair gleamed in the lights, catching shafts of silver when flames flickered, but tresses fell across her face and throat, unnoticed by her and she did not even brush them away.

Livius watched her, seeing that it was from her that this tension and silence emanated, like some mysterious aura that flooded the room. Nothing could reach her, and because of her, and because of things left unspoken, the atmosphere between him and Commodus was increasingly charged and tense.

Commodus spoke with his mouth full. "You are very silent, Livius."

Livius wanted only to avoid the unpleasantness he saw was ahead. He had tried to get drunk, he had put away more wine than Commodus, but it didn't affect his senses. Steadily he became colder, more sober and aware, sensitive to every change in the brightly lighted room.

He said, placating Commodus, "Perhaps I've been a soldier too long."

"No. Perhaps it's just because you don't like the things I say—what I just said, and," he spoke deliberately, "what I now repeat. The Roman empire has no real meaning." He smiled, pleased, when Livius leaned forward, cold and rigid. "If there is any logic anywhere, Livius, why haven't our provinces rebelled long ago?"

"Because they are not fools. Before we came to them, most of them were savages." Unconsciously, he jerked his head toward the terrified Tauna, cringing at the tension in their voices, following each movement of their hands or heads. "We've brought them roads. We've brought them law. We've—"

"That was centuries ago, Livius," Commodus said wearily. "But now—they could build their own roads, and make their own laws, much cheaper. Why should they pay us taxes and tributes? Who are we?"

Tauna, trembling, set herself and sprinted toward the door. A guard stepped into her path, caught her roughly, and pushed her back to her place near Xenia. Her princess did not look at her, and neither Commodus nor Livius gave Tauna or the guard a glance.

"We are Rome," Livius said.

"Rome!" Commodus laughed. "A myth holds the empire together! The truth is the provinces no longer need us. Only we never let the colonies suspect it. My father strides about, the great image of a god-like father, going about doing good for all, for them and for Romans, bringing their leaders to state functions like this—or to Rome itself—dazzling them with games and banquets . . . and then if they still seem suspicious—crush them."

"No. The more you talk, Commodus, the more I see your father is right. Crushing them, taxing their strength away— that's not the sane answer. We *must* find new ways . . . change—"

"My father!" Commodus sat forward, shaken by sudden cold fury. "He is always talking about change—learning to love and understand even those who harm us! That is the one thing we must not do—change. As a matter of fact, we in Rome are living far beyond our means. If we stop, our creditors would tear us to pieces. No, no, Livius—what's the saying?—live while there's still light. Let's laugh while the gods are laughing."

Livius' face was gray. "I don't hear the gods laughing, Commodus."

Commodus held his gaze, their eyes clashing. They faced each other. Commodus' cheeks were pallid. "We're not saying everything we know, friend Livius. . . . Something weighs on you. What is it?"

Livius was as pale as Commodus, but he did not speak. Tauna whimpered in the thick silence. Commodus shouted, "Well?"

"You've been too much at Rome, Commodus. You—should be more with your father."

Commodus roared. "Will you tell me how I must live? Must I try to live as you do? Like a pupil, drinking in every word of my illustrious father's? Like you do!" His voice was hoarse. "Oh, I've heard all the rumors. Why Father has gathered everyone here. . . . *Why* you were at his side." His voice broke suddenly, his mouth twisting. He shook his head. "No. . . . No, Livius, don't let it come from you. . . . I need you as my friend. Don't tell me any more . . . I don't want to hear it."

In the pregnant silence, Livius sighed, deeply moved. "I am your friend, Commodus."

Commodus stared at him, his mouth pulled petulantly, for a long time. Suddenly then, he shook off his thoughts and heeled around, staring at Xenia.

"Ah, Princess," he said. "You boast that you are a nation of warriors. . . . Well, then, warrior, every soldier knows that sometimes his side loses—and he becomes part of the spoils of war—even a princess becomes a slave, to be used as the master wishes." When she did not move, he shouted at her. "Do you hear me? You are lost. You are prisoners of war." He stood up. "Come here to me."

Xenia did not move. There was no way to tell from her expressionless face even if she heard him at all. His voice rose. "Come! Drink with me. You may as well accept that you are lost. You may as well relax." He laughed. "You may as well enjoy it. Wine will help put a brighter edge on everything. . . . Drink!"

When the slender young girl still did not move, he went around the table to her.

He knelt, offered the beaker of wine, but she turned her head away, stiffly.

Commodus caught her head in his hand, tried to pour the wine down her mouth. It ran trickling across her lips, filling her nostrils, discoloring her cheeks.

Suddenly, gasping, she struck at him savagely, spilling the beaker of wine all over him.

Commodus yelled at her, like a child in a tantrum. "I am still Caesar's son! Do you understand? I could have you burned alive."

Commodus slapped at the droplets of wine spattered upon his clothing. His eyes were wild, fixed on her, his mind churning with the indignities that would degrade her, show her the depths a woman could reach when she fought him.

Suddenly he realized that Livius was watching him silently, shocked at his lack of self-control.

Commodus, trembling, managed to get hold of his emotions. He moved his gaze over Xenia's body and then turned slowly to face Livius.

His voice was casual. "I don't want this one after all, Livius. I thought I did. She rouses me more to rage than to passion, and—that doesn't fit my mood tonight." He jerked his head toward Tauna. "I'll trade you—even before I've used the *princess* at all. . . . This little blonde animal quivering like a frightened hound is more for me."

Livius nodded. "Take Tauna then, Commodus. She's yours."

Commodus stared at Livius another moment. Then he walked to Tauna and grabbed her. She bit her lip, but did not cry out. She was quivering and kept her eyes closed. Pleased, Commodus knelt, swung her easily up into his arms and strode out of the room into his quarters.

Livius was shaken. It was as if Commodus were full of hatred and his only satisfaction came from venting it upon the helpless.

Livius took a long drink of wine, but it was tasteless, less than water. He was troubled, wondering if he would remain cold, and beyond the touch of wine for the rest of his life.

Xenia stirred slightly across the table and, remembering her, he turned, looking at her. He said gently, almost teasing, "Is it true, girl, as Commodus fears—that you think?"

She got slowly to her feet, came around the table to him,

knelt between his knees, mouth parted, looking up, pale, as if waiting.

Livius did not touch her. He drew his tongue across his dry mouth, seeing the way she trembled before him, waiting, and he remembered this morning when Marcus planned with Lucilla to give her in a marriage-alliance to Sohamus of Armenia. The only woman he had ever loved; he had feared all his life he would never marry her, now his fear was grounded, and he would not. What else mattered? Perhaps Commodus was partly right. If only *he* could hear the gods laughing as Commodus did. Perhaps this girl's kiss might waken him, and make him forget for a little while.

Throat taut, he lifted his hands, cupped them over Xenia's ears. He turned her pallid face up, holding her with more force than he realized, but she did not protest.

"A warrior who thinks?" he said. "You're a fool—that's what you are—just as I am a fool to forget I'm only a soldier, and trying to think. What will it get us? Where?" He shook his head. "But I will not threaten to burn you alive—just for your crime of thinking." His mouth twisted. "I will offer you a more generous treaty of peace. A treaty of peace. Rome and the barbarian who thinks." His hands tightened on her head. Her eyes searched his face, shadowed, in fear and misunderstanding. Cruelty she could understand, the force of his hands, the use of her body, all this she understood—but the tone and quality of his voice troubled and frightened her. She drew her tongue across her parted mouth, trying to move closer to him, waiting.

Suddenly Livius got to his feet. Xenia fell back, eyes wide. Livius stepped over her and walked past the guard, going out of the tent. Xenia stared after him, bewildered and chilled.

V

GROUND MISTS obscured the world, the earth giving off gray light in pre-dawn of a cold raw morning.

Contingents of the Northern Army, like parts of greased machinery, moved with unerring proficiency, into place.

Mounted, Livius sat in saddle, holding reins to quiet his horse, unnerved by the mysterious clatter of sounds. Livius was not aware of the chill. He had been months away, and all his old pride and love for this Northern Army swelled through him. His heart pounded faster, and the blood was pulsing through his veins. A thousand years of glory, and this was Rome's finest army.

He watched them fall into place, a formidable power unmatched on earth. In the earliest days the army had consisted of one thousand men in each of three legions, one legion recruited from each of the three tribes in old Rome, each legion with a detachment of one hundred horse-soldiers.

The earliest army had been made of patricians, but soon all citizens were made liable to serve, and they were divided into five classes according to their status—important since these divisions still held, though the worldly means of the soldiery had no part in determining it. The richest served as cavalry, next richest as heavy-armed infantry, and so down to the poorest who were light-armed skirmishers. And there remained an even more humble class who were to be called only in times of national peril.

This gave four legions of infantry, with cavalry in addition. They fought in solid formation, known as the phalanx, with a frontage of five hundred men and depth of six ranks.

The phalanx proved clumsy and the legions were divided into maniples—handfuls—arranged in three groups, according to battle experience. Skirmishers entered action first, prepared the way for men of the first line, the *hastati,* with spears and sword for close fighting. The second line, more experienced men, the *principes,* were held waiting in reserve. If this wave failed, the most experienced fighters, the *triarii,* came into action.

As the battlefronts moved farther from Rome, the campaigns lasted longer, the great losses in life and wealth caused Marius to reorganize the army completely again. He threw the army open to all willing to serve for pay. Men adopted arms as profession, for fifteen to twenty years, pledging oath to their general in person. The old method of grouping men according to experience was dropped, though the names of the groups remained in use.

The spear was replaced by the javelin. Legions were divided into ten cohorts, each containing three maniples, each of which in turn was divided into centuries. The cavalry was no longer composed of the patricians, but came from foreigners, mainly Spaniards and Gauls.

Now, sitting in the gray wan fog, Livius watched this formidable force gather under the centurions, the tribunes, the legates. They moved fluidly, the archers, the infantry, the cavalry. Voices of tribunes could be heard in the awesome ground fogs calling the movements. Listening, Livius felt he could distinguish the voices of his friends, Victorinus and Polybus.

A new sound broke across the continued rhythmic clatter of the regular army.

Catching his breath, Livius jerked his head around. Commodus and his gladiators—on foot and headed by Verulus, took a position near the front ranks of the army.

Livius scowled watching Commodus move among the gladiators, laughing too loudly, trying too hard to appear to be one of them, displaying rough camaraderie.

Commodus and Verulus paused, watching as Livius gave last-minute instructions to Polybus. The young officer moved away in the growing light. Polybus silently inspected the army which was drawn up now in attack position, full strength.

Polybus stopped before the archers, reviewing them with cold, undeceived eye. The archers stood at rigid attention as he moved past. He heeled quickly to the javelin throwers, letting his gaze go over them searchingly. Polybus nodded briefly, galloped on through the ranks.

Only when he had reviewed the battle-ready forces did Polybus appear to notice the gladiators near these front ranks. Now he rode swiftly across the rough terrain to them.

Commodus stood with a twisted smile of challenge about his mouth. At his shoulder, Verulus lounged, watching the young tribune warily.

Polybus stared first at Commodus, then at Verulus, and finally moved his gaze across the gladiators. They were nothing like the men they seemed in the sand of an arena. Close, they were grim, battered men, standing half bewildered, sullen.

Polybus caught his breath sharply.

Commodus watched each of the young tribune's movements. Polybus pulled his horse around, faced the waiting prince. He spoke quietly, field officer in command: "Move your men back behind the lines, Prince Commodus."

Commodus laughed at him, and there was contempt in the sound. "We're veterans. We've fought in the arena. We've faced death before. We came up here for the excitement of hunting man-beasts."

Polybus remained calm. "My orders are from the high command. They don't require explanation." He sighed heavily. No matter what else Commodus was, or was rumored to be, he was the emperor's son, and Polybus knew he would explain. "We have been chasing the barbarians for years, especially their leader Ballomar."

Polybus lifted his arm, pointed below through the mists toward the enemy camp. "We think Ballomar has come to do battle after his terrible losses of last week. We think he's there now. We must have battle-tested veterans when we move into that valley. They will be used as bait. Their orders will be to stand and draw out Ballomar."

Verulus cut him off. "Who is this Ballomar? What kind of animal? We've killed hundreds like him."

Commodus nodded defiantly. "I'll lead my men—as your bait. I'll show these legions what it is to be Caesar's son! I have the blood of emperors in my veins."

Polybus glanced over his shoulder toward the silent, grim-visaged army. He spoke coldly. "Well then, if you really want to fight."

"We'll show you how to fight," Commodus said.

Polybus nodded grimly and pointed to a densely wooded thicket below them in the fog-hazed valley. "Then it's really very simple. At the command, you and your gladiators will move forward into that forest there in the valley. At first, the barbarians will think it is a trap. But you will keep moving ahead until they are convinced it is a single scouting unit safe for them to attack. Then—you will stand against them until we can get to you."

Polybus sat quietly in his saddle waiting for Commodus and Verulus to digest this—to understand its terror and horror and to withdraw behind the lines.

Commodus was pale, but without glancing at Verulus, nodded, accepting the orders.

Polybus hesitated, then gave a grim answering nod, wheeled his horse about, galloping away.

Commodus laughed and hurled an ugly, defiant gesture from the gutters after him. Laughing, Verulus aped him.

Behind them, the thinly clad gladiators stirred uneasily as

Polybus rode away. Verulus moved among them, his tongue lashing at them, trying to whip them into some semblance of military order.

Commodus, watching, only laughed. His gladiators didn't need army discipline to kill half-human animals in a forest.

Galloping at top speed, Polybus rode to where Livius, Victorinus and other officers of the line were gathered.

Polybus outlined curtly to Livius what had happened. Glancing beyond the tribune's shoulder, Livius saw Commodus and Verulus standing defiantly. From old, he knew better than to attempt to reason with Commodus when he was in such a mood.

Polybus, Livius and Victorinus, unsmiling, coldly studied Commodus and Verulus and their ragged, sullen band of killers. The silence deepened, settling like the ground mist over the seemingly unending ranks of men.

Sighing deeply, Livius pulled his gaze from the hulking gladiators to the perfect ranks of trained forces awaiting his command.

A sudden gleam of light, reflected from the earliest sun, caught Livius' eye. The others around him noticed and glanced up, seeing two bronze-collared vultures circling patiently overhead, riding the updrafts.

Victorinus said to Livius, "Two vultures our men recently captured on a battlefield. They put bronze collars on their necks. They keep following the army."

Livius stared a moment, along with his officers and men at the strange, black carrion birds. On the far flank, the gladiators stirred uneasily, suspicious and wildly superstitious.

Livius glanced once more along the line of archers, javelin men, cavalry, and then gave the signal to move out.

Polybus rode forward, calling to Commodus and Verulus: "Forward!"

As gray as the fog now, Commodus heeled around and faced Verulus and the gladiators behind him. He gestured the men forward.

The gladiators broke ranks and shambled forward, not holding back, but without heart for what was ahead, the unknown and the ugly symbol of vultures like lookout kites above their heads.

Moving forward in cadence with his men, Livius, Vic-

torinus and Polybus watched. The gladiators went down the
incline as the morning light lifted, showing the depth and
melancholy dark of the forest.

Commodus plunged ahead with Verulus at his side. They
entered the first line of thick undergrowth into the trees, and
the gladiators straggled into it behind them. None spoke, all
alert, tense, listening in the deep forest silence.

Neither Commodus nor Verulus spoke as they thrust aside
the tangled limbs, penetrating more deeply into the unearthly
stillness. Commodus glanced over his shoulder. His intellect
was far superior to his men's and he saw from the terrain
that help could not come quickly when the barbarians attacked. Soon even the slow-witted gladiators became aware
of this truth and they glanced about, eyes distended, mouths
parted, as if deafened by the overwhelming silence.

Commodus gave a signal that was passed along and the
gladiators drew their swords, drawing some comfort from the
cold weapons in their fists. They pulled their shields close to
their bodies and held tight-ranks, making as compact a group
as the trees would permit.

They were forced to move single file, and to break the
silence they spoke in low tones to the men nearest them,
words without meaning or intelligence, sounds made only to
reassure themselves.

Suddenly Commodus stumbled on something. He caught
his breath, brought up his sword. Before him was the body
of a Roman soldier, dead for some hours.

Commodus blanched, staring at the body. The others drew
up behind him, made a semicircle, unable to move forward
or to retreat. Laboriously, unmoving, they counted the bodies
of five dead soldiers, mutilated, decapitated on the ground.

Unable to pull their gazes away, they stared in fascinated
horror at what the barbarians had left of the five men.

They held their breath as one man, listening, reacting in
terror to the rustling of a branch, the crackling of a twig.

The gladiators turned all the way around, searching for a
way out. Commodus spoke under his breath and finally they
were able to move forward again, looking everywhere at each
step for the foe they realized had surrounded them with the
same silence as the fog. The barbarian was out there—somewhere—watching them, following every movement they
made. Waiting. Like those circling vultures.

At the crest of the incline above the forested valley, Livius halted his men. He sat, mounted, along with Victorinus and Polybus at his side, the trained legionnaires poised, ready to plunge downhill into action.

Livius swore under his breath, scanning the valley in the dawn light. There was nothing to see, even as the fog lifted, and the sun drenched the trees and shortened the shadows, shifting them and graying them out.

He squinted, occasionally finding the glint of a shield in the dense thicket, the only evidence of Commodus and his gladiators in that purpled silence.

He was aware that Polybus shifted impatiently in his saddle, troubled because he had given Commodus the command to take those untrained ruffians into the forest. Whatever happened, Polybus was living with an inner guilt.

Inside the forest, Commodus jerked his head and his men moved across the mutilated bodies of the soldiers and deeper into the valley. As they walked, lifting their feet warily to keep from making noise, they heard sounds from the thick curtain of undergrowth surrounding them. But when they stopped, holding their breath, there were no sounds at all, only green, unbroken silence that was more terrifying than the yells of Hun warriors could have been.

Commodus glanced across his shoulder, feeling a wild sense of helplessness. He knew these men, but he had never seen them like this before. They were on the verge of panic.

He swallowed hard, unable to blame them because even the thick stillness itself was unnatural. He shared with those men the deep instinct that death was close to him, stalking him.

He gave a sharp signal and they moved forward, paused, stopped, listening. There was nothing. No sound, no movement, a serene sense of peace and security as false as it was deep.

Commodus moved forward and, straightening, beheld an open plain ahead through the trees. He pointed, and his men, feeling safe again once they were in that open, breathed out heavily, sighing with relief. One or two were able to smile, life coming back to them.

Suddenly the stillness was shattered by a guttural roar. It was made by uncounted voices, but sounded like one voice. It seemed animal-like, but no animals could make such a sound. It came from all sides, plunging closer like nerve-shattering storm-waves crashing across the gladiators.

The barbarians, clad in black, and strangely ornamented with teeth, skulls and bones from animals, erupted as if from the earth itself. They rushed out from behind trees, small brush, rocks, sometimes seeming to the terrified gladiators to appear directly before them in some weird devil's magic, screaming, yelling.

The gladiators fell in wild disorder, panic. Some dropped their shields, others threw away their swords in sheer fright and surrender. Those who saw any chance at all forgot to fight and plunged into the undergrowth, running.

Commodus yelled at them. Verulus moved among them frantically, slashing at them with the side of his sword trying to restore some sanity, trying to keep them in place.

Commodus, seeing his men in flight, swung his sword as if replacing ten men, his mouth twisted with rage, his eyes black.

He swung around and before him appeared a man who seemed a giant, shoulders wide and hairy, his body battle-scarred, his crude broadsword glinting in the sun.

For a moment, as if in a trance, Commodus stared at the huge man. No one had to tell him. This was Ballomar. He had accomplished his objective: he had flushed out the Marcomanni leader the Romans sought.

His mouth pulled bitterly because he had small hope at the moment of ever living to be rewarded for this achievement.

Ballomar roared, sounds that were unintelligible to Commodus, but were understood by his black hordes who swept past him on those guttural commands, pouring in upon the disorganized band of gladiators.

Above the forest, the guttural roars of Ballomar's warriors struck at the legion. These men did not even flinch. They were poised, waiting for the command to charge. They had met the Marcomanni and Huns like them for eight years now, and if they had ever feared them—any more than re-specting them as warriors—they had learned to control that fear.

Victorinus swept up his arm. "Ballomar!" he yelled at Livius. "We've pulled him out of hiding!"

Livius nodded, and Polybus, already straining forward in his saddle, spurred his horse, plunging downslope even as he shouted the command to charge, gesturing with his sword toward the forest.

The sound swelled from a bubble of sound to a torrent as the forward flanks of the legions raced downslope, followed by wave after wave of thundering, even-paced soldiers.

Caught in the closing whirlpool of black-clad Huns, Commodus could not hear the thunder of Roman legions pounding to his aid. He heard nothing but the cries of panic from his own men, the unearthly war-cries of the barbarians.

Driven back into the narrowing circle, the gladiators saw Commodus fighting without cease. They sensed at once that fighting as Commodus fought was their only chance of staying alive. They put their backs to the center of the closing circle, striking at the waves of Huns overwhelming them. But the numbers were too great, and not even the savage fierceness of Commodus and Verulus could rally the gladiators. They bolted, running in terror, striking out with their swords, but now only to clear a path to some kind of safety outside this swirling forest of wailing animal-men. Demoralized, they sobbed, running until lance or arrow or axe felled them.

Verulus wept with uncontrollable rage. "The fools! They've let the whole Hun army fall on us. Run, Commodus."

Verulus, swinging his sword, parrying thrusts with his shield, tried to force Commodus back from the attacking Huns, but Commodus shoved him away savagely.

Commodus and Verulus, swinging sword and shield, were engulfed as the barbarians screamed past in pursuit of the retreating gladiators.

Commodus, looking forward, saw no hope. It was like a nightmare. From the forest gushed what looked like an endless stream of black-clad, screaming animal-men.

Verulus, still weeping in rage, yelled at Commodus. "Run! Save yourself!"

Commodus kept fighting at Verulus' side. He wanted to run, as badly as Verulus did, but neither gave an inch, except as they were overpowered, overwhelmed, driven back step by step by uncounted savages attacking them.

The Roman legions, broken into maniples, came into the forest on every side from the high ground. Now the thunder of fighting men shook the earth, and even the screaming Marcomanni warriors heard it.

Livius, and mounted soldiers with him, galloped into the

ring of trees, racing toward the first line of the barbarians.

As Livius reached the depth of the battle, he could see Verulus and Commodus, fighting like wild men in a churning sea of black-clad Huns.

Livius gave a signal and his men plowed forward, riding over barbarians in a straight line toward the place where Commodus and Verulus alone were standing ground.

Livius, swinging his sword, cut his way directly to Commodus and Verulus, followed by his horsemen, the savages falling back before the ferocity of the attack by mounted men.

Livius rode directly to Commodus, leaned down, caught the prince about the waist and bodily lifted him upon his horse out of the danger as Roman reinforcements plunged past them, driving the Huns back or chopping them down where they stood. Victorinus swung the still raging Verulus up behind him.

Livius hesitated one moment, only to see in anguish that the huge Ballomar and his aides had pulled back, and were going to escape his snare.

He did not speak, feeling the trembling Commodus clinging to him, dazed and overcome with terror, now that the danger was past. With Victorinus behind them they fought their way back through the forest, trying to reach the hill and safety.

VI

COMMODUS WALKED OUT of his tent in the late morning and surveyed the encampment. He was freshly shaven, had taken two hot baths and washed away even the memory of the terror of that battle in the valley. He had thought he would be haunted by the vision of the craggy, scarred monster Ballomar for the rest of his life, but even Ballomar now seemed only part of a very bad dream.

Joined by Verulus, who still looked ashen-faced and shaken despite a cold bath and fresh clothing, he walked toward the west gate where only a few hours ago they had slunk back from defeat, riding behind Livius and Victorinus.

"What were our losses, Verulus?" Commodus said.

"The army is not yet back."

"I don't mean the army. I don't care about the army. I mean our losses. Our men. My gladiators."

"Heavy. But not so bad as we deserved."

Commodus shrugged, the old petulant pull drawing his mouth down. "We did as well as any, Verulus. Never forget that."

Verulus glanced at Commodus, but did not answer. He supposed the younger man's intellect was keener, but his own memory was better. He said nothing, watching the orderly return of the legion from the encounter in the valley. They were sweated, some bloody, some wounded, but they kept ranks, marched with pride and discipline. Verulus was astonished that he would feel the tingling of pride. He had no idea he had ever cared what happened to Rome or the Roman army. But you could not help admiring these gallant men. He thanked the gods they had swept into that forest at the moment they had.

He followed Commodus to where Livius and Victorinus stood, surveying the returning troops. They were combat-exhausted.

There was a heavy silence, except for the sound of wagons, horses, metal and gear, and the thunder of legion-marching vibrating the earth.

Polybus and other young tribunes, some bleeding from wounds, left the ranks and moved to Livius to report on the battle.

Polybus let his gaze touch for a moment on Commodus and Verulus. When he spoke to Livius he was hoarse with fatigue and bitterness. "Ballomar escaped."

Livius nodded.

Polybus glanced coldly at Commodus and Verulus. Forgotten was his sense of guilt now that they were alive and safe. He now considered only the sorry part they had played, and their failure. He said, louder than necessary, "We lost two hundred men. It was not worth it."

"Are you blaming us?" Verulus said, stepping forward.

Polybus ignored him, but said, "Two hundred legionnaires dead. And we failed our mission."

Verulus spoke in fury, voice rasping. "No one could have held!"

Polybus stared straight at the aging gladiator now. "Our

legionnaires could have held." Polybus jerked his head around and stared at the demoralized remnants of Commodus' gladiators bunched together near Commodus' quarters. "They were cowards!"

Verulus lunged forward, roaring. "A lie! A lie! We were not cowards."

A breathless silence fell on the group of officers. Commodus looked on, as if aloof, his mouth twisted in an amused smile.

"You lie," Verulus said. "You put us in a place where no one could have stood, and you lie."

At the sound of his roaring voice, the two bronze-collared buzzards soared upward, wings creaking rustily.

Livius faced Verulus, spoke warningly. "That's enough, Verulus."

"He lies," Verulus raged, scarcely seeing Livius.

Livius' voice went harsh. "That's enough. The tribune Polybus is a commander of a Roman army—"

"I don't care who he is," Verulus said, face gray. "What is that to me? Even if he were Caesar and called us cowards, I would say it." He almost spat the word in Polybus' stricken face. "Liar!"

Livius lifted his hand in a gesture toward two young lictors to have Verulus dragged away, but Commodus snagged his wrist, holding him firmly, delaying him.

Commodus spoke in low tones, his voice chilled, even as he wore a casual smile. "No, Livius. No one touches Verulus."

Livius was deadly white. He stared at Commodus' hand locked on his wrist. His voice was low. "You know better, Commodus. I cannot permit this."

"The heat of an argument," Commodus said, still smiling, but steel showing through. And when Livius would have given the command to have the gladiator arrested, Commodus spoke fiercely, but very low: "No one touches Verulus!"

Livius glanced at his officers, at the gross, defiant gladiator watching him with contempt. He pulled his gaze back to Commodus and shook his arm free. He let his hand drop in resignation to his side.

Commodus' smile deepened, and Verulus, seeing that no one truly dared oppose Commodus, laughed aloud, color returning to his swarthy cheeks. "We'll show you soldiers who are cowards! Let twenty of your legionnaires who dare, fight twenty of us!"

Livius, pallid, surveyed the group about him. This was a kind of insanity, and he knew better. They were not here to accommodate men like Verulus—or Commodus—with games. War was deadly serious, and it was his profession, not to be ridiculed by feats of bravado like this. And yet he knew inside a terrible rage that needed to be released in violence. He saw this same tension on the faces of Victorinus and the other tribunes. When his gaze touched Polybus, he saw the young officer was silently beseeching him to agree to the contest.

He hesitated a moment longer, then hearing Verulus' laugh of contempt, he nodded grimly. "Get your men together," he said. He gestured toward Polybus. "Find twenty legionnaires who'd care to fight gladiators." Polybus almost laughed aloud, and wheeled away, exultant.

Livius stood, chilled. What sort of insanity was he constantly allowing Commodus to push him toward? Why did he do it?

Thunder rumbled up from the bowels of the earth, and the wind bent trees, and he lifted his head, seeing the swollen black belly of storm clouds piling up on the horizon.

Thunder clapped and white streaks of lightning rent the sky above the open plain outside the encampment. Livius, Polybus, Victorinus, and seventeen other Roman legionnaires lined up, each in a chariot, each trembling with raging anxiety to overpower the gladiators, gathered in chariots across the field, along the brink of a steep cliff.

The army, duties forgotten, the earlier battle out of their thoughts, stood making wagers, watching the two rows of chariots.

A dead silence stretched tautly across the plain, broken only by a whip-snap of lightning and ensuing volleys of thunder.

Livius lifted his arm and let it fall. He rolled forward in a steady, straight rank with his nineteen charioteers.

The gladiators also advanced, swords beside them, lines secured about their waists, and escape-knives gritted between their teeth.

The two files of chariots converged slowly and steadily, Livius in the center. He jerked hard on his lines when he recognized Commodus facing him in the middle of the gladiators.

Livius rode directly toward Commodus.

Commodus stared at him, his face pale. "I didn't think my opponent would be you, Livius."

"I am the commander of the Northern Army. Who else could it be?"

Ashen, Commodus said it again. "I didn't think it would be you."

Livius was pale, too, and his voice was less harsh. "Nor did I think it would be you, Commodus. . . . There is one answer. . . . Only one. . . . Withdraw now, Commodus."

Commodus stared at him intensely, head tilted. "No! No. I cannot withdraw."

Livius held his gaze. "We must not fight each other, Commodus, and I cannot withdraw."

For a moment their gazes clashed, held in silence, filled with old memories and a hundred things neither had voice for.

Commodus straightened. "It has fallen this way. What is it Father teaches? Resign yourself to the will of the gods?" He spoke with hard contempt. Then his voice lowered. "Perhaps it is best this way, Livius. Now you and I need not make the choice that we have not spoken about—and yet which we both know would destroy our friendship. . . . Let the gods decide which one of us it shall be."

Livius winced, staring first at Commodus who was pushing him again into some insanity he was powerless to combat, then he turned, looking at the gathered army waiting in the distance behind him, the double lines of chariots, gazes fixed on him, awaiting his signal.

Thunder grumbled, the ominous roar of displeased gods. Lightning burst blindingly white, searing the world.

Livius' eyes were sad. He nodded. "Then let the gods decide, Commodus."

Commodus' face was expressionless. They gazed at each other for one more moment, reached out, touching in friendship, and parting.

Pulling his head around, Livius swung his chariot out in a wide circle. Behind him, his charioteers followed.

Commodus and his arena-scarred gladiators swung in the opposite direction. Fire chains of lightning lashed down upon them and the plain as the two lines of carts raced head-on at each other, the rumble of thunder lost in the wild pound of hooves and wheels.

Two chariots raced at each other, one trying to force the second toward the brink of the cliff. The charioteers lifted their swords and slashed at their opponents. The horses reared and plunged frantically, trying to veer away from the precipice. Neither soldier nor gladiator would yield.

At the very last second, both charioteers pulled at the lines, trying to head their horses, turn them. It was too late. Chariots, horses, both riders, screaming, fell over the cliff, smashed on the rocks below.

Without even glancing toward the place where the two young men had lost their lives, other charioteers raced at each other. One rider cut his lines, leaped to safety from his overturning cart only to be trampled under another racing horse and chariot wheels.

A rider was thrown from his chariot before he could cut himself free of his lines, and was dragged along by his uncontrolled horse, smashed against rocks and bounced over the rough ground. The suicide carts upset, splintered or leaped over boulders and broke apart when they struck the ground, drivers fighting to free themselves.

Livius gripped his lines, slapped them across the rump of his horse and raced toward Commodus.

Commodus was pulling him in a long arc toward the brink of the cliff. Livius did not slow his racing horse.

The two chariots almost collided. At the moment they were about to crash, Commodus pulled on his lines, swerving. He lunged out with his long sword as he turned, slashing it across the reins of Livius' chariot, severing them. Helpless to control his horse, Livius braced himself. His frantic horse, freed of leash, rushed on blindly.

Commodus pulled close alongside, wheels almost locking. Commodus swung his sword at Livius' head. Livius parried the blow and struck back, chopping off a section of Commodus' cart. They fought savagely, neither even glancing ahead to the brink of the cliff, Commodus because he was on the safe inside, and Livius because he could not control his horse anyhow. His only thought was to beat Commodus off and jump to safety somehow in the next few moments.

The horse galloped to within feet of the brink of the cliff.

Some instinct caused the foaming animal to swerve from the precipice. One wheel of the chariot hung for a breathless second over the void. The horse scrambled insanely, squealing, managed to pull the wheel back over the rim of the cliff.

Commodus pressed hard, trying to turn the unreined horse again toward the cliff-edge.

Commodus was laughing now. Parrying Livius' savage thrusts, he slowly, but inexorably forced the other chariot again toward the brink of the cliff. A wheel of Livius' cart veered along the rim, slipped off the side.

Timonides charged alongside them in a chariot. The Greek's face was white, eyes distended. Hoarsely, he was shouting: "Stop! In the name of Caesar! Stop this insanity!"

Timonides drove directly alongside of Commodus. The prince was hardly aware of him. Face flushed, drunk and wild with sense of impending victory, he ruthlessly crowded Livius' chariot closer to the brink.

Timonides raged at Commodus: "In the name of Caesar!"

Commodus paused, turning his head slightly.

When Commodus turned his head, Livius leaped from his own chariot into Commodus'. Only that split-second move saved his life. His chariot plunged out into space.

Livius fell, off balance and helpless in the careening chariot. Commodus forgot Timonides again. He pulled his head around, saw Livius sprawled helplessly, trying to regain his footing.

Screaming with insensate laughter, Commodus wielded his sword above his head, ready to chop down across Livius' prostrate form.

Timonides screamed at Commodus, all the agony in the world in his raging voice. "Stop! Your father—Caesar— commands you, Commodus. Stop! Under penalty of death, stop!"

Commodus heard the tone of the Greek's words, even more than their meaning. In that instant he sensed that his father would not hesitate to put him to death for the murder of Livius Gaius Metellus. Some glimmer of reason ate through the lust to kill, and he shook his head, lowering his sword.

By now, Livius had gained his footing. He gave a quick

glance at Commodus' hesitating, at the savagery in those black eyes, the twist of that mouth. He looked around him. A driverless chariot swung past as if hurtled along on the wind.

Livius drew one deep breath, set himself and leaped outward. He toppled into the riderless chariot and for a moment bounced with it, and then caught the lines, pulling the frantic animal to a halt.

Timonides turned his chariot and headed again toward the encampment. Commodus circled his own cart, following the rigid-backed Greek, and Livius pulled in behind him. They rode in silence back to the assemblage of soldiery.

Livius caught his breath. He did not see the soldiers. He saw only one man, standing before them, silently waiting.

It was Marcus Aurelius.

Caesar's face was twisted with disgust, and bitter disappointment.

Livius glanced upward, tears burning his eyes. Silently he beseeched the gods to open the earth and swallow him up, anything so he did not have to face the great, wearied man after this latest display of insanity.

Timonides, then Commodus, and then Livius pulled their chariots to a halt in a line before the gray-faced emperor.

For what seemed an eternity to Livius, Aurelius did not speak at all. He stood, a slender, handsome man, embodiment of gentle understanding and great wisdom, now sick with despair at what he saw: his son who would be emperor, and the bleeding, battered young soldier to whom he had hoped to entrust the fate of the civilized world at a time of the most bitter crisis in man's history.

Aurelius spoke in a low tone to Timonides and then turned, his wide shoulders slumped, walking away, sorrow like a burden on his back.

Sick with shame, Livius watched the emperor walk away. The storm rumbled ominously, the swollen black belly of the clouds directly overhead. The air was thick, gusty, agitated.

Neither Livius nor Commodus could face the other. Livius wondered if he would ever be able to stand up as a mature man again before the distressed Caesar. He dropped the reins and stepped out of the chariot. He was overcome with remorse for the thoughtless, insane way he had behaved. He felt Commodus' eyes on his back as he walked away. He could not care what Commodus felt at this moment. All Livius could think was that it was as if the great, good Aurelius had found him out in some shameful way, leaving him stripped of armor, exposed for what he was—what he himself had been forced to see he was.

VII

THE STORM HUNG suspended above the earth, growling, flashing in livid white from black clouds ready to burst as night came.

Livius walked alone through the encampment, glad for the early darkness over the face of the world. The soldiery, auxiliaries, the wings, the visiting dignitaries were all withdrawn to their quarters. Pale lights glowed across the *castra,* but Livius kept himself to the shadows.

He could not remember ever having felt so lonely, so abandoned. He felt the hot flush of shame crawl across his face, even in the chill wind. The emperor had silently rebuked him before the whole Northern Army, and the gods knew he deserved it.

Lightning flared, but he strode on, wincing against its fire, but not slowing, not seeking shelter. The gods hadn't yet created a storm to match the one going on inside himself.

How in the name of the gods had the good Aurelius ever considered him capable of administering the affairs of the civilized world? And worse, how could he even secretly have tried on that purple toga for size? What a stupid fool to imagine himself ready in the least way to replace the godly Aurelius. What did he know of the troubles of the empire, the commerce, the industry, the treasury, the building, the political dealings with the senate and the magistrates of all the provinces? He was no statesman, only a soldier, and he had proved to the world today, not even a very disciplined one.

He walked faster, as if trying to escape his own hounding thoughts. He heard the sentinels on duty, but he moved past without glancing toward them. He heard the enlisted men off duty yelling and arguing, perhaps drunk on their sour wine.

He did not slow his steps. He found a broken javelin. He paused, knelt, picked it up and walked again, holding it in his fist. It seemed to him this weapon was itself a symbol of the men who made the Roman army great. Marius had joined the metal point of the javelin to the shaft with a wooden pin that snapped when the hurled javelin struck; Julius Caesar had made the head, except for the point, of soft iron that bent on impact of a blow. Javelins used by Roman soldiers could never be used against them. These men had made such inspiring contributions to the army and the profession of warfare. What had he done?

He swore back at the raging thunder. Much about the present day army distressed him, but he had no answers. It seemed to him the centurions had too much responsibility and authority, and they abused it. Still, Julius Caesar had taught that the centurion was responsible for discipline, and you could not weaken their power over their men. But sometimes the brutality and immorality of these petty officers sickened him. He had seen men flogged almost to death for misdemeanors. Men of the ranks had to bribe the centurions to avoid floggings, avoid extra duties, to get any privileges. Centurions had come to count on bribes as part of their income, and some of them became inhumanly cruel and vicious. He had no answers even for such a minor, yet far-reaching problem. He had been a fool to consider for one drunken moment the possibility of his becoming Caesar of the empire. The gods forgive him.

Livius flung his head back, staring at the storm-riven sky, needing to be purged of ambition, vanity.

A metallic flash of lightning suddenly stood the encampment watchtower in stark relief against storm-torn sky.

Livius, gazing at the structure, caught his breath. At first he thought it was an hallucination, a need of his own anguished mind in his loneliness. Lucilla stood alone on the tower platform, as alone as he in the night storm.

He held his breath, waiting. A second burst of lightning revealed her again. Livius ran suddenly, going to the foot of the tower, clambering upward in the wail of wind.

When he came off the ladder onto the railing-enclosed platform, Lucilla for one moment remained poised against the sky, like some unutterably lovely statue of a goddess.

When she heard him, she swung away from her intense

study of the vistas below her, and heeled around to face him.

For a moment, neither of them spoke, facing each other, removed up here from all the rest of the world, like two distant stars alone in a black firmament. The thunder shook the tower supports as well as the pillars of the earth.

Livius said, "Maybe I should have stayed away. I have no right—"

"I was thinking about you."

He exhaled heavily. "It's no good. I've known that, even when I was a boy. I knew then you were never intended by fate for me. Ever since I saw you again here, I've tried to fight it off—the way I feel about you. . . . But I can't. . . . It seems all I have that's good on earth—the way I love you. . . . I love you, Lucilla. I've loved you—forever—as long as I have any memory of you, I've loved you."

He took a long stride across the platform toward her. She fixed her gaze on his face in the darkness and sudden glare of white lightning. He took her in his arms, feeling her shudder.

Her face lifted up to his and he kissed her, more roughly than he intended because his love was so intense.

The storm raged, and yet was paled by the storm that had built for so many lonely years inside them.

Suddenly Lucilla cried out, wrenching away from him.

Livius stood, bereft, unable to move, staring at her. She had to come back to him, close in his arms, he was less than whole without her, and there was no longer any denying that she knew this now.

A savage shudder shook Lucilla and she turned away from him, going to the railing, almost as if she meant to walk out into space and end the brutal conflict inside her.

Livius walked to her, pressed himself against her, feeling her tremble, feeling the resistance against him go out of her. He pulled her about to face him.

Lucilla cried brokenly. She had no strength to fight him, only the desperate knowledge that she must. "No. . . . No. . . . No."

Livius held her closer, whispering. "You love me—you *know*."

She tried to pull away, tilted her head back, her slanted eyes brimmed with tears. She spoke tiredly, as if her will and energy were spent, leaving her without spirit. "Yes. I love you. I want you. It has always been you. First. Only. Always. I want no other man. . . . But I—I've been afraid, too, that this day would happen." The tears spilled, slow drops on her high-planed cheeks. Her mouth trembled. "There were times—knowing it—I didn't even want to live . . . Not without you. . . . It made me doubt life—or any reason for living. . . . Oh, I doubted life, but I—never doubted the way I loved you." She stood straighter. "I am pledged, Livius. You know that. I promised my father—"

"Come away with me," Livius said. "Now. Anywhere. Wherever a man and a woman can be alone."

Her eyes distended, her voice showed her shock. "I—am Caesar's daughter."

Livius tried to smile. "I'll make a woman of you. That is a much higher rank."

Lucilla shook her head, crying. "I couldn't live that way."

"I could. I could live any way, as long as it is with you."

She breathed out, disengaging herself, leaning against the platform railing, slowly regaining control of her emotions. Her voice was truly incredulous. "Run? Hide? Give up everything?"

"What do we really have—on this earth—except each other?"

"Forsake our vows—our pledges?"

"Gladly. Gladly."

There was such force, such power and need in his voice that Lucilla felt helpless against his will, his strength. "How long does this madness last?"

"Forever." He drew her closer. "But even if only for a month—a week—"

"You'd trade your duty and your honor for this?" She stared at him, frightened. "And you are the man my father wishes to be his heir."

His laugh was bitter, tormented. "I'm not the man to take his place, Lucilla."

"Of course you are. Father knows you'll grow, learn—who else but you?"

"I don't know. But not me."

"You are the only man, and you'd throw it away like this."

"Let me tell you the truth, Lucilla. If I had to choose between being Caesar's heir—or your love." He shook his head, holding her closer, convulsed with a sudden shudder.

"I'd choose your love. . . . If that makes me finally less than what your father believed me . . . then I am not fit to rule an empire. . . . Without you, it would be nothing. . . . I am empty and lost, and incomplete without you. I am chilled with cold when you pull away from me here." He kissed her eyes, pressing his face into the luxurious texture of her faintly scented hair. "Only this is real." He whispered against her mouth. "For the sake of all gods, let us be wise enough to know that." His lips moved over her face, and her eyes, along the chiseled line of her jaw to her throat. "All else is half-life—emptiness . . . not living at all. Only loving you is real—"

Lucilla whimpered, a sound of anguish, no longer afraid of him at all, but filled with dread at the storms he had loosed to rage in her mind and her heart.

"That—is only my body. . . ." She shivered visibly, trying to control herself by quoting her Stoic father. "But *I* am more than that. *I* can reason. *I* can rise above that."

Livius kissed her with brutal hunger. "There is *nothing* above this. When the gods bring two people together like this—there is nothing above it for mortals . . . and not even the gods can help those who throw it away . . . for *anything*."

Lucilla broke away from him, moved distracted across the storm-lit platform, pressed against the farthest support.

She did not speak to him, but to the storm-clogged dark. "No. Not true. Not true. I cannot rise above this. . . . I don't want to. . . . I don't want to reason. . . . I want to love him whom I have always loved—him only. . . ." Thunder reverberated from the earth, rattled against the roof of the sky. "I won't listen! I won't hear other voices! I no longer hear any voice but his!" She tilted her head, her hair wild, her eyes fixed defiantly on infinite sky. She shouted her defiance, exultant. "Do you hear me, gods? *I love Livius.* . . . Do you hear me, world? I love Livius." Her voice lowered, fervently. "I'll pray to Venus. Of all the gods, she'll understand. She loved the god of war, didn't she, Livius? And not even the ridicule of the world when she was hung in a net in his arms could change that—she'll understand my love. . . . I'll bring sacrifices to her shrine. Venus will help us. . . . The goddess is close to me. She's always been because I've loved you so deeply, so sincerely, so forever. . . . Venus loves me because I love you above all else. She loves me and she won't let me lose you. . . ."

She stopped abruptly, covering her face, sobbing into her hands.

Livius came to her, took her in his arms. Exhausted, she rested her head against his chest.

Her voice was lower, but she spoke with hope, as if purged from old doubting. "And in the morning, I'll speak to Father. First above all he loves me—he'll release me from my pledge—" She pressed closer, whispering, "Hold me, Livius, don't ever let me doubt, don't ever let me be afraid again."

Lightning erupted in a violent streak, ripping the blackness from one horizon to another, but they didn't hear it; they pressed closer and closer in the blinding whiteness.

Cleander paced inside the tent of Didius Julianus, moving with the uncertain manner of the blind and the instinct that was a kind of sight of its own.

Near the tent doorway, the huge Lentulus lounged, silently watching Cleander. Outside, the storm raged, the wind howled, the walls of the tent pulsed as if breathing.

From couches, Claudius, Julianus and Niger watched the blind man. They had been reclining on pillows, but now all three sat forward, gazes fixed on the white eyes that seemed to burn with gray flameless fire.

"—I was there, outside his room," Cleander was saying. "I heard it all. I know what I heard, and I make it my business to hear all that will help me." He gave a brief laugh. "Twice I made noise, once accidentally, and then waited. They were quiet in there—Caesar, his daughter and this young tribune he means to make his heir in your dear friend Commodus' place. Then, after a moment, they resumed talking, and did not check on my presence at all. What I tell you is the truth. The Caesar is dying—and he does not mean to leave the empire in the hands of Commodus."

"How can you know all this?" Julianus said. "You pretend even to know the state of his health."

"I do know the state of his health!" Cleander stopped and turned his head, as if fixing sightless eyes in the direction of Julianus' voice. "The Caesar is in constant pain, he has had fever for days. He now knows he cannot last much longer."

"Then you think he'll proclaim Livius his heir any moment?" Julianus said.

"I know it—unless he is stopped." Cleander nodded.

"If he does proclaim Livius his heir, then Commodus will not be Caesar," Julianus said. "What will happen to us?"

"It is not going to happen," Niger said. "We've made up our minds to that. We're not going to let it happen."

"How can we prevent it, if we allow him to go on living— ill as he is?" Julianus inquired.

Niger stood up. He spoke savagely. "What difference does it make how long he might last? The important thing is that we decide—what must be done."

There was silence, the only movement was the pulsing of the tent walls as the wind raged, the slow pacing of the blind Cleander.

Julianus said, "It's been decided. Here. Tonight. He must be stopped—before he makes an unfortunate choice."

Claudius laughed in a delighted tone. "How droll you are, Julianus. No wonder the emperor hates you."

"No. I'm serious. We all know that poor Aurelius is too trusting. Didn't he name Lucius Verus as joint ruler? What a disaster! We're only saving him from himself actually!"

Claudius giggled audibly, giving Julianus a playful shove. Julianus scowled, glancing at Niger. "Though some of us don't seem to realize how deadly serious this is—we must have some plan."

Niger pulled a knife from his girdle and laid it across his palm. The other men leaned forward, staring at the snake embossed on its silver handle. Claudius giggled again, this time a nervous sound, and pressed his scented handkerchief against his nostrils.

Niger said, "It has been settled. We have a plan. It is this."

"A knife?" Julianus protested.

Niger smiled. "A deadly poison has been smeared on one side of this blade. Cut fruit or meat or bread with this knife, and then offer the poisoned side to—your victim, yourself take the other half—"

"Oh, how clever you are, Niger!" Claudius cried.

"—it can be done before hundreds of witnesses. You, yourself, eat the other half. You can't be suspected."

Claudius shivered and drew closer against Julianus' side. The knife was passed from hand to hand in the silence. Only

Claudius was unable to touch it. The knife rested at last in Cleander's palm.

Julianus asked, "Who?"

Niger stared at their faces. "Someone from whom Caesar will accept fruit or bread or meat."

Julianus shook his head. "I am not that close to Caesar."

"Nor I," Claudius said. "He detests me. He made horrible charges against me—had me exiled to the provinces."

"Nor am I close to him," Niger said.

Cleander's voice was calm. "I am."

Niger's head came up. "But you are blind."

"I have only to feel the handle to know which side." A faint smile of contempt twisted Cleander's lean face. "And who better than a blind man?"

They stared at him in awe. After a moment Niger nodded, and smiled, feeling secure, as if the deed were already accomplished. They sat in silence, listening to the wailing of the wind.

VIII

TIMONIDES WALKED into the command room behind Marcus Aurelius, deeply concerned for the emperor, and only vaguely aware of the change that permeated the busy office when the *imperium* entered it.

The slave scribes—*amanuenses*—were bent over documents, writing feverishly, quill pens a constant scratching sound that seemed to be heard above everything else. Couriers, envoys, officers, all weary, but exhibiting the results of impressive discipline and organization, hurried in or out, collecting or depositing documents.

Near the general's table, Aquila the eagle sat unblinking on his perch. He cried out like a watchdog at the sight of Caesar and the room was momentarily silent as soldiers and slaves came to attention.

Timonides watched Aurelius make the slight gesture that released the men and set them again into feverish activity.

Though the storm was raging full-force, its fury seemed distant, diminished in here to Timonides. The fury of the wind and the chill of cold seemed to him reflected in Aurelius' tired face and in the strange melancholy that hung over him.

He's only tired, Timonides thought, and why shouldn't he be mortally exhausted? Few people understood, and the Greek slave was fearful that few would ever know the extent and the overwhelming fearfulness of the problems of empire Marcus had inherited from Antoninus Pius.

The whole world loved, revered, respected Pius, and talked of the calm of his rule; his enemies were quiet, his relations with the senate and all the provinces were harmonious, Pius was the most universally loved of all rulers; he was blameless, and got along well with all the world. Ah, but this was the rub!

Antoninus let the army become slack, discipline lax, left provinces to a kind of self-rule, allowed the barbarians to become strong all along the northern frontiers.

Disasters broke upon the empire when Aurelius began his rule; troubles struck from everywhere. Aurelius had been trained by Pius to accept the responsibilities of emperor, but Aurelius had no inkling of what rigors awaited him. The slack army had to be whipped into shape with barbarians attacking from the North and orientals from the East. Aurelius found good men to head the army and there were victories, but all of them were costly, and all of them drained the strength from Caesar.

Aurelius was a meditative man who was never permitted to rest. His victorious armies returned from the East—bringing with them the Black Death, a scourge and epidemic that infected the Roman world. While Aurelius was fighting this pestilence, a coalition of northern barbarians attacked along the whole Danube frontier. This crisis demanded the presence of the emperor. Thirteen years of fighting followed.

Timonides glanced at the rounded shoulders of the slender, tired man. Working ceaselessly, Aurelius had quieted the Quadi and the Marcomanni along the Danube and worked out a plan to further prevent such uprisings. But before his plan could be completed, one of his most successful generals in the eastern campaigns declared himself emperor of the Roman world, and Marcus was forced to abandon his incompleted works in the North and drive East to protect his empire. While he was gone from the north country, all his work there was undone, and he had to return, tired, deadly tired, and set about doing all of it again.

Timonides shook his head—a tired man, his heart weary and weakened, fevered in a camp here at Vindobona—a man who had given his whole life to his people, dying up here so far from his beloved Rome.

Angered, Timonides stared about at these working men. Couldn't they see how ill Caesar was? Couldn't they know he was exhausted fighting to save them from ruin?

But Timonides saw that none of these men noticed how fatigued Aurelius was. The emperor sat himself at his simple table and officers crowded around him bringing him their problems and the latest state documents.

To hide his rage, Timonides turned and glared at the huge maps of the civilized world covering all the walls of the command room.

He turned back then, and interceded himself between Caesar and the couriers, greeting them, accepting their messages and documents. He glanced through them quickly, passing on only the most urgent to Aurelius.

Working, Timonides found a new cause for rage. He did not speak because he was only a slave, and Cleander had long been a trusted friend of the emperor.

Timonides scowled. If history found a weakness in this great emperor, it would be in his ability to judge men, for he permitted Cleander a freedom that Timonides would never tolerate.

Reading state messages, Timonides saw Cleander and his ever-present Lentulus bending over a table where slave scriveners read to Cleander from parchment documents.

Timonides could contain himself no longer. He bent forward, meaning to call this fact to Caesar's attention, even when he was sure he would get only reproof from Aurelius.

At that instant Aurelius fell back in his chair as if an unseen fist had struck him forcefully in his chest.

Timonides forgot Cleander, Lentulus, confidential papers. He stepped closer to the emperor's chair. For a moment, Marcus swayed, as if rocked by a physical blow.

He put his hands on the table, steadying himself and stood erect, slowly.

The room was charged with a static silence. No command was needed. Slaves, soldiers, scriveners all understood the emperor must be left alone with his pain.

The room was cleared quickly. Timonides stood watchfully beside Marcus' chair but did not touch the emperor.

Aurelius was struck again, and he swayed under the impact of the pain. It was unendurable. Caesar glanced only to see that he was at last alone, and he yielded to the agony in his chest, let the seizure master him. He sank slowly to the table.

After a moment he toppled back in his chair, breathing through grayed lips. He glanced up at Timonides and a wry smile twisted his ashen features. He spoke quietly, as if out of breath, defeated at last by an enemy too formidable for him.

"You—a man to—enjoy an irony, my dear Timonides? Consider then—Marcus Aurelius, emperor of all Rome, become no more than the least slave, writhing and helpless. And what is it then that makes itself my master?" He indicated his solar plexus. "A fever, a spot, a point, perhaps no larger than a grain of sand. What is the wisdom of that?"

Timonides did not trust himself to speak, and anyhow, he had no answer.

"No answer for that, Timonides? Nor do I. . . . Think. . . All we have read and pondered—you and I. . . . And the endless talks, Timonides. The hours and hours and months and years of words we have spoken to each other. Surely . . . it should have prepared me for—" he touched at his chest, "—for this. But it has not, learned Greek. . . . I am not prepared. . . . Why was that, Timonides? In all this talk we made, did this topic slip our minds? Or did we have some hidden and unuttered knowledge that our wisdom would be of no avail before this mystery of mysteries? . . . And if once we had admitted that, then would we not have been forced to admit that—all other knowledge, wisdom, skill —all of it is trivial, empty and meaningless? And then we would not have thought—or talked—or read—or wondered. . . . Perhaps it is just as well, my Timonides. . . . For if men do not think, read and talk, above all else— talk to each other—they are no longer men."

The emperor was again rocked with a paroxysm of pain. He pressed his face into his hands and stayed bent over for a long time. Timonides did not move, helpless as the most ignorant savage.

Aurelius looked up at last. "He stands there—alongside of you. . . . He has come for me, the silent boatman, to row me across the shadowed river." He straightened, face showing gray rage. "I am not ready for you!" He pointed to the unfinished document before him. "Ballomar the chief of the Marcomanni has met with the Vandals. . . . Don't you see? If they should make a treaty, the whole North would become a place of terror for the empire, and the world. . . . I can't go yet. . . . I am not ready!" He gasped, struck again by pain, crumpling under it. He whispered in agony, "No . . . wait. . . ." He lifted his trembling arm, pointed to another document. "The Persian sits on our eastern frontiers like a hungry jackal. . . ." He cried out this time when the sledge-hammer agony hit him. Shattered by it, he sank helplessly into the shadow of his chair. After a long time, he spoke in a reasonable voice, "Come. . . . I was always a man to talk, even to my enemies, to speak sanely with them. . . . Come, sit here by me, and let me show you how much—how much there is yet for me to do. . . . Can we not—make a treaty? You and I? On your side—I ask you to wait—that's all. . . . Two years? One year? Oh, I cannot do all this in less than a year. . . . I will not say to you—let me have children, or a woman, or my friends, or any pleasures. . . . I will speak only of Rome. . . ." The pain wracked him and he cried out, speaking hastily. "When I say Rome—I mean the world—the future centuries. . . . I do not ask that you be easy on me —only wait a little while. . . . On my side, I am prepared to live on in pain—such pain as this—if only you will wait, for you can see I—have so much yet to do."

He sat, waiting like a reasonable man awaiting an equally sane reply. But the answer when it came was an overwhelming streak of fire in his chest, and for a long time, he crumpled forward, unable to speak at all because of the pain.

"A year!" he cried out, gasping. "A year! What is a year to you?"

He toppled back as if beaten, the pain so great he was no longer able to speak at all. He sprawled against the chair, defeated, too tired to fight any more. The agony ebbed, and when it subsided, he forgot its terror in his rage against it. He pulled himself to his feet, his eyes blazing with fury.

He shouted, "Blind, stupid, vulgar, unreasoning being! Ugly, disgusting, mindless! You to whom no reason can make appeal! You who make of human beings—dust—rocks—nothing! You do not belong in this world of man."

Sighing, he sat down at his table, by sheer and incredible will controlling himself.

His mouth twisted with that old wry smile. "Was it I who asked—did not I ask, 'Is it not within the nature of the fig-tree to give figs—as the honey-bee to give honey?' So it is in the way of things for you to come to me. . . . It is the price we pay for our humanity. . . . I am one of those small truths I spoke about. . . . Yet, this I know. . . . There is a greater truth behind it all. A truth we have not yet divined." He stared out at the deepening shadow. "Forgive me, boatman. . . . I did not know you were blind and deaf. Come for me when you will. . . . It will be my hand which will lead us."

He sighed again and lapsed into silence. He put his head back, closed his eyes, seeming to sleep.

Timonides did not move. His eyes were dry, and he thought how true it was that we weep for the small things, but there is an agony too deep for tears.

When at last he saw that Caesar was asleep, he tip-toed from the room, leaving the tired man to find rest where he could.

Aquila perched over Aurelius, unblinking. In the room, silence and shadow deepened, the storm pounding as if from a far distance.

Lentulus led Cleander into the command room. They closed the door behind them and for a long time stood in the heaviest shadow, studying the room.

Aurelius opened his eyes. He started, surprised to see them standing before him.

"It is only us, Caesar," Cleander said. "We did not mean to disturb your rest." ·

"It's all right, Cleander. You didn't waken me. . . . I was chilled . . . or perhaps I dreamed it. I wakened cold."

"Are you in pain, my lord Caesar?" Cleander asked from the shadows.

Aurelius hesitated a moment, almost as if Timonides were at his shoulder, cautioning him against the duplicity of men, his own belief in their innate goodness. He sighed. He had known Cleander so many years. He nodded. "I am, Cleander. I am in great pain."

Cleander moved into the faint light around the *imperium's* table. From his woolen *tunica*, the blind man drew first an apple, and then after a moment, from his girdle, the snake-embossed knife.

His voice was soft, filled with pity and concern for his old friend. He said, "Share this fruit with me, Caesar. It will ease your pain."

Aurelius smiled, face gray, and nodded.

Cleander hesitated a moment, his hand fumbling along the hasp of the knife, fingering the blade. He cut the apple in half. Again, he hesitated briefly, almost as if weighing the halves in his slender hands. He extended the sliced apple to Aurelius. Aurelius thanked him, glad Cleander and Lentulus were with him in the shadows and loneliness. Both men bit into the apple.

IX

THE RAIN was blown away on the wind. The world was a dark and hollow cave, its single eye of light a widening orb of torches, lamps, fires, concentrated outside the praetorium. Men came running from everywhere. They moved in stunned silence, king, consul, legate bumping slave or soldier, and none of them speaking, rank and class forgotten in the static silence and frantic disorder of the courtyard where death stalked, a disdainful leveller.

"He is dead—"

"Caesar is dead—"

"Not dead, but dying—"

"I heard it said he was dead for hours, and only now the whisper has escaped—"

"No. He is inside. They have carried him to his quarters. He lies helpless, unable to speak, but alive."

"God spare the great Caesar—"

King Sohamus, followed by his aides, pushed his way to the entrance of the praetorium. Silently, the king was refused admittance by the guards. Angered, his face cold and set, the youthful monarch heeled around, staring across the heads of the milling crowd.

Marcellus and Virgilianus, who already had been refused admittance, joined the king. None of them spoke, speechless over the lack of protocol, the confusion.

Sohamus spoke to Commodus, attempting to convey some of the deep pity he felt. Commodus stood dazed, hardly aware of the young king of Armenia.

Julianus stepped away from Claudius and Niger, part of the half-dressed group accompanying Commodus. Julianus addressed Sohamus with humility and a look of deep sorrow. "Commodus is unable to speak, your majesty."

Sohamus stared at Didius Julianus a moment and then waved his hand. "I understand his grief, Senator. I hope the terrible loss to all Rome in the death of this good man is not wasted on any of us."

"We are all stricken," Claudius said.

"Not the death of our own father, nor the death of all our gods would desolate us more," Niger said.

Sohamus glanced at their faces once more, and heeled around, turning his back on them. He saw Lucilla hurrying through the crowd and moved toward her before he recognized Livius with her.

Sohamus watched emptily as the tribunes Victorinus and Polybus cleared a way for Livius and Lucilla to the entrance of the praetorium. Near the doorway, Cleander reached out his hand toward her and Lucilla hesitated.

Lentulus led Cleander forward to where Lucilla stood. Cleander sank to his knees before her, weeping. He caught the hem of her garment, kissing it, crying out. "I was the last one with him. Oh, why couldn't the gods have taken me in his place?"

Sohamus, glancing around, saw the way the three aides with Commodus looked at each other, as if hiding contemptuous laughter for Cleander's behavior. Sohamus was angered for a moment, but then admitted with honesty that he was not deeply impressed by Cleander's weeping, either.

Lucilla touched the blind man's head for an instant, and then hurried to the praetorium door. The guards delayed them only a moment. In that brief space of time, Lucilla gazed around as if seeking someone. Her glance settled on Commodus. Commodus shook himself, took a step toward her and then stopped.

The guards hurried Livius and Lucilla into the praetorium.

When Lucilla and Livius entered the room where Caesar was lying motionless on his cot, both hesitated involuntarily.

Left alone in the room with the dying man, they moved slowly forward and knelt on each side of his cot.

For a long time there was silence. Sounds of confusion in the courtyard seeped through the walls.

Aurelius opened his eyes. He stared at Lucilla's face, as if memorizing each feature of it. He struggled, but was unable to speak or move his hands.

Lucilla was pale, but she felt overwhelmed with relief seeing her father was alive. Word had come to her that he was already dead. Now she was able to believe that he would live; she was unable to imagine life without her father's gentle wisdom a part of it.

She touched her father, whispering, "You will get well."

His smile was like the gray memory of a smile in his taut face. He moved his gaze from her eyes to Livius, and back again.

Lucilla whispered, "Father, I love Livius—"

Aurelius kept his gaze on her face. His eyes showed no hint of surprise.

"Can't you—release me from my promise?" she pleaded in that strained whisper. "I cannot endure losing you—or him. . . . I know that now. . . . Is there nothing you can say to me?"

Aurelius was unable to move.

She tilted her head, eyes brimmed with tears. "I love him, Father. I want to live with him. I cannot be without him—now."

Aurelius closed his eyes for a moment, and then when he opened them again, tears stood in them. A tear slipped across his lashes, along his cheek. He was unable to move.

"Oh, Father," Lucilla wept. "Talk to me . . . I don't mean to make you cry. To hurt you. . . ."

Aurelius struggled, trying to move his lips, shake his head. His eyes showed the agony of the attempt, but he could not stir and lay there, helpless.

Lucilla cried out. "Oh, Father, don't leave us like this!"

Aurelius' breathing was more labored, painful. His eyes closed and he was unable to open them again, unable to move at all.

Lucilla looked up, her gaze locked on Livius. "Oh, Livius, he—he's dying."

Livius got to his feet. He came around the cot, lifted Lucilla in his arms, drew her away from the dying man into the shadows. He held her, letting her cry against his chest.

She whispered brokenly, "Livius, what if he dies—what if my father dies—before he can declare you his heir. . . . What will you do?"

Livius held her. He shook his head, eyes tormented. "I don't know. . . . There is nothing I can do. . . . He didn't name me. . . . Commodus is his heir."

"He wanted you!"

"There would be doubt. No matter what I said, there would be doubt. Caesar must be undoubted Caesar, Lucilla."

Lucilla spoke fiercely. "*I* will be your witness. I will tell the world my father wanted *you*. I am Caesar's daughter. They will know I do not lie."

Livius exhaled heavily. "And if you come forward—and if it were only your word—what would the world believe? Commodus is much loved in Rome—wouldn't they whisper that *we* had conspired together—against your brother?"

Her mouth twisted with her scorn. "My brother!" She pulled away, speaking with contempt. "This boy—this athlete—this companion of gladiators. . . . Can you let the empire fall into his hands?"

Livius was silent a long time. At last he said quietly, "A dozen times on the battlefield, I've seen a boy—an athlete—a soldier—forced to become a leader, and before my eyes become a man—"

"Father was about to name you—"

"Yet he did not. And he knew that his heir had to be undoubted Caesar. That is why he convened everyone here—"

"My father did not want Commodus! He wanted you!"

Livius' voice was deadly quiet. "He wanted the good of Rome."

Lucilla trembled, clutching his arms. "And what will happen to us? In the wreckage my father leaves, how could I forget the pledge I made to him?"

Livius stared at the man on the cot. He spoke prayerfully. "He still lives . . . the gods will not let him die this way."

But Lucilla spoke flatly, her face expressionless. "No. My father will not live . . ." She heard movement across the room. She turned and went quickly back to the cot. Aurelius lay motionless. She knelt beside him. She whispered against his cheek. "Don't leave us yet. Can't you wait—just a while longer?" Her father did not move. Her voice was soft, yet firm. "Father—if the gods find no man to carry on your dream—I will carry it on. I vow I will."

Aurelius opened his eyes, looking up at her. His features seemed to relax faintly, softening.

Lucilla rose to her feet. Livius walked up close behind her. Lucilla stared down at her father, then looked at Livius a moment without speaking. She walked past him, going slowly out of the room.

Livius stood staring after her, and then looked down helplessly at the dying emperor. After a moment he knelt beside the cot, covering his face with both his hands.

Lucilla walked into the command room where the slave scribes and *imperium* aides were silently, doggedly at work again under Timonides' direction. Timonides' face showed that he had his grief leashed and as long as he worked, he was all right.

Timonides and several slave scribes were searching through piles of parchment documents on the tables, moving with frantic haste and rigid silence.

Timonides looked up when Lucilla entered the room. She saw the frustration and defeat in his face. He had learned to control his emotions, he did not permit himself to think about her father's death, but whatever it was he was searching for was not to be found.

There was a moment of hesitation as Timonides and Lucilla faced each other.

Lucilla said, "You were looking for a document, Timonides? A state paper my father left—in case of his death?"

Timonides nodded, speaking cautiously. "Yes, I was."

Lucilla searched his face, frightened. She said urgently, "You must find it—"

"We have looked everywhere."

"There must be such a document. There has to be. You know there was. You knew Father better than anyone. . . . You know there was. Look again! Look everywhere! Look quickly."

The intensity of her tone startled him. He stared at her, and shook his head. Before he spoke, he pawed one more time before the pile of documents.

"There is no such document, Princess."

"There's got to be! There must be. You must have seen him make it!"

Timonides' face was haggard. He finger-combed once more without hope through the stacks of parchment. He looked up and spoke flatly, "There is no such document, Lucilla. . . . At least, I cannot find one."

Behind them, someone moved past the guards, entering the command room. Timonides and Lucilla glanced around.

Livius came directly to the table where they stood. He heard what Timonides said but asked no questions, finding their answer in the bleak gray of their faces.

A sudden wailing started outside, swelling across the entire expanse of the encampment.

Lucilla cried out, pressing close against Livius.

"It's the soldiers," he said, drawing her against him, feeling her tremble.

She nodded. Though she'd heard how the legions used the hollow of their shields to amplify sounds, she had never been caught inside its hurting fury of sound before.

"My lord Caesar," Timonides whispered. "Caesar is dead."

Caesar was dead, and the legions mourned. Across the *castra*, every soldier knelt weeping into the bowed hollow of his shield—a sobbing painful to hear, increasing from shallow murmur to depth of guttural moaning, an agonized animal growl, sorrow without comfort, wild and unbridled passion of men not afraid to weep aloud and boldly, protesting the distress of human life and mortal loss, voicing hurt in a fearful melancholy lament that cast a pall of gloom and filled the dark void between earth and heaven.

None of these battle-scarred brutes alone could have put his anguish in words—their pain could not be expressed in eloquence, for they had none—but for this blind, grieving monster with uncounted heads bowed into shield-hollows, the discordant, yet measured and continuous sob pulsed, their wretchedness a monument to Caesar's greatness and their own immeasurable loss. Slow, deep and unbroken, with rage in its force like a sullen madness, the weeping lifted and they purged themselves with this oratorio of grief, this storm of tears that purified the air of the plain.

Lucilla slumped against Livius' chest, sobbing brokenly.

At last, she looked up, eyes shadowed with deep fears. "What will happen to us now?" She knew she was like a child left suddenly alone in the dark, helpless without security or reassurance from the one whose strength she'd always looked to, and she tried to control her fear. She tilted her head, looking challengingly at Livius through her tears. "My father is dead—now what will you do?"

But Livius did not answer because he could not. His grief was too deep for words, and not even the raging sobs of the legions, magnified to heaven and hell, could express his sense of numbness and personal bereavement.

The resonant sobbing of the legion quieted. Every dignitary gathered in the courtyard stood in taut silence as in the strange half-light, Livius, Lucilla and Timonides left the praetorium.

Commodus did not move. He was surrounded by Claudius, weeping into his scented handkerchief, Julianus, Niger and Cleander with Lentulus slightly behind them, anxious, watchful.

The soldiers remained on their knees, heads bowed behind their shields. Before them, Victorinus, Polybus and other tribunes and legates were in military lines.

No one spoke, all watching the praetorium doorway. After a long time, the imperial guards came through this exit carrying the Caesar's dead body high above their heads.

A deep sigh rushed ahead of them to the soldiers. Their unbearable lament swelled again, filling the night.

Commodus moved slowly, walking behind the guards. These soldiers carried their burden in a slow pace before the line of army officers, the gathered dignitaries and the army, then moved back into the praetorium. The sobbing sound from the soldiers subsided, and a flat, complete silence settled across the encampment, and those who moved about at all, milled around aimlessly, lost. . . .

The sun appeared gray, and its light gray in the overcast morning. The sky was streaked and smudged with clouds like piles of dead ashes. Rain fell gently, but the gathered army, dignitaries and slaves were not aware of it.

The imperial guard placed Aurelius' corpse on the funeral pyre. His body was wrapped in the purple, denoting his great rank, adorned with crowns and honors he had won. The last rite paid to him—the ceremony of *conclomatio*—crying aloud for seven days the name of the dead emperor, was completed. Though it was daylight, custom dictated the pro-

cession carry lighted torches. The pyre was made of olive-
wood, juniper, pine twigs and laurels over which sulphur
had been cast. It remained now only for the dead Caesar's
closest relation—*his nearest heir*—to set a lighted torch to
the perfumed and sweet-scented pyre.

Commodus stood before the lines of mourners, waiting
with stony face. Near him Cleander held the emperor's pet
eagle Aquila, ready to release it. Timonides held the burning
torch which was to be cast upon the resinous wood.

In the taut-stretching silence, Commodus glanced about,
fee…g the rage swelling in him. The high-ranking officers of the army stood unmoving. The tribunes, Victorinus
and Polybus among them, gave no sign of acclamation for
the youth suddenly heir to the most important throne in the
history of civilization.

Commodus moved his head, finding Livius, but the young
officer stood rigidly straight, staring ahead. Near Livius, Lucilla watched as though holding her breath.

The tension spread and the dignitaries stirred, watching
avidly.

Livius at last surveyed the faces of those nearest him intently, as if trying to read some secret there. He found
those faces impassive, expressionless.

Commodus shifted, stood proudly, waiting defiantly for
the torch.

Livius glanced at Commodus, at the torch in the Greek
slave's hand, at the bier atop the funeral pyre, then turned
his face heavenward, feeling the soft rain.

After a long moment, Livius lowered his head. When he
moved, a sigh spread across dignitaries, officers and army.

He walked slowly to Timonides, took the torch from the
slave, held it high. He turned toward the pyre and Commodus
directly in line.

Lucilla's lips moved in a silent prayer as Livius walked
with the torch toward Commodus and the pyre beyond him.

When Livius reached Commodus, he stopped. Lucilla ut-
tered a cry of protest, pressed her hand over her mouth.

Livius extended the torch, putting it into Commodus'
hand. Then he stepped back away from him, his face fiercely taut, eyes savage, touching for one moment, Lucilla,
the consuls, his officers.

Livius shouted, defiantly: "Hail the undoubted Caesar! Hail
Commodus!"

There was still one breathless second of defiant silence from nobles, officers, army. Livius straightened, fixing his gaze upon them.

The voices rose, and the gathered dignitaries cried out acclaiming Commodus. Lucilla stood stunned, then shook her head, horror showing in her eyes. She backed away from Livius as the army in chorus took up the shouting: "Hail Caesar! Hail Commodus!"

With a satisfied smile, Commodus marched to the pyre, touched the torch to the wood, watched it burst into flame, the fire reflected in his eyes.

Behind him, Cleander released the eagle. With a wild scream, Aquila spread his great wings and flew heavenward. There was a whispered sound of awe as the eagle was lost in the overcast skies.

The only group which had been silent were those around Commodus—Cleander, Claudius, Didius Julianus, Niger. At last they began to realize that it was over, Caesar was dead, Commodus was his heir, the future held nothing but glory for them. They cheered, their voices rising exultantly. "Commodus! Hail Commodus."

The faces of the consuls, Virgilianus and Marcellus, were grim. They did not even glance toward their new monarch, but kept their gazes fixed on the leaping flames.

Lucilla pressed her hands over her face, tears streaming down her cheeks as the fire consumed the bier, the purple toga of her father.

Commodus turned at last, gazing at Livius with deep gratitude. He thrust out his arms, embracing Livius. He wept, laughing. "I'll never forget what you have done today!"

Livius nodded, gaze pulled toward the flames in the pyre. "Rule wisely, Commodus," he said in a low, prayerful voice. "Rule honestly."

Commodus, tears standing in his eyes, whispered fervently, "I will. I will."

Commodus breathed deeply, straightened. He strode forward with the flaming pyre at his back and, with upraised arm, gestured for silence.

The silence fell slowly, heavily, broken by the sound of flames, and a distant mourning.

Commodus shouted: "Let this be heard over the four corners of our emprie! I, Commodus, now Caesar, do proclaim Livius Gaius Metellus, commander in chief of all the Roman armies, proconsul of the whole Roman empire, second only to Caesar himself."

The assemblage cheered, but only Lucilla remained chilled, queenly, aloof and alone, fearful with the tragic sense of impending doom. She stared at Livius, whispering almost to herself, "Livius, Livius, what you could have done——" but none heard her because her whispers were lost in the sound of flames and cheering.

Standing apart from the shouting dignitaries, Virgilianus and Marcellus watched the celebration as if studying some kind of madness from a safe distance where they could not become contaminated.

Virgilianus stared at Commodus' exultant face. "Now what will happen? What's to become of Rome?"

Marcellus' mouth twisted into an ironic smile. "Why, the boy emperor will return to Rome for a dazzling coronation. Livius will go back to the cold countries and carry on this war. You and I will return to Syria and to Egypt."

"After that," Virgilianus persisted.

Marcellus shrugged. "After that, we will see." He shook his head, watching Didius Julianus, Claudius, Niger and the blind Cleander surrounding Commodus and Livius, the funeral fire behind them forgotten.

Mourning trumpets blew, breaking across the exultant laughter of Commodus' friends. Staring at them, Lucilla shook her head, crying. She turned from the spectacle and ran blindly.

Livius pushed free of the mob around Commodus, seeking Lucilla. Seeing her running away, he moved after her, and then stopped. Lucilla ran directly toward the gaudy entourage of the king of Armenia. Sohamus, seeing her, stepped forward, arms outstretched. Lucilla glanced once across her shoulder and then blinded by the rain and her tears, she ran into the embrace of the young king.

BOOK TWO

X

"Remember, thou art only human—"

The steady murmur of the priest at his shoulder was the last thing Commodus wanted to hear, but those words intruded upon every other sound or sensation.

Commodus stiffened, trying to ignore the words and the priest. This was his day, the supreme hour of his life to this moment—though his mind swirled with plans for greater spectacles, greater pleasures for his senses even than this celebration of his return to Rome as its emperor.

Commodus Emperor. Commodus Caesar. He turned his head from the whispering priest, glancing down at his raiment. He smiled, pleased. He'd never thought himself ugly, but the purple of his toga, embroidered with the palm tree, the gold of his laurel crown, surely set him apart from ordinary mortals.

"Remember, thou art only human—"

Commodus smiled, wondering how much—how little— this priest really knew? Did the man know, for instance, how he had challenged the gods to remove him from life if he were not to be ruler of the civilized world? The gods had brought him to this moment, this place.

The pageant spread out for acres upon the field of Mars, the Campus Martius. Wasn't this the place of gods, the space for military exercises, the site of columns, arches, statues to the great of the greatest empire known to man?

Commodus sighed, seeing the procession form and move past the Circus Flaminius toward the Forum Romanum at the foot of the Capitoline Hill. The Via Nova and Via Sacre were packed with humanity, and people were still pouring from the ten-storied *insulae*—racing along the narrow, twisted streets to get one look at him. A million people waiting along the path of this parade to glimpse his face, to cheer him. The gods knew the Romans had had the equanimity of Pius, the austerity of Marcus long enough, they were ready for the youth and pleasures of Commodus Emperor. These people already adored him, looked forward eagerly to the long, heady party. This spectacular entry was only the beginning!

"Remember, thou art only human," whispered the priest.

Commodus' ivory chariot, decorated with precious stones and drawn by four pure-white horses moved forward now toward the lustily screaming throngs, and Commodus was glad. Custom dictated that a priest ride at his shoulder, incessantly repeating those words to remind him of his fallibility, but he did not have to listen. They sent a priest along in the chariot of a general returning for one of the rare state-approved triumphs. All a heritage of the rugged simplicity of early Rome where no man was permitted to believe himself set apart from other mortals. Commodus hadn't given the practice a thought before, but he saw now how annoying this presence was.

He tilted his head, seeing the vanguard of the procession passing through the arch of triumph, followed by trumpeters, their long, tubular instruments gleaming in the sun, blaring.

Behind the trumpeters the empire dignitaries marched in portentous decorum Commodus had once found hilariously comic. He saw now their stateliness fit the occasion. The magistrates, the aediles, the senators, the patrician leaders in their togas. For a moment his gaze touched on Didius Julianus who gained a certain dignity and austerity simply by being in the company of the older senators. Claudius remained a simpering, giggling ass, but Niger was extremely handsome in ceremonial robes. Even Cleander's blindness set him apart, made him seem the worthiest of senators, leaning on the arm of the giant Lentulus.

This group passed through the arch and were followed by the white oxen, gleaming, destined for sacrifice to the gods in name of Commodus Emperor. The oxen were led by young boys in purple-bordered robes.

The coin bearers were next, carrying containers of the new coinage and banners displaying the new coins, all with the likeness of Commodus Emperor. Commodus felt his heart swell, pumping faster: silver and copper from Spain's Sierra

Morena and copper from her Rio Tinto. All those mines to be put on double shifts from Portugal to Cantabria.

"Remember, thou art only human—"

Commodus watched the governors and delegations from all the lands and provinces of the civilized world. Men of every color, skin and kind of dress, from Africa, Greece, Asia Minor, Dacia, Gaul, Britain, the Danube countries, the Fezzan. No homage ever paid to Marcus even approached the splendor of these entourages. It was as if the leaders from as far away as the Euphrates understood the electric charge in the atmosphere, a new day was dawning in the Roman world, a time of pleasure, a time for enjoying the *annona*— the harvest of the boundless majesty of the Roman peace: *"Immensa Romanae pacis maiestas." I, Commodus, am bringing this new moment to the empire. These people understand and share my tastes, they already love me. . . . They already deify me. It is in their faces for me to see.*

He watched the Armenian Escort march past, going through the arch to the awed whispers of the people, dazzled by the oriental magnificence of Sohamus' retinue.

Sohamus, with Lucilla at his side, held his head high, aloof and untouchable. But Commodus grinned to himself. He had heard how the young Armenian king had arrived in Rome, prepared to belittle its glories in comparison to those in the Near East. It hadn't happened that way. Sohamus had been impressed. He had been unable to restrain a cry of admiration and envy upon the sight of Trajan's Forum, and in honesty admitted there was nothing to match it in the oriental world.

Commodus let his gaze pause for one moment on Lucilla's face. The months seemed to have thinned her, given her eyes a far-away, dreamy quality, as if she found it more endurable to live with her thoughts than with reality.

The procession was halted for a moment and Lucilla was jolted, almost losing her balance in the regal Armenian chariot. She put her hand on Sohamus' arm to steady herself. With a twisted smile, Commodus watched the by-play. Sohamus turned quickly to Lucilla at her touch, his heart showing in his eyes, but Lucilla instantly withdrew her fingers, and Sohamus dragged in a deep breath that Commodus recognized in glee as frustration, and set his face ahead once more. The new king and queen of Armenia were not living happily ever after in their marble castle. This was clear enough, even if it were lost on the insensitive Roman mob.

The voices raised, cheering Lucilla. She gave them the barest nod of recognition, gazing across them, eyes sad as if they were being betrayed in the midst of all this grandeur.

Commodus swore under his breath. . . .

The procession moved forward again and Commodus was happy to see the last of his serious-minded sister.

Twenty-four lictors in full scarlet dress galloped into the column of marchers. Ahead of them a hush fell, and the moment had come for Commodus' escort to accompany him to the ceremony at the forum.

The acclaim before had been as whispers compared to the unceasing thunder as the crowd went wild. Flowers were hurled, people darted out just to touch his chariot. Young girls, hoping to catch the new emperor's eye and attention, ran into the street in front of the horses, tearing off their clothing to expose the fresh beauty they longed to offer him. Praetorian Guards dragged the naked girls out of the street, and Commodus could hear them crying out to him even after his chariot had passed, even through the frantic, hoarsely-yelling cheering.

And he could hear the whisper at his back, causing hackles along his neck: "Remember, thou art only human—"

Ahead, he saw Lucilla glance back along the narrow, humanity-jammed street, seeing the frenzied crowds, the young girls hurling their nude bodies into the line of his vision, the display, the madness of the growing mob. Her eyes filled with tears. But when Sohamus asked concernedly what was the matter, she brushed them away, and did not speak.

Sohamus sighed, watching her, disturbed.

The procession entered the Via Sacre, going into the forum.

Commodus found himself stunned at the size and insensate screaming of the hundreds of thousands of people crowded into the forum. It was like a swelling sea, caught inside the temples, arches, columns, the Tabularium—the hall of records—the temple of Saturn, the treasury of the city with its banners showing the new coins of Commodus, the curia beyond, the great halls of the basilicae—roofed halls divided into aisles by mammoth columns—the courts of justice, merchants' exchanges, the public meeting places, but all business forgot as the people streamed in to pay him worship. It was his, all his, and the wildly cheering mobs certified it.

Commodus glanced across his shoulder with contempt at the priest who continued to whisper, "Remember, thou art only human—"

The procession moved past the temple of Concord, the Tabularium, the twin libraries.

At the library of Roman art and culture, the procession halted, the magistrates, senators and notables taking their places along the marble steps.

Lucilla stepped down from the Armenian chariot and walked up the steps toward the place where the chief of scriveners and the amanuenses in full ceremonial dress awaited her. She was followed by slaves carrying cases of scrolls. The chief scrivener spoke the ritual words to her, asking, "Princess Lucilla, why have you come to this place today?"

There was a hush in the library area and Lucilla's words echoed.

"In these buildings you store all the law and all that which has been written and which is beautiful, by the great men of Greece, and the great men of Rome. I bring you now the writings of my father, Marcus Aurelius. Whatever happens in the days that are coming, I charge you and beg you that you let not this work be destroyed. For this is the future—"

The slaves brought the carrying cases, the chief scrivener led the way and the huge doors of the Tabularium were opened. The slaves, the scriveners, the amanuenses moved into the interior with the works of the deceased emperor. The doors closed behind them.

Lucilla stood for a moment on the steps and then returned slowly to the chariot where Sohamus awaited her, and the procession advanced.

Before the temple of Jupiter at the south summit of the Capitoline Hill, the procession stopped again. Commodus stepped from his chariot, happy to escape the whispered harrying of the priest. He strode to the entrance of the temple, deposited a laurel branch before the statue of Jupiter. The white oxen were slain for the sacrifice. The crowd roared, acclaiming the new Caesar.

Commodus stood straighter, feeling taller than the columns, greater than the idols of the gods, excited and exultant in the deafening acclaim. Suddenly behind him, the priest whispered, "Remember, thou art only human."

Commodus swung around, as if ready to strike him across

the head with the back of his hand. He did not lift his arm, only stared at the priest with contempt, the cheers finally completely drowning the sound of the hated voice.

Commodus turned his back on him, heeling about. He no longer heard the priest, but his gaze touched Lucilla's face and he was consumed with rage when he saw that she was openly crying.

He moved about, staring out across the assemblage, denying the sound of the priest's whispers, ignoring Lucilla. He had never realized before how deeply he hated her. The thing to do was to put her out of his mind. No amount of her tears was to be permitted to spoil things for him today. Nothing could spoil it, not her crying, nor the voice of this stupid priest.

On the farthest reaches of the Danube frontier, the Roman legions found themselves filled with a despair, which for the first time in twelve centuries came from within. They had been cold before, faced overwhelming odds, gone farther from home, met defeat, but for the first time they huddled in the desolate marshes into which their pursuit of the Marcomanni had led them, feeling cut off from hope, depressed and dispirited because whisper had it Commodus Emperor was ending support of the north campaign.

No man liked to enter such a swamp of desolation, but disciplined fighters went where the battle was. Never before had they faced the probability of abandonment by Rome.

There was no warmth in this chilled land. The marsh was wild, infested with death and unseen terrors, all of it blanketed with low-lying fog.

Behind the soldiers in a picketed prison pit, the captive barbarian women and children huddled together against the cold.

Livius moved past the prisoners, gazing at his soldiers, but not speaking to them. He went through the dank encampment, sharing the loneliness of his legions, but haunted by something he had lost that most of them had never even known.

A light glimmered from a tent ahead of him in the fog. He walked toward it without any sense of anticipation.

Through the slit of the tent-flap, Livius saw Timonides and the barbarian princess, Xenia. Timonides was reading by the inadequate flickering of a swinging oil lamp. Before the Greek teacher, Xenia sat rigidly. Her eyes glittered with sullen hatred. Holding a wax tablet and a stylus clumsily, she watched Timonides intently, trying to gather some gleam of sense from all he was teaching her.

When Livius entered the tent, Xenia's eyes darkened. The look of hatred in them became even more intense. Livius saw that glitter impaling him, but ignored it.

When Timonides saw it was Livius, he put away the document from which he was reading. Sighing with relief, Xenia instantly dropped stylus and tablet.

Timonides stood up, a warm smile lighting his dark face. "I am teaching the princess how to read and write."

Livius nodded, glancing at Xenia with a look of curiosity. She averted her gaze.

"I am teaching her Greek," Timonides said with a smile. "That is my way of trying to make a Roman out of her."

Livius exhaled in weariness. "A Roman out of her?" He paced morosely, both of them watching him. "This is a war without end—no matter what they say in Rome. You think you have Ballomar beaten, he disappears only to come back stronger than ever." He heeled around, face gray with rage, his dark eyes fixed on the savage princess. "What sort of people are you, Xenia? You have no homes, no families. You live on horses."

Xenia straightened on the ground. Her voice was tinged with contempt. "We are warriors—"

"Warriors?" Suddenly Livius strode over to her, grabbed her. He pulled her to her feet before she could struggle at all. "Don't you ever yearn for a man?" He held her savagely against him, his face gray and taut, and no sign of pleasure in his eyes, his mouth a gash of rage. "To be held like this? To be loved?"

For a moment, breathless, Xenia pressed against him, her heart hammering, her untamed emotions violently and quickly roused.

Her fingers dug into his arms, she clung to him. But this lasted less than the space of a harried breath. In that time she was flooded with raging memories. She remembered the way she had gone on her knees to him, waiting for him to act the victor claiming his rights over a female prisoner. This was the treatment she understood, and even when she fought him—if she had opposed him that night in that tent at Vindobona—she would not have hated him because there was no man even among her father's people to match this splendid man. Her opposition would have been half-hearted, but her passions would have been of a violence he would never know in the effete cities of the South. She had offered herself, even if he were her hated enemy. Nothing could ever erase the memory of the strange treatment he'd shown her, acting as if she were not only unlovely, but not a woman at all.

Defiantly, she writhed free, hurling her words and her hatred at him. "No! No."

Livius stepped toward her. He saw Timonides watching them, but Timonides would not attempt to deter him, no one could stop him if he meant to take her. A man needed a woman worse than ever in this desolate place, even a barbarian like this one.

Suddenly he spoke somewhat more gently. "Then what do you live for? Even warriors must yearn for peace?"

Xenia crouched defiantly, voice shrill. "Peace is for pigs. We live for victory."

Livius pushed her away from him roughly. The sudden fire that had flared to instant life was even more abruptly quenched. He didn't want her. He didn't want any woman. It was a hellish truth he had learned, when you feel rage toward the only woman you could love, you hated all women with that same fierce intensity.

He needed something, but it wasn't this half-wild creature. He drew the back of his hand across his forehead, for that instant almost overcome with dizzying weariness. His clothing was intolerable, the weight of his flat, short sword unbearable. With a tired movement, he removed the sword, placed it on the table without even glancing at it.

"You're tired, Livius," Timonides said. "You need rest more than violence." He smiled, "Even the violence of my little tigress."

Livius didn't look at Xenia again. He watched Timonides, puzzled. "Don't you ever need anything, Greek? Aren't you roused by animals like that?" He jerked his head toward Xenia, still without giving her a glance.

"I have my problems," Timonides said. "The Greeks are a jealous, proud, race-conscious people. I am like that. I was like that. I learned a great deal from Marcus. I taught him much, but I learned more from him. Resignation. Acceptance."

"Lessons I'll never learn." Livius pressed his fingers hard

against his eyes, seeing lights and prisms of color from the pressure. He stared at Timonides. "I've fought in battles for eleven years, and faced death many times. I have overcome much, many fears. Yet you seem more at peace, more certain of yourself than I am. Why?"

Xenia moved with the lithe grace of a lynx, soundless as a shadow. Timonides had grown accustomed to her presence, and Livius was too exhausted to care what she did. They were deeply absorbed and did not see her lunge suddenly, before Timonides could answer the *imperium*. She grabbed the sword. It whistled free of its scabbard, glinted in the yellow light as she sprang toward Livius.

The only sound Xenia made was the hissing inhalation as she threw up her arm to strike. It was enough, too much. Timonides swung around and thrust his arm in the same movement between Xenia and Livius.

Livius, roused by Timonides' silent wheeling about, moved with the instinctive speed of a combat-trained soldier. He sprang upon Xenia, turning, and could only partially block the sword thrust.

Timonides bit his lip, face twisting in pain. The sword laid open his upper arm. Blood spurted, spilling over his *tunica*.

Livius glanced at the slave, moved past him, reaching out with quick, deft movement, snatching the sword from Xenia.

In a fluid, continuous motion, he brought his other arm up, backhanding Xenia across the face and sending her sprawling.

Xenia struck a tent support, almost toppled around it, clutching at the wood for balance. Then she slid beyond it, moving into a shadowed corner, crushed, cringing, numb with physical shock as she watched Livius stalk toward her, blood-smeared sword red in his fist.

The fiery green passion of hatred died in her eyes and she slumped inward, watching dully for the death stroke.

Livius' face was cold. He raised the sword over her.

From behind him, Timonides cried in anguish, "No! No!"

Clutching his blood-covered arm, Timonides ran to them. He caught Livius' upraised arm. He shook his head, mouth gray. "I don't want her punished, Livius."

Sword still upraised, Livius stared at him incredulously. "But she tried to take your life. She's wounded you. You must kill her."

They both stared at the girl crouching numbly in the corner.

Timonides spoke carefully, "There are three possibilities—" He held one finger up. "One—we kill her, we destroy the miracle of a living thing, reduce her to one with rock, dust—"

Livius stared as if not believing what he heard as Timonides held up a second finger. "Or two—we punish her severely, in which case she will hate us, and so do again what she has now done." He held up a third finger and quoted, "Or three—'Ye have heard that it hath been said, Thou shalt love thy neighbor and hate thine enemy. But I say unto you, Love your enemies, bless them that curse you, do good to them that hate you'."

Livius glared at him uncomfortably. "Do good to them that hate you. And give her another chance to kill you?"

Timonides smiled. "I shall be more careful now." He gazed at the princess. "And sooner or later, my love will triumph over her hatred, as it must over all hatred."

Livius shook his head as if Timonides were speaking riddles in his native tongue.

Suddenly, Xenia slumped to the ground, sobbing.

Livius jerked his head around, staring at her in amazement.

From the ground the quivering girl whimpered, "I no longer want to be a warrior."

Livius had already heard more than he could comprehend. He demanded grimly, "What is it you want to be?"

Xenia answered, but her voice was almost inaudible, as though all this were too new for her, feelings she didn't understand and had no words for, and was almost ashamed of uttering. "A woman. . . . I do not want to kill any more."

Livius knelt, lifted her easily by her shoulders. He held her at eye level, inspecting her suspiciously. "Give up your arms and live in peace?"

Xenia avoided his eyes, mumbling. "I want—to live in one place—with one man—the way the Romans do."

Timonides, tending his slashed arm, glanced up at this with a wry smile. "The way the Romans say they do—"

But Livius was staring at the girl. He lowered her slowly until she was back on the ground. His expression was a mixture—suspicion, disbelief and faint, replenishing hope.

Timonides, watching the young warrior's face, remembered suddenly something Aurelius had written: "Look well into thyself; there is a source of strength that will always spring up if thou wilt always look there." He saw how true this was as he watched Livius Gaius Metellus slowly, unwillingly finding within himself the strength and wisdom that the immortal Antoninus had always seen there. Livius was learning all that Marcus had been sure he would learn. It was slow, but he was learning, and in his exultancy, the Greek forgot the blood dripping along his arm.

XI

THE LEGIONS marched slowly upon the paved road. The road was straight and in the distance they could see the river and the place where the road ended at the river. Beyond the end of the road was an unknown world for them; where Roman roads ran out, civilization no longer existed. The men did not talk, and the mule trains rattled on the road in a gray and empty world. There were marshes along both sides of the river, the trees thick with jungle-growth and netted with fog, separated by the black water that was deep and fast. Up there the engineers were already building pontoon bridges and they would cross those bridges where there was a narrow channel and sand beds visible in the swift current.

The line of march seemed unending back along the road. Mounted officers moved through the cohorts and maniples and companies, seeing to discipline in the silence.

The prisoners were herded along in drab wads, their dull animal-skin clothing like puddles of mud in the colorful lines of the archers and javelin throwers.

Livius, near the front of the column, halted and looked back along the crowded road. The road was aswarm with silent soldiers and prisoners and there were walls of forest and undergrowth matting on both sides. The sun was almost lost in low overcast. He turned, watching the engineers at work on the banks of the river. The ground was low there and the current looked treacherous.

"What's the matter?"

Livius jerked his head around when Xenia pulled her horse near his. He bit his lip to keep from ordering her back among the prisoners, or at least with Timonides. But he did not speak. He frowned, staring at her with a puzzled, thoughtful look about his eyes.

Lines of marchers moved grimly past them, eyes front; the pounding of sandaled feet made a rhythmic thunder on the road. He watched them, hoping the bridges would not jam in that swift river. They had troubles enough without having to fight the current and marsh sand.

From the tangled undergrowth two couriers ran, breathless and exhausted. Livius lifted his arm, summoning them. They panted, for the moment unable to speak.

"The tribune Polybus—and his legion." Gasping, the boy pointed toward the marshes.

"Ambush!" the second said, staggering.

Livius nodded. He whirled his mount around, calling out, "Sound the alarm!"

Roman horns of war sounded, blasting the fog-shrouded stillness. The legions, responding, came out of their lethargy. Heavy packs were deposited on the mule carts, and the cohorts sprang into battle-readiness.

Livius and Victorinus spurred their horses to the head of the columns of men. The soldiers jogged along the road, going into the gray mists of the marshes.

Livius, Victorinus and the other officers rode into the marshy swamp, tense and watchful. The legions behind them did not slacken pace. There was a charged atmosphere of silence. Livius lifted his arm, giving a signal that was repeated through the companies and the men were slowed to a cautious but steady advance into the fog and thigh-deep marsh.

A lookout shouted ahead and Livius and Victorinus hurried forward. Moving in, they stared at Polybus with a handful of haggard survivors floundering in the bogs. Livius shouted for aid, men ran to the exhausted troops. Livius swung down, caught the weakened Polybus, held him up.

Polybus stared into Livius' face for a moment as if he didn't even recognize him, then mumbling, raised his arm, pointing in mute horror.

The officers moved slowly forward, sickened at the sight of the grasping hands of Roman soldiers extending in silent pleading above the mire. Horses floundered, helplessly sink-ing; armor, swords and broken javelins floated on the muddy surface.

On a mound of dry ground in the slough a charred altar stood blackened from the human sacrifice to Wotan made upon it.

Livius stared at the carnage, recoiling in horror.

Skirting the slime the soldiers moved past the altar. They stopped again, stunned at what remained of Roman legionnaires. Mutilated men and horses were strewn about in the swamp, horror revealed through breaks in the streamers of fog.

Livius moved forward toward the river, which was strewn with fragments of spears and other broken weapons. Bodies had been hacked, nailed to trees. He stood staring in agony at a pit in which dozens of Roman hands protruded imploringly. He remained here for a long time, the unbroken marching of his men behind him. Victorinus near him, he strode on again, seeing how the ambush had been accomplished, the evidence of needless cruelty, barbaric inhumanity.

The legions crowded into lines, waiting. Victorinus, glancing at Livius' gray face, spoke suddenly in cold fury, gesturing toward the tortured, mutilated bodies. "Romans—let us avenge them. Romans! Forward!"

A wild roar like a tornado on a still day burst through the swamp and the soldiers plunged in pursuit of the barbarians.

The empty night world was dark along the river, broken by fires in spots across the battlefield. The barbarians had retreated from the death marsh, but the Romans had overtaken them, driven them all afternoon to the site of their temporary camp on a wide plain. In the fire-lighted darkness, the screams of barbarian women, the terrified wails of children mixed with the sounds of battle. From every burning tent and hut, seething masses of women fled with their young, screeching like animals in panic. At the brink of the camp, the captive Marcomanni women and children had been brought up and forced to watch the retributive slaughter of their people. Near the guarded prisoners Xenia stood in silence beside Timonides.

She did not speak, watching Roman soldiers led by Victorinus implacably pursue her people, slaying the women along with the warriors, burning huts, the primitive straw and wood hovels flaming up, quickly consumed by the Roman fires. In the weird light she saw a detachment of Romans working with deadly ferocity assembling crosses. The daily plain was strewn with bodies of dead men and horses as far as she could see. Corpsmen of the legion were moving among them, carefully removing the Roman dead. Swordsmen moved in a half-run, killing all the enemy wounded, lopping the head off any barbarian that showed a sign of life.

Livius stood with Polybus beside him, overlooking the fire-struck battleground. Victorinus ran to them, face exultant, eyes glittering in the firelight.

"We have them!" He pointed. "Ballomar himself is somewhere there in the camp. He won't escape this time. Now we can destroy them all—wipe them out forever."

Livius gave him a tired nod, watching enemy women and children being herded toward the stockades. Those who protested or lagged were struck down and trampled. The screaming of children rose to a crescendo, seeming to burst inside Livius' head, unendurable.

As he watched, a little girl suddenly broke from the ranks of prisoners, screaming in wild terror for her mother, running back toward a woman sprawled dead on the ground with an arrow in her.

A soldier, javelin poised, heeled around, took three long strides and with unconcern hurled the spear after the child.

Livius shook his head, almost sobbing out his protest. He lunged forward, clutching the child by the hair and whipping her to him as the javelin screamed past.

The child grabbed at Livius, clinging to him in hysteria. Livius hardly realized what he had done, what strange instinct he had obeyed almost involuntarily. His face twisted with puzzlement, he stared at the sobbing child and then at the faces of Victorinus and Polybus. He recognized the looks in the eyes of his under-officers. Incredulity. It was what he himself felt.

He pulled his gaze away, peering at the carnage all around them in the lunging red fire light. He was afraid he would vomit because he had seen all the agony and horror of war he could take. He had heard Marcus Antoninus talk of hating the killing, but he had never seen it before, he had seen only the battles, the glory of victory, all the things he and Polybus and Victorinus had been taught to see.

His manner strange and upsetting to his under-officers, he set the child gently on the ground, motioned to a corpsman to remove her to the prisoners' compound, see that she was cared for.

Neither Victorinus nor Polybus spoke. Livius stared at a hut, suddenly illumined in the fires, a place larger than the tents and shacks around it. He saw the Roman torchmen approaching the large shanty, fires ready. He broke into a run, going across the field. Victorinus and Polybus hesitated a moment, looking at each other, faces expressionless and then they followed him, not because they wanted to, but because they had the long habit of discipline.

Livius ran across the battlefield, the night illumined by fires, the hysterical screaming of the wounded and the crackling flames hammering at him. He did not slow until he reached the closed flap at the largest hovel in the barbarian village.

He thrust open the flap, burst into the room with Polybus and Victorinus at his heels.

He strode forward inside the single room of the hut. He slowed involuntarily at the sight of the huge Ballomar at the head of a crude log table. Before the Marcomanni leader was his ill-kempt wife and three terror-stricken children. On the table in front of each was a large hand-formed goblet filled with sour wine, laced with poison.

None of the people at the table stirred when the three Roman officers entered the room. Livius took one glance at the barbarian ruler, the goblets. He stepped forward and grabbed the table, pushing it over. The goblets flew. The children whimpered, but Ballomar and his wife snatched up their cups before they could fall.

Livius slapped the goblet from Ballomar's grasp before the big man could close his fingers on it. He heeled around but Ballomar's wife, holding the cup in both hands, gulped it down. Livius stood numbly, staring at her. Ballomar lunged to his knees, grasping at the goblets.

Polybus stepped near, caught the huge man by the hair and jerked him over on his back, away from the goblets. Victorinus strode forward with drawn sword. The children moved closer to Ballomar, whimpering like animals. Ballomar gathered them to him, but did not look at his wife. She sank to the floor, writhing. Ballomar did not even glance at her when she was dead.

Ballomar stood slowly, towering above the Romans. "One

day my people will join with the Vandals and the Goths. We will teach them things of war they don't yet know." His face twisted with contempt. "That—together—with them, we can destroy Rome. . . . One day our horses will march over the ashes of your city. One day you will be our slaves."

Victorinus and Polybus laughed at the man's bravado. But Livius, watching the zeal burning in the half-savage eyes, shivered as if a chill wind had rustled through the hut.

He spoke quietly, gaze holding Ballomar's. "Your people will never join with the Vandals—or the Goths."

Ballomar laughed in his face, an exultant hoarse sound. "Neither you nor anyone will be able to stop it." He straightened his magnificent shoulders. "You will never drag us through the streets of Rome in chains."

Livius held his gaze, neither flinching. Behind him, the flap was pushed away, Timonides and Xenia entered. The princess remained unmoving, her gaze fixed on her father's face.

Livius said, "I pledge you, on my honor, Ballomar, you will never be in chains, nor will you or anyone of your people be slaves."

Victorinus and Polybus glanced at each other, then stared incredulously at the young general. It was quiet in the hut, roar of the fires and screams of the dying sounding distant.

Victorinus said, "If they're not to be slaves, then what will you do with them?"

Livius did not answer, standing rigid for a moment listening to those sounds from outside the shanty. He spoke urgently to his second-in-command, "Stop the killing—stop the burning, Victorinus."

A sharp inhalation from Victorinus was the only answer from the incredulous officer. He did not move. Livius spoke louder. "No. No. At once, Victorinus."

Victorinus shook himself from his trance, then stunned, moved from the hut to carry out the order.

Livius exhaled heavily. "Gather the prisoners of war together, Polybus. Treat them kindly. They are coming to Rome with us."

If Livius' voice had not held such quiet authority, Polybus would have considered him a victim of shock, fatigue. He had seen this happen in battle. He had known Livius many years, had never seen him behave so strangely before. Still, Livius was the commander, he appeared rational, even if he sounded insane. Polybus hesitated a moment, then dazed and bewildered by orders he did not comprehend, he left the hut. The truth was, he was glad to get out of there into the sanity of the battlefield.

Commodus stepped from his sedan outside the Tabularium —the marbled hall of records. He paused for a moment at the foot of the inclined steps, waiting for Julianus, Niger and Cleander, led by Lentulus, to join him.

The sun felt pleasant on his shoulders. The Via Sacre was crowded at this hour, and the subjects who spied him and his regal entourage, bowed low, hailing him. He smiled because they adored him. These first months of his reign had been smooth and bright, rewarding for Romans and himself. There was no doubting that his living among the gladiators, carousing with the youth of Rome in the baths, games, streets and clubs had provided him with an insight into the common people that his learned father lacked. He knew what his people wanted: food and fun. A harvest and a circus. At last they had the emperor who understood them and would give them what they wanted.

Commodus waited until the young boys gathered the folds of his toga—no minor garment since it was eighteen feet long and seven feet wide—and then with his party, went up the steps. Near the entrance he paused, surveying the buildings at the foot of the Capitoline Hill with proprietary pride.

The chief scribe, the scriveners and amanuenses came out to meet him, the tall doors of the hall of records opening slowly and with ceremony.

Commodus' party followed the scribes into the courtyard of the Tabularium. Surrounding this space, dozens of small rooms were all occupied by slave amanuenses, busily scribbling upon parchment at writing tables.

Commodus gave them a glance, followed the chief scribe into the main room. This enormous cavern with vaulted ceiling, huge columns, was lined along all walls with bookshelves. These were divided into sections, one for each province: Britain, Gaul, Syria, Egypt, Africa—

In the center of this room and dominating it was a large map, depicting in many colors, all the countries which formed the Roman empire. Around this, busts of the great Roman rulers were carefully disposed—Tiberius, Julius Caesar, Augustus, Nero, Trajan, Hadrian—and behind each bust the major laws, and essays of the ruler. The atmosphere was one of deep reverence, of dedicated men who realized they were the custodians of history.

Commodus gave the busts and statues mere glances, concentrated on the huge map, pacing back and forth before it. The others waited in respectful silence.

At last, Commodus spoke in low tones. "You are my friends and therefore you must know this: When it was known my father was dying, I spoke to the gods and said, 'I have made no secret that I am not like my father, and if I am crowned Caesar, I will change all he did'—and I offered my life to the gods saying that if it is not for the good of Rome that I be Caesar—kill me. . . . But the gods spared my life and acclaimed me Caesar. . . . Therefore, the gods have clearly spoken to me. Rome will change.

"Let us rid ourselves of the old men who surrounded my father! Let us make once more of Rome the city of light and gaiety—beauty and strength. The strength and courage of the gladiators! Let us have games, and let the people of the city be fed. Let us this day record—and send word to all the colonies and provinces they must forget the weakness of my father! There will be no weakness in Rome. We will give them strength and glory and power—and pleasures. But let us tell them plainly that these things cost money, and Rome must have that money in taxes. We wish to burden no one, but we believe that the taxes on all provinces can be doubled without hardship anywhere. They must double the shipment of grain they have been sending, if we are to feed the people of this city."

There was a brief, tense silence. Commodus heeled around, found the senator Didius Julianus scowling, fretting. "Well, what's the matter with you?"

But Julianus only shrugged, forcing a hypocritical smile.

Cleander spoke with deadly calm. "I'll tell you, Caesar, what troubles the senator Julianus. First I must state that I agree with your measures in full, and in no way oppose them. But Senator Julianus and I both know that additional taxes are being opposed in the senate." He held up his hand. "I can handle the senate for you—and I will. I know what to put in what hands, and I can promise you the senate will back you. . . . But the fact is that the governors of Egypt and Syria—and the king of Armenia, your brother-in-law,

Sire, have petitioned help from us. They send word of famine among their people."

Commodus stared at the blind eyes for a moment and then spoke coldly, "Their people? Rome is their people." He swung his arm in a grim gesture, almost like a gladiator with trident, "Let there be no hesitation among them—unless they wish to be thought traitors—I am Caesar, by divine will of the gods I am Caesar, and I speak with the voice of the gods! I want this matter handled at once."

Julianus nodded, gestured toward the chief scribe, and slave scriveners were summoned. They scurried into the room, ready to transcribe the Caesar's latest edict.

Marcellus stood with his aides waiting as Caesar's emissary and his entourage approached along the quiet street before the palace. The town was silent with the stillness that belonged in an empty place, dark-skinned Syrians standing in sullen quiet along the curbs. Marcellus watched the company of gaily bedecked ambassadors parade their pomp and splendor before the harried eyes of his hungry subjects. Not too long ago, Marcellus had been a legionnaire, and he swore like a soldier now, though under his breath.

The sun was metallic on the oriental city of Antioch-on-the-Orontes. Here was the crossroads of traffic between Europe, Asia and Africa, where huge caravans crossed mountains and desert bringing goods of India and the Far East to the Mediterranean. This offered a sight of exotic wonder to the Romans, but Marcellus knew they were marching through it not to see, but to be seen, displaying their own wealth, arrogance, ugliness.

"They make it so easy for me to remain governor of a people with not enough to eat," he told himself in bitterness. Still, he straightened with the memory of an old military pride when the lictors galloped forward, chariots emblazoned with the imperial insignia of Rome. He was one of them, even when he wasn't always proud of it.

Didius Julianus stepped down from his chariot and was escorted up the steps to the shade of oriental canopies. There was a brief moment of tension when Julianus waited for Marcellus to come down the steps to him. But Marcellus did not move.

Julianus' face was rigid when he stepped forward, forcing a graceless smile, and handed the governor of Syria a parchment document with Caesar's seal upon it. Marcellus left the seal intact, stood holding the message, making no move to read it.

"I've been expecting you," he said.

Julianus was hot, irritated by the snub and lack of protocol. "No word was sent ahead of me."

Marcellus tapped the document against his calloused, soldier's palm. "These things don't have to be delivered in person. Not when they are as flagrant as this. We can smell them months in advance. . . . This delivery has happened everywhere in the empire. I suppose I should be flattered that a senator delivered mine. I suppose I am. But I must warn you, it means nothing here—"

"What are you talking about?"

"This message from my lord Caesar, Julianus. What else? The emperor may with good cause believe himself the chosen of the gods. I myself have never believed I have any such special protection of our deity. If I were to carry out these orders—"

"What does that mean—if you carry out these orders?" Julianus trembled in righteous outrage. "They come from Caesar."

Marcellus shrugged, calm. "If I carried out such orders, we risk having the whole province rise against Rome."

Julianus brushed a speck from his tunic. "Are you making threats, Marcellus?"

"It is not I who threaten, Julianus. Look around you. You are outside Rome now. Remove those scales from your eyes. Look. See. Those people down there—it is they who threaten. They and the people of all provinces across the Roman world. We haven't legions enough to protect Rome if rebellion broke out from the Euphrates to Portugal—"

"Concern yourself only with your own province. Caesar will concern himself with empire."

Marcellus stared at Julianus a moment, then laughed in a harsh, cold tone that was devoid of mirth, but as contemptuous as spittle in the face. He turned his back abruptly and walked away.

The document conveying Caesar's will concerning taxes was delivered in Armenia by Pescennius Niger.

Lucilla stood at the side of King Sohamus when he read the document Niger handed him. As Sohamus read, Lucilla

glanced at Niger, at his entourage, telling herself they per-
sonified the decay, and self-indulgence practiced in her
brother's court at Rome. Niger was getting puffy, bags under
his eyes; he was eating and drinking too much—as was the
whole court. In contrast, the handsome people of Armenia
were slender, hardened, tempered.

Sohamus read the document through again, then word-
lessly handed it to Lucilla.

He watched her as she read it quickly. He did not know
what influence she might wield with Commodus more than he
himself, and he would move cautiously no matter what he
permitted her to do. Word of the murder of Arrius Antoninus had recently come from Rome. With more honesty than
wisdom, Arrius Antoninus had attempted to disclose to Commodus the true character of Cleander who seemed more and
more in control of the mind and movement of the emperor.
Enraged, Cleander had used all his powers of persuasion and
flattery, convinced Commodus that his own kinsman was his
worst enemy and caused his death. Sohamus was afraid even
for Lucilla to return to Rome, but this tax edict was vicious.

When Lucilla looked up from the document, her face was
cold, white. Sohamus caught his breath. He had not seen
Lucilla display so much fire and passion in all the months
since she'd agreed at the Vindobona encampment to become
his wife. She'd seemed detached, dreamy, barely aware of
what was happening to her, where she was. Anger was an
emotion. Sohamus was pleased to see it: any sign of feeling
was hopeful, and she was truly enraged. She let the document snap back into its roll and then she thrust it out, returning it to Niger.

Sohamus spoke quietly, hoping to give Lucilla time to
calm down. He was afraid she would say something that
Niger could report to Commodus—something the emperor
might assess as treasonable, unforgivable. "You in Rome
seem to have forgotten, Senator Niger, that Armenia is an
independent kingdom. We are not a province of Rome."

Niger gave him a blandly innocent smile. "But we have no
desire to change that."

Lucilla's voice lashed at him. "If these orders are obeyed,
we will be neither kingdom nor province."

Niger stared at Lucilla a moment as if she were an insolent
slave girl rather than Armenian queen; then, without even
deigning to answer her, he turned to face Sohamus.

"You are king only by the tolerance of Rome."

"This comes as news to me." Sohamus stood straighter.

"Then accept it as earnest news. We can find a dozen other princes of Armenia who would do our bidding. If you doubt this, oppose us. . . ." He waited a moment, mouth twisting. "How does my lord Sohamus wish it to be?"

Lucilla stepped forward, face gray and rigid. Sohamus gently stopped her. He spoke in that same quietly inscrutable way after a moment. "We will try to avoid bloodshed for my people—and danger to Rome."

Niger was not deceived. He may well have fared better against Lucilla's overt outburst of rage. He recognized Sohamus' tone and words as the supreme art of diplomacy. They were a calm, civil reply—that could mean anything, from compliance to declaration of war.

Niger inhaled deeply, surveying the dark king and his lovely, bitterly unhappy queen. He held them in his gaze for some moments, critically. They waited, regal and aloof. At last, Niger nodded with grim satisfaction, turned and strode out, followed by his entourage.

Lucilla waited only until the Roman entourage was clear of the chambers, then she heeled around and ran from the room. Sohamus stood a moment as if stunned, sensitive to the charged silence of his palace subjects, then he hurried after her, his face deeply shadowed, troubled.

Lucilla returned to Rome in early fall. The roads were damp from night rains and the trees stood bare along the way. Mulberry trees stood leafless in brown fields. Olive trees were wet, and the laurel and juniper looked desolate against the sodden earth. She saw the city ahead, and crossed the river going into it at the Forum Boarium, the old cattle market but now a place of business. The city seemed chilled and cheerless, the tall *insulae,* ten floors of ugliness and crowded humanity on twisted narrow streets. She saw the new baths, circuses, places of amusement that Commodus had ordered built under Cleander's prodding. Cleander said incessantly to the Caesar, rumor had it, that the people—dazzled and preoccupied by all the splendor and entertainment—would forget the woes of pestilence and famine. Lucilla found herself pervaded by a fevered sense of melancholy and loneliness. She felt as a stranger inside the hills of her own city.

All vehicular, animal-drawn traffic was forbidden inside

Rome during daylight hours, and so from her man-hauled sedan, Lucilla watched the town move past: seeing the queues of people lined up before one of the government halls for the *congiara*—public distribution of food and money. Money poured in from excessive taxes, and grain from starved lands as far away as Egypt. She let her curtains fall in place, shutting out the sight.

It was two days before Lucilla could get an audience with Commodus. She spent the first night sleepless, listening to the rumbling horse-drays making deliveries all night, the teamsters shouting, the animals rasping because the harnesses choked them under heavy loads. The clatter continued till dawn. Lucilla longed for nothing except escape from Rome. It held nothing for her any more but agony and painfully sweet memories.

She was besieged by old friends, by people coming with whispers and confidences concerning her brother, the emperor. She brushed them all aside. They sickened her, but her only concern was the intolerable burden of taxes and grain-levy upon the people of Armenia.

She entered the gymnasium near Commodus' palace on the Palatine Hill, a *palaestra* especially built by Commodus for the training and pleasure of his gladiators.

When she found him, Commodus was in the uniform of the *secutor,* opposed by Verulus with trident and net. For a long time she stood in silence watching Commodus and Verulus hack at each other with loud, raucous cries of pleasure. She admitted that Commodus equalled the most skilled of the gladiators. But her mouth pulled with contempt because she did not feel this was a great accomplishment for the ruler of a beleaguered world.

Tiring of this senseless display of dexterity and speed, she moved her gaze about the huge barren gymnasium, finding only the bust of the goddess Faustina—goddess by decrees of Marcus and assent of the senate after her death. Marcus Aurelius had caused her to be represented in the temples of the gods, declared her to have all the attributes of Juno, Venus and Ceres. He even decreed that on the day of their nuptials, youth of either sex should pay their vows before the altar of their chaste patroness, Faustina. Staring at the bust of her mother, remembering the monstrous infidelities to which only her beloved father remained blind in all Rome, she shivered convulsively, finding another reason for dreading her return to Rome.

Beyond the statue of her faithless mother, it seemed somehow fitting and symbolic to Lucilla that dozens of almost naked gladiators trained in pairs. Faustina would have liked that, she thought, mouth twisting.

Commodus charged Verulus. With a cry, the aging gladiator stepped nimbly aside. Verulus laughed, but his look of triumph was cut short as Commodus, feigning to stumble, got him off guard, then struck at him cunningly—a blow which could have killed Verulus, except that Commodus gleefully arrested the blow in mid-air.

Verulus nodded, wildly pleased. He saw he could have been killed, and he burst into harsh guttural admiring laughter, applauding Commodus. Commodus laughed, too, and Verulus watched him in pride. "If he had not been born Caesar, he would have been one of the great gladiators of our time!" he shouted.

Commodus wiped sweat from his glowing face. "Coming from the greatest gladiator of all, that's no small praise."

Lucilla stepped forward. Her voice was chilled. "Since you force me to meet you in these surroundings, let me speak quickly."

Commodus glanced about angrily. "Where would you rather meet? In some dark library? You're behind the times, Lucilla."

"I know. Gladiators are all the fashion in Rome these days."

"Gladiators! Yes. What's wrong with gladiators? Do you know the heritage your philosopher father left me? Because of his endless wars and legions kept guarding frontiers of value to nobody, the imperial treasury is empty. Peasants have abandoned their land and come in to Rome where they must be fed at public expense. That's what your philosopher father did for Rome!"

"And how does the gladiator answer? With games and festivals in the city and famine in the provinces—"

"Damn you. I don't want such talk in my presence. Famine in the provinces?" He was white with fury. "Have you come to plead for these people? Pity? You?" He laughed, a sound almost as raucous as Verulus' harsh laughter. "Pity? Not you, Lucilla. Oh, no. It does not become you."

She stared at him in bewilderment. He laughed again and

spoke in low, taut tones. "I was there, Lucilla. I was in that room when Mother was dying."

Lucilla winced, swaying as if he'd struck her across the face. She was shocked, caught off guard, and she saw Verulus staring at her, his face reflecting Commodus' rage.

Commodus swung out his arm toward the bust of Faustina. "I was there, Lucilla, that night she died. I saw her hold out her hand to you—I heard her beg of you, 'Tell me what I've done to turn you from me, Lucilla—tell me why you hate me so, and if I have hurt you, forgive me.' She begged you—for forgiveness. Just one word of forgiveness, Lucilla. Pity. . . . And you let her die—" He stepped close to her, cheeks pallid, "—without one word of comfort. Your own mother."

Lucilla retreated a step, badly shaken. There was an ominous silence in the *palaestra*, and she looked about, stunned, getting herself under control.

At last, she waved her hand, almost as cold and harsh as Commodus.

"All right, Commodus. Then let's not speak of pity. Let me then say that hundreds of thousands in the provinces will die of starvation. . . . But they won't. Rather than die by famine—they'll choose rebellion."

Commodus slashed downward with his hand, cutting her off. His eyes blazed with fury. "I hope there will be rebellion. Open rebellion. Because then I'll show the world that the Rome of old is not dead. Punitive expeditions—that's what they were called once. Punishing armies. Whole states sacked. Cities burned. Forests of crosses. Whole nations destroyed forever without a trace. Wiped out."

She shook her head, her eyes chilled with horror, seeing what he forecast, threatened. She whispered it, "A gladiator's world."

Verulus had been listening intently and containing himself only with difficulty. He stepped forward, belligerent, sweated. His chin was thrust out challengingly. "And what's wrong with the gladiator's world, Princess? Kill or be killed. The whole world is like that, but it's only in the arena where it's open and honest."

He slashed out in a gesture of defiance and disgust toward her. Commodus laughed indulgently, appreciatively at the gladiator's outburst. Lucilla stared at them with overt contempt.

"Verulus," she said. "Not only a great gladiator, but something of a philosopher, too." Her chin tilted defiantly. "That's not my world, nor the world all our people have made such sacrifices for."

"Sacrifices?" Commodus laughed at her. "Why, Lucilla, if you find your life in the East too hard—remember, I am Caesar now. I could dissolve your marriage if you find it unpleasant. It would be one more way of showing the strength of Rome. . . . And I'm sure we could find other ways the sister of Caesar could serve—"

He stopped talking abruptly, made a gesture to indicate the discussion was closed, the interview ended. She waited but he refused to speak to her again. It was as if she were in Armenia, no longer existed for him. He looked at the spot where she stood and did not see her. Suddenly, he grabbed up his sword and whirled upon Verulus, crying out.

Verulus, moving faster than a man half his age, leaped to defend himself. They spun before Lucilla's gaze as they slashed skillfully and violently at each other.

She stood for a long time watching them, and then turned and walked slowly out. Behind her, Commodus for one fraction of a second paused, watching her leave. His face was expressionless. He turned back to his training with Verulus, slashing, thrusting, faster than ever.

XII

THE FORCED MARCH brought Livius' Northern Army to the gates of Rome in the ninth month. Messengers had gone ahead to Commodus. The legionnaires were preparing their encampment when Commodus' emissaries appeared, inviting Livius and his major officers to a hero's welcome at the emperor's newly-completed *palaestra*.

Orderlies arrived at Livius' quarters to help him don the full ceremonial dress of imperial commander. It bothered him to have the slaves and orderlies working on his person while outside the haggard legions built the encampment, and the Marcomanni captives made their own rough living quarters. Victorinus in bright uniform, bedecked with medals, arrived while Livius was still being dressed. Victorinus laughed. "I would rather face the Quadi in some Danube marsh, eh, General?"

Livius tried to smile but could muster only an impatient nod. "I've always hated a toga," he said.

A full company of polished soldiers awaited them outside the praetorium. Livius got slowly into his chariot, moving like an old man because he was hampered by the toga.

The escort moved through the growing encampment. No general in the last few hundred years had been permitted to enter Rome with his legions: many an ambitious general might be tempted to seize the government; since Marius made the legions an army of professionals, the enlisting men had sworn oath to their commanding general personally, and often in the case of men from provinces, this was where their only loyalty lay. The law remained rigid, applied to all commanders and their legions. By now, the senate saw the mistake Tiberius had made when under the influence of Sejanus. He'd allowed the Praetorian Guard to be housed within the fourteen regions of the city. The Guard had expanded, developed, and taken increasing power, so that the commander of the Praetorian Guard often became in reality the most powerful man in the empire. Ruling class fear is behind all law, and the rulers of Rome had learned to fear acutely the very men to whom their debt was greatest, the legion generals who kept order, manned and maintained frontiers and commanded respect, collected revenues and taxes for the emperor.

As he rode past the prison compound, Livius saw Ballomar at work with his people, building rude animal-skin shelters. Ballomar did not look up; he was outside Rome; he no longer believed in anything, not his god Wotan, certainly not the vow of an enemy commander. Nothing showed in Ballomar's face except sweat and old bitter hatreds.

Near the picket lines, Xenia stood beside Timonides. Livius glanced at them, not needing the chariot slowed to see the fears and doubts in Xenia's face. There was only the slightest difference between the Princess Xenia and her father—Xenia *wanted* to believe.

Livius lifted his arm in a brief salute, and gave her a smile that he hoped would reassure her. Her people were *not* going to be driven through the streets of Rome in chains. He nodded, as though she'd questioned him anew, pleading,

and he had given his answer again, and it was the same
vow. He saw her exhale deeply as if she'd been holding her
breath, and she made a gesture as if amazed at his physical
splendor in full ceremonial dress.

The caterwauling of sounds inside the mammoth *palaestra*
was more painful to Livius than the wails on some nightmare
battlefield.

The gymnasium was the same place where Commodus had
held brief audience with Lucilla, but only the half-naked
gladiators and the bust of Faustina remained to prove it, for
the flooring, walls and ceiling had been covered, decorated, altered so it was converted into a huge banquet hall.
The dominant motif of its decor remained still the gladiator,
as if indeed Commodus meant to make of the empire a
gladiator's world. The muscled athletes were everywhere, their
nakedness and the nudity of young girls and pretty teenage
boys seducing attention from the sumptuous banquet on
the tables.

Livius attempted to appreciate all the splendor because it
was in his honor, and it was the first such celebration in
his career, and it was the first affair created by Commodus
he had attended since the prince became emperor. He was
impressed, fearfully impressed. But there was too much for
the eyes of one man to contain: the opulence was even
more overwhelming upon the senses than the noises. Hundreds of guests, many of them a new breed of friends of the
emperor and unknown to Livius from the days of Aurelius.
He recognized the senators by their toga, but only a few
of the elders to whom Marcus had entrusted Commodus for
instruction and counsel were in view. Livius decided he
could understand this: whatever else Commodus was, he had
been a shy, timid boy, and he hated the wise sages from the
senate though he recognized them as supremely intelligent;
they made him feel like a fool, he was uncomfortable
around them; it was unlikely he would have them at a gala
such as this. Still, their absence troubled Livius because it
went unexplained, almost as if the sage senators no longer
existed in the empire. Livius shook himself, knowing he had
to avoid such doubts.

The senators and magistrates he saw were more concerned
with the pretty young girls or simpering young boys on
their laps than with affairs of state. Syrian musicians played

exotic melodies that even though half-drowned in wine-steeped laughter and shrill conversations, still gave the strident sensuality a kind of sanity; it seemed to have reason and purpose in this place, as if the world of reality beyond these walls didn't really exist anyhow.

Commodus held tightly to Livius' elbow, propelling him through the dancing girls, performing dwarfs, acrobats, all executing their turns as if they believed the guests were truly watching them. A small army of slaves scurried about between the dancers, performers, strollers, musicians and diners, pouring wine, serving exotically prepared fish, sea food, pigeons, geese, swine. Other slaves, rigid as machinery, agitated fans of peacock feathers to drive flies off the piles of food along the tables.

Livius glanced at Commodus, seeing he had gained weight, but had not grown soft. Commodus probably kept in shape better than his soldiers, training daily with the gladiators. And talk was that the young emperor was the cleanest of Caesars in his person, taking as many as eight baths a day, in the perfumed company of young boys to lather him and young girls to amuse him. He had never looked handsomer, resplendent in silk costume, but his face was a conflict of pride and barely controlled rage.

Livius had sensed this tension in Commodus from the first moment of greeting and he himself was drawn, distracted, lost in this gaiety, stared at as an oddity by the young aristocracy of Rome.

Commodus made a sweeping gesture, as if challenging Livius. "Have you ever seen anything lovelier? All for you, my Livius."

"I've never seen anything like it."

"Of course you never have. There's never been anything like it."

Livius sighed, and Commodus spoke in a sharp tone. "Well, Livius? What is better than feeling yourself among your own —and with them."

Livius glanced quickly about him, the nude women, the cord-muscled gladiators, the young Roman patricians. He managed a rueful smile.

"This is surely more comfortable than a cold campfire and the cunning of the barbarian, my lord Caesar."

Commodus was not placated, the note of challenge grew. "Know that I am your true friend—as always. . . . It would have been so easy for me to have listened to all the wild rumors about you. But I chose not to listen."

"Rumors?"

"Rumors about some insane plan you had for putting those Marcomanni captives in some Roman city—to live among us—us, civilized people among such savages—"

"How can you judge it since I've told no one about it?"

Commodus stopped, staring at Livius aghast. The shrill cries, laughter and music swelled, but he didn't hear it. He shook his head, spoke in a hoarse whisper. "Surely there was no truth in such rumor?"

Livius held his gaze. "Let me first tell you what my plan is."

Commodus slashed downward furiously. "No. No. I do not wish to hear of it." He swung his arm out wildly toward the senators and aediles present. "Everybody will oppose it."

Livius nodded. "Then don't defend me. I don't ask that of our old friendship, Commodus. Let me go before the senate. Let them decide. Then—it won't be your responsibility."

Commodus shook his head, eyes fiery. "Am I not Caesar? Can I not rule alone? The gods have chosen me! Why will you fly in the face of the gods? Why will you risk our friendship?"

Livius straightened, angered. "Why should it risk our friendship?"

In the wailing party noises they were silent. Commodus said, "Know this, Livius: I do not wish you to do this." He made an effort to smile, said eagerly as he'd spoken when he was a boy, wanting his way, "Give this up, Livius!" He smiled, softening, certain Livius would relent. "Enjoy life! Look around you, see all the pleasures. There is so much I want to do for you!"

Before Livius could speak, Commodus gestured, and a loud gasp erupted from the assemblage, and everything else was forgotten as a shower of flowers, petals, golden coins came raining down from the ceiling, scattering over the guests. There was a wild burst of gaiety as the guests scrambled for coins and flowers, screaming and shoving.

Slaves bearing the two-handled, tight-necked, big-bellied and narrow-based wine vessels came running to refill glasses. The amphores of wine were tilted, pouring wine everywhere.

Commodus gave Livius an expansive smile of forgiveness, as though convinced that Livius had yielded to his desires, and watched, delighted as hundreds of half-nude dancing girls unseen before, came swirling in, writhing among the guests like bejeweled serpents.

Commodus swung his arm, gesturing toward the guests. "*This* is what they want," he said loudly above the noise. "This is what they want."

Dancing girls pirouetted about them. Livius looked at them, his face gray. Commodus spoke eagerly, "Don't you see, Livius? I want you to be happy. There's no one I trust like you . . ." His voice became gentle. "Don't drift away from me, Livius."

Livius didn't speak at all. There was nothing to say as this loud and fantastic display surrounded and drowned them, and they were borne along as if in a swift, churning current.

The leader of the senate declared that body in session, and Livius stood waiting, tense, knowing battle lines were as surely drawn as if he were on a campaign in the north. Only here in the *curia* he had no legions of archers and javelin-hurlers behind him. Virgilianus had arrived from Egypt and Marcellus from Syria, but even with his old war friends backing him, he knew how alone he was. For the first time he understood a strange and terrible brand of loneliness, that of the man making a decision, fighting for something he believes in. Marcus Antoninus had spent his life in such loneliness, and Livius was sweated in it already.

The body of the senate sat in colorful pageantry, but were strangely austere, unapproachable in their places, and the solemn atmosphere was charged with tension. Livius glanced across them, trying to find a familiar face from the time when he accompanied Aurelius on state business. He recognized Caecina, frail, withered, almost lost in his toga, looking to be ninety, at least. Caecina did not return his glance. Near the elder was Senator Titanicus, a grave man in his late thirties.

Livius turned, seeing Commodus, dressed in full pomp as Caesar, with gold crown, purple silk toga. His boyish face was white with fury and he restrained himself only with difficulty. He had asked Livius to drop this matter of slave-rehabilitation, yet found himself facing his supreme commander before the senate.

Commodus stared directly at Livius without a flicker of recognition in his angered eyes. Clustered around the emperor were Cleander with Lentulus at his shoulder, and Commodus' friends of the senate, most prominent among them Didius Julianus.

Livius winced at the snub from Commodus, but his gaze touched the group of young barbarian chieftains and Marcomanni women on display along with Ballomar before the senate. Near them, Xenia stood erect, a defiant, savage young princess. Livius straightened, knowing why he was fighting, and knowing he would not back down. Still, there was the sure sense of defeat in the charged atmosphere. He had felt it crossing the forum to the *curia* at its north. Thousands of Romans packed the forum, and all had heard the whispers of Livius' plan to integrate the wild Huns with the Roman citizenry. They were silent, uneasy, restless as he strode through them. In the whole mob, Livius saw one friendly face, the Greek Timonides.

Julianus getting the leader's permission, addressed the assemblage. His voice was modulated with heavy sarcasm laced through it.

"Honorable fathers of Rome—have you heard what is being proposed?" He glanced at them in a moment of silence. "Livius Gaius Metellus has asked that we take these savage people—these barbarians, little better in intellect and way of life than wild animals—" he pointed toward Ballomar and his people. The whole senate followed the direction of his gesture, staring at the defiant group of captives. This was the first opportunity many of the elders had had to see the Huns who had cost Rome so much in time, money and men these past seventeen years. "He wants us to take them to live among us—these wandering murderers—he would ask us to take them into the Roman city of Ravenna, there to settle them, so they may live *as* Romans, *among* Romans!"

He shook his head, smiling as if unable to credit the whole scheme as anything but a monstrous joke. A deep silence spread across the chamber.

Livius pulled his gaze from Julianus to Commodus who was trembling with barely concealed rage, and the senators Cassius, Antonius and Marius, whispering among themselves, faces showing shock.

Julianus continued with monumental sarcasm: "Take these half-animals in, to treat them—these savages—as brothers

—equals! What kind of sword will it take to enforce such brotherhood? How safe will we be in our own beds with them among us? And what of our other provinces? What of Gaul, so loyal to us? And Syria, and Egypt, which sends us our grain? If we make Romans of the barbarians, can we withhold citizenship from them? Then what becomes of that precious prize Roman citizenship once was? It becomes a cheap, common thing—to be handed out like bread!" His voice rose. "No! We are Romans! Warriors! We are civilized human beings. Let us cast out from among us these poisonous ideas which come from slaves and Jews and Greeks!"

He paused, flooded in a storm of approval from one side of the senate. He nodded, smiling, and shouted over the roaring, pointing toward Ballomar and his people, "You want to be kind to them, and to others who would emulate them in fighting us? Then crucify them—their leaders—for the world to see. Let the Hun know what his opposition will buy him! Burn some at the stake. Let the smell of their burning flesh ride the wind north as our warning! Sell the rest as slaves, so the word will spread that Rome is stronger than ever, not weaker!"

Xenia, her face rigid, moved over and joined her countrymen. Julianus spoke coldly, "Teach the Vandal once and for all what it is to make war on Rome!"

Another roar of approval echoed through the *curia*.

Commodus, Cleander and the others of the group around them nodded, grimly pleased. Julianus returned to them, and accepted their congratulations with a chilled smile.

Livius stepped forward, pale and shaken, the roar from the senate like the battle cry of wild hordes on some cold plain. He took his place, and spoke levelly.

"I am not an orator, only a soldier. I never realized before my learned friend Julianus spoke, how little an orator I am. I hope I am a better soldier. But as a soldier, this I know: a hundred times in eleven years have we taught the barbarian that lesson Julianus suggests, what it meant to make war on Rome. A hundred times have we burned their villages, crucified their leaders, enslaved their young. . . . My friends, the fires go out, the dead are buried, and the slaves die slowly, but the hatred we leave behind us never dies. Hatred means wars. Wars mean tribute torn from our provinces, taxes falling on the people, farmers abandoning their weary land. Hunger and disease brought to Rome itself."

He moved, crossing in long soldier strides to Ballomar and the others. The senate stirred with interest, and currents of excited whispers flowed unevenly among them.

Commodus leaned forward. Beside him, Lentulus whispered to blind Cleander, and the lean senator's face showed gray.

Livius nodded and Ballomar stepped forward from the other captives. The two walked to the center of the stage and stood side by side, the towering, awe-inspiring Ballomar and Livius.

Livius resumed speaking to the senate. "One million beings now live in Rome. Six hundred thousand of them are slaves." Suddenly he ripped away the rough fabric of Ballomar's cloak, revealing the scarred, fantastically powerful torso. "Put this man in chains and we have one more slave. Even now there is no work for hundreds of thousands of Romans who must live off public charity."

Marcellus stepped forward, handed Livius a folded toga. Livius shook it out and tossed it across Ballomar's bare shoulder, instantly transforming Ballomar into a magnificently regal man.

Livius waited a moment, gazing at the changed barbarian, allowing the senate to peer at him, awed.

"Ravenna is an abandoned city," Livius said. "It is surrounded by rich, deserted farm lands. Let us put him in that city, on those lands. Let us make a Roman of him. We will have a prince, an ally! And with twenty thousand others like him living among us—we will have a nation of allies!"

A buzzing of excited whispers spread through the banks of seated senators.

"A nation which will spread among others of their people and tell them how much better it is to live as we do! Then shall we have our human frontiers against the Vandals! Then shall we have an empire of equals, a family of free nations living together! Then shall we have our *Pax Romana*—the Roman Peace Marcus Aurelius Antoninus spoke of."

The whispers died. Livius, with the giant Ballomar close beside him, moved his gaze across the faces of the senators. Cassius, Antonius, Marius, Virgilianus and Marcellus. They were silent, watching with keen interest.

Julianus openly moved close to the emperor. Heads swiveled and eyes were trained on Julianus and Commodus as they whispered together. No one listened any more to Livius and he was silent.

Julianus stepped away from Caesar, moved out before the senate, a smile of supreme confidence lighting his face, interrupting, calling for the floor: "In the name of Caesar!"

Gazes returned to Livius in the dramatic silence and Livius yielded the floor.

Julianus glanced across the faces of the senators. "Our Caesar has just asked me—when was Rome greatest? When has Rome been stronger?"

The senators straightened, a charged thrill surged through the chamber. It was evident now to the least of them the way Caesar wished them to vote, clear also that a vote for Livius' plan would mean a vote against Caesar.

Livius felt his shoulders sag, and he felt more alone than ever since Commodus had thrown him a direct challenge.

Julianus spoke in supreme confidence. "And so I say in answer to our Caesar—never has Rome been greater or stronger. What is it that has kept our empire together? Our strength, our might—and the fact that we have not mongrelized our blood by mixing it with inferiors—or with half-animal savages. Why then should we take in our enemies among us, so that the whole world will consider us weak? Then they will fall upon us from everywhere! It will be the end of Rome!" His voice broke dramatically. "The end of Rome. . . ."

Julianus allowed his voice to trail away, but he could not completely conceal his smile of triumph as he relinquished the floor.

From the rows of senators, the aged Caecina rose and stepped out to claim the floor. Heavy silence greeted him.

Caecina's voice rose pure and clear. This was a battle-ground he knew well, his memories going back to the struggles in these chambers during the reign of Pius, and before. History of the thousand years of Rome was bright in his mind—the wrongs, the evils, the triumphs, the building, its past and its destiny.

"The end of Rome? How does an empire die? Does it collapse all in one terrible moment? No . . . No. But there comes a time when its people no longer believe in it, when they live only for the pleasures of the moment, apathetic toward dangers, reveling in gaudy display of their worldly wealth; when, instead of searching for means to protect the empire, they think only of means of grabbing more, of protecting what they have taken to themselves. Then does an empire begin to die, slowly, slowly." He pointed toward Ballomar. "There are millions like him waiting at our gates. If we do not open these gates, they will break them down and destroy us. Instead of taxing our people, our provinces, beyond endurance, let us take in new blood that will make us stronger. Instead, let us grow ever bigger, ever greater. Let us take these new people among us. Honorable fathers, we of Rome have changed the world. Can we not change ourselves?"

One after another the senators rose to their feet, cheering the old statesman. For him there was an acclamation.

Commodus clutched at Julianus, whispering to him, their faces sick with anger and frustration.

Livius nodded toward Caecina, thanking him for coming to the rescue of his plan, and of the Roman world. The old man gestured tiredly, returning to his place.

The senate leader rose after the vote: "The honorable fathers of Rome have voted for the plan presented by Livius Gaius Metellus."

Commodus stood up, unable to speak. He was surrounded by his friends, stunned, incredulous, but already whispering plans for reprisals against those who opposed him.

There was clamor and excitement as senators descended upon Livius from all sides, congratulating him. Messengers scurried through the throngs of chattering lawmakers.

Commodus stood a moment, then white with fury, turned and stalked out of the senate chambers. The Praetorian Guard, led by their chief, Cornelius, and taking their cue from the stormy attitude of the Caesar, pushed senators roughly aside making a path for Commodus and his friends. Before the swift-moving emperor, the senators fell silent, backing away. Across the chamber, Livius, seeing Commodus leave, hurried, trying futilely to push his way through to him.

XIII

LIVIUS ENTERED the palace on the run, brushing aside the guards, rushing up the staircase. He burst into the entry of Commodus' private chambers. Except for slave girls at work on his wardrobe, Caesar was alone, standing as though awaiting Livius, a strange excitement in him.

Commodus spoke at once, voice flat. "You've defeated me."

Livius bowed, shaking his head, face rigid. "Since it was for Rome, it cannot be your defeat."

Commodus forgot his self-control. His mouth, grown more sensual than ever, twisted in petulance and contempt. "For Rome!"

When Livius tried to speak, Commodus slashed downward with his hand, stopping him. His voice was cold, with rage roiling under its surface. "The senate has spoken. I cannot now stop the move to place these barbarians in a Roman city—among Romans. The gods like to play such tricks on the empire." His voice changed. "Also on you, Livius."

Livius braced himself.

"You are no longer in command of the army of Rome," Commodus said. His tone was as casual as if he were refusing him a second cup of wine. Blood seeped from Livius' face, and he stood tall, gray. Commodus shook his head, speaking almost sorrowfully as if forced to mete out punishment against his own will. "No longer second to Caesar himself. . . . Nor will you live in the city of Rome. You will live with the barbarians whom you seem to prefer to us—in Ravenna. For ever. . . . Or until I see fit to recall you."

Commodus shifted his toga, waiting for any gesture of protest, of refusal. None came. Livius did not move and the two faced each other. After a long time, Livius spoke quietly: "You are undoubted Caesar."

He nodded, bowed, and turned to leave the room.

Commodus shook his head, shadows flickering in his eyes, his mouth trembling. "Livius!"

Livius stopped and half turned, waiting.

Commodus Caesar took one step toward him, eagerness in his manner.

"Listen to me, Livius. There is still one way we could stop it all. If *you* were to appear before the senate—" He was almost pleading. "If you were to say you were wrong about this whole Ravenna scheme. That you were misled by the philosophers, the weaklings—" Excitement mounted in his voice. "You would say it was the poisonous influence of the Greek, Timonides—my father's friend." He waited, but Livius' face remained cold. "Perhaps you would also mention the influence of Polybus. . . . It would not be bad to show the army, too, that we are not afraid of them. Since Timonides is Greek, we would crucify him. You see, we would have to. . . . Since Polybus is Roman, we would have him thrown from the Tarpeian Rock to his death. . . ."

Pleased with the outline of his infallible plan, Commodus watched Livius' face.

Livius shook his head, voice quiet. "No."

Commodus went into an instant rage. "Wait! Wait! Don't answer yet—" And as Livius scowled, puzzled, Commodus turned, motioning Livius to follow. "Come."

Livius hesitated one moment, then followed. Commodus strode quickly across his private suite, along the gray corridor. He paused before a closed door, glanced over his shoulder, waiting with an odd look of triumph on his face.

Commodus threw open the door, stepped through it, beckoning Livius to follow.

Livius stepped inside the scented, silk and lace adorned chamber and stopped, numbed, when he saw Lucilla standing there as lovely, and yet as unreal as she had been in all his dreams this eternal, lonely year.

Commodus glanced from Lucilla's ashen face to Livius, smiled, and spoke quietly. "When I heard you were returning to Rome, Livius, I insisted Lucilla wait here rather than return at once to Armenia. . . . I was certain you would have so much to say to each other."

Commodus stood another moment, watching them, drawing some sensual pleasure from this cruelty to two people who had tried to exist separated from each other. He turned then and closed the door behind him, leaving them alone and for some moments wordless.

It was as if neither dared to speak, not trusting their voices, or the tears behind them. Lucilla's face was strained, tormented, showing some signs of the great inner turmoil. She had known Livius was coming home, she had prayed she would see him, if only for a moment, in a crowd somewhere, and yet had dreaded it, too. For a taut moment she stood rigid, aloof, then suddenly she was in his arms and he was holding her close.

She sobbed against him. "Livius . . . Livius. You are well and alive. . . . I keep dreaming you are on a battlefield, you call to me, and when I come to you—you do not move, and I see it is—my father—"

He kissed her hungrily, speaking against the delicious texture of her face. "No—I am alive—alive." He held her for a long time, but as nothing compared to the empty months away from her. "You've been well?" He didn't wait for an answer. "A queen. . . . The world hears that you have charmed the East . . ." And then he gave it up, "Oh, Lucilla, why? Did you have to hurl yourself into a marriage with Sohamus? You were hurt, the world was turned upside down, but—the gods know . . . we might have found a way—we might have found a way."

Lucilla shook her head, pulled herself from his arms, shivering faintly in the chill, wanting desperately to press again into his warmth, but wanting as desperately to escape. "There was no other way. . . . I am still pledged as wife to my husband Sohamus."

As Livius moved toward her, she backed away.

"Oh, Livius, can't you see why Commodus brought you to me and left us alone? He hopes we will be weak—because that's what he understands and trades on—weakness. . . . He wants us to abandon our honor."

Livius stared into the slanted pools of her eyes, mouth wry. "He almost succeeded."

"It's the only way he can succeed. The only way he knows to have what he wants from us—is to destroy us, Livius, to make us—what he is—weak and without honor."

"Without you, honor doesn't seem very much."

"Oh, Livius, without honor you and I would have nothing in this—this terrible new world Commodus is making." Her voice lowered. "Now you see what Commodus is, what he has become—" The words tumbled out. "Now it's clear. He'll destroy the empire. You must stop him, Livius. Only you can do it." She whispered, frantic. "The army is with you. March against Commodus."

Livius retreated a step, watching her face. Her eyes were fevered, glazed. Rome had become a trap, a maze, and for her there was only one escape, the way of rebellion. She was distracted with fears, and yet he could not see where she could reconcile rebellion and honor.

She caught his arm, pleading. "Become Caesar. In the Rome you would make there might even be happiness for us —with honor—as Romans."

She trembled, her tear-struck eyes searching his face in the silence.

He shook his head. "No, Lucilla."

She was stricken, without hope if he failed her. "The senate is with you! All Rome is with you!"

Again he shook his head. A man had to see deeper than the surface, and several truths had made cold impressions upon Livius since his return to Rome. The city was on one long binge; they indeed had what they wanted, no matter what kind of belly ache or hangover awaited them when the party ended. Pius had given them equanimity, and Marcus had given them austerity. Commodus delivered precisely what he promised: fun and food. He spoke quietly, but with certain knowledge. "Rome is not with me."

She looked about, distracted. "Take power, Livius. It's waiting for you. But it's much more than this. More terrible. The Roman world needs you, or I'd never plead with you like this to take power while something remains, while it is waiting—"

"What would be waiting is Roman fighting Roman. Civil war. It may come, Lucilla, but not from me. It's not power I want—"

"But once you are in command, you could impose a thousand Ravennas! You could force hundreds of thousands of barbarians to be accepted in Roman cities—"

"I could not. Nobody can. You cannot force people to accept something that is repugnant to them except by education and enlightenment—that is something which must grow slowly—"

"There is no time!" She gazed about her in desperation, the walls of the maze closing. She backed away from him. "Oh, Livius, there would be no honor in it—if you were an ambitious or mean, or a self-seeking man. . . . There is honor in saving our world from ruin." Her head tilted and her jaw squared in an angered line that made her lovelier—and more lost to him—than ever. "Why do you hesitate?"

Livius drew the back of his hand across his mouth, putting into words the thought that troubled him. "It would mean the death of Commodus."

She burst into helpless tears. He took a step toward her to comfort her, stopped. His tone changed.

"I would not be in command after insurrection, Lucilla. . . . The army would be Caesar."

She brushed away her tears, lifted her head, whispering.

"Commodus will never live out his life. . . . Someone will kill him. There will then be insurrection, ruin, and it will be too late. Livius, millions of lives are at stake."

He shook his head, face grim. "No . . . we are not there yet. At least I am not."

She sighed deeply and for uncounted moments they stood looking at each other. This was the place where everything finally ended between them, and neither could deny it any more. Livius knew he could remain a faithful soldier to Commodus only by heeling around, running, away from the scent of this room, the fragrance and beauty of her, the allure that was like derangement, where a man tossed off honor, self-respect, integrity like old garments. Yet if he walked away from her, his life stretched ahead of him as empty and abandoned as some Roman road through a distant wilderness. He had to run, he wanted to grab her in his arms, and so he didn't move at all.

Lucilla looked at him and saw the court at Armenia and the role she played as the perfect queen. She saw the moment when they were young and she had begged him to love her, when the overwhelming desire in her at this moment, strident and screaming, was just born—strident and screaming. It had been like that forever for her. It would be forever. She had to begin now, living with her need, without him to satisfy it, and she began by fighting down her desire, holding herself away from him.

Her voice was cold, level. "What should we do, Livius? Bow to Commodus' plan? Abandon everything but each other? No. I will not. It would be Commodus' victory. He has never won over me. He never will. I would become something I have despised all my life." Then she cried out, unable to surrender her last hope. "Why won't you act, Livius?"

His face was expressionless. "Would you want me to become something I have despised all my life?"

Her mouth trembled and her eyes filled with tears. She searched his face, studying it, remembering it, denying it. She managed to shake her head, standing tall and regal, and alone.

Livius turned and walked across the room. She held her breath until he opened the door, closed it behind him. She pressed her fist against her mouth, crying out. She wanted to run after him, but she did not move. She didn't have to run after him now, it would not do any good, and besides there was plenty of time for running after him—she would do that in all her lonely dreams from now on.

BOOK THREE

XIV

RAVENNA. . . .

The whole world heard that name in the years after Livius
Gaius Metellus was exiled there along with his Marcomanni
captives.

There was every reason for the experiment to fail, and the
empire waited for the failure. Ravenna was already a tired
town when the Marcomanni arrived there. In the province of
Ravenna, the walled city itself was on the flat Romagna
plain only thirteen feet above sea level. The Adriatic Sea was
four miles down river to the east. Sixty-five miles north-
east of Florence, seventy-five miles south of Venice, it had
grown swiftly after Augustus Caesar based one of his two
fleets at nearby Classis. Ravenna then assumed importance
to the expanding Roman empire because of its protected position amid marshlands and its ready access to the sea on a
part of the coast devoid of other good ports.

But this was history, and while Ravenna was the market
center for the rich surrounding agricultural area, it was
struck hard by the Black Death brought west by Marcus'
conquering armies. It was a desperate struggle to stay
alive, and the town lay almost forgotten until the Marcomanni's arrival made it the center of tension and discord.

From his government palace overlooking the town, Livius
stared across the city, the river and the plain in growing
despair. Nothing ran smoothly in Ravenna except time itself; time was always slipping away from him, always running out, always his enemy. Sometimes when one more day,
one more week, another month would make the difference
between a major defeat and one minor victory, he had everything on his hands except time.

He awoke an hour before dawn—a habit formed when he

was a schoolboy in his Palatine Hill home back at Rome,
and due in his classroom at the light of day. With Timonides
and sometimes Xenia when she wakened early enough, he
ate a light breakfast, freshly baked bread dipped in wine or
eaten with honey, olives or cheese. While the others were
still eating he would "ask for his shoes," leave the table
and attack the latest problems of the town, the unending
conflict between the Ravenna citizens and the barbarians who
had been forced upon them at his suggestion and upon the
vote of the senate. It made it no easier that all Ravenna
knew the Caesar himself had opposed the whole scheme.

In the middle of the morning, grown tired, he strode to a
window overlooking the market place and stared wearily,
yet hopefully, upon the mixture of the fair-skinned savages
and the black-eyed Italians.

The market place was alive with humanity. To Livius it
seemed all life revolved about the fountain on the square
which dominated the place, its water making it the center of
activity because everyone came here to fill his jugs except
the very wealthy who had private wells in their own court-
yards.

It was easy to distinguish between Ravennan and barbarian; the dark-skinned Romans walked with a certain tension, watching every move of the blond people with suspicion. On the other hand, the barbarians after all these
months had lost none of their own suspicious curiosity, their
superstitions or their childlike awe at the wondrous wares
displayed for sale.

"Have you heard the latest talk from Rome?" Timonides
said to Livius, at his shoulder.

Without turning, Livius answered curtly, "I don't want to
hear it."

"Maternus and some of his rebels were captured and
killed," Timonides reported as though Livius had begged for
news.

"I told you, I don't want to hear about some renegade
officer and his band of tattered bandits who robbed and
killed the very people in Gaul and Spain that he'd vowed to
protect. I have my own woes."

"No woes like those they have in Rome itself," Timonides
said in his gentle way.

"Still, they do me—"

"Do you ask *where* Maternus and his men were captured?" Timonides didn't wait, hurried on. "Inside the gates of Rome itself."

"What?"

"There. I knew I'd excite your interest. Yes. It is said Maternus and his men were almost captured in the Alps, but disguised themselves as peasants, filtered south and into Rome where Maternus planned to kill Commodus and declare himself emperor."

"Then death was what he deserved."

"Perhaps. But do you think he will be the last? Or is Maternus just a symptom of the terrible unrest?"

"I don't know. I don't care, Greek!"

"Oh, you care. You sit here far from all of the hurts that inflict Rome, but you care. With all your heart! You don't sleep at night, you have a hungry, restless look—the look of a man eaten and consumed by inner hungers—a man who has gotten little from life he wants or deserves, and who can make his life endurable only by driving himself day and night, like a madman. Oh, you care, all right."

"Greek, I order you to be silent!"

"If I were silent, where would you hear the truths that you must hear?" Timonides shook his head. Daily, he did this to Livius, reciting the rumored excesses of Commodus relentlessly, as though they were assignments in geography, social sciences, history, and government which had to be drilled into his unresponsive pupil as he taught Xenia Greek, graces and philosophy. Having unwilling pupils did not dismay the Greek slave-teacher; he'd had few of any other kind.

Livius found he listened to Timonides whether he wanted to or not, because in Ravenna there was no place to escape the persistent Greek.

For many months Timonides had been bringing word of Maternus and other common soldiers like him in all provinces, deserters who took taxes and tribute from the people they'd been hired to protect from despoilers; robbing travelers and raping cities along the Roman roads. Rather than send punitive forces to deal with these rebels, Commodus listened to Cleander and Claudius and abandoned the distant provinces to their fate. Cleander and Claudius exaggerated the hardships, dangers, uselessness of the campaigns in the wild countries beyond the Alps, or the Danube. They assured the emperor that the terror of his name and the arms of his lieutenants would keep order along those far, cold frontiers.

Commodus had ordered the last of the legions removed from the Danube outposts. Livius had written him long, impassioned letters of protest, but received polite, barbed replies inquiring about the weather in Ravenna.

"Commodus no longer even respects the senate," Timonides began one morning and Livius could not shut him off.

Timonides reported that an attempt had been made on Commodus' life, the assassin screaming as he raised his dagger, "The senate sends you this!"

The assassin was seized by quick-moving Praetorian Guards, and under the pressures of inhuman inquisition, admitted the senators were guiltless, the plot hatched inside Commodus' own palace, the knifer hired and rehearsed in his lines. But even though the senate was not guilty of any plot against him, Commodus never afterwards trusted any of these men except his own close friends, suspected the august body as his secret, plotting enemies. Hired informers, spies, men with grudges were used by Commodus to learn all he could about the senate and its movements. Suspicion became equivalent to proof, smear campaigns without basis in truth ruined distinguished careers; trial became condemnation. The people heard of the unbridled accusations against Commodus' political opponents, but they were never told when the charges were disproved or dropped as false.

"Commodus has declared that anyone bringing him news of rebellion, defeat or any other ugliness in the provinces will be subject to death," was the topic of another of Timonides' morning dissertations. "Commodus has assumed the very ugly character of his evil advisers."

Livius heeled around. "I've known Commodus since he was a child. He may have been weak, but he was never evil."

"His father was poisoned in his name—"

"That has never been proved, Timonides—"

"Nor ever been disproved." Timonides spread his hands. "Whether he was an evil youth, or only unprincipled, he now spends his days slaughtering wild animals in the gladiators' arenas. People are starving and do you know what laws Commodus is interested in getting on the books? He wants to make it a law that every Roman attending the circuses, the forum, the Colosseum must wear a toga. A toga! The most urgent matter on the mind of the Caesar."

"Where do you get such rumors?"

"Oh, believe me, they come to me like filings to a magnet. Because I want to hear them. I must hear them."

"And do you bother separating chaff from wheat, Greek?"

"I'd as soon try to separate the smoke from the flame, my lord general. As you suggest, perhaps Caesar's timidity and not his evil allowed unprincipled advisers to control him—"

"This has to be the answer. You know as well as I that Commodus put off for months going into Rome after Marcus died because he was too shy to face the ovation, the triumph of his coronation."

"A long time ago. Much wine has run since then. His timidity may have made him slave to his debased friends, and they then corrupted his mind. Cruelty, even when it at first only obeys the dictates of others, degenerates first into habit, second to pleasure and then becomes the ruling passion of a man's soul."

Livius stared at the Greek a moment and then stepped past him, striding across the room.

"Where are you going?" Timonides cried, and Xenia leaped up from the couch, troubled.

"I'm getting out of here," Livius answered. "I'm going down in that dirty market place to get a clean breath of air."

When Livius strode into the market place, the Italians glanced up from filling jugs or drinking at the fountain. The blond savages turned from the displayed wares in the stores, standing as if awaiting sudden doom as Livius approached. It had been an interminable time, but the Marcomanni believed no more in good now than they had on the day they entered Ravenna.

Livius slowed, feeling tired. He was aware of Xenia and Timonides close behind him, almost as if they were his bodyguard, ready to die for him, but not ready to allow him a moment of freedom, a full breath of air.

He glanced at Xenia from the corner of his eye. She no longer looked like a child though she was still a young girl. She had the look now of a woman, and he winced, knowing he'd given her that, driven into her arms, trying to find a forgetfulness that always eluded him. He never forgot anything, not even when Xenia screamed and wailed in her anguished pleasure.

He drew his hand across his face, sweated. It was a failure, all of it.

Timonides gestured toward the market place where the crowds of blond and dark people were stirred together, yet obviously in no way integrated. He spoke hopefully, "See how well they live together, General. Blond and dark people—"

Livius was silent, grimly surveying the peaceful scene, a peace entirely of the surface, boiling underneath, ready to erupt.

"Oh, Great Livius! Oh, Great Livius!"

Livius went tense at the cry of a young female voice. A blonde child, not yet twelve, hurled herself from a crowd of the barbarians, ran across the stones and clutched her arms about his hips, pressing her face against his body, kissing him.

"Oh, I've looked for you every day," she cried, tears streaming down her cheeks. "May I come and live with you now? Will you make me your own slave, until I am old enough for you to marry? I'll be as no woman ever was for you. My whole life will be yours."

Frowning, Livius lifted the child in his arms, holding her out at eye level, studying her. "Who are you?"

"Don't you remember, Livius?" Timonides said when the child wept inconsolably. "She is Griselda, the child you saved from a javelin—"

"But you were only a baby!" Livius said, holding her in his arms until her sobbing ceased. "How you've grown."

"Children grow fast," Xenia said.

"And I will grow much faster now," the little girl said, talking brightly into Livius' face, stroking his cheek. "In this wonderful place you have brought us, I'll soon be grown, and I'll be lovely—and you will want me."

"I'll never be worthy of your loveliness," Livius told her, smiling. "Are you happy here?"

"Oh, yes. It is heaven here. We have everything, and I remember when we had nothing, only cold and misery all the time. I worship you, sire. Not only for saving my life—but for all you have done for all of us."

Livius, his eyes burning, kissed the girl's cheek and set

her on the pavement. "You run along and play and grow. Don't ever speak of being anyone's slave—except the man you love—"

"It is you I love," she said. "I'll never love anyone else."

"Then you be happy," Livius said. "For I love you." When she was gone, he smiled for the first time in months. "A child. Of course it's easier for her to adjust than for her parents. But maybe it will work, after all."

"It is working," Timonides said. "The parents will learn civilization, and the children will forget they ever lived otherwise."

Pleased, Livius gave Xenia and Timonides a brisk nod of approval as though they were responsible for peace and order in Ravenna, as though this whole experiment were somehow particularly theirs.

He turned and strode away from them, anxious to find new signs of the slow spread of success.

Xenia did not move. Her face was shadowed. Timonides laughed at her. "Do not be jealous, Xenia. It doesn't become a princess. . . . Besides, it was only a child he kissed."

"A child today," Xenia said. "Yesterday she was a baby."

"Do not be jealous—"

"I cannot help that I am jealous. You are my teacher. You insist upon teaching me the ways of the Greek. The proud and jealous Greeks—"

At the sudden wailing of the Italians, Livius stopped a few yards from the market place fountain. The barbarians stood watching silently, the impassioned Ravennans yelling in protest as an impassive barbarian, heavy, stolid, his hair the color of wheat, and as unkempt, led a huge, plodding horse across the square past the gaping, protesting crowds and with great difficulty persuaded the horse to climb into the fountain.

Amid the outraged and horrified screams of the Italians, the barbarian took a cloth, dipped it in the water and began methodically washing his horse.

"In our drinking water!"

"A horse in our drinking water!"

"Washing his horse in our drinking water!"

"Kill him before he kills all of us with his dirty ways!"

"Get that horse out of our water, you filthy animal!"

The Italians streaked across the square toward the fountain, shouting. The barbarians moved closer, not truly understanding what all the impassioned screaming was about, but ready to fight if one of their own was attacked.

An Italian man lifted a rock to hurl at the impassive barbarian, and a blond youth near him struck him in the face with his fist. The Italian forgot the man soiling the fountain and the first fight broke out in earnest.

The man at the fountain continued washing his horse without glancing toward the fights erupting all over the street.

Livius did not move. Xenia and Timonides ran past him, pushing their way through the fighting crowds all the way to the fountain. Timonides ordered them to stop fighting in the name of the *imperium* Livius, but it was only when they saw that Livius was standing watching that the fighting gradually ceased and the people stood in two groups, torn, bleeding, glaring at each other from opposite sides of the fountain.

Timonides walked to the base of the muddied pool where the barbarian continued to scrub his huge horse.

Timonides spoke reprovingly, "You must not wash your horse there."

The barbarian glanced up, incredulous. "But my horse is dirty."

"Exactly." Timonides pointed to the water. "And that is drinking water." He lifted his hand as if holding a cup, gesturing as if drinking to be sure the man would understand. "People drink that water."

The barbarian stared at him a moment, then nodded. "I've seen them." He went on washing his horse.

"You are making the water dirty—"

"But my horse is getting clean—"

"Pig! Cow!" Xenia pushed close to the fountain, screaming at the stolid Marcomanni. "Stop washing your horse in that fountain!"

She stepped forward, going into the pool, ready to assault the man. Timonides snagged her arm, holding her back. When she finally subsided, he made a patient gesture to placate her. "No. No. He must understand why he must not wash his horse in the pool." He turned, facing the man. Beyond him the Italians watched Timonides in suspicious distaste. "When people try to live together, there are three possibilities—"

As the Greek philosopher held up one finger, Livius sighed heavily, turned and strode away. Xenia watched Timonides a moment, then, staring anxiously after Livius, she heeled around and followed him, running.

Livius was mounting his horse outside his palace when Xenia overtook him, signaling a slave frantically to bring her a saddled animal.

Livius glanced at her, his face showing his weariness and defeat. "They don't seem to learn—"

There was an edge in Xenia's voice. "Give us time. Give them time."

Livius winced. He barely saw Timonides hurrying along the street to them, glowing with a smile of triumph.

Livius shook his head, staring at Xenia, but not really seeing her. "Time! Time! Months! Years! How much time do you think we have?"

From his saddle he stared down at them, the blonde, almost childlike young woman and the sad, wise and tired philosopher. His face was expressionless. Only his eyes were lost, not seeing them, or the surrounding city. He pulled his horse around and galloped away toward the gates and the Romagna plains beyond.

"We must go after him," Xenia said.

"Perhaps a moment alone—"

"We must go after him!"

"Perhaps a moment to think, to breathe, to regain his strength—"

"Something might happen to him!"

This convinced the Greek, and he shouted for a horse. Mounting up, they rode swiftly, following Livius.

As they left the town behind them, with Livius far in the lead, Timonides slowed his horse and unwillingly Xenia matched his pace.

"Why are you slowing down, Timonides?"

"Let him alone a little while, Xenia. If you really love him, you must let him alone a little. Don't cling to him—"

"I can't help it. Don't lecture me about that. Wise as you are, you don't know my heart—"

"I know your heart, and I know his. He is a lonely man, tired, feeling defeat and loneliness—"

"I don't want him to be lonely."

"You cannot help it. You can do much for him, I grant, but his loneliness—"

"Don't you think I know that!" she cried out. "He takes me in his arms, and I am transported, and yet he is lonely. I speak of love, and he doesn't even hear me. He is kind to me, and his kindness is the worst kind of cruelty—"

"Maybe you'd be happier if you went away from him."

"Don't talk like a fool, wise man!" She spurred her horse.

Livius rode his horse at full gallop until the magnificent animal faltered. He slowed then, knowing he hadn't ridden fast enough to escape his angers and frustrations.

Ahead of him he heard a sound like thunder, yet it was almost intelligible. He reined in, staring across a poorly ploughed field.

The huge Ballomar was behind a horse trying clumsily to plough a field. He was unable to keep the furrow straight. He was raging, voice bounding across the fields.

He glanced up, found Livius staring at him, and then Timonides and Xenia riding up behind the general.

When Ballomar saw them watching him, he roared with rage. He ripped the harness free of the plough, lifted the plough easily above his head and beat it against a tree, trying to smash it. It was bad enough being unable to plough, but unendurable to be a comic figure.

Xenia screamed at Ballomar as the plough bent. She dismounted and raced across the broken field toward him.

Ballomar turned defiantly, ploughshares like small sticks in his fists. When he saw her running toward him, he dropped the plough and waited for her challengingly.

Raging, Xenia screamed at him. "Dolt! If I can teach these hands of mine to hold the plough, why can't you?"

Ballomar bellowed back at her. "Because I am not a cow!"

Xenia's face flushed violently red beneath her blonde hair. She glanced quickly from Ballomar to Timonides to Livius and back to the giant Ballomar. In a white fury, she caught up a cudgel, and advanced on Ballomar, her voice mimicking the logic of Timonides: "There are three possibilities!" she raged. She struck Ballomar with the cudgel. "One."

She struck him again. "Two."

With all her strength, she struck him again. "Three."

Roaring, Ballomar deflected the blow and struck out at Xenia, backhanding her across the head. She went sprawling across the rough-ploughed ground.

Livius leaped from his horse without stopping to think. He wanted violence, not cerebration. As he ran across the broken soil, he wondered if he was moving to Xenia's protection, or merely seeking an outlet to his own pent-up frustration and anger.

He drove forward, swinging into Ballomar without speaking. They fought silently, viciously.

Xenia, more angered than hurt, picked herself up and brushed the soil from her clothing. Timonides came forward slowly and they watched, wincing when Ballomar struck Livius in the temple and sent him sprawling.

Xenia moved toward him protectively, but Timonides caught her arm, warningly.

Livius took a moment to clear his head, then got up warily.

He warned himself that Ballomar had all the force of an enraged bull. He had to be smarter than to walk into those battering-ram fists. He moved in, feinted with his left and drew Ballomar forward, off balance.

Livius brought his right fist up from his thigh, putting all his rage in it. Ballomar was coming forward in a fury and the sound of knuckles against the jaw was sickening in the open field.

Ballomar straightened, shook his head, his eyes not focusing. His knees gave under him first and he crashed on the ground, helpless even to break his fall.

He stayed there for some moments and when he got up to his knees, shaking his head, he eyed Livius with more respect. Ballomar moved in anew, his heart willing, but his flesh weak and unsure. When Livius faked again, and was bringing up the right cross, Ballomar suddenly backed away, battered, staring at him. He shook his head, holding up his hands. He was bettered, beaten, and he knew it.

Xenia screamed at Ballomar. "You are fit only to be leader of pigs. Go to work now."

Ballomar snarled, made a menacing movement toward Xenia. Hands like talons, Xenia rushed at him, but Livius caught her, holding her off. Ballomar stared dully at Xenia, Timonides and Livius, then he spat on the ground at their feet. Xenia fought furiously, trying to get at Ballomar.

Ballomar, scowling, stared at them. Then he turned, walked over to the plough. He picked it up, knocked it into shape,

attached it to the harness, without speaking. Then he started
unsteadily again to plough the unfinished furrow. He staggered and weaved like a drunk.

Timonides laughed exultantly. "You see! You see, Livius!
They learn! They learned! They are learning. They will
learn! They are building, we are succeeding."

Livius watched Ballomar's huge back wearily. "Perhaps."
He drew his hand across his eyes. They were learning, but it
was too slow. Time was running out, not only for these people at Ravenna, but for the empire. He could not remain
deaf to the dire reports from Timonides: the excesses in the
court of Commodus; the lavish entertainment to amuse the
emperor while starving people died in the provinces; citizens
revolting against the Praetorian Guard outside Commodus'
palace and the Caesar unaware of it, refusing to listen when
advisers attempted to tell him. And he, left here in Ravenna,
forgotten among people who could not even learn to live in
peace and plenty.

"It's here where the real war is being waged," Timonides
said, as if following the direction of Livius' thoughts.

"That's what I've been telling myself, Timonides." His
smile was grim. "But it gets harder all the time to persuade
myself to listen."

XV

LIVIUS STRODE into the state room at his Ravenna palace and
found Claudius awaiting him, along with an entourage of officers and aides from the imperial court at Rome.

"Claudius," Livius said. "It's good to see you."

Claudius simpered. The reason why Livius was exiled
here in Ravenna was clear to him. "We've missed you in
Rome," he said. "Caesar is distraught that you are not
with him."

Livius was aware of Claudius' aides peering at each other
with knowing smiles. He glanced at the effete men without
truly seeing them. Claudius was in a position of power now
so he could select his company from those of congenial
tastes.

Claudius took a parchment document from the case of the man beside him. "We've ridden across Italy without rest to get this to you, Livius. I trust it will make you as happy as it will make us in Rome. . . . Orders from Commodus Caesar."

Livius took the document, read it through quickly, and then reread it with growing excitement. He folded the message, put it in his tunic. His eyes glowed with renewed life, his shoulders straightened; suddenly he looked ten years younger, and he forgot the fatigue that began every new day with him.

"Make your company at home, Claudius," Livius said. "If you will excuse me, I must prepare to leave Ravenna."

"Of course," Claudius said. "We all understand. We couldn't be happier for you."

Livius glanced back once toward the walled city on the banks of the river. He felt as if a long term of imprisonment had ended. With the scarlet-clad lictors of Claudius' company, he rode at the head of the fast-traveling troop. He was on the road to Rome again. They could not travel fast enough for him.

Still, he was filled with regrets, and memories that would die hard, as painful as the way Xenia wept, the way Timonides stood silently, only his eyes reproaching him for deserting the experiment which the Greek was certain alone could save Rome and civilization.

A horn sounded on the road ahead, and Livius jerked his head around, Ravenna forgotten.

Before him, in glory and color of combat-tried magnificence marched the entire Northern Army: heavy artillery, swordsmen, javelin troops, archers, wagons, engineers—a war machine unexcelled.

Livius felt his heart pounding. He had not in all these long months allowed himself to think about his army, or his feelings toward it. But now it rushed back over him.

He slowed his horse to a halt, waiting with the sun against his eyes. He heard the command filtered through the ranks, halting the huge force before him. The two generals of the Northern Army, Victorinus and Polybus, rode forward to him, sedately at first and then galloping as they saw him at the head of the Roman entourage.

Victorinus and Polybus rode close on each side of him. They touched arms, but did not speak, for there were no words. They turned their horses and the three of them rode together back toward the assembled troops.

The veteran legionnaires recognized Livius and, using ~~ir shields to amplify the thunder of their welcome, they bellowed his name, a sound that rocked the heavens: "Livius. Livius."

Livius, Polybus and Victorinus rode the length of the armed might, the thundering acclaim swelling around them. "Livius."

Polybus shouted to make himself heard above the cheering. "Welcome. Welcome back, Livius Gaius Metellus. Have you come to take command again?"

Livius shouted in answer: "My orders are only to accompany you to Rome."

Polybus laughed, and shouted, pointing toward the cheering troops. "You need no orders for that."

They reached the end of the march, rode again its swollen length to the point position. The command to move was given and the huge force stepped out, a lift and snap in them just because Livius had returned.

Livius breathed deeply as he inspected the marching army, all faces turned toward him in welcome.

Polybus said, with puzzled excitement, "It was beginning to have its effect, Livius, the work you were doing in Ravenna. The whole world has been talking about you—and your town. The word was spreading north through the barbarian country that Rome was willing to take them in—let them live like Romans."

Victorinus spoke even more grudgingly, "The barbarians do not want to fight us the way they once did."

Polybus nodded. "A few more years and you never know —we might have human beings to deal with."

Livius looked at his old friends, unable to conceal the deep pleasure he got from these words. He glanced across his shoulder one last time toward Ravenna beyond the east horizon, and then, caught up in the joy of the reunion and the excitement of the moment, he shouted with laughter, galloped down along the line of veterans. As they saw him, the men cheered louder and louder until on the Romagna plain there was a delirium of acclamation. There was only one silent area in the whole range, and this was in the group around Claudius. Claudius watched intently, scented handkerchief pressed against his nostrils, wondering how wise Commodus Caesar had been in bringing Livius back to Rome, wondering if the emperor had any idea of how popular Livius was even after his long exile. . . .

A detachment of Praetorian Guards met Livius, Claudius and Claudius' aides at the bridge over the Tiber and accompanied them through Rome to the emperor's palace on Palatine Hill.

As Livius was escorted up the palace steps, he glanced out at the yellow eyes of Rome by night, the flickering candles and oil fires, the thick shadows and the glow of torches illumining the obelisks and temples. He was home and he felt as excited as a small boy.

Claudius remained with him as the Praetorian Guards escorted them across the entry into the state room where slave girls and the patrician youth of the city drank and laughed together. But as Livius came in sight, the laughter ebbed and silence spread over the place like a shroud.

Cornelius, the chief of the Praetorians, came forward, and led Livius alone along the corridors to Commodus' private chambers.

This suite looked out on the *palaestra*, as though Commodus was truly happy as long as he was in sight of the gymnasium and his gladiators.

The spacious room was softly lit by oil lamps suspended on delicate chains from the ceilings and walls. Commodus looked lonely, a brooding figure in the shadowy chamber. Behind him on the cavernous walls were huge maps of all the Roman provinces.

Commodus did not look up, seeming not to notice that Livius and Cornelius had entered his presence. Cornelius glanced at the emperor, then at Livius. He withdrew, leaving Livius alone some distance from Commodus.

Commodus spoke in low tones. "Oh, Livius. My friend— my brother! Why did you leave me?"

Commodus descended from the throne, moved slowly toward Livius. Livius hesitated only a second longer and then rushed to him. They embraced fiercely, then parted.

Livius, only now looking at his great friend, realized how much he had missed Commodus and all he represented. Gazing at Commodus, he found it hard to credit all the rumors and whispers Timonides had retailed to him at Ravenna.

"I am alone, Livius." Commodus' voice was odd, ready to break. "This is a fiercely lonely place I exist in, Livius. I try to lighten my terrible burdens with some pleasures—music, gladiators, excitements—and terrible talk starts about me. I imagine you have heard much of it—even as far away as Ravenna."

Livius smiled. "I've heard whispers."

Commodus sighed. "And I suppose you disapproved, too?"

"I didn't believe everything I heard."

"But you disapproved what you did believe?"

"It was not for me to approve. You are undoubted Caesar. You must become disheartened, tired—"

"Oh, I do, Livius, you'll never know how tired I become. If it were not for my pleasures, I couldn't endure it at all. . . . Still, I can see by your face that you don't approve."

"You can't see that, Commodus, for it is not there in my face. I have no right to censure you. You do not live as I would, but your tastes are not mine."

"How I've missed you, Livius! Why can't the world understand me as you do?"

Livius didn't speak, and Commodus persisted. "What's the matter, Livius, is it my fault the world does not understand?"

Livius shrugged.

"I need you here, Livius. I am so alone. There is no one like you. No one I can trust. No one I can talk to, ask advice, speak my heart to. They all want something of me. I can never know what they're thinking." He smiled at Livius, great love showing in his face. "Only you, when you speak, I know it's the truth—and for my good."

"I have not wanted to be away, Commodus." He spoke tensely. "I have been isolated. I have heard only rumors. What really has happened?"

Commodus' face shadowed, tightening in helpless frustration. He spoke in a whisper. "Rebellion—the whole East has rebelled. Syria, Egypt."

Livius shook his head, staggered. "Syria? Egypt? That is Virgilianus, Marcellus. It cannot be! They were soldiers with me. They were the most loyal."

Commodus laughed in rage.

"They were loyal to my father. Now they are raising

armies against me—against Rome." He glared about him, eyes bitter. "They've always hated me. Marcellus. Virgilianus. They've waited all these years for the right moment."

Livius turned away, prowling the huge room as though it were suddenly a breathless cage. He was deeply disturbed.

Commodus said, "Even Sohamus has joined them." When Livius heeled around, scowling, Commodus peered into his face, studying it. "He forced Lucilla to flee with him."

At the sound of Lucilla's name, Livius felt something flare inside him and he winced as if an old wound that had lain dormant were suddenly ripped open, raw and bleeding.

Commodus stared into his face. "And there is more, Livius. More I haven't told you. The rebellion is spreading in your name."

"What?"

Livius looked squarely at Commodus, their gazes clashing. In the deep silence, the remote sounds of the *palaestra* filtered through the heavily curtained windows.

At last Livius said in a quiet, hard voice, "Rebellion cannot be made in my name, Commodus."

"Yet they are using it that way. Your name has spread over the whole East—as the new Caesar." His mouth taut, Commodus quoted, " 'Bring in the new Rome—the Rome of Livius Gaius Metellus.' And now there are echoes of that same cry in the North and West. Do you say you have not even heard it?"

"I do say that, Commodus. I remain loyal to my country, my Caesar, my oath." He prowled the carpeting, staring at the map of the provinces, the shadowed walls, the oil lamps, the emperor waiting. He heeled around, mouth bitter. "Why do you recall me, Commodus?"

"I wanted to hear from your own mouth that you loved me still, Livius."

"You knew that."

"The whispers are shouts, the rebellion is real, growing."

"Why do you call on me, Commodus? Where is your Eastern Army?"

There was protracted silence. At last, as Livius waited tensely, Commodus gave a weary gesture of his hand. "Our Roman legionnaires have been so long in the East, they are no longer Roman." His voice lowered, becoming almost inaudible. "The Eastern Army has gone over to the rebels."

Livius retreated as if struck physically, staggered by this

news. Commodus straightened, eyes bitter. "Why do I call on you, Livius? Because you are the only man the Northern Army will follow in battles against—other Roman legions."

Livius stared at the emperor in the thick silence. At last he said, "This is a filthy task you impose on me—to throw Roman against Roman."

"It must be done. If the empire is to survive, it must be done. And even more, Livius. It will have to be as in the old days of punishing armies. Cities destroyed. Every living thing killed. Before the rebellion spreads. Before our enemies attack. The whole world must know we have again become the Rome of old."

Commodus waited, but Livius did not speak. Commodus lowered his voice to a wild, urgent whisper. "We are fighting for survival."

Livius was shaken. "That Rome should have to fight for survival."

"It's true! I haven't told you all. I—had to behead the chief of the Praetorian Guards and—give that head to the people of Rome to—to quiet them. We are in desperate trouble, Livius—everywhere. Even here at Rome. We must show them that we are strong, that we will destroy our own people if they oppose us."

Livius barely heard him. "I've fought a dozen battles alongside of Virgilianus and Marcellus. They were my friends."

Commodus swung his arm in a savage, cutting arc. "Friends? Jackals ready to destroy us. No. No. Destroy them! What other way is there?"

Livius stared at the emperor in the shadowed room, feeling his face ache with the ruts pulled into it. "What other way is there?" Neither spoke because there was no answer, they had said it all.

XVI

LIVIUS SAT astride a white Arabian horse at the head of his generals and aides on a wide expanse of gray beach.

Below them the breakers thundered and dashed themselves

to spume against the rocks and the shore. The sun seemed lost somewhere in the sullied basin of the morning sky. The wind whipped spray across them.

Behind Livius, Victorinus, Polybus and Timonides waited with some impatience for the contingent of horsemen approaching along the distant beach. Pervading them was a sense of uneasiness, but only Didius Julianus, as representative of the Caesar, showed irritation and ill-concealed anger.

Livius gave Julianus a glance, moved his gaze to his company of Roman cavalrymen in attendance. The banners and imperial pennants whipped in the sea breeze. He felt pride being again in the paludamentum of the imperial general, but little comfort because the entire remaining Roman army was at this place with him, no longer spread as a bulwark across the face of the civilized world.

Julianus had been controlling himself with great difficulty and finally could no longer restrain his rage. It had not pleased him that Caesar had reappointed Livius as supreme commander of the legions—Livius was too popular with the soldiers, Livius was too much like Aurelius Caesar, always looking for some way to compromise rather than to smash the enemy first and parley with him later on Roman terms.

Julianus glared at the approaching horsemen. His face was rigid. "They are rebels. In rebellion against Caesar. What good can come out of meeting with them like this?"

Livius turned, the wind riffling the plumes of his helmet. His desperation showed in the gray of his cheeks. "They know what to expect of me, Julianus. And still they have asked to meet with me. There must be something they will propose that can settle this without setting Roman against Roman—"

"What can they propose?" Julianus inquired with the same sarcasm he'd used to such advantage against Livius in the senate. "It's a trick. I see no reason to meet with them."

Livius held his breath a moment, and then, still furious, gestured towards the horizon. "The Persians are two days' march from us. They are this moment praying that Roman will fall upon Roman, so that they may strike at us and destroy us. Can you see that, Julianus?"

With one more penetrating stare at the senator, Livius turned his back on Julianus. The other officers were speaking quietly, in tension, among themselves, but as the horsemen of the rebel leaders approached they fell silent.

Livius sat silently in his saddle, hearing the wind whipping the imperial pennants, the roar of waves against the rocks, and, it seemed to him, the sound of his own heart under his breastplate.

When the rebels were still a hundred yards away, Livius abruptly reached a decision, turned deliberately and gestured that Julianus was to return to his quarters, the meeting would be held without him.

"I am Caesar's emissary!" Julianus said.

"I will have you removed, under arrest," Livius said in a tone that was deadly quiet.

Julianus hesitated one more moment, and then wheeled his horse viciously, and rode away. He was suddenly not unhappy to depart this fruitless conference: the talks would accomplish nothing; his being banished from them would harm Livius badly when it was reported to Caesar.

None of the officers or aides turned to glance at Julianus. They kept their faces straight, waiting impassively.

The horsemen were riding swiftly and they did not slow their mounts until they were within a few yards of the Romans.

These rebels were Romans, but looking at them one would not suspect it. Their uniforms showed oriental influence. As Commodus had said, the legions had been so long in the East they were no longer Roman, having assumed all the characteristics of the Eastern provinces.

When the company halted, their flags and banners furling and crackling in the wind, Livius recognized Marcellus and Virgilianus. He felt a sense of pain and loss seeing the way their faces were set stubbornly against him, against Rome.

At the head of the contingent, the leaders dismounted while their guard remained in their saddles.

Livius lifted his arm in a signal. His officers and aides dismounted. He swung down from his saddle, standing at the head of his party.

With his subordinates following, Livius moved toward the large brown tent which had been set up on the seashore as a conference place.

The rebels hesitated outside the tent, entered it. When they were inside, Livius led his own company inside. The tent, carefully decorated with imperial insignia, pennants and other signs of Roman might and history, was divided into two parts, the rebels aligned along one side and the Romans on the other. As they took their places, Livius glanced at Marcellus, Virgilianus and the others, but none spoke in greeting.

Seated, Livius moved his gaze over the faces of the rulers, regents and commanders of the rebel territories and armies. He addressed Virgilianus. "Where is Sohamus?"

"The Armenian king is awaiting word of the results of this meeting. He does not care to attend unless there is some prospect of agreement." Virgilianus waited, but the silence stretched painfully thin.

At last Livius waved his arm impatiently. "It was you who asked to meet. Speak."

"You were prepared to do battle against us, Livius," Virgilianus said, his face rutted with puzzlement and disbelief, "even before you spoke to us?"

"You have rebelled against Rome. What have I to say to you?"

Virgilianus stood up, his voice still showing his shock. "You speak as if Rome had any meaning any more—"

"It does to me. I vowed my life to its protection—as did you, Virgilianus, and you, Marcellus."

"This was when Rome was an empire and not a rotted core starving the rest of the world. You must be aware of what is happening—the unfair burden of taxes, the steady drain of our resources, the Roman armies without discipline, plundering rather than protecting, our people treated as slaves, enemies even, rather than a part of Rome. You must see, Livius! Was it not Marcus Aurelius who spoke of an empire of equal nations—human frontiers? Were you not fighting for that along with the rest of us?"

Livius stared at him coldly. "What did you take that to mean? A Rome that would tolerate rebellion?"

"Rebellion is not our aim. We are not rebelling against Rome, but against those who would destroy it from within, Livius. We are trying to save ourselves, and our empire. We tried reason with Caesar, and failed, we tried everything and failed. We were caught—"

"Caught in treachery," Livius said, voice cold.

"No!" Virgilianus said. "You cannot be treacherous against treachery. Livius, I beg you, please hear why this—this rebellion as you call it—this fight for restoration of Rome as we call it—won't you hear why it came about?"

"That is not my task."

"What has happened to you, Livius?"

"I am as I always was. I vowed to protect Rome, not destroy it. Wrongs cannot be righted by other wrongs." His voice lowered, harsh. "Why did you ask me here?"

Virgilianus spread his hands, face grave, eyes sad. "We had hoped as old friends to have some influence over you, to make you see the evils you are now blind to—"

"Then you are not only traitors—you are also fools. What can I offer you in the name of our old friendship more than the promise of a quick death?"

"Death may come to us, Livius," Virgilianus said, "but it comes in honor, and not to us alone."

Livius controlled his feelings only with great effort. He moved his gaze from Virgilianus to Marcellus, anguished. "How did you come to this?"

Marcellus stood up beside Virgilianus, his face gray and rigid. "Perhaps you have some information that this is a hasty thing, Livius, a hotheaded fight against Caesar, against our homeland. Nothing could be further from the truth. We have been driven to our position, and in it we stand unalterable. You speak of a quick death for your old army comrades, Livius. I must warn you. We are not alone in this. There are others with us."

The conference ended in impasse as both sides must have known it would from the first. Virgilianus said he had made the last effort to save Rome without bloodshed, his heart was heavy, but his conscience clear. He strode out, followed by his aides. Other consuls, generals, stood up and departed. At last only Marcellus remained. He ordered his aides to leave, and then came across the tent to where Livius stood. His face showed his distress and heartbreak. For one moment the two old friends looked at each other. Marcellus said, "We have made every effort to convince you of the right of our cause, Livius. I understand and approve only your loyalty to our homeland. The others stand ready now to destroy all we've spent our lives to build. I find myself with them because I believe in their aims, their ends. But I cannot turn my back on you, Livius, and our long friendship, and our own mutual love of our empire, without making one last effort."

He waited, until finally Livius nodded, dismissing his aides.

Then he led Livius through a tent flap into another section
of the conference place.

Marcellus held open the flap, allowed Livius to enter ahead
of him. Marcellus did not follow, but allowed the material to
fall closed.

Livius paused, his face showing his shock at finding Lucilla standing there. She was tall, calm, regal, only her eyes
haunted by the old memories between them.

Her voice was level. "Why should you be shocked to see
me here, Livius? I made a pledge to my father to make of
our empire what he dreamed for it. He hoped—and I prayed
to our gods—that you would be the man to save this great
nation. But since you would not act—"

"Act? To make a rebellion?"

"It is called rebellion only if it fails! We will not fail. We
cannot fail because we have the manpower, the organization,
the driving need to win. We won't fail. You look upon us as
a small band of rebels! How blind you are! We are more
than that—we are the Roman people." Her tone became pas-
sionate. "Don't turn away from me, Livius, in your stubborn
clinging to some ideal of Rome that is dead—no longer
exists, is being killed, starved, destroyed! Don't turn away
from me, Livius! Listen. We are breaking away from a Rome
that is rotted and already lost. We will make our own empire
here in the East."

Livius shook his head, stunned. "Your own empire?"

"An Eastern empire—here—"

"You won't make anything but chaos!" Livius paced the
carpeted room, overwhelmed by shock. "Why should Cap-
padocia, Egypt and Syria join you? What would hold you
together? What will you accomplish except one thing—you
will divide the empire. You will render it weak and helpless
—and then the Persians will fall on us and tear the world
apart."

Lucilla stared at him for a long time, tears glittering in
her upslanted eyes. "The gods have sent you here at the
head of all that remains of the Roman legions. The gods
have willed it that you bring these armies to join the other
Roman armies against the traitors who destroy the empire.
We'll have all of Rome. Join us! Rome will be greater than
ever and we'll have our *Pax Romana*—our Roman peace!
We will build my father's empire together—"

"What have you done, Lucilla?"

"Why are you afraid?"

"Because in the name of the gods, I see the world on fire, Lucilla! Ignited by people who mean well—without even knowing what they are doing!"

Lucilla stood straighter. "If you cannot join us—if you won't—then take your army back to Rome. Let us make our own destiny here in the East."

"I am commander of the Roman armies—all Roman armies. I cannot let rebellion go unpunished."

Lucilla exhaled heavily, standing for a long time with her hands at her sides. At last she spoke in a low voice. "*I* am part of this rebellion."

Livius took a step toward her, face dead white. He let his hand fall at his side. "Then persuade the others to lay down their arms—"

"They will not, and I will not try. And if I did, what would happen to me? What slow and cruel death would my beloved brother devise for me?"

Livius winced. "Get out of the empire, Lucilla. Run. Hide somewhere—now before it's too late! Because as certain as death, we will assault the rebellious armies and punish them."

Lucilla shook her head. "I do not run, Livius." Her mouth grew taut, her voice choked with tears. "If I were weak, I could have run from my vows a long time ago. I do not run."

Livius stared at her in the deep silence. At last he spoke almost inaudibly, "Then may the gods grant that we never meet again."

She did not look at him, stood unmoving. Livius waited, staring at her, anguished, at last turned and walked out.

After a long time, Lucilla left the tent and joined Virgilianus, Marcellus and the other leaders before their mounted guards. She did not say she had failed. They did not ask her. There was no need for words. They stood silently watching Livius, Victorinus, Polybus and Timonides gather with their company.

Before he swung up into his saddle, Livius paused for one last look at Lucilla and his two old friends beside her. His face was gray, haggard, lines of infinite weariness about his eyes. His face remained expressionless, and neither Marcellus nor Virgilianus spoke. Livius made a brief salute of farewell, mounted his horse and rode away at the head of his company.

At one sharp command from Marcellus, the rebellious leaders mounted and rode along the beach, returning to their own encampment. They arrived as Sohamus approached with his companies of Armenian soldiers.

Marcellus, awaiting Sohamus, glanced at Lucilla. "Why does Sohamus bring so many soldiers with him here? Doesn't he even trust us—his own allies?"

Sohamus rode into the encampment, dismounted. He went at once to Lucilla, bowed over her hand and then studied her face intently. "You did not succeed in convincing Livius to join you?"

She shook her head, eyes grim. "No. I did not."

Sohamus sighed, glancing at the other leaders in the ensuing silence, black eyes almost sad. "I knew he would not. He is a Roman—"

"We are Romans, too!" Lucilla said.

Sohamus nodded. "Now the moment has come to risk our lives, our nation, I must face the truth."

Lucilla watched his dark face, frowning.

"We Armenians are not of the West, Lucilla," Sohamus said.

"What are you talking about?"

"The truth I must face. Armenia belongs to the Orient." He straightened, glancing at Marcellus and Virgilianus with slight aversion. "I am sorry, my lord consuls, I am no longer a part of your rebellion."

Virgilianus clapped his hand over his sword, rage flashing in his face. Shocked, Marcellus nevertheless touched his friend's arm, cautioning him to silence.

Lucilla's face was white. "What does that mean?"

Sohamus spoke levelly. "Armenia will join the Persians."

Virgilianus retreated as if he'd been struck. Stunned, Marcellus backed away, too, as if truly facing treachery for the first time.

"Betrayal," Virgilianus whispered.

Sohamus remained calm, inscrutable. "Betrayal? No. I am joining my own kind. My people are strong and Rome is dying."

Neither Virgilianus nor Marcellus could speak. They had

backed away from Sohamus as if his touch would contaminate or infect them.

Sohamus stared at them coldly. "I have come to you with an offer. Bring your armies to us. The Persians will welcome you. I have their assurances. You will have wealth and power." When neither spoke, Sohamus said harshly, "You now know what reprisals await you on the Roman side."

They looked at him a moment as if they had seen something like him before, but only in the snake pits of the circuses. Marcellus and Virgilianus turned at once, almost with the discipline they had learned in long ago legion days, and strode to their horses. No one stopped them.

The back of her hand pressed against her mouth, Lucilla moved after them, but Sohamus caught her arm, stopping her.

At Lucilla's protest, Virgilianus and Marcellus swung around.

Virgilianus grasped his short sword in his fist, and Marcellus waited for Lucilla to ask him to intervene.

She fought against Sohamus for less than a second, seeing the Armenian soldiers advancing upon Marcellus and Virgilianus in overwhelming numbers. She bit her lip and did not speak.

Virgilianus swung up into his saddle, and after a moment Marcellus followed. The armed Armenians formed a phalanx now between them and Sohamus. Virgilianus and Marcellus, outnumbered, rode away.

Lucilla was numb, incredulous, still unable to believe what had happened. She stood limply, watching Virgilianus and Marcellus leave.

Sohamus said, "It is all right, Lucilla. You are still my queen."

She glanced at the armed men surrounding her. She shook her head, gazing into the king's dark face. "The Persians represent everything we're fighting against! They're worse than the Rome of Commodus. They don't want to build anything. They want only to conquer, to enslave. . . . Sohamus, you've betrayed me."

Sohamus remained unmoved. "And you, Lucilla? Have you not betrayed me—from the first—from the day you came to me in your father's encampment at Vindobona?"

"I have been your wife all these years—"

"But what was it kept you my wife—pushed you on? Was it just your father's dream of a new empire? Is that what it was, Lucilla?"

"I have been your wife—"

"Or was there not always behind that dream—another dream, of one man—"

"No!"

"—a man who finally abandoned you—and your dreams today?"

"No! No! No!"

She cried out in rage, sobbing, but Sohamus remained impassive, looking at her distantly, not believing her, but not caring any more, his mind already on his future with the Persians.

XVII

LIVIUS RODE with Polybus and Victorinus at the head of the grimly silent Northern Army. Near him and at the front of his aides was Timonides.

There was a silence about the world that the rumbling, marching army seemed only to intensify.

Livius found his mind going back to a distant summer when he had been a boy at a villa south of Rome. Rome was impossible in the summer, a place of humidity, odors and threat of disease. Everyone who could escaped for the hot months. Near his father's villa was the summer place of Marcus Antoninus, not yet Caesar. It was the finest summer in Livius' memory. They rode horses, he and Lucilla, and sometimes permitted Commodus to tag along, as young as he was. They discovered secret places, ate ripening grapes in the vineyards and sat in a kind of ecstasy of pleasure in the long lazy afternoons, with their hands touching on the ground between them. He wondered now what they talked about, but perhaps they hadn't talked at all, too shy for words, too filled with awe at the discovery of what excitement there could be in letting their fingers brush, or their gazes touch. They had no need for words.

"Flames, General!"

Polybus' voice dragged Livius back to the moment, the Syrian road, the stark plains, the brilliant, hideous hues of flames beyond the horizon. Livius gave a signal to double-time and galloped forward, the others following.

When they rode over the knoll they could see the Syrian village in flames. The narrow street was littered with dead and those still alive were fighting each other like animals trying to escape the place. As Livius and his officers rode into the settlement, a wounded man staggered toward them, silhouetted against the fires, the heat intolerable behind him, the cries of the wounded and the dying mixed with the rage of fire.

Livius jerked his head and a young tribune leaped from his horse, supporting the wounded man. His hair was gray, and he was stocky in his camel-hair coat which was bloodied and caked with red dust. He sagged against the young soldier and was barely able to speak. "Persians! The Persians have attacked! And Armenian soldiers among them. . . ."

Livius nodded, staring at the holocaust.

Polybus swore bitterly. "Persians. . . . Like something you've known all along was going to happen. . . . They've waited over a hundred years for a moment like this—a time when Rome would be truly divided."

Victorinus did not pull his gaze from the fire-gutted village. "If the Armenians have really joined Persia, then they've chosen wisely. . . . With the army of Sohamus, they outnumber us."

Livius pulled his head around, giving Victorinus a quick, wry glance. "Rome outnumbered, Victorinus. It's as crazy as everything else that's happening. It doesn't make sense. . . . It's been centuries since a Roman officer admitted his army was outnumbered." He sagged for a moment in his saddle, then straightened, eyes tormented but his mouth grim. "Not yet." He lifted his arm, turning, his voice sharp, carrying back across the first columns of his troops. "We march at once for the Persian frontiers."

Victorinus scowled, staring at Livius, and when the commander hesitated, waiting, Victorinus put his fears into words. "And what of the rebels? What if they attack us from behind while we're fighting the Persians?"

Livius spoke drily, considering the question that had no answer. "Then we'll be caught in a trap, Victorinus. . . .

Something a good commander tries to avoid. . . . Give the order!"

His officers pulled their horses around, moving away to obey him.

The forced march seemed never to end. Livius changed horses several times, but remained in the saddle without rest. He lost track of time, did not know how long he rode, only that he and his army moved swiftly.

They had no trouble following the trail of the Persian armies, because they left behind a long line of abandoned towns, wrecked bridges, and dead bodies in houses and fields.

The night was chilled, but signs of the pillage were concealed from the sight if not from the nostrils. In the dawn the weary army came to a road that led to the Euphrates River. The river was high and the stone bridge had been hacked away around its center arch.

Livius gave the order and his army stirred, getting itself into battle formation in frantic preparation, for they found the gaudy, combat-ready forces of the Persians like an unending wall between them and the Euphrates. There was not a place for miles along the route of the river that Persian troops were not deployed, awaiting the signal to attack.

Livius expected the charge to come in the darkness but it was not begun until the sun was up. He saw this was only the supreme confidence of the Persian commanders. The Persian cavalry, riding great horses in a solid line of spiked iron armor, fretted with impatience to strike.

Livius watched the enemy columns and the frantic preparation of his own wearied troops. He moved among the soldiers, giving orders, trying to rouse them. They milled about, veterans aware that they were outnumbered by an army with superior equipment.

Livius gazed across the Euphrates as the dawn sky lighted the world. Long lines of Armenian cavalry reinforcements moved toward the bridge which Persian engineers had repaired. These troops would come in upon the Romans from the rear.

There was a thunder of sound from the lines of Persian cavalry and the heavily armored lines moved slowly toward them, gathering speed as they came.

Livius yelled an order, swung his arm in signal to advance. Behind him Roman trumpeters sounded the battle call. The legionnaires, though not completely prepared, swung frantically into position. For the first time they were choosing neither place nor time for battle. The Roman cavalry charged and the Persians continued toward them in unbroken line.

They clashed on the plain above the river under powerful driving impact that jarred the earth. The Roman cavalry buckled in the center, pulling the onward-moving Persian line deeply within.

The center of the Roman cavalry continued to waver and retreat. The howling Persian horsemen rode faster, pressing them. Roman foot soldiers, shields before them, swung around from both sides, coming in behind the formidable armor of the Persians.

Livius stood on high ground, Timonides at his side, watching uneasily, fist knotted against his breastplate as if ill.

Timonides said, "But the Persians are fools. Drunk with overconfidence. Fools."

Livius could barely speak. "They are not fools."

Virgilianus and Marcellus brought up their rebel forces during the first hours of that morning. Below them on the plain the Northern Roman Army, fatally outnumbered, was in battle with the Persians.

Marcellus swung down from his saddle, glanced back at the massed forces of their Roman soldiers. His face was twisted, eyes tormented, and he cried out, as if answering Virgilianus, his own conscience, his gods, in terrible rage. "No! We cannot join Livius. We must not. No matter what happened, we would be treated as traitors—dishonor and a slow death on some cross."

Virgilianus, on his horse, seeming not to hear Marcellus, glared moodily at the unequal combat before him.

"And yet it is Roman against Persian—while we stand by."

Marcellus heeled around. "Not our Rome, Virgilianus." He swung his arm furiously toward the battle. "Let them kill each other—Roman, Armenian, Persian. . . . We'll ride over those dead to a new empire—"

He stared beyond Virgilianus, suddenly stopped speaking when he saw Sohamus and his reinforcements galloping toward the bridge across the Euphrates.

He gazed as if stunned, unable to speak.

On his horse, Virgilianus turned, following the direction of his horrified gaze.

Virgilianus pointed, his mouth dry, eyes anguished. "Sohamus—the Armenians. Livius will be caught in a trap."

Marcellus managed to shake off the agony. He spoke in a rage. "Good—"

"In the name of the gods," Virgilianus whispered in agony, "Livius—our friend Livius—and the Romans—"

"Good!" Marcellus' voice rose with tears and exultation at conflict in it. "Good!"

He stood, legs apart, as if braced, as the Roman cavalry, stunned by the force of the first Persian onslaught, reeled, reforming with desperate slowness.

Regrouped, the bloodied horsemen galloped forward again for the charge to drive the Persians back into the Euphrates.

Watching them, holding his breath, Livius was aware of a frightful new thundering sound. He heeled around and saw Sohamus urging his Armenian reinforcements across the bridge, ready to come up behind the already staggering Roman forces.

Livius did not even hesitate. He yelled desperately, "Fall back! Retreat! Quickly! Retreat!"

The horns of retreat sounded, a fearfully mournful wail, carrying across the heads of the Romans, pulling them up to a halt, sending them into uncertain retreat.

Livius swung into his saddle and rode down into the center of his retreating men, the retreat call still blaring from Roman trumpets, growing louder and more frantic as the Persians pressed their advantage, trying to turn the recall into a rout.

Polybus rode close to Livius, fighting beside him, but the young officer's face showed his despair. The Persian cavalry with the withdrawing Romans off balance was inflicting heavy losses.

The frantic retreat call wailed. Polybus and Livius, fighting from their horses, shouted at their men, trying to encourage them. Suddenly, a new sound, a new set of Roman trumpets blaring the attack call broke across the wailing of defeat.

Livius hesitated, sword raised above his head, startled and puzzled, trying to find the source of this insanity. From the hills behind them, he saw the bright colors of the

Eastern Roman Army, its columns of men, banners, arms, racing downward, moving toward the Euphrates and the bridge.

For one hideous second, Livius thought the Eastern Army had joined with the Persian-Armenian alliance to cut off their last hope of escape.

But the forces of Romans under Marcellus and Virgilianus converged on the plain before the bridge over the Euphrates. The bridge was narrow, confining. Marcellus and his men reached the span before Sohamus' army could cross it.

Marcellus' forces held the charging Armenians bottlenecked on the structure. Marcellus led his men forward, yelling at Virgilianus on the plain behind him. "Cut the bridge after us!"

Virgilianus hesitated, for the moment stunned by the implications of Marcellus' orders. Marcellus was issuing his own death warrant.

Virgilianus swung his arm and his engineers and demolition men surged forward with axes, hacking frantically at the huge beams supporting the bridge. One support buckled, fell into the swirling stream, was caught by the wild current and driven down the river with savage force, and the bridge broke. Marcellus and his forces, chance of retreat destroyed, fought grimly and without hope of survival, pushing Sohamus' men back across the Euphrates.

The men fell slowly, chopped down by the superior numbers, but fighting gallantly. Marcellus fell under a sword, toppled over the bridge, his body whirled away down the bloodied river.

The sound of attack grew louder, coming from trumpets of all the Roman forces, now rejoined. Livius wheeled furiously, Polybus beside him, and followed by Virgilianus and his legions. The combined Eastern and Northern Armies, acting under Livius' command, attacked the embattled Persians. The charge was invincible, sending the Persians reeling back all the way to the banks of the Euphrates. Heavily armored horses and riders plunged into the river.

The engineers having repaired the bridge with heavy trees, Livius led a company of Roman forces against the Armenians. These men, demoralized by the savage holding maneuver of Marcellus' men, and by the sight of Persians sent relentlessly into the Euphrates or to their death, milled about, fighting less than halfheartedly.

Sohamus turned his horse, attempting to reach a place of safety deep behind the Armenian lines. But the fast-charging Romans cut him off, drove him back among his trapped cavalry. The Romans advanced savagely, killing any Armenian who stood against them.

Livius did not hesitate at the rim of the battle, but moved into its core where the trapped Armenian noblemen were fighting for survival. Livius looked around, but could not find Sohamus. It was evident that the Armenian ruler had been thrown off his horse. Livius dismounted quickly, fought his way through the thick of the battle until he saw Sohamus.

Livius shouted, thrusting his way through the combatants until he confronted Sohamus. He lifted his sword, shouting in wild savagery, "Where is Lucilla?"

Sohamus slashed at him, and Livius yelled it again, striding forward, his sword flashing.

Sohamus was forced to retreat, stumbling slightly, his swarthy face ashen.

His voice raged back at Livius. "We've lost Lucilla," he cried as they fought. "She's lost to both of us." He lunged with the sword. "If I kill you, she will never forgive me—"

Livius fought harder, knowing at least that Lucilla was still alive. Sohamus retreated, staggering when he tripped over a dead body, catching his balance, slashing out frantically.

"If you kill me, Livius," he shouted, breathless, panic making him wild, "if you kill me, Livius, know this—" He glanced over his shoulder, seeking some escape, and cried out involuntarily as Livius knocked his sword from his hand, "If you kill me, you'll never have her! She'll be killed! At once! You'll never have her!"

Sohamus staggered backward, unarmed, awaiting the death stroke, trying to accept it without losing his dignity, without begging for his life.

Livius threw his sword above his head, brought it downward before he realized what Sohamus meant. *You'll never have her!* Sohamus never tired of reminding Romans that Armenia was not of their world. Livius saw the terrible meaning in Sohamus' threat. Lucilla would be killed at once upon word of the king's death, because when an oriental king died, his queen was always buried with him.

Livius stopped the downward thrust, let the sword fall harmlessly at his side. For a moment he stood in the cater-wauling screams of battle, unmoving. He backed away from Sohamus, face pale. He was appalled that he had almost killed him. He couldn't kill him at all, he had to keep him alive.

Sohamus, reading Livius' agony, straightened, pulling his robe closer about him, his mouth twisted into an ironic smile.

A Roman javelin hurtled past Livius, piercing Sohamus. Livius gasped, crying out in agonized protest as Sohamus went hurtling back full length on the ground, javelin impaling him.

Livius did not know how long he stood there staring down at the unmoving king. He called out frantically, "Soldier! Soldier!"

A soldier ran to him and Livius nodded toward Sohamus. "Soldier, help him."

The soldier didn't question Livius' order, moved quickly to the motionless Sohamus. He knelt over the king, touched him.

Livius took a step forward, staring into the soldier's face. The soldier glanced up, indicating Sohamus with a nod. "He's dead, General."

Livius nodded, turned away. There was a strange silence from the Armenian horsemen. Livius saw that one of the riders had stared at the dead king a moment, then wheeled his horse, galloping away at top speed through the knots of fighting men.

Livius looked about frantically, caught the bridle of a riderless mount. He ran along beside it, swung up into the saddle and spurred the horse, racing after the Armenian cavalryman.

XVIII

LUCILLA STOOD in the Armenian pavilion, waiting for news of the battle. Perhaps a more timid woman would have waited at the palace in the Armenian capital city, and had Sohamus been less certain of a Persian victory over divided Roman forces, he would have stayed apart from his army in this behind-the-lines pavilion.

Lucilla glanced around, standing tall, regal, aware of the fateful turn of the tide against Sohamus and the Persian invaders. It was too late now for regret, or conjecture, or second-guessing. Anyhow, she could not have stayed away: her hope of life was bound up in the outcome of the battle today, as well as her dream of creating the empire her father had planned and projected. It was all over now.

On either side of her stood two Armenian slave girls, jewelled daggers drawn, and beside them eunuchs on guard with drawn swords.

There were loud noises of pitched battle, brutal fighting and confusion all around the pavilion. The last of the young noblemen who had been left as her personal guard by Sohamus had been killed or driven away. The few remaining palace knights, wounded, bleeding, fled in wild disarray.

Lucilla saw the Armenian horseman riding from the battleground, galloping through the disorder about the pavilion. She read the truth instinctively, in the rutted agony of his face even before he spoke, shouting to the slave girls beside her: "Kill her! Kill the queen! The king is dead! Kill her!"

Lucilla did not even glance at the two slave girls. She stood taller, tilting her head, waiting. Then in the dust-clouded distance behind the Armenian horseman, she saw a Roman officer riding at breakneck speed toward the pavilion.

The horseman yelled again, signaling furiously to the two slave girls. "Kill her!"

Lucilla trembled, reacting in momentary horror and dread, then she stood motionless, knowing she could not beg for her life. But the two slave girls did not move. Raging, the horseman rode directly toward them.

The girls stared at the horseman, at each other and then at Lucilla, tears brimming their eyes. They let the daggers slip from their fingers, refusing to slay their queen.

Lucilla's lips parted as she recognized Livius racing toward her.

The eunuchs cried out in protest, throwing away their scimitars, standing unarmed rather than use the blades against Lucilla.

Screaming at them, all his training outraged, the horseman straightened in his saddle, armed his crossbow, sat for one moment taking aim. He was jostled by the skittish horse, side-stepping in the noise and confusion. The horseman let fly his arrow, slightly off-balance.

Lucilla was struck in the shoulder by the arrow, knocked back under the terrible impact of it. She fell against a draped upright, screaming in agony.

Still riding forward, Livius hurled a javelin, transfixing the Armenian horseman. The rider straightened in the saddle, his face going gray. His hands relaxed on the crossbow and it fell to the ground. He twisted slowly in the saddle, and then tumbled from his horse, the animal squealing in panic, trampling him, trying to get free.

Livius rode close to the fallen horseman, dismounted, breathing through his mouth. Hands reached for him, and blades swung. He hardly saw them, fighting them off as he ran in panic across the pavilion to the place where Lucilla had fallen.

She lay on the ground, soaked in blood. The two terrified slave girls stood over her numbly. One of them held the bloody arrow; she had jerked it from the queen's shoulder and did not realize yet that she had done it.

Livius knelt beside Lucilla. She was only half conscious. He lifted her against him, holding her head up, praying, searching her ashen face.

Lucilla whispered faintly, "I have lost—let me die."

"No. No," Livius said. "No, I want you to live."

She was incoherent. "To die . . . I want to die. . . ."

"Lucilla! Lucilla!" Livius tightened his hands on her, as if he would hold her from death physically, as though he were all that stood between her and death, and he was all she needed.

The Northern Army marched first into Antioch. Behind them in long, dusty columns stretched the remaining companies of the Eastern Army with Virgilianus still in command.

Victorinus and Polybus rode at the head of the conquering armies, and near them rode Timonides and Livius' aides-de-camp.

Livius did not have his mind on the city or the army. He rode alongside the purple-draped imperial wagon in which Lucilla lay, feverish, delirious even under the sedation administered by army medical men.

Livius pulled his mount close beside the imperial wagon, parted the drapes, reached out and quietly touched Lucilla's fevered forehead, smoothing her hair from her temples.

Delirious, Lucilla whispered: "Livius?"

"I am here, beside you."

Her voice was weak. She whispered in frantic urgency: "Help me. . . . Tell her to leave me."

Livius sighed but did not speak. Lucilla was alone in the wagon.

"Tell her to leave me. . . . I want to die in peace. . . . She keeps tormenting me."

Livius felt ill, wanting to call out for the doctor, but Lucilla clung to his hand and he did not speak.

"Tormenting me. . . ." Lucilla pointed before her. "See? Look how she keeps stretching her hands out to me." Her whisper had terror and agony in it. "It is my mother, Livius. . . . She is dying—she wants me to forgive her."

Lucilla twisted on the mattress. Her voice rose as she tossed in her delirium. "I will not! There is wrong and there is right! We are creatures of reason. . . . We are not animals. . . . We are creatures of reason! No! No! I cannot forgive you." She screamed out suddenly, "I will not forgive!"

Mouth parted, she rolled on the pad within the wagon, and then abruptly she realized it was Livius leaning over her. She tried to smile, but it was a wan failure. "Livius? You must not forgive me. I have no right to live. I was part—of the rebellion. Tell me, Livius. Tell me you will not forgive me!"

Livius stared at her in agony but did not speak. She would not hear him anyway, she was completely wrapped in a ball of agony inside herself, and he was helpless to draw her out, or even to reach her at all.

Her voice became imperative when he did not answer. "Livius? Speak to me. . . . I command you. . . . I can understand, speak to me—"

"Once I was as sure of right and wrong, good and evil, black and white, as you, Lucilla," he said, almost speaking to himself. "Everything was either right or wrong. Now—I don't know. The rebels I came out here to crush—gave their lives for me, for us. Now they seem to me greater than the Romans of Rome. . . ."

Lucilla's head rolled on the purple silk pillow. "No . . . No, Livius, no. Don't you see? If you forgive them—if you forgive me, then I was wrong. . . . I should not have let my mother die that way . . . wanting forgiveness . . . denied it . . . I should not . . ." She tossed deliriously, weeping. "Her hands . . . Make her leave me in peace. . . ." She cried out, wailing, "Her hands. . . !"

Livius stroked her head tenderly, and she fell back into fitful sleep. Livius rode slowly beside the wagon, watching her pale face, hardly aware of the rising sound of music as the army rode deeper into Antioch. Polybus called to him, and Livius looked one last time at Lucilla, then rode away to join his officers.

Livius and his major officers rode to the Antioch quay. Here he paused at the sight of Roman splendor and pomp, as though there had been no disastrous campaign fought along the Euphrates. His officers pulled up, watching his face.

He stared at the commission from Commodus Caesar disembarking from a Roman ship, preceded by musicians filling the waterfront area with their triumphant strains, by scarlet-clad lictors and regal escorts.

The escorts came forward to greet Livius, his officers and aides led by Timonides.

Livius gazed for one moment at Didius Julianus and Pescennius Niger, in full ceremonial toga and decorations as leaders of the Caesar's commission. His gaze moved from them to the gaunt, hollow-eyed Egyptians watching in hostile silence as their grain was being loaded with feverish haste onto the waiting Roman vessels.

Livius shivered with the terrible sense of wrong that seemed to haunt him constantly these past months.

Senator Didius Julianus and Senator Niger came forward

to greet Livius, faces wreathed with smiles for the leader of Rome's victorious armies.

The dock workers continued loading Egyptian grain upon Roman ships, but everyone else along the quay was silent as Julianus stepped forward, calling out in a frenzy of admiration: "Hail Livius Gaius Metellus!"

From behind Niger came bands of Syrian musicians, hundreds of dancing girls, acrobats and gaudily dressed dancers strewing rose petals. They raised their voices in a chorus that shook the whole pier: "Hail Livius Gaius Metellus!"

Livius made no reply to the ovation and his officers watched stonily as Julianus, in an even greater display of frenzied admiration, shouted: "Hail Livius! Liberator of Syria! Liberator of Armenia! Liberator of Egypt!" His voice rose in a climax of frenzy, "Hail Livius! Conqueror of the Persians!"

Again the voices of the hundreds of dancers chorused: "Hail Livius." The ground trembled with the thunder of acclaim.

Livius glanced at his officers, stonily silent, at the musicians, dancers, the beautifully clad dancing girls, to the workers loading tribute grain, and the emaciated crowd, sullen and silent.

The cheers died away, and Livius waited until the silence stretched across the sun-struck quay. He did not even acknowledge Julianus' acclamation. Instead he spoke curtly to Victorinus: "Unload that grain. It is not to go to Rome."

There was stunned, incredulous silence. Even the musicians stopped playing, the acrobats ended their acts, standing awkwardly in the deepening quiet and tension.

Livius spoke louder, addressing the hungry crowd. "Let that grain be distributed in Syria and Egypt."

He could not have created greater consternation among the members of the commission had he blasphemed the Caesar.

Julianus stood speechless, shaking his head. An intelligent man, he had ordered the grain hurriedly loaded on the Rome-bound ships so that it could be accomplished during the celebration for Livius. He had hoped to avert any demonstration among the Syrians or the Egyptians by giving them something else to think about—the victory party, the dancing girls, the acrobats. He could not minimize the importance of a hero's welcome for Livius, but he knew the shipment of this grain was of greater importance because upon it depended the survival of Roman citizens.

He saw his horror reflected in the faces of Niger and the others of the Caesar's party.

This was a moment to assert his authority, but as he hesitated, he saw he was lost. At a signal from Polybus, the first maniples of the Northern Army marched grimly forward, all the way to the water line.

Along the docks, the crowd began to understand what was happening.

Livius gave another silent command, and Polybus led a group of combat veterans forward. They surrounded Julianus and Niger. Musicians, dancers and acrobats retreated in terror as Polybus, with practiced speed, removed the short sword from Julianus' scabbard, tossed it contemptuously to the ground at their feet. With equal facility, he disarmed Niger.

Julianus and Niger stood perfectly still, stunned to silence at this display of undisciplined brutality on the part of Livius' army. Julianus stared at Livius, waiting for him to call the soldiers off, but Livius seemed unaware of what was happening. Soldiers brought chains, binding Niger and Julianus as if they were captives or slaves.

A thrill of excitement rippled through the crowd. They whispered to each other, shaking their heads, smiling uncertainly, grimly, as Livius marched forward when Niger and Julianus had been securely trussed with chains.

Livius surveyed them, face cold and gray. "If you are still alive when you reach Rome, I have a message for you to deliver to Commodus Caesar from me. You will tell our Caesar that there will be either a new Rome—or a new Caesar!"

The silence lasted another breathless moment and then the crowd roared with approval as one voice all along the Antioch quay. Niger and Julianus were dragged away aboard one of the ships. The cheering broke loose again, wilder, louder.

But Livius seemed as unmoved by this acclamation as he had been by the simpering cheers of Julianus and his friends. He touched Timonides' arm, leading the Greek aside. He whispered urgently to him. "Take a few men, Timonides. Go quickly ahead of the army to Ravenna. . . . Commodus may try to strike back at me through Ravenna. If he does—if he tries—" his voice lowered to a grim growl,"—tell him I am only a few hours behind you—with the army."

Timonides nodded, smiling as he had once smiled obeying orders of Marcus Aurelius Antoninus, commands he knew to be selfless and for the good of a needy people.

He hesitated, and then stepped forward. He and his pupil embraced quickly. Timonides turned and hurried away, not looking back.

In the middle of the howling mob on the Antioch quay, Livius stood alone, lonely, watching moodily as Timonides left him.

XIX

COMMODUS STRODE through all the corridors of his Palatine Hill palace, giving orders, changing them, and changing them again, almost happy for the first time in all the long months since the night Livius had returned to him from exile in Ravenna.

He paused when Cornelius spoke his name, the tone of the chief of the Praetorian Guards bringing to his mind the hateful memory of that priest reminding him of his human fallibility on the day of his coronation.

"What is it now, Cornelius?" But even as his tone hinted his petulance and displeasure, Commodus was forced to admit fairly that Cornelius had his welfare in mind, following him about the palace like this, staying alert to every altered plan in the coming journey to the Port of the Tiber.

Cornelius spoke softly, reminding the emperor subtly of the dangers inherent in a trip like this outside the city— in fact, outside the palace as matters now stood with the disgruntled populace.

There was the tension of overt scandal in Rome. Commodus glanced about impatiently, barely heeding Cornelius' soft tones. The party between Commodus and the Roman citizens was over; it had lasted a long time, a lot of loud, gay years, but it was ended, and the people stood sullenly in the lengthening lines at the *congiara*. They barely applauded the emperor now when he slew lions and jaguars with arrows or javelins at the arenas; they talked in whispers of his excesses when they met in the public toilets or in the baths, bars and galleries of the *thermae*. One of the emperor's ugliest waking nightmares occurred during the trial of an Egyptian. Present to see the man sentenced, Commodus had been insulted and humiliated before the world. The Egyptian, convicted, ordered executed on a cross, appealed suddenly to Commodus, asking without hope, but with great sarcasm that the emperor set him free, do one humane act in his wasted life. The crowd gasped, strained forward to see; the court officers attempted to quiet the prisoner, but he was heard before he could be effectively silenced. When Commodus merely stood, staring, stunned, the Egyptian shouted at him, "You are no emperor! You are not fit to be Caesar, not fit to wear the toga of your sainted father!"

Commodus felt heated and would have turned away, moving in hope of escaping his own unpleasant thoughts. But Cornelius was still talking, and Commodus paused, sweating, pretending to listen to the Praetorian chief.

Commodus glanced about, troubled, even in the security of his own palace. Only when he was with Verulus, or among the gladiators was he truly at peace, for he no longer trusted anyone except these scarred fighters.

He shrugged his toga up on his shoulder. He did not trust Cornelius, or even the officers beneath Cornelius in the Praetorian Guard. They had too much power, and they always wanted more. They denied it, and yet this national police force wanted to rule the city, and the empire; this was what they truly wanted, no matter how piously they disavowed it.

Commodus had his youthful friends, and liked them younger every year, but sent them away when they became blasé, sophisticated—or ambitious. He no longer trusted them—whom could he trust?

For a moment his mind touched on Marcia. She was his favorite, and had been for a good many years. She was a strange young woman, full of complexities and contradictions, warm as fire, cold as ice, and a devout Christian.

And yet he did not even truly trust Marcia. It pained him

that he couldn't trust her. He had done so much for her. The fools in the senate bleated about the good, just reign of his father, and yet the Christians for instance had never fared as well as they did now, during his rule. He was unimpressed by them—as unmoved as he was by the customs of the national religion—and yet he tolerated them, and they came out into the open for the first time since the death of their Messiah over one hundred fifty years ago. He simply did not care what they did, their religious practices didn't interest him, and it thrilled Marcia that her influence with the Caesar made life endurable for her persecuted sect.

When people inquired of Marcia about the wide gulf between her behavior as the favored concubine in Commodus' court, and her avowed Christianity, Marcia told them that she would rather be alive, entertaining Commodus, knowing her people were secure and growing stronger, than die, pure but helpless. She had great power in Rome, and she knew it, but Commodus watched her carefully, afraid to trust her.

And it was worse, because instinctively, Marcia sensed this lack of faith, and in turn, she was afraid to trust him. She saw others favored one day and destroyed the next, banished, exiled or slain on some caprice or whim of Commodus, or because of some lie peddled to him that the emperor chose to believe without investigation. She had lasted a long time, and yet there was not a moment of her life when this fear of death wasn't hanging by a slender thread over her head.

If only he could trust someone—especially Marcia, for he loved to have her drinking with him, performing for him, because her abandon and her art fired and delighted him. Even when in a mood of depression, suspicion or fear, he would order her from his presence temporarily, he always sent for her again: Women were not all the same; some were cows; some had imagination and fire and excitement in their blood, like Marcia the wild young Christian. And there was more. No matter what he ordered Marcia to do in his presence, she accomplished it with great art and excitement, giving him the pleasure and forgetfulness he needed. But away from him, Marcia was chaste and untouched. He had the sworn word of his spies and his police for this. Outside the emperor's suite, no man could touch her, she kept herself entirely for the pleasure and amusement of the Caesar, and the whole palace knew this.

Why then couldn't he trust her wholeheartedly? He didn't, and knew she was afraid to trust him, and sometimes covertly studying her, he found Marcia watching him. . . .

He touched his throat, feeling as if he were choking.

He spoke abruptly, cutting off Cornelius: "All right. All right. Make what security plans are necessary. I don't care. Only don't try to delay me. I want to be at the Port of the Tiber when the ship returns from Antioch. It's the first good I've had to think about in months—in years, and I won't let anything spoil it, Cornelius. Nothing must spoil this."

He trembled, feeling the need for the security and peace he experienced only now when Livius was near. He felt protected, removed from the ever-present threat of treachery when Livius stood between him and the world.

Yet even with Livius there was this apprehension. He was reminded a dozen times a week by the blind senator Cleander that Livius Gaius Metellus was a dangerous man because of the Roman army's devotion to him.

Commodus shook this fear from his mind. Hadn't the rebellion in the East been instigated in Livius' name? Livius had gone there and put down the insurrection—in the name of Commodus Caesar.

Commodus trembled in anticipation. Livius would not be on this ship docking at the Port of the Tiber, but word of Livius would come with the return of his ambassadors.

Perhaps he might announce the celebration of a full triumph for the commander of the Roman armies. This would please the citizenry, take their minds off their empty bellies, placate the army, and much of the glory would redound to Caesar because Livius' conquests in the East had been made in his name.

Commodus turned all the way around in the corridor, trying to think how he could speed the start of this journey.

A hundred flaming torches lighted the quayside at the Port of the Tiber as the ship from Antioch was moored in the night.

On the docks, Commodus had had the ugly place transformed into the bright, gilded setting for a celebration. From Rome, he had brought in his party only the youthful men and women who could add charm and excitement to the occasion. Not one gray or bald head of the elder statesmen could be found in the wild orgies along the piers.

The bands played, but Commodus' emissaries did not at once disembark. Instead, the cargo was swung from ship to dock and at the screams of pleasure from his friends, Commodus forgot the ambassadors. He could deal with them later. At the moment, cages of roaring lions, tigers, jaguars were being unloaded.

Grabbing staffs from the pennant bearers, some of the young nobles ran at the cages, taunting the imprisoned beasts as their cages were set on the dock. They raked the staffs across the bars, setting the animals to wailing in frenzy. They poked them with the stick-ends to enrage them, and shrieked with delight when the frustrated animals lunged against the bars, roaring in rage.

Young men grabbed girls and swung them up close against the cages, letting the screaming animals claw at them; the enraged beasts swiped at the air, barely missing, or ripping away at expensive *stola,* sending the onlookers into gales of hysterical laughter.

Commodus, laughing loudly, and for the moment forgetting the pressures behind him at Rome, grabbed a staff and rushed at a cage being lowered to the waiting carts.

His young friends crowded around him, shouting, urging him on. In the shadows, omnipresent but unnoticed in the gaiety, Cornelius, chief of the Praetorian Guards, stood with a group of his security men, calmly alert. When the emperor rushed toward a caged lion to torment it with a staff, Cornelius nodded and a Praetorian Guard stepped forward silently, javelin ready to impale the animal should the cage bars break.

Along the entire expanse of the quayside this thrilling game of torturing the animals infected everyone. Commodus Caesar had joined the sport, giving it supreme status in the night. Only Cleander, calmly standing with Lentulus near the gangplank, waited in cold silence.

Suddenly a gasp from the crowd broke across the shrill merriment. People nearest the ship jerked their heads, staring upward, and then faces were upturned the length of the piers. Silence spread over them because they were too shocked, too stunned to speak.

Commodus stared upward, unable to believe what he saw, and then decided it must be a joke, a jest played on him by his returning friends—it was just the sort of foolishness that Claudius might dream up. It had to be a prank.

Commodus could not pull his gaze from the cage hanging from a crane. The cage swung out from the ship and was slowly lowered near where the emperor stood.

Commodus shook his head, recognizing Senator Didius Julianus and his ambassador Niger chained inside the cage like animals.

Commodus remained unmoving as the cage was lowered to the ground. He did not speak in the taut silence. He looked about him, shaking his head. Then he grabbed an axe from a dockworker and ran forward, smashing at the bars of the cage.

Praetorian Guards rushed to him and helped Julianus and Niger from the broken cage. The two men were sick, pale, bearded and still locked in their chains.

Commodus retreated a step from the ugliness and stench of them only to see a second cage with more of his emissaries being lowered beside the first.

Commodus was sick with horror. He recoiled from the cages, from the men, from the truth that this was no prank, no nightmare, nothing he could turn his back on.

He was unable to speak, and none of his party made a sound. The silence stretched, broken only by the roaring of the wild animals, the steady slap of water against the underpilings. The crowd stared in horrified fascination at the chained men and the cages.

Julianus, staring at Commodus, cried aloud. There was none of the charm and art of oratory in his voice. It broke, almost hysterically. "Livius did this, Caesar! It was Livius who did this to us! Livius Gaius Metellus! We told him we had been sent by Caesar himself! But he mocked you, Caesar!"

Commodus pressed the back of his fist against his mouth to keep from vomiting.

Julianus wept. "Livius mocked you, Caesar!"

Commodus' mouth twitched and he pulled his gaze from Julianus, glared about at the silent crowd, the flaring torches, the cages, the ship he'd been so sure was bringing him solutions to his most pressing problems.

From deep in the crowd came the faint, snickering sound that cut Commodus like a whiplash. He jerked his head around, finding malicious pleasure in the faces of the people he had chosen as his dearest companions. He moved his gaze from one face to the next, the terror growing in him, and showing in his eyes.

Commodus spoke, almost inaudibly, "Livius! Livius! How could you do this to me?" He sobbed, deep in his chest. "Livius, my friend, my brother. . . ."

Commodus saw how alone he was, betrayed and abandoned by Livius, and the terror changed to rage in his face. The smiles around him disappeared and the snickering whispers ceased as even the dullest in the crowd saw the sick anger consuming Caesar.

Commodus shook his head, took a backward step from Julianus and the cages, moved as if to run away into the shadows. Then he stopped, as if lost, gazed about frantically, seeking something in the faces around him that he knew he would never find. He turned all the way around, running again, returning, as if not knowing where to turn.

Sick, Commodus moved closer to Julianus and Niger. His voice was petulant. "Why did you let him mock me, Julianus? Are you a Roman? Do you not defend your emperor?"

He stared into Julianus' face, moved his gaze to Niger and to the others who had been helped from the cages. Julianus frowned, watching Commodus, but not speaking. A sudden ray of hope lighted Caesar's eyes, momentarily dissipating the glaze of madness. He spoke, accusing his ambassadors, "You went over to the enemy. That's it. You went over to the enemy. You were traitors. That's the reason. That's why Livius sent you back to me in cages."

He nodded, pleased with this explanation. But Julianus stood up and the others backed him, none retreating.

"We did only what Caesar ordered us to do," Julianus said. "It is Livius who has joined the rebels."

The look of hope died in Commodus' face. He stared at Julianus intently but was unable to doubt him, no matter how devoutly he wanted to. He shook his head again, speaking in a monotone, "Livius has joined the rebels." He repeated it stupidly, "Livius has joined the rebels."

Commodus looked at the unshaven, sick men before him. He shook his head, face gray and expressionless. He backed away from them into the shadows, repeating it over and over, "Livius has joined the rebels."

Julianus' voice followed him, battering at him. "Livius sent you a message, Caesar." Commodus stopped, ceased speaking, and stepped forward again, nodding, awaiting the message. Julianus said, "Livius commanded us to tell you— there will be a new Rome, or a new Caesar."

The words rang in the silence of the Tiber dock. It was some moments before their full impact impressed the stunned emperor. He stared blankly at Julianus a moment, and then he struck out, his fist smashing downward into Julianus' face, sending him sprawling.

Commodus waited, standing with fists clenched at his sides. No one spoke and no one moved.

Commodus turned, looking about the crowd until he located the blind Cleander standing with Lentulus near the empty gangway.

Commodus strode toward the blind senator, almost running. He caught Cleander's arm, speaking brokenly, with sick urgency. "Get me gold, Cleander . . . from everyone . . . from everywhere. . . ." He whispered, nodding, "Strip all the public monuments of gold." He swallowed fearfully, then said, "Even the temples. Strip the gods and goddesses."

He heard Lentulus' sharp intake of breath as the giant reacted in fear. Commodus glanced at him, then looked again at Cleander, gaining some hope from the way the blind man stood impassively, his composure not even disturbed by this fearful and unprecedented order to strip the sacred temples of their gold.

Commodus nodded, tightening his grip on Cleander's arm. "Enough gold to drown Livius, to suffocate him, to crush him and his *new* Rome. New Rome! New Rome!" He glared about him, and his voice rose, almost incoherent with rage. "Praetorians! Praetorian Guards!"

He grabbed a torch, the light falling across his face, glittering in his distended eyes. The national security police came running.

"You Praetorians!" Commodus shouted. "Do you know where this *new* Rome is? Do you? Ravenna! That's where his new Rome is. Ravenna. Where Livius has entrenched his barbarians and his plans for rebellion. I order you to march against Ravenna. Let us rid ourselves once and for all of this new Rome."

He stared at them, at Cleander, the crowd of stunned

young people, the cages and the broken men around them, then he ran through the knots of onlookers, rushing toward his chariot, the torch flaring brightly in the wind.

XX

TIMONIDES RODE at the head of an escort of Roman mounted troops. Saddle weary, he stared ahead, looking for the Romagna plains and Ravenna, seldom glancing back the way he had come. It was strange the way you lost track of time and distance when you moved steadily and at top speed possible for men and animals. They had ridden out of the heat and dust of Antioch, following the Roman roads across Cilicia, Galatia, Thracia, changing horses often, at Anycra, Nicomedia, Byzantium, Thessalonica and at most garrisons in Macedonia and Dalmatia. They reached Italy fatigued and hungry, but it had not occurred to Timonides to slow his pace, nor to his escort to question him.

He glanced over his shoulder. A Greek, an ex-school teacher, he was nevertheless respected and obeyed by these tough Roman soldiers because of his position as slave-aide to their general. He'd seen this situation so often throughout the Roman world it was no longer remarkable to him. Contemptuous of slaves in general, the Romans often found themselves deferring to, bribing and buttering-up the slaves of their betters.

As he rode, his gaze seemed to focus nowhere, his body jarred and ached in the army saddle, and his thoughts turned inward, to his life in Greece, the simple joyous time of growing up in the splendor and the pleasures offered the mind and imagination of a young boy. He had spent years in his early slavery yearning back toward the rocky heights of those hills of Greece, and had talked with other slaves of insurrection, escape, flight, of returning home. But the only time he had returned to Athens had been with Marcus Aurelius Antoninus, as his slave-aide and as his friend. Aurelius kept no halters on him; he had long ago set him free, returned his own name to him; he could have walked away, in the night or the broad light of day, and Aurelius would not have stopped him. Yet he was still among the Romans, having served Marcus, and now doing the bidding of a younger man of power and strength and potential for vast good. Strange. How strange life was.

He shook away his thoughts because even after all these eventful years, the memory of Aurelius still had the power to disturb him and make him melancholy. The endless hours of their arguments in logic, law, philosophy, religion, sex, manners, morals—they talked of everything in the world together, and Timonides envied no other man his existence.

He sighed. He and Aurelius had been at odds in their views on many subjects, and yet there was only one they never discussed and which Aurelius viewed as Timonides' unforgivable weakness. "Every man has his weakness, Timonides," Aurelius would say when the Greek tried to draw him into discussion, "and you have yours. Perhaps your Greek temperament explains it. I know my own Roman mind rebels at it. But we need not discuss it; it shall remain a closed matter between us."

Remembering, Timonides smiled, his dark eyes brimmed with tears as he remembered, and he released the reins a moment, clutching something at the neckline of his tunic, closing his fist on it. He almost laughed aloud. His guilty secret!

He heard the shouting of the tribune in charge of the escort and he drew rein, halting his mount.

For a moment it was as if he were still racing along, even the thunder of hooves against the road reverberated inside his head.

The tribune extended his arm, pointing across the plain to the walled city of Ravenna. At first, Timonides was aware of an exultancy. They were back in the town where the new civilization was being hatched. He tried to count back the days of his riding from Antioch north and west, and failed, but the important consideration was that they had made it and he would execute the orders Livius had given him: a slave fighting with all his heart and soul to hold the Roman world together. How strange life was.

After a while the entire company had halted along the roadway behind him and Timonides became aware of a vast and upsetting silence, not only here among the men of his escort, but in the walled city of Ravenna itself. The town was silent, with a tenuous, frightening silence that seemed ready to erupt into violence, that existed in its own tension. Not a sound of life or movement came from within the walls.

Timonides shivered, clutching at his tunic neckline, chilled by this sudden premonition of evil.

He shook off the feeling, gestured forward, already riding past the young tribune as the others spurred their horses into a gallop, following him.

Ravenna's city gate stood open and Timonides rode through at the head of his escort company. There was no sign of life in any of the houses or *insulae*, nor along the twisted side streets. Riding, Timonides glanced about in alarm, spurring his horse and bursting into the Ravenna market place.

All life of the town was concentrated here in the area around the public fountain. People swarmed, a seething mass of color, blond Marcomanni and dark-haired Italians mingling side by side, bargaining, buying, arguing, working.

Timonides threw up his arm, calling his company to a halt. For some moments the soldiers remained mounted, staring at the fruition of Aurelius' dream and Livius' laboring.

Overcome with relief, Timonides swung his leg over the saddle and slipped to the ground, smiling, beaming upon the mingling people as if they were his own children. For some moments he simply stood there among them, watching them, nodding and smiling at them.

The word spread that he had returned. People shouted and others came streaming into the market place from everywhere, surrounding him, greeting him joyously.

His eyes filled with tears he made no effort to conceal, Timonides saw Xenia pushing through the throng trying to get to him and behind her Ballomar and young chieftains of the Marcomanni.

Xenia thrust people aside. Timonides held out his arms and she flew to him, holding him, almost dancing with him, weeping and laughing at once. Ballomar and his young chieftains looked on in pride and admiration. Holding Xenia, Timonides lifted his head seeing the blue eyes fixed on him in adulation, and the respect in the black eyes of the Italians.

The tears brimmed his eyes, spilled. Timonides tried to speak, for the first time in his life discovered himself without words. He opened his arms wide in a gesture of gratitude, an expression of well-being, satisfaction, of embracing them all,

all his children, taking them all to his heart, these people whom he had come to love so deeply, these people who had changed from animal-like barbarians to useful citizens, rebuilding a town and an empire.

Suddenly Ballomar and the young chieftains grabbed Timonides as if they were exuberant children, and pulled him along through the market place. They stopped often, speaking boastfully, displaying the produce they had grown on their farms, and even more proudly showing the work of their artisans. Timonides continued nodding, nodding, pleased, agreeing, excited by everything, aware of Xenia remaining close at his side, as if somehow Livius had returned to her because another who loved him was here and had recently seen him.

Ballomar and his chieftains drew aside into a knot, watching Timonides carefully as they indulged in a heated discussion. Finally a decision was reached and Ballomar yielded reluctantly. The men came toward Timonides and Xenia, carrying tankards of wine brought up by women. In a group, they moved into a hut.

Xenia glanced about troubled, seeing that somehow the blond people had completely excluded their dark-skinned neighbors, encircling the Greek.

A young Marcomanni chieftain poured full mugs of wine. He handed one to Timonides, and took one himself. Mugs were quickly passed to Ballomar and the others in the crowd.

There was a tension within the group and Timonides glanced about uneasily. Xenia seemed strangely pale, and Ballomar remained silent, impassive.

Timonides lifted his tankard, drank with noisy appreciation. "Come!" he said. "Come now, admit it! Is this not a better life than what you knew before?"

The silence continued, no one replied. Timonides frowned, glanced at Xenia, at the others. He shrugged and with another show of gusto, drained his wine mug. The wine began to go to his head, and his voice showed his excitement:

"Now you have shown once and for all how quickly it can be done. Now we can say to the senate, to the empire—to the world—'Behold Ravenna! There live together in peace the blond people of the North and the dark people of the

South! What we have done in Ravenna can be done the world over!' "

He was smiling brightly, a little drunkenly he admitted, but he ceased talking when he saw his words were greeted without any particular enthusiasm. The silence deepened around him.

A young chieftain spoke to the others of the encircling crowd, his voice hard. "The army of Gaius Livius is marching on Rome. Roman will fight Roman. What better moment for us to strike?"

Another nodded, his blond hair falling about his face. "Messengers have come from our people in the North. They, too, tell us that this is the time for us to fall upon the Roman—"

"What kind of talk is this?" Horrified, Timonides backed away from the two young chieftains. "But you have everything here. All a people could want. Why should you destroy it? Why should you throw it away? But you must not do this." He breathed deeply, getting himself under control. "Let us look upon this situation logically. One—"

He held one finger high and then stopped abruptly as the young chieftain gave a signal. Timonides jerked his gaze to Ballomar, but the huge man towered above the others, waiting impassively.

The crowd parted and several Marcomanni men came forward bringing a heavy, carefully covered object. They carried it gingerly, deposited it with great reverence on a stone table.

Xenia recoiled from it and Timonides stared at it in puzzled uneasiness as a young chieftain pulled off the rough cloth covering and revealed an expertly carved statue of Wotan, the barbarian god of war.

Timonides shook his head, his eyes showing his distress. "But this is Wotan. Your god of war. You mustn't do this. You are forbidden by state laws to have this god any more."

Ballomar spoke at last, his voice low but deep and harsh. "The moment has come for us, Greek. . . . We either stay here forever, and become Romans—or we strike out at Rome —for our freedom!"

Timonides shook his head, recoiling. He turned his head, searching for Xenia, but she had moved back, silent among the surrounding hostile faces. They waited again, watching the Greek in that reflective, heavy silence.

At last Ballomar spoke. "If we are to give up our ways, Greek, if we are to abandon our gods, we must know that your god is stronger."

Ballomar gestured, and several young men seized Timonides.

Startled, Timonides offered almost no resistance. He merely watched, not believing what he saw as a wooden apparatus was brought into the circle of people. He winced, recognizing the bottom half of a cross.

The young men moved rapidly, stripped away Timonides' tunic and *subucula*, leaving him standing in leather sandals and *licium*, his linen loincloth.

Xenia shook her head, watching with stricken eyes. But she did not speak.

"You must not do this! You must not!" Timonides said, voice hoarse.

Ballomar and the other chieftains settled themselves around the idol and the half-naked Greek. They watched the proceedings with the detachment and curious objective air of spectators at a theatre or some other interesting spectacle. They showed no hatred, anger, or bitterness, simply this deep curiosity. They were unmoved, in fact paid no attention at all to Timonides' protests and writhings, considering them aspects of this matter completely to be anticipated.

Xenia moved away, standing among the women, silent, her cheeks gray.

Timonides found himself half naked, arms stretched wide, tied to the cross bar, his feet secured to the vertical bar. His eyes widening, he watched the younger men bring forward instruments of torture.

Ballomar spoke in a most reasonable tone. "If your god is strong, he will give you strength to resist."

Timonides did not look at the irons heating in a brazier. He said, "But we want to do so much for you—"

A young blond man touched the odd object on a fine cord about the Greek's neck. He closed his hand as if to jerk it loose, but Timonides gasped, shaking his head, his eyes darkening, and the youth stepped back, scowling.

"It is not happening, but is a bad dream. This cannot happen," Timonides said aloud. "It must not happen."

A youthful executioner lifted a white-hot iron from the brazier, stepped toward Timonides. The teacher recoiled, watching the fiery tip. The crowd became silent, each man holding his breath.

Ballomar's voice remained level. "You have only to reach out and touch our god Wotan, admit that Wotan is stronger, and we will free you. You will not be hurt."

Timonides stared at Ballomar, at the idol, at the young executioner with the white-hot iron. He swallowed hard, speaking levelly, "Let us look upon this logically." He held up one finger. "One—what will you know if I touch your god? Only that I am weak." He held up a second finger. "Two—"

Ballomar jerked his head in a silent signal. The executioner stepped closer to Timonides and applied the burning iron. Timonides' fingers closed as with a fantastic effort of will; he made no sound. He did not cry out. It was Xenia who screamed.

The others did not glance at her or appear even to hear her outcry.

The executioner stepped back. Holding the cooling iron, he, Ballomar and the others waited patiently for the scream that would indicate that the searing pain had become unendurable. But Timonides did not scream.

The young chieftain and the others nodded to each other as if finding deep significance in this.

After a moment Ballomar gestured for the executioner to continue. Again the blond-haired men waited, watching with the same detached, objective interest to see how Timonides, who now had been taught the meaning of this particular pain, would react to a second dose.

Sweating in agony, Timonides watched the executioner's iron approach with a deep dread, trying to avert his gaze as the white-hot iron came closer, but finding it impossible to tear his distended eyes away.

The executioner approached with deadly calm, and slowly, slowly applied the iron. Timonides bit his lip until it bled, but again it was Xenia who screamed.

Timonides made no sound.

Ballomar and his young chieftains glanced at each other, deeply impressed. But once more Ballomar gave a signal, almost reluctantly, and again the tormentor approached Timonides.

With one more fantastic effort, Timonides kept from screaming, and spoke hurriedly, but kept his tone down, reasonable, logical, as if what he was saying was more an explanation than a plea for mercy.

"No . . . no . . . you must not continue to hurt me like this. . . . Even though I have been a slave—I—I am not accustomed to pain, you see . . . No—"

"Then touch Wotan," Ballomar said.

"The pain is too much," Timonides said as if not hearing Ballomar. "Although I am a philosopher, I am weak."

Again the executioner applied the iron.

Timonides writhed, his eyes for a moment going upward in their sockets, his face rutting, his body shaking convulsively. But he bit down on his bleeding lip, making no sound. The hiss of the burning iron on his flesh and Xenia's broken sobs were the only sounds.

The young chieftain stepped closer, staring at Timonides as if trying to see his breaking point. Ballomar stood up, and all stared at Timonides, waiting for his cry.

Timonides' head rolled from side to side. But he spoke in that reasonable tone, as if thinking it out, finding the explanation that would make it possible for him to endure this torture. His voice remained low, but the hysteria was under it as the pain undermined his self-control. "No, no, they are not worthy of it. They are not worthy." Suddenly his voice rose, lashing at them. "Barbarians. Monsters. Animals."

Ballomar said, "Touch Wotan. Confess he is stronger."

Timonides seemed not even to hear the stolid voice. He continued his reflections, speaking in that calm tone with the hysteria edging it. "Why should I endure such pain for—these? Why? And yet we fought for them. And yet—"

Again the iron was applied, this time he no longer saw it, his eyes not focusing on anything. He continued speaking aloud, "I cannot. No, no. It's no use. I cannot endure this. It is beyond all human endurance."

Again the iron was pressed against his flesh. He writhed, rolling on the cross bar. "They should not be Romans. . . . They do not deserve to be." He whimpered slightly, turned his eyes heavenward. "I cannot. . . . I cannot."

The executioner stared at the glowing iron tip, adjudged it not hot enough, heated it again. In those moments, Timonides, barely lucid, continued talking in low, even tones. "Oh, Livius, Livius, what a terrible world when its future rests on such as these. . . ."

For a moment his head sagged against his shoulder, and he lay there, eyes closed. The executioner withdrew the iron from the brazier, stepped toward him. The extreme heat seemed to revive the Greek. His eyes flew open, he stared at the white-hot metal growing larger, coming nearer.

Timonides shook his head suddenly, threw out his arm, touched the idol of Wotan.

A deep sigh rolled across the watching crowd. Timonides stared at his own hand grasping at the idol. He shook his head in amazement. "I had no intention of doing that. I—"

There was a sign of triumph from the young chieftain. Nodding, Ballomar walked to Timonides, slashed the ropes binding him to the cross bar. Timonides sank into a semi-coma. Ballomar lifted him gently, placed him on a table. For a long time Timonides did not move, did not speak, and only at last opened his eyes and stared at the roof of the hut into which they had moved him.

His mouth twisted and his eyes filled with bitter tears as he realized he had failed. His voice broke. "I had no intention—only, only—I have failed. My faith was not strong enough. . . . What is the value of all my thoughts, of all my beliefs, of all I am, if I could not triumph over this? What is the good of all I have learned, known, believed?"

His body shook and he sobbed uncontrollably, the pain forgotten in his self-hatred and despair.

There was the sound of crackling fire and then flames. He turned his head, staring at the dancing shadows of flames on the ceiling. He pushed himself up on his elbows, turned and saw the idol of Wotan burning. He shook his head, staring at the blond men in amazement.

The giant Ballomar's voice was almost gentle as he explained. "Your gods gave you much more strength than our god could have given us." He shook his head in disbelief. "You did not even scream." Suddenly he roared out. "Now, here, in this moment, we pledge our eternal loyalty to Rome! Now are we blood brothers for all time with the Romans. Now will we live in peace with them."

There was an answering roar, a pledge, from the assemblage.

Timonides shook his head, speaking brokenly, "But I—"

He stopped, watching Wotan burn, hearing the sigh of awe as the idol was consumed by fire.

From the rim of the crowd a blond boy, breathless,

agitated, pushed his way forward. He was sweated, disheveled, exhausted from running.

Ballomar spoke. "Now will the gods of the Romans give us strength to endure such great pain—"

"No. No." Timonides cried out, sitting up on the table. "But that is no reason to take our gods. That is no reason to change your ways."

Ballomar, who was nearest him, stared at him in amazement, and spoke in an outraged whisper, "Don't you want us, Roman Greek?"

Timonides stared at them for a long time and then sank back wearily, defeated. He whispered, "Miserable, uneducated, superstitious, half-men! You are not at all what we fought for. And yet—" He paused as Ballomar, shoulders sagging round, moved away from him, and quickly added, "Yes. Yes. We want you. We want you! Want you!"

The blond boy pushed his way through the crowd, grabbing at Ballomar's arm. He cried out, "Romans. An army of Romans! On horses! Coming here!"

"What are you talking about?"

The boy pointed desperately. "I saw them. I saw them."

Watching the boy, Timonides sagged heavily, feeling the deplorable weight of failure again because it was as if the youth had described the men, the punishing army sent out from Commodus in Rome.

XXI

TIMONIDES PUSHED himself up slowly, his body seared and welted with blisters. For a moment the room spun about his head but he shook away the hands that tried to support him.

"We must hurry," he said to Ballomar.

The giant scowled, staring at him. "Why must we hurry? They are Romans. What have we to fear from the Romans?"

Timonides peered at him helplessly. There was so much to say, the whole history of progress and intrigue, of small good emerging from whole slimy rivers of evil, the difference between men, the difference between Romans. There wasn't time. He shook his head. "Close the city gates," was all Timonides said. "Bar the city gates."

Ballomar nodded, jerking his head toward his finest young men. They turned, sped from the hut and across the market place.

Breathing through his open mouth, Timonides first looked for his tunic and *subucula*, then gave them up because their weight and fit against his seared flesh was impossible to consider. He crossed the room, wearing only the linen *licium* and his leather strap sandals.

He heard the gasps of the people in the market place at the sight of his blistered body. He ignored them, walking with painful slowness toward the city walls. He tried to hold himself erect, but listed, staggered, and almost fell.

He reached the wall, rested for a moment on the lowest of the stone steps leading to the parapets. Gasping for breath, he heard the sounds of dray horses, saddle animals, the shouts of Roman soldiers beyond the walls. Closing his mouth tightly, he fixed his gaze on the top stone and slowly ascended the steps.

Alone on the wall, Timonides stared down at the assembled Praetorian Guards and heavy weaponry commandeered from Roman army garrison and supply. For a long time Timonides remained there, awed at the sight of the gaudy Praetorians galloping forward and bringing the implements of war into place.

He caught his breath, recognizing in the rear Commodus Caesar himself. Like a reed in the wind, Timonides swayed on the wall, staring at Commodus and his company—Julianus, Niger, and Cornelius, chief of the Praetorians—directing the siege below him.

Timonides turned, looking down into the sullenly silent market place where blond and dark men stood, alike puzzled, caught in a conflict they didn't even understand.

He gazed down upon them, filled with infinite sorrow. They did not speak, faces turned upward. He saw the hatred in their eyes. He shook his head, completely despaired of ever understanding either men or life though he'd spent all his existence in study and contemplation of them both.

He swayed a moment, then called out, raising both arms above his head.

For a moment the Praetorians fell silent in a wave that extended all the way out to Commodus and the commanders. They stared upward at the swaying figure on the wall.

Timonides shouted hoarsely, "Men of Rome! Go back! Do not touch these people. They have become your brothers! Do not destroy them and this city! Let them live in peace! They are Romans now!"

He paused, breathless, watching the Praetorians. There was one more moment of hesitation, and then the officers shouted orders and the great crossbows, with flaming javelins, were wheeled forward into place.

Timonides shook his head, desperately shouting, "Do not do this! You will only destroy yourselves! Listen to me. Livius and the entire Roman army are only a few hours behind me. Do you understand? They are on their way here. They will punish you cruelly!"

The soldiers continued rolling forward scaling ladders and bulky catapults.

Timonides lifted his voice, pleading: "Do not harm them! Rivers of Roman blood will pay for this! The whole Northern people will answer you with death and fire! Their hatred will live for centuries. You will make nations of killers out of them. Put away your swords. Let us live together in peace!"

There was an answer, one answer. In the rear lines Commodus nodded fiercely, a tribune relayed the order and Timonides got his answer from the Praetorians. A flaming javelin streaked through the air, transfixing Timonides.

Timonides clutched the shaft of the javelin, shaking his head, incredulous, whispering still, "Peace . . ."

He stumbled backward across the parapet and toppled from the wall. He was dead before he struck the stones below.

For the space of one long breath there was taut and stricken silence in the Ravenna market place. The people edged forward, gazes riveted on the dead Greek, eyes distended in horror and disbelief.

The barbarians growled first, a hurting animal sobbing from their entrails, and then suddenly bellowed as one man their old war cry—a sound they had not made in all their years at Ravenna.

As if in reply to the war call, a shower of flaming javelins rained over the walls, falling among them, followed by another storm of fire. The people broke, screaming, and ran for cover. They went wild in their terror, clutching at their children, looking about for loved ones, running one way and then the other, distracted in the hail of fire.

Only Xenia did not move. She had walked forward rigidly to where Timonides had fallen, and stood stunned, incredulous over his body. Fire and stones fell about her, but it was as if she were in a catatonic trance, she did not move her gaze from the face of her beloved Greek.

Outside the walls, Commodus' company, finding no resistance to their attack, raced forward to the front lines. The gates were smashed open and men swarmed up ladders, scaling the walls, storming into Ravenna.

Livius and his officers found the broken gates of Ravenna hanging open in silence and destruction.

The massed Roman legions, silent and grim, stretched out across the plains below them.

Livius, followed by Victorinus, Polybus and other officers, rode through the smashed gates. They were stunned, shocked, and they moved slowly into the utter desolation, the city crushed in smoldering ruins, the bodies of unarmed men, women and children scattered in the streets and littering the market place of the ravaged town.

Livius gave curt orders, sending searchers seeking any survivors, commanding troops to enter the city and bury the dead. He spoke in a hard, low tone, as if only by keeping taut leash on his emotions could he speak at all.

Suddenly, he stopped speaking, staring at something near the wall. He shook his head, moved forward, his silent officers watching.

He paused, standing over Timonides, looking at the body welted and seared with blisters, transfixed by the javelin.

Livius knelt beside Timonides' body. He gazed down at the sage's lined and gentle features, shaking his head, seeing the half smile that was like a benediction and forgiveness forever fixed on his mouth.

Livius breathed deeply, clenching his fists at his sides. For some moments, unmoving, he gazed at Timonides' body. Frowning, he reached down and lifted the small wooden cross secured on a fine cord about Timonides' neck. Livius' eyes brimmed with tears and he remained, head lowered. This was the answer to the old arguments between the Greek and Marcus Aurelius—the weakness about which Caesar had taunted his slave.

Livius spoke softly, under his breath. "What happened, gentle Greek? Did you try to tell them there were three possibilities? Didn't you know there was—a fourth possibility?" With savage moment, he tore out the javelin. "This!"

Livius got to his feet. His cheeks were pallid, rigid. He gripped the javelin. "This is the way they answer reason. This is always the answer to reason."

He hurled the broken javelin from him. It clattered across the stones in the deep silence.

His officers stared at him, and said nothing because they knew him, they knew war, and there were no words. He strode away from them, going across the market place, and they did not look at each other and did not follow him.

Livius didn't know how long he walked, only that he strode away from his thoughts, his memories, of this place, and that good and gentle man dead back there. He did not see how he could speak to anyone just now, or take up his life again.

He walked the twisted streets, his fists clenched at his sides, the only sounds the striking of his leather sandals against the stones. The sun was hot against his shoulders and yet he was chilled in his military tunic. The shadows of the *insulae* and the houses darkened long shafts of the narrow lanes. The silence pressed in on him, and distantly he heard sounds of troops burying the dead.

He caught his breath when he walked out of the shadows into an open court littered with blond and dark-haired dead. He winced. He had tried to walk away from the carnage just for a little while, but all the streets in the ruined city led to the same place, to more scenes of terror and desolation. He stood looking around at the slain people, mingled in death, brought to death because he had chosen this place for his experiment with human beings—human frontiers. Well, those frontiers were pushed back now, the gods only knew how far back. He swallowed hard, tears spilling through the dust caked on his cheeks.

He heard a sound behind him and heeled around.

"Livius."

He drew a deep breath, watching Lucilla, pale, weak, lovely, walk toward him.

She came close to him, touched his arm gently.

Her voice was low, edged in bitterness. "My brother Commodus understood better than I did the meaning of what you were trying to do here—"

His bitterness was cold. "It seems not many understood—"

"They understood. They did understand, Livius. That's why they had to destroy it. They had to destroy you."

"They've done well."

Her voice had tears in it. "You are not destroyed, Livius. You are not like other men. I know that now. I hoped it, but I was afraid to believe, even when my father said it. I know now. You are like my father—the gods have touched you, too."

"Oh?" His smile was twisted and bitter. "If that is so, then the old saying is true, it's not always a blessing to be touched by the gods."

He stepped closer to her, despairing and defeated. He took her hand, as if clinging to her. She spoke gently, "It must be lonely for you—for men such as you."

She stepped nearer to him, and he held her close against his body. He felt her tremble. "We better go back," he said.

The troops inside the city were in military formation when Livius and Lucilla entered the Ravenna market place.

Livius walked slowly to them.

Victorinus stepped forward. His voice was low, solemn, yet granite hard. "Give us the command, Gaius Livius. Your army will sweep through Rome. We'll teach Commodus and his corrupt what it means to kill Romans."

There was a growl of approval from the other officers.

For a moment, Livius straightened, his eyes glittering, fixed on retribution and vengeance, the cleansing blood-bath of violence that would make him whole again.

He moved his gaze across his loyal officers and the waiting troops inside these ruined walls, and the endless legions beyond them. But he saw, too, the destruction Commodus had left behind him here, the senseless slaying of innocent and unarmed people. He shivered, aware of the chilling threat of disorder, of anarchy, the final and complete destruction of everything he had vowed to uphold.

He shook his head and spoke sharply, because there had to be an end to this talk of punishing armies, it had to end here.

"No. I am still in command. The word to destroy Rome won't come easily from me."

The officers glanced at each other, looked again at him. He was silent, prowling before them as if this desolated town were a cage and the confining bars were closing in on him.

They watched him in silence. At last he looked at them, at Victorinus, Polybus, the others.

He spoke quietly, but with finality. "I will go ahead of you, alone into Rome. You will prepare the army to march without halt—until the gates of Rome. On the day of your arrival at the Tiber, you will come forward to the gates at midday. You will wait that day at the gates of Rome until sundown. . . . If I have not returned to you from the city by sundown . . . only then will you lead the army into—Rome itself."

He waited, but none spoke. They heard and digested what he said, and they respected him and his orders. They watched his face but saw nothing in it because it was carefully, coldly expressionless.

BOOK FOUR

XXII

COMMODUS LEAPED from the chariot as it pulled in along the curb outside the imperial mint.

He ran across the wide forecourt in the lengthening shadows of late afternoon and sped up the steps. Behind him, Lentulus helped Cleander from a second chariot, and with the blind senator clinging to the giant's arm they hurried after the emperor into the work rooms of the government building.

Julianus stood in the center of rows of molds, lines of bubbling caldrons and metal racks. Slaves and laborers pressed into service moved frantically under the lash of Julianus' orders and threats.

Huge golden heads of the statues of the gods lay like outsized, broken toys along the flooring, waiting to be fearfully transported by superstitious slaves to bubbling caldrons and melted down. Other slaves were ladling molten gold into molds to be minted. Rows of workers at the racks were swiftly sacking the newly minted coins and piling the sacks of coins into waiting imperial wagons.

Commodus walked past Julianus, glancing toward the fiery caldrons, the molds, the priceless heads of idols created in antiquity and now rolled carelessly on the floors. He went directly to the racks where the coins were being sacked, realistically going straight to the end results of this whole operation.

He stepped close to the line of feverishly working slaves. When they did not glance around, too busy to be aware of him, he shoved one of them roughly aside and picked up one of the coins, inspecting it closely.

His face relaxed slightly at the feel and perfection of the coin bearing his likeness.

Behind him, Lentulus handed Cleander one of the newly minted coins. Cleander's sensitive fingers circled, tested the face of the dinari. He read aloud what his fingers told him, mouth pulled in an ironic smile, "Commodus Caesar—Conqueror of Persia."

Commodus nodded in satisfaction and then tossed his coin back into the growing pile.

He spun around, facing the sweated Julianus.

Commodus' voice rasped at him. "Faster, Julianus. They must work faster."

Julianus nodded, turning, and shouted at the slaves carrying the golden heads of the broken idols.

"Come on," Commodus said over his shoulder. "Let's go, Cleander. We—"

He stopped, catching a glimpse of the avidity in Cleander's lean face. He paused, watching Cleander feel the gold coin in an almost sensual way, gratified by the touch.

Commodus laughed. "There will be enough for you, too, Cleander."

Cleander stopped smiling, his face becoming once again imperturbable. "I know, Caesar. I know."

Livius entered Rome alone, aware of a darkness of the soul that matched the ugly shadows in the narrow, twisted streets. He had paused on the bridge over the Tiber, stared into the swift, turbulent water discolored with the mud that it carried down from the mountains. The river was dark, and the day was, and the world was. Not even the screaming crowds celebrating at some decree of the emperor gave any color or light to the town.

He went along the Via Nova to the forum, pausing outside the temple of Jupiter at the summit of the Capitoline Hill.

Heavy formations of Praetorian Guards stood at attention along the approaches to the temple.

Livius pushed his way through the growing crowd forming in the square. When he reached the steps and moved up them, guards stepped forward, swords drawn menacingly.

Livius paused, and some of the guards recognized him. He was asked to wait, word was sent inside the temple, and after a moment, Cornelius came out, smiling.

He greeted Livius, bowed, motioning the general ahead of him up the steps.

Walking slowly ahead of Cornelius, Livius entered the

vast, roofless temple. At the entrance, towering to the top of the wall, stood a statue of the god Jupiter, awe-inspiring, scowling, immense. Soft oil light glowed everywhere.

Suddenly Livius stopped walking, staring at the idols. All around the shadowed temple, statues of the gods, in various sizes and colors, had been beheaded, and their heads replaced by likenesses of Commodus.

Livius stood speechless, with the chief of the Praetorian Guards at his back. At last he moved forward, shaking his head in the gloom, going from god to god, staring incredulously at the graven heads of Commodus.

He paused finally beside the statue of Jupiter. He straightened when he recognized Commodus in the deep gloom of the shadows.

"I've been waiting for you," Commodus said.

"What is your answer?" Livius said, holding himself stiffly erect. He was aware that Cornelius was keeping his fist closed on his short sword, but he did not give the Praetorian chief a glance. He kept his chilled gaze fixed on Commodus' face.

"Answer?" Commodus shrugged.

Livius spoke, voice sharp. "I sent a message to you, Commodus. I must have your answer."

Commodus' voice remained impassive, as if he barely heard his general and didn't even understand him. "I've been made a god, Livius. Did you know?"

Livius winced, staring at the expressionless face, the bleak, empty eyes.

Commodus moved his arm, gesturing toward the court before the temples of Jupiter and Juno. "I have ordered thirty days of celebration to mark this day. Rome will have the greatest games ever seen."

Livius watched the emperor carefully.

Commodus smiled. "First they need a Caesar who will give them bread and festivals—then—they need a god. They must have someone to trust, someone they can believe in, Livius."

Livius shook his head impatiently. "I have no time for this. Leave now. Leave Rome at once. I can still spare your life."

"What is it a god can do that I cannot?" Commodus inquired, moving his gaze from the face of his general to the Praetorian chief and back. His voice remained calm, warm. "I can kill. I can destroy whole cities."

Livius, puzzled, angered, glanced at Cornelius. The alert

guard stared at him impassively. Livius gazed at Commodus again, trying to get through to him. "Commodus. Do you understand me? The army—my army—loyal to me and to new Rome—is at the gates of the city—"

"What is your army to me?" Commodus tilted his head, his voice showing a flash of petulant rage. But he smiled again, his eyes empty, and his manner changed, becoming warm. "Of all the people around me, Livius, only you—my Livius —only you could have been a god with me." He smiled, considering this. "Two gods together ruling the world."

Livius frowned, seeing that Commodus was somewhere beyond his reach, and that Cornelius had stepped forward, threateningly. He spoke to Commodus, but his words were a chilled warning to the Praetorian chief. "It will not help to kill me, Commodus. Even if you kill me—you will not escape. If I don't return to the encampment outside the gates before sundown, the legions will march on Rome."

Commodus shook his head, sadly, distantly, only faintly troubled, but genuinely puzzled. "Why will you do this? For Rome? What is that—Rome? A half-million slaves whose only hope is to die quickly? A half-million free Romans who live on public charity and whom I buy with a few games? A few wealthy senators who are rich only because I permit them to be—"

"Thirty thousand men will be turned loose on the city." Livius gazed into the emperor's face, seeking desperately for a glimmer of reason. He sweated. "Do you understand what that will mean?"

Commodus straightened, crying shrilly, wounded. "You could have been a god! I offered you everything." His voice rose to the edge of hysteria. "What is it you want?" He pointed his finger at Livius. "You! You are the real enemies of the empire! You are the real threat. You who *believe*— you who have fool *ideals*. . . . What is there more than this? To play—to eat—to make love—to die—"

"We are men and men are more—" He shook his head, seeing the futility of arguing with Commodus. He spoke abruptly, "The time is short. I will order the Praetorian Guard to summon the senate. . . . There must be some love for Rome left within them—"

"The senate?" Commodus lifted his head, glanced around as if listening for something neither of them would ever hear again. "If we were to go before the senate—it will all be over—for you—it would be your Rome or mine . . . your life or mine."

"Commodus, hear me well. Your Rome will never be. Either we change, or there will be no Rome at all."

Commodus shook his head, his vague gaze fixed on Livius as if he were a stranger. His voice sounded plaintive. "I loved you, Livius . . . why—no man could have loved his own brother more."

Livius breathed deeply, but did not answer.

Commodus nodded, as if reaching a decision inside his confused mind. His mouth tightened, face grim. "Your life or mine."

Livius nodded, turned on his heel, moving past Cornelius toward the exit to the courtyard. Commodus reached out his arm after him.

"Livius—"

Livius paused, glancing over his shoulder, his face agonized but chilled and determined.

Commodus' voice was soft, "The senate . . . the honorable fathers of Rome." He held this plaintive mood a moment, then tilted his head, stared at Livius and burst into laughter. "You said once you had never heard the gods laughing. . . . Then listen."

Commodus laughed again. He put his head back, letting the frenzied sound of hysterical laughter erupt from his mouth, the crazy wail echoing and re-echoing in the vast temple, seeming to come from all the heads of Commodus so strangely placed on the bodies of the old, lost gods.

XXIII

THE SENATORS arrived at the *curia* of Julius Caesar in unwilling, unhurried and ill-humored groups.

Livius stood with four young tribunes forming a semicircle behind him in a shadowed antechamber near the *curia* entrance off the forum. He watched the fathers of the empire crossing the great square, striding through the festive crowds, purple-edged togas giving them at least the look of dignity and honor. But meeting with their peers on the ap-

proach-steps or in the hallway they grumbled, questioning
any sense at all in holding an extraordinary session during
the season of Commodus' thirty-day holiday celebration.

Livius watched the men falter in the corridor, moving into
the senate chambers unsteadily, laughing and joking. Most
had come from interrupted parties on the Hill, and came
reluctantly, more than a little drunk.

Livius clenched his fists at his sides, staring across the
entrance foyer toward the antechamber where Commodus
waited with his friends, Julianus, Niger, Claudius and
Cleander among them. There was the air of a gala over
there, too. Only Commodus' gray face showed any signs of
tension at all.

The sacrifices and preliminary prayers concluded, the senate was declared in extraordinary session at the request of
the emperor, and the commander of the Roman armies,
Livius Gaius Metellus.

The senators rose from their seats, the rings of places,
three hundred set in rising tiers.

Commodus nodded toward Livius, crossed the foyer and
paused at the senate chamber entrance. Livius followed, standing behind him, watching the elders over Commodus' shoulder.

Inside the *curia* there was a frenzied sense of festival,
feverish, brightly gay, even the air itself tainted with the
heavy-sweet smell of wine. The senators were in full ceremonial dress, those who had chosen to answer the sum-
mons and show up at all.

Livius stood silently behind the emperor, waves of the
hysterical excitement flooding down upon him. He scanned
those faces anxiously, hoping to find some sign from them
that they understood the fearful gravity of the threat that
hung over Rome. But there was only laughter, whispered
joking as the senators leaned across each other to greet
friends and even enemies with a great display of elegant
warmth and pleasure.

Commodus gathered the silken folds of his toga about
him and stepped into view of the tiers of senators. When
they saw him they yelled, a roar of frantic acclaim, shrill,
as if they regretted that their voices were only human and
could supply no greater volume.

Commodus stood a moment in the thunder of cheering,

then he smiled faintly, his white face and empty eyes giving him a look of regal, infinite sadness.

The acclaim dissipated slowly as Commodus moved to the throne and seated himself, for the moment alone.

Livius, his four tribunes moving closely behind him protectively, walked out to the center of the senate forum. There was a polite cheer for the hero of the Persian campaign, but during it most of the senators were settling themselves in their places.

Livius waited until there was a strained, polite silence, broken only by sudden whispers and uncontrolled bursts of laughter. It was as quiet as it was going to be under the strange circumstances.

"Honorable fathers of Rome. I have not come here seeking power, nor do I wish it. Yet you must understand, the empire is in peril of its life. It is my desire to avoid bloodshed. It is my wish to avoid violence. It is my supreme prayer that we can change here in Rome in time to save our beloved city, and our world as we know it today."

He paused, but got no response from the senators. Their gazes were fixed on him, but showed nothing more than impatience and contempt.

"Only you—the great leaders of Rome—only you can now stop the army which is a few hours from the city. Once more Rome must speak from your lips."

A silence, like a wall of stone, greeted these words.

Livius set himself, pulling his shoulders back, tilting his head, his voice flinging his harsh challenge at them: "Caesar must be deposed."

He got a reaction now from the senators, a horrified gasp of disbelief. The fathers moved their gazes from Livius to the emperor to see how he reacted to this treasonable declaration. But Commodus was relaxed on the throne, a faint smile on his mouth, his empty eyes lost, fixed on distant thoughts as if not hearing anything Livius had said.

"Caesar must be deposed! The army has been able to put down rebellion in the East and to hold Rome together—but only long enough for Rome itself to change. Caesar has been unable to understand the terrible need for this change, unable to change himself, and so Caesar must be deposed or Rome will be destroyed. It is now up to you, clearly up to you to bring in the Rome that was the dream and ambition of Marcus Aurelius."

The senators glanced at each other, but this was their only reaction to Livius' plea.

Sweat poured along Livius' forehead. His heart beat erratically. He drew a deep breath, trying to control the irregular pounding of his heart, the spreading tension in the pit of his stomach.

He shook his head, moving his gaze across the faces of the senators, and they were like faces seen in a nightmare.

He stared at them, his voice lifting harshly, as though trying to waken them from this dream-state of unreality that seemed so serene to them and such a nightmare to him. "Hear me, fathers of Rome. The army is at the gates of the city!"

The faces of the elders remained stolid, impassive. Livius licked his dry lips, ceased speaking. He realized something was desperately wrong, as if all reason and intelligence had been removed from this august body, leaving a motley gang of clowns to simper and giggle.

He glanced around, bewildered.

Commodus moved on the throne, making the barest suggestion of a gesture with his fingers and Julianus jumped to his feet.

Livius caught his breath, hearing the stir of gracious and conspiratorial anticipation that greeted Didius Julianus. It was as if this whole affair were prearranged, even to the contempt they showed him.

Livius stared at Commodus. The emperor lounged on the throne, a dreamy, half-contemptuous smile on his face.

Julianus strode to the center of the forum. He waited, gazing at Livius with an odd, bleak smile, devoid even of recognition, until the general stepped back, yielding the floor.

Julianus stood a moment then, staring at Commodus with tears brimming his eyes. He remained so until all gazes were fixed on the emperor, and then he spoke, voice quivering with emotion, charged with ill-controlled tears.

"Glorious Caesar—who has been named Lucius Aelius, Aurelius Commodus Augustus Pius Felix—Pacifier of the Whole Earth, Invincible, and Paulus, most celebrated Secutor of the most colossal gladiators, the Roman Hercules, High Priest, Emperor—Father of Our Country—and now Conqueror of Persia—"

Livius stared at Julianus in growing horror, seeing the

bland, eager faces smugly nodding, cheering each appellation spoken by Julianus, oblivious to everything else.

Julianus bowed toward the throne. "We are convened here in extraordinary session for the one purpose, Divine Commodus, of asking a kindness of you, kindliest, most godly of all."

Commodus inclined his head in a slight nod.

"We are gathered here to beg permission of our Divine Caesar that he, in his holy grace may authorize us to proclaim that from this day forward our empire be called, not the Roman empire, but the empire of Commodus, and this city be called, not Rome, but the city of Commodus."

The chamber rang with the senators' roar of approval.

Livius, sweating, gazed about as if he found himself suddenly transported into some insane pit of hell.

Niger rose from his place among the senators, his face wreathed in smiles, and ran forward to stand beside Senator Didius Julianus.

Niger offered exultantly, "And we beg that from this day forward, we here be called not the senate—but a Commodian Body!"

Commodus nodded indulgently, smiling down upon them. "You have my permission."

The wild acclaim thundered through the *curia*.

Livius retreated a step as if he had been struck. His shoulders slumped round and he stared about him, sick with disgust, bewildered.

Commodus lifted his hand for silence and finally all sounds within the *curia* died away. Commodus glanced toward Livius and then stood up before his throne.

His voice held a strange, gentle quality, and a tone completely out of reach of reality. "Honorable fathers, you are the voice of the people of the new Rome—the city of Commodus. It is through you our empire speaks."

He nodded, glancing about them with that distant, aloof smile. "There is a matter of great importance which I wish to propose to you."

The men in the tiers of seats cheered.

"Yesterday," Commodus said in that dreamy tone, "I was served the fish which is known as 'mullet.' It was prepared in such a delicate, delicious fashion that it passed through my mind that to prepare or serve mullet in any other fashion would be a crime. I, therefore, would that you, Honorable fathers, declare it to be the law henceforth that this fish be prepared only in this manner."

The senate applauded and Julianus said with deep emotion, "It will be so recorded, Divine Caesar."

Commodus turned suddenly, the wan, lost look gone and his face hard and chilled, unsmiling. He stared across the forum space at Livius.

Livius straightened, his gaze meeting Commodus'. He was ill because for the moment Commodus had won. Even the Roman senate had been perverted, debased, demoralized. They were so spiritless they failed to see they had signed their own death warrants and sealed the doom of their existence.

Commodus gestured toward Livius and from the foyer Cornelius and Praetorian Guards appeared. They marched toward Livius and silence settled across the *curia*.

Commodus and the senators watched in silent fascination as the Praetorians moved toward Livius. They flinched, startled, when a voice rang out across the chamber, crackling like some dry whip. Even the Praetorian Guards halted, staring at the aged Senator Caecina who had walked down to the place where Julianus and Niger had stood in the center of the forum.

In the chilled silence the old senator surveyed the faces of the other politicians wrathfully, letting his fiery gaze linger accusingly on each man.

His aged voice lashed at them. "What are you? Who are you? What have you let yourselves become? Heirs of a great empire. You have here today destroyed and despoiled your heritage. You are worse than the hordes of Vandals which stand poised to the north! You are worse than all the enemies of Rome who are armed on all our frontiers. You are traitors! Traitors!

"You are traitors, each of you. Traitors not only to your nation—but betrayers of the whole civilized world and of centuries to come. Generation after generation will weep in misery and curse your memory. Cowards! You are cowards! Cowards who did not come forward when Rome called you."

He moved his bitter gaze across them. He shook his head. "I will not live to see the horror you have sown, the tumult and convulsive agony that will come after you."

The Praetorian Guards, prodded by Cornelius, moved in

on both sides of Livius and led him slowly toward the foyer.

Caecina stared at the guards surrounding Livius, heeled around, gesturing at the senate. "I will not live to see it, but you will!" He rocked himself, in terrible mourning, "Some day when the Vandals enter Rome—they will not find a city —only its tomb—for you have today killed Rome. Rome is no more!"

The old man swung around, gesturing at the senators and finally throwing out his arm, pointing at Commodus before the throne.

Julianus was standing a few feet away. He cried out in rage when Caecina pointed accusingly toward Caesar. He drew a dagger from his girdle and sprang suddenly, the knife upraised before the stunned gaze of the senate, and plunged it into the old man's back.

Caecina straightened, let his arm drop to his side. His gray head twisted, not to see who attacked him, but as if to look one last time upon the place where he had spent most of his long and honorable life. He staggered and fell.

Julianus wheeled around with the stained dagger and stood over the crumpled body. He lifted his voice, shouting, "Hail Caesar!"

There was a hesitation of less than a fraction of a second and the entire senate cried out in answer, acclaiming, "Hail Caesar!"

The Praetorians led Livius through the doorway and out of the *curia*. He glanced back only once, looking at Commodus. The cheers rang around the emperor, but Commodus, shuddering, was gazing at the dead body of Caecina.

XXIV

LUCILLA RODE in a covered imperial coach behind the legion on its forced march angling southeast across Italy toward Rome.

She leaned out of her curtained window often, glancing at the sun, at the dust and confusion ahead of her and, far in advance, the generals, Victorinus and Polybus riding hard and never even looking back.

Lucilla was tense as the coach jogged along, each passing moment increasing her tension. And she did not relax when the legions reached the Tiber and were set at once to making an encampment outside the gates of Rome.

Time seemed to spin, out of reason, on some wild caprice of the gods. There was so much that must be done, and so few hours of sunlight remaining. It made her ill to contemplate the vast space between the needed reforms and Commodus' will to alter.

Lucilla set herself tautly as if willing the sun to hang longer along the western slope of the world. But the blindingly bright orb seemed to plummet downward, and all along the east horizon dark clouds banked higher and higher as if drawing eternal darkness between earth and heaven.

She saw the staff officers, led by Victorinus and Polybus, gather at the head of the troops on the road leading into the city. She ordered her carriage driven forward. As she rode she saw the legions being brought to attention, battle-ready in wave after wave.

Victorinus glanced toward her carriage and was about to order it to the rear of the lines, when he recognized Lucilla. The officer said nothing. Polybus swung down from his horse, opened the coach door for Lucilla.

She stepped down in the waning sunlight, staring toward the tall buildings and the hills beyond the walls.

A tribune rode forward, reporting the troops ready to march. Polybus accepted the information silently, but glanced once more toward the sun, and again at the gate as if praying Livius would ride out of it.

A man spoke, pointing along the road toward the city gates. The officers leaned forward, staring, and behind them the legions stirred restlessly.

Four chariots came thundering down the road into the army encampment. Lucilla caught her breath—Livius was not among the approaching charioteers. She recognized instead, the red coats of lictors. These young officers held high for all to see the laurel branches and fasces which were symbolic of imperial power.

As they came near, racing along the roadway, the lictors shouted, proclaiming: "Claudius Marius Albinus, Envoy of the Emperor Marcus Antoninus Commodus. . . . Attend.

. . . Claudius Marius Albinus, Envoy of the Emperor Marcus Antoninus Commodus—"

Lucilla, frowning, deeply troubled, stepped forward and could see the white chariot, the white horses, the insignia of imperial Rome emblazoned on it, and Claudius holding the leather lines limply, almost daintily though his team galloped at full speed.

Behind Claudius she saw a dozen other chariots, piloted by young men very like Claudius, all laughing drunkenly, and calling out as if the thirty thousand assembled legions comprised some enormous party.

Lucilla stood unmoving as the cavalcade of chariots roared past.

She saw in the confused faces of the generals and lesser officers that they were deeply puzzled by this strange, insensate behavior. The chariots drove deep inside the ranks of the soldiers, the youths crying out to the soldiers, teasing them with offers of sensual pleasures.

Heavy rumbling sounds of wagons thundering toward the army in the wake of the chariots made Lucilla put the lictors from her mind and heel around staring at the rumbling carts.

Claudius swung his chariot around and raced back to where the silent officers stood grimly watching.

Claudius waved a parchment document, on which the seal of Caesar was clearly visible. The other chariots were swallowed up in the ranks and some of the legionnaires broke the lines, surging around the shouting, taunting youths.

Claudius shouted toward the officers, the legions behind them: "From Caesar! An urgent message from Caesar!" He waved the document. "A change of command! Gaius Livius is no longer your leader. The Roman legions have a new commander!"

There was a rustling of disorder all across the ranks as the word blazed through the legions. A new imperium. Livius no longer supreme commander.

Lucilla stood straighter, watching Claudius. She pressed her hands into the folds of her *tunica* to conceal their trembling.

Victorinus, unable to hide his own self-seeking ambition, licked at his mouth, stepped forward, gaze fixed on the document. "Who then is our now leader, Albinus Claudius?"

Claudius laughed, shouting it: "Caesar! Caesar himself!"

Victorinus paused, stunned, hearing the news spread through the ranks of the soldiers.

Claudius jerked his head around, arm stretched out toward the heavily laden carts lumbering toward them.

Lucilla bit her lip, now able to recognize on the canvas covering of the first cart, the insignia of the imperial treasury. These wagons had come from the temple of Saturn.

Claudius turned, projecting his voice across the officers toward the enlisted men. "Gold! Caesar has sent gold to pay his soldiers of Rome!"

The cry spread among the legionnaires: "Gold! Gold!"

Polybus stepped toward Claudius, shouting at him. "We have given our blood for Rome. Does your Caesar think he has enough gold to pay for that?"

An expectant silence spread over the encampment. Lucilla watched Claudius, his face wreathed in smiles of assurance and confidence—and behind him the wagons rumbling toward them. The legionnaires hesitated momentarily, watching Claudius in his chariot.

Claudius waved his scented handkerchief at the dust before his face, shouting, "Three thousand dinarii in gold for each soldier! Three thousand dinarii!"

It was as though Claudius had struck the men around Lucilla in the belly, for a sudden gasp went up from all of them as one.

Claudius laughed, seeing the way their faces lighted. "And there's more from Caesar's godly bounty. Time of army service has been cut! All men with fifteen years' service are free to retire with a grant of land!"

There was a stunned silence. Victorinus stepped forward, eyes distended, mouth parted, incredulous. "No! It is a trick!"

Claudius laughed. "It is no trick, my fair general!"

"You do not have enough gold." Victorinus shook his head. "There is not enough gold in the whole world."

Claudius swung his arm triumphantly toward the first of the loaded treasury carts. "Look! Look! See for yourself all the gold in the world!"

The wagons rumbled past at Claudius' signal, in a long, apparently unending line between the encampment and the treasury in the temple of Saturn beyond Rome's walls.

Claudius leaned forward, face bright red, throat cords

standing tense. "Enough for all! Gold! Three thousand dinarii for each man. Gold."

A thunder even louder than that of the lumbering carts and heavy dray mules rose in rowdy lawlessness as the legionnaires surged forward, completely forsaking all military discipline, rioting.

Polybus stepped close to Lucilla trying to protect her from the heedless mob running past them. Lucilla was struck, knocked against Polybus, and he set himself, legs apart, to keep from being trampled.

The legionnaires swarmed around each arriving wagon where payers from the treasury counted out the gold pieces and handed them over. The soldiers were yelling, but as each was paid, he was struck dumb, staring at the pile of gold incredulously. As they moved away from the treasury carts, fresh waves rolled forward.

Lucilla leaned against her carriage with Polybus beside her, trying to get out of the wild current of insensate soldiers. They bumped her, pushed her without seeing who she was, no longer caring.

The first hundreds of soldiers were paid and they moved past the wagons, churning about aimlessly, milling in a maze of dust and disorder. After some moments they regained the power of speech and they shouted to each other, counted their dinarii again. As they gazed at their gold they made a delirious sound, half-whining, more animal than human, a cry of exultation that filled the whole encampment, and swelled as more and more soldiers were paid and joined the commotion.

Polybus leaped up on a wagon. He shouted hoarsely toward the animal-wailing soldiers and those shouting hordes yet unpaid, "But what of the years you've given? The blood you've shed? Your comrades who have died? What have they died for?" He yelled in a fury that cut through the wailing. "Will you throw all this away? Won't you obey your officers? You are legionnaires! You are Roman soldiers!"

A centurion stared up at Polybus, spat toward him. A grizzled, battered man, he roared at his general, "I've fought seventeen years! My children are grown, and I've barely seen them! My time has come! Our time has come—and to hell with you!"

Lucilla ran forward, screaming at them. "Time? Your time? Time of betrayal! Deserters!"

Victorinus heeled around, staring at her, his face as rigid and wild as that of the centurion. "How can you call us deserters?" He waved his arm toward Claudius, the imperial treasury wagons. "We obey our Caesar!"

Polybus stared at his old friend, unable to speak. But Lucilla moved toward Victorinus. "Your Caesar! Your Caesar is buying you! I—the daughter of Marcus Aurelius —tell you—if you touch that gold you are traitors! Traitors! Traitors to Rome."

From the milling crowd someone shouted at Lucilla, vile obscenities churned in crazed laughter.

She straightened, staring at them. A rock was hurled from the rioting men. It struck Lucilla on the shoulder and she staggered back against the wagon, gasping in pain. Polybus leaped from the cart bed to her side, but she barely saw him. She grabbed the rock, hurled it back into the ferment of rioting men. A roar of anger rose from the legionnaires.

Lucilla, overcome with rage, looked around wildly. She picked up rocks, hurling them at the legionnaires.

Polybus shouted curt orders and a small group of officers ran in with him, forming a circle about her. Victorinus and the centurion, faces gray with soul-sickness, drew short swords and ran toward the circle of loyal officers.

The legionnaires went mad with a frenzy of yelling, screaming, laughing, some of them joining the savage fighting just for the sheer excitement.

Lucilla stood trembling and helpless in the center of the tumult, the small circle of officers driven back in upon itself.

Polybus turned to speak to her. But he did not utter a word. As he heeled around, an arrow transfixed him. He gasped in mortal pain, staggered under the impact and fell to his knees. Other loyal officers around him were hacked down, left wounded, and the legionnaires and commanders forgot the battle, ran to the carts still rumbling in endlessly from the treasury.

Lucilla leaned against the wagon. As far as she could see the legionnaires had broken ranks and were surrounding the treasury carts in insane confusion.

Through the maze of men she saw Claudius in his chariot. He had his handkerchief placed against his nostrils, but his eyes were bright with triumph.

Lucilla sank to her knees beside Polybus. His glazed eyes barely focused. He was dying and he spoke urgently. "Run, Lucilla. Get out of here somehow. Save yourself. . . ."

Lucilla cradled his head in her arms, whispered brokenly, "The army—the great army—this cannot be. . . . Not our army . . . my father's army." She moaned, agonized. "Oh, Romans, Romans."

Polybus gasped, face twisted. "There's nothing left. . . . Darkness. . . . Death. . . . Run—run, quickly, Lucilla. . . ."

His voice ended as blood choked him. His body moved convulsively in a death tremor. He sank heavily against her, dead.

Lucilla stayed for a moment as if buried in a tumultuous mass of seething human beings. She got to her feet, pressed against the wagon, looking around in bewilderment. Victorinus was scrambling, gouging, fighting among the enlisted men, oblivious to anything except the wagons of gold.

None of the young officers who had rallied to her side at Polybus' command were left standing. She stayed against the wagon, staring upward toward the darkening heavens as if making a solemn pledge to her gods.

She looked around, stooped down quickly and pulled Polybus' dagger from his belt. She stood up, hiding it in the folds of her robe.

She inched along the cart, around it. A few feet from her stood an empty chariot, forgotten in the triumph. The raging wail of the legions, the growl of the men still fighting to be paid, the confusion and turmoil showed how completely Commodus had triumphed.

Lucilla ran to the chariot, mounted it, catching up the lines, gazing one last time at the spectacle of a corrupted army.

She whipped the horses, wheeling the chariot about and rolling through the crowds on the road toward Rome.

XXV

THE FRENZIED caterwauling in the teeming forum outside the *curia* had the violence and turbulence of civil disorder. Livius stood surrounded by armed Praetorian Guards look-

ing out across the rowdy commotion, seeing it was not a riot
but the celebration of a soul-sick people who no longer saw
any hope beyond the public doles and public parties of this
moment.

He shook his head. Here was a people with a long and
distinguished history who could no longer stir itself to meet
one more crisis, or find any reason for looking beyond tonight. The lengthening shadows across the forum seemed bitterly symbolic to Livius, for as the sun set and darkness
spread, the cries increased, the laughter was louder, wilder,
deranged and without sanity or control.

Behind him, on the approach-steps to the *curia,* Commodus
stood in deeper shadows with Niger, Julianus and Cornelius.
They did not speak but there was an air of expectant waiting.

A cry went up across the square, and lifting his head,
Livius saw what the emperor awaited. People scrambled to
safety when a white chariot, drawn by white horses and
bearing the insignia of the imperial family, careened off
crowded Via Sacre and thundered across the forum toward
the *curia.* The startled people fell away, stunned because for
hundreds of years horse-drawn vehicles had been forbidden
on the streets of Rome until after nightfall.

Livius recognized Claudius as the charioteer. Claudius
urged the horses to the lowest steps before the *curia* and
when Commodus stepped forward from the shadows, Claudius gestured triumphantly, calling out that all was well, his
mission accomplished.

Livius, watching Commodus' face, saw the tensions ease
about the emperor's eyes and mouth.

Niger hurried down the steps to where the guards stood
with Livius. He jerked his head toward them and at the
same time spoke with overdone pleasantness to Livius, "The
sun has already set, Gaius Livius, and see, no army is marching upon Rome." He walked past, gesturing for the guards
and the prisoner to follow. "Come, General, we are taking
you—home."

Livius did not move. The Praetorians pressed toward him,
short swords drawn. He exhaled, moving inside the knot of
guards after Niger.

The Praetorian Guards opened a way through the masked
and shouting celebrants toward the center of the forum
square. Here slaves were still heaping firewood in a pyramid
pyre.

Livius faltered, staring at the stakes in the mountain of dry wood. Xenia, Ballomar, young chieftains, and the blonde child he recognized as Griselda were among the Marcomanni captives brought from the siege of Ravenna to be sacrificed in fire. Along with the barbarians were philosophers who had alienated the imperial family, slaves and freedmen of Rome who had in some way made political enemies.

Livius stood, emptily staring up at them.

Niger spoke at his shoulder, face pulled in taunting smile, "Don't you recognize them, General? They are your people. You belong with them."

Two Praetorians seized Livius, pushed him roughly toward a stake where two others expertly bound him. The guards then withdrew, faces impassive in the insensate cheering of the mob.

Livius looked about him, stunned to find the man staked beside him was a tattered, beaten senator whom he recalled as especially friendly toward Commodus' legislation. "Why have they brought you here, Cassius?"

The senator spoke quietly, lips bloodied. "We are Christians."

Involuntarily Livius recoiled, withdrawing from them; his whole training caused him to despise and shun the followers of the Galilean rabbi. The white-hot memory of the wooden cross about dead Timonides' neck flashed through his mind.

Livius stared defiantly, angered, toward the captured member of that persecuted underground sect, the Christians; they had opposed, circumvented, broken Roman law for over a hundred years; there was no more humiliating disgrace than to be executed in company with this rabble. "What have I to do with you? I am a Roman—all I have done I have done for Rome."

Cassius spoke more softly than ever, "Perhaps we did belong together, Livius, more than either of us knew. . . ."

Lucilla drew her horses to a halt just within the gates of the city, unnoticed in the frantic celebration. In the deepening shadows, she dismounted quickly from her chariot. She glanced about her, paused a moment to adjust the folds of her *palla*, carefully concealing the dagger, and then she moved quickly, almost running through the twisting, narrow street.

She turned a corner, pausing, looking both ways. As the

darkness increased she felt as if she were falling under the heavy weight of a shroud. The farther she ran from the gates the more she seemed to be running from the actual world into strange unreality, and she began to feel lost. The night-dark was like the thickening shades of fog in some nightmare place where she had never been before, and she whispered, "Oh, Livius."

She heard bursts of laughter and people spilled from the doorways of the *insulae,* hurrying past her as if she did not exist, as if she were a dark wraith in the fog and they did not see her. The streets were poorly lighted. In a way, she thought, this was a blessing, for all the flaring brightness was concentrated in the forum and she had only to keep running toward it.

Through the twisting street, she saw the brilliance of the forum, and she drew a veil across her face. She went swiftly across the dark cobblestones and rounded a turn, finding herself oddly at the foot of a small hill. She stared upward breathlessly.

She went up the gradual incline of the hill, her body feeling taut with unnamed fears and unthinkable terrors she had no words for, even in her own mind. Her nerves felt raw, exposed, and every time a hurrying celebrant bumped her she almost cried out in rage.

At the rim of the square she paused, blinking against the brilliance of lights, the thunderous sounds of people converging from everywhere.

She moved through the crowd and then stopped, seeing that an invisible line held the mob back from a huge pyre of firewood with human beings staked there for sacrifice. For a moment, horror clutched at her heart and she thought she would faint, seeing Livius staked up there with barbarians, slaves and other condemned.

She stood motionless, watching Praetorian Guards moving about the mound of firewood, pouring thick oil on the pyramid. She glanced about helpless, as if she'd walked waking into a nightmare and was unable to escape its horror. She wanted to turn and run away, somewhere, somewhere find safety and the old sanity and security she'd known in her father's world.

She walked slowly forward, staring upward at Livius. He did not see her, did not glance down at her, or any of the other gibbering, screaming people around her. His gaze was fixed on something far across the night. She turned, pushing her way through the crowd, going toward the Capitoline Hill and the temple of Jupiter overhanging the Tarpeian Rock at its summit. A mammoth idol of the god Jupiter had been brought out to overlook the jubilant celebration in the forum, and it towered there, its head lost in the darkness above.

Lucilla hurried past, staring at the temple of Vesta. She paused for a fraction of a second, murmuring a quick, silent prayer, feeling as if her lungs would burst. High above her the sacred flame burned within the serene and peaceful confines of the temple, a place where she had once sought refuge that was now forever denied her.

Lucilla hurried on, not looking back.

She leaned panting against an obelisk, sobbing for air, then moved out of the crowd, fleeing into the darkness toward the emperor's palace.

Darkness closed in around her again, and mists from some forgotten rain dripped from the eucalyptus trees as she ran across the palace grounds and moved up the wide stairs.

The Praetorians standing guard saw her coming and stiffened to attention, weapons drawn.

Reaching the head of the steps, Lucilla pulled away her veil and the startled Praetorians, recognizing her, stepped aside, permitting her to pass.

She moved into the lighted palace, half running, her veil drifting out behind her. It was as though something clamped tighter and tighter upon her the deeper she entered this gaudily lighted place. In her father's day she had looked to the palace of the emperor as a haven embodying everything that was good, but here in Commodus' world there was no strength, nothing enduring, no tenderness, compassion or security. That world was forever gone, lost, ended.

Praetorians along the corridors stepped forward, recognized her and then relaxed again, giving her a slight bow as she hurried past them.

Outside Commodus' private chambers, Lucilla stood a moment, composing herself, straightening her hair, her flowing skirts, trying to catch her breath and slow the ragged pounding of her heart. She set her head regally, pushed the door open.

The room was only dimly lighted, and the door swung open soundlessly. Lucilla stepped through, closed it behind her.

She caught her breath, startled when she saw a silhouetted figure at the half-darkened end of the room, kneeling, hunched over in brooding silence with his back to her. Commodus praying! She had not known what she might find when she entered his chambers, but to find her brother on his knees had not even entered her mind.

Before the crouched figure, lighted with the soft glow of several small oil lamps was the bust of Faustina.

The figure did not stir, and frowning, puzzled, Lucilla stood for some seconds staring at him. At last she drew the dagger from the folds of her dress and walked stealthily forward, holding her breath.

The hunched figure did not move. Lucilla crept slowly until she was directly behind him, the broad shoulders rounded, the head sunk forward in his hands.

Biting her lip, but her eyes dry and cheeks rigid, Lucilla raised the dagger high above her head and then plunged it downward.

The figure, startled by the barest whisper of air, or Lucilla's indrawn breath, or old instincts, heeled about with lightning suddenness and professional agility. A powerful arm thrust out with an unerring instinct and caught her by the wrist, stopping the blow in midair.

He came upward slowly from his knees, twisting her arm. He flung her from him and she fell half across the room, striking a wall, the breath knocked out of her. The dagger clattered to the floor, painfully loud in the silence.

She leaned against the rough texture of the wall staring at the man who had looked exactly like Commodus kneeling before the bust of Faustina. She saw now that it was not her brother at all.

It was Verulus.

Verulus was stunned, startled as she, and for a moment neither of them spoke.

Lucilla shook her head, but did not move. Her voice quavered, "I thought it was—"

"You thought I was Commodus." Verulus' gaze impaled her. He stepped toward her in the thick silence. He glanced at the dagger on the floor, looked at her again. "Commodus is your brother. Why would you slay him? Why do you hate him so? What has he done to you?"

Lucilla's head tilted, her gaze struck against his, defiantly.

"He does not deserve to live. He must not live."

She leaned forward, but the moment she started toward the dagger, Verulus anticipated her move, caught her easily, holding both her wrists as if she were a small child.

She writhed, making a desperate effort, and broke free of his grasp. She lunged for the dagger, and Verulus smiled, taunting her. He kicked the dagger away.

Lucilla stared up at Verulus, wondering how she could reach a man trained in a world without pity or compassion. "He will kill Livius." She ran again toward the dagger. "It's my only hope."

Verulus caught her effortlessly, held her dangling at the end of his scarred, muscled arm, studying her strangely.

"Livius? Why would you kill your brother to—save Livius?"

"I love him."

His voice struck at her. "Oh? So at last you know what it is to love?"

He moved his gaze across her and then thrust her from him in savage contempt. "You had no love, no forgiveness for your mother." His head lifted. "Yet you now love this —man. . . . Maybe now you understand why your mother and I—" he caught himself, stopped speaking, staring down at her.

She shook her head, her mouth twisted. "My mother? You. . . . Who are you?" She felt the sickness gorging up inside her. "What were you doing in this room? What did you know about my mother?"

He shrugged awkwardly, he was not intelligent or imaginative enough to lie well. "Once—in the arena—when I could have been killed . . . your—mother saved my life. . . . I—have thought of her often."

Lucilla stared at him, seeing that he was lying, seeing the way he had been kneeling abject, lost before the bust of Faustina—and with growing horror—she saw how much he had resembled Commodus. She had thought he *was* Commodus. She made a sound of revulsion, shaking her head. "You—were—with my mother—a lover."

"No." Verulus shook his head. "No. No."

"You . . . a gladiator . . . a killer."

He gestured bitterly toward her, his fingers splayed in tension. "A gladiator—a killer." His head came up. "Yes. Your mother loved me."

Lucilla pressed her hand over her mouth. "No . . . no."

Verulus glared as if he could read her thoughts, see the way she compared him to her brilliant and noble father. He mimicked her. "No! No! No! Why not? You think you know what it means to love? You don't! You know nothing."

Shaking her head, Lucilla backed away from him.

Verulus moved after her, stalking her. "Do you want to know what it is to love a man? You believe he must be great of mind—respected by the world? What do you know of love—of what it is and what it does to you? . . . It does not matter. Nothing counts." He stared into some past moment, musing. "Nothing counts . . . to love with an open heart." His mouth twisted as he looked Lucilla over. "There are not many in this world who can love that way." He turned, gazing at the bust of Faustina. "She knew what love was—because she was ready to give up everything for it —her palaces, her fine summer places—her silken gowns, her riches. She knew what love was.

"And I. *I* knew . . . because I loved her so much I could not bear to have her give up everything—for me. . . ."

He shook his head, his face haggard, his eyes agonized with loss. He moved his gaze across Lucilla.

"And your father knew."

Lucilla shook her head, incredulous, but Verulus' voice struck at her disbelief, ripped it away.

"Yes. He knew! Your father knew what it means to love. Because he forgave her. He took her back. He forgave her. Forgave her!" His face twisted with rage, agony and unutterable contempt for Lucilla. "You did not."

Lucilla sagged inwardly, backing away from him, trying to run away from his voice and the unbearable truth.

Verulus stood, legs apart, muscled columns, as if he were in the blood-smeared sand of the arena. He poised defiantly, stronger than the good men of this earth, but lost without the only woman he had ever loved.

"And now, as my life is coming to an end, I truly know what it is to love. . . . And I think I was wrong. . . . She and I—we should have been together—Faustina—and Commodus my son—and I."

There was a cry of outrage in the room and both Verulus and Lucilla heeled around, staring at Commodus who had run into the room. His eyes were distended, his face rutted with wild hatred and rage. He screamed at Verulus.

"You lie! You lie! My mother would not even have looked at you! You low, vile animal! No! I am not your son. I am the son of Marcus Aurelius!" He looked about distractedly, and then crouched, drawing his short sword. "I am Caesar. I have the blood of Caesar in my veins. You lie. I'll kill you. I'll kill you both!"

Commodus raised the sword and ran toward Verulus. Verulus watched him a moment and then he stepped forward in front of Lucilla. Commodus growled, raging, crying, and slashed savagely.

Verulus feinted, side-stepped the attack, grabbed Commodus by the upper arm and heaved him past him, hurling him against the wall.

Commodus struck the wall with fierce impact, thrown with all the strength in Verulus' body. His face raked along the stone, his neck snapping back. Stunned, Commodus crumpled along the wall to his knees.

Verulus gave Commodus one hasty glance. He clasped Lucilla by the hand and ran with her across the room, through the door and into the corridor.

Commodus stayed pressed a moment against the cool, rough texture of the wall, bruised, gazing with glazed eyes about him, only half-conscious. After a moment he shook his head, stared at the sword, grasped it. He leaped to his feet and ran across the room, sobbing under his breath.

XXVI

As COMMODUS ran he was barely aware of external matters—the Praetorian Guards, the startled servants in the corridors, and far along the shadowed hallway, Verulus rushing Lucilla beyond his reach.

Commodus knew people spoke to him, and lights flared into his vision and died away as he ran, but it was as if he could attend only the confusion of voices and disorder of chaotic scenes within his own mind.

He saw Verulus standing in his shadowy room. "—and

Commodus my son," Verulus had said, sending Commodus into an instant frenzy, a need to kill, destroy the man he'd loved and admired as a gladiator since his youth when he had gone to live among the gladiators on the Caelian. But his son! Commodus felt the sickness gorging up in him.

He trembled, hearing the screaming of the mob, as he had been made a god—to be worshipped by the people. What terrible irony, his being made an immortal—for he was not Marcus' son at all, but the bastard progeny of a gladiator!

His whole life had been a lie, as ugly as the truth about Faustina that he'd spent his adult years denying—to himself and to the public.

He shook his head. It had to be a lie. He held the lives of human beings in his hands—he had the power of death over millions of people. And yet which of them could he trust—which had trusted him? Just today his spies had given him a full report on lovely little Marcia. She had plotted to take his life—not because she didn't love him, but because she was afraid to trust his whims. And she had been close to him in the palace, and not alone in her plotting. With her was Eclectus, his chamberlain, and Laetus, a prefect in the castle Praetorians. Their motive? They felt the emperor must die before he decided to take their lives on some caprice. This was in the report! They planned to poison him—Marcia to administer the lethal drink, Eclectus to spirit away the corpse and the evidence, and Laetus to protect them officially. Commodus had laughed when he heard the plot. With a gesture he sent Marcia from Rome, imprisoned Laetus and ordered Eclectus executed. As simple as this—for the emperor, for the son of Marcus. Only he was not Marcus' son, he was less than Marcia!

Inside his head he heard the ringing voice of the crucified Egyptian, Appianus, hymnasiarch and priest of Alexandria, shouting in scandalous defiance when Commodus ordered him executed, "You are not emperor! The divine Marcus had every right to call himself emperor, but you have no such right—you are the antithesis of Marcus— you love vice, filth and brutality!"

Commodus moaned aloud, running. He staggered, running with the sword gripped in his fist. Clearly, he saw the storm-riven field outside Vindobona when he was in mortal combat with Livius. He had dared the gods to kill him if he were not meant to be emperor—and he had lived, almost slain Livius, with ease. But it was not the will of the gods at all, but the gods' joke, another cruel, cosmic jest of drunken gods.

How the world—through all time—would laugh and scorn the name of Commodus—the immortal! Commodus the bastard son of a gladiator caught in the bed of the empress!

He lifted his head, hearing shouting, frenzied screams below him in the forum. He could not let the world learn the truth about him. Perhaps he could yet defeat the gods, keep Rome from learning the truth, if he could kill Verulus and Lucilla.

This was the answer.

This was the only answer, the only way he could save his soul and his sanity. They had to die, he could not let them live with this filthy knowledge.

Verulus and Lucilla ran toward the mob fermenting inside the forum, Verulus hoping to find haven among the hundreds of thousands of milling, screaming citizens.

The great square was lighted by immense torches. Alongside the huge statue of the goddess Cybele—mother of all things—could be seen columns topped by the heads of Commodus. Standing on each side of the goddess, two actors on stilts, each wearing an enormous mask, were executing routines.

Verulus roughly cleared a way for him and Lucilla through the rim of the churning crowd. He glanced over his shoulder, his face paling. Behind them the crowd was magically giving way as they recognized the purple robes and gold laurel crown of the emperor. Commodus, sword in hand, followed by troubled Praetorians, plunged into the crowd. Verulus paused, looking around helplessly, more desperate than he had ever been as a *retari* in the arena.

Lucilla, gasping for breath, gestured toward the temple of Vesta. Verulus nodded and, clinging to her hand, fought his way through the crowd toward the sacred sanctuary.

Lucilla was staggering, breathless as they reached the steps of the great temple of the virgins. Verulus suddenly thrust her up the steps ahead of him.

For a moment off-balance, Lucilla stared up at five vestals who appeared as if in a miracle at the head of the steps.

Then hearing Verulus' cry, Lucilla jerked her head around as Commodus overtook them.

She saw the gray agony in Verulus' scarred, rigid face. The survivor of hundreds of battles in hot arenas now tried to confront his beloved son, unarmed.

Verulus whirled, trying to speak to Commodus.

Commodus lunged forward. His sword was driven through Verulus' body. Verulus, mortally wounded, staggered back his full length and then fell halfway up the temple steps.

Lucilla ran up the steps.

Commodus paused for only one moment, staring down at Verulus, then he followed Lucilla, his sword dripping blood.

When Commodus reached the top step the chief vestal stood before him.

Commodus hesitated, holding the bloodied sword. The other vestals joined her and they remained in a semicircle, faces expressionless. Suddenly, Commodus shook his head, backed away, plodded into the crowd and disappeared, swallowed up in it.

Lucilla stared down at Verulus. His gaze was fixed on her, his arm outstretched toward her in an imploring gesture.

Lucilla stood unmoving, unrelenting, staring at the fallen gladiator, but seeing the way Faustina, dying, had reached out beseechingly toward her like this—forgive, forgive, forgive.

Lucilla, her eyes bleak, brimmed with tears, tilted her head. Then she saw the dying athlete's hand slipping downward. Lucilla moved down the steps, knelt beside Verulus.

He opened his eyes. They were pale with death, already glazed. He whispered, "Lucilla . . . Do not hate me . . . do not hate your mother."

Lucilla cradled the dying man's head in her arms. She sobbed brokenly, and whispered, "I no longer hate her. . . . I don't hate you. . . . It is *you* who must forgive me. . . . Verulus, forgive me. . . ."

Verulus' eyes widened and he looked at her strangely, a smile spreading across his rugged features. Slowly his hand reached up and touched her cheek, tenderly. He moved his gaze across her, awed. "Yes. You look like her. Now you

look like Faustina . . . with an open heart—for love. . . .
Now you will know love."

He cried out and Lucilla tightened her arms about him.
She felt the death tremor, heard the death rattle and he
died. Lucilla cried, looking up from her mother's dead lover
to the compassionate faces of the five vestals.

Livius stared across the swirling mob beneath the pyre
where he was chained near Xenia and Ballomar toward
the dark skies of the north. A sudden silence settled over
the assemblage and from the silence erupted a tumult of
brassy music. The crowd stirred, a thrill of anticipation
shooting through the square. The music and screams grew
louder. The crowd parted in awe to make way for a procession of priests carrying whips, their faces painted in
grotesque colors, their half-nude bodies lacerated from
savage, self-inflicted flagellation.

Livius stared down from the pyre as the frenzied priests
came near, whipping themselves. All around them was a
thunder of drums, clashing of cymbals, dissonant blaring
of horns.

A file of slaves pulled frightened animals for sacrifice,
calves, raging bulls, struggling rams. The cries of the animals
added to the fantastic bedlam. The procession crossed the
square and halted before the god Jupiter.

The crowd quieted again, row after row of masks, strange,
alien faces settling into a profound silence. The masked
actors, towering on their stilts, with built-in megaphones
amplifying their voices, giving them an unworldly tone,
spoke, declaiming in perfect unison: "Know then that before all else was the god Saturn, god of time, from whom
come all yesterdays and todays, and from whom will come
all tomorrows. There came into being Cybele, the Mother
Earth Goddess, who gave birth to many sons."

The actors gestured and all eyes turned toward the
Mother Goddess, and the crowd moaned.

"And as this day consumes the day which came before,
so will this today be consumed by tomorrow and so it
was that the god Saturn consumed each son that Mother
Goddess gave him, eating them that they might not menace
him."

The moans of the crowd grew in depth and intensity.
Suddenly, the lower part of the Mother Goddess was

thrown open, and Commodus, wearing the costume of the god Hercules, appeared, holding high a flaming torch.

The crowd gasped, pressing back in awe at the sight of their young Caesar emerging from the goddess.

The masked actors declaimed, "Then was our god Jupiter born and our Mother Goddess ordained the clash of hollow cymbals and of hoarse-throated horns, so that the cry of her son might not be heard by the fierce Saturn. . . . Thus was our god of Rome saved. Thus was our god born."

The musicians broke into an orgy of dissonant sounds which grew in loudness and intensity as Commodus, burning torch held high, walking at first slowly and then increasing his pace, made his way toward the staked people to be sacrificed on the pyre.

The crowd stirred as if holding its breath. Abruptly, the music ceased, and the crowd, troubled, puzzled, turned and looked around. Some of them cried out as Lucilla and the five vestal virgins moved from the temple and formed a human barrier between Commodus and the pyre.

Commodus hesitated for a moment, confronted by the silent line of priestesses. The mob waited tensely, watching Commodus.

Commodus glanced around, gestured. A group of half-naked gladiators appeared at his command. He jerked his head toward the line of women. The gladiators walked toward the vestal virgins. The crowd gasped in horrified disbelief, and the gladiators slowed, hesitant when the vestals did not even flinch.

Commodus made an angry, threatening movement toward them and the gladiators advanced. They caught the women and hurled them aside. The mob growled, a roar of anger, incredulity, as the gladiators roughly forced the vestals back from the pyre, clearing the path between Commodus and the mound of firewood below the staked-out human sacrifice.

Commodus strode forward with the flaming torch. Lucilla screamed his name, fought, trying to run to Commodus, but the gladiators restrained her. And for the moment Commodus was forgotten as a woman screamed, wailing, pointing toward the temple of Vesta: "The sacred flame has died!"

All eyes turned, staring at the darkened temple.

Though the immense torches set all about the forum

glowed as brightly as ever, it was as if a sudden darkness had fallen over the square. The mob, suddenly milling in chaos, roared and moved like an avalanche toward Commodus at the rim of the pyre.

Commodus raised the torch to toss it on the mound of wood. He turned, seeing the raging people bearing down on him, shook his head, recoiling, visibly trembling.

The Praetorians ran between Commodus and the mob, joining the gladiators around him.

Commodus hurled the flaming torch. It landed well up the side of the pyre and the oil-soaked wood burst into flames.

Lucilla screamed, broke away from the knot of vestals and rushed toward the flaming pyre.

At the pyre, Lucilla fought her way to Livius, worked frantically at the cords. Behind them, around them, the flames were consuming the dry wood, bursting and crackling, leaping upward. The bound prisoners screamed in terror as the fire reached them. Below them the crowd rushed forward, overwhelming the gladiators and Praetorians surrounding Commodus.

Commodus broke away from the guards, ran, merging into the mob.

The cords fell away and Livius was freed. With Lucilla, he worked frantically unchaining those nearest to him, Ballomar, Xenia, the child Griselda. But the flames became too thick, and Lucilla choked, half-blinded, overcome by smoke, swayed and almost fell forward into the fire. Livius, heeling around, caught her up in his arms, carried her away into the rioting mob, unnoticed in its frenzy.

Livius kept walking with Lucilla clinging to him until they reached the safety of a dark corner outside the square.

Kneeling there beside her, Livius saw others running from the mob and recognized Ballomar and other barbarian women and children.

Xenia was not with them and Livius turned toward the pyre. He saw her, caught in the flames, unable to get away from the stakes now surrounded by bursting fires.

Livius leaped up, ran through the crowd, fighting at them, aware suddenly of someone running beside him. He glanced over his shoulder. It was Ballomar.

The flames were mountainous. Livius was unable to see anything and the heat was intense, unbearable. But he ran through it, Ballomar beside him. Ballomar was coughing, roaring like an animal.

Livius reached Xenia first, stumbling. Xenia extended her arms to him, sobbing, her clothing and body afire. Livius caught her up and, with Ballomar half-pushing them, ran through the flames.

Livius kept walking until they reached the shadowed area near the place where he had brought Lucilla. Ballomar spoke his name. Livius paused, gently put Xenia down.

Ballomar knelt on his knees beside the girl. Livius heard h / enraged growl. Ballomar looked up, gestured helplessly ..iat Xenia was dead.

Behind them there was a roar as the pyre collapsed, consumed in flames, swallowing women, children, martyrs on the mound. Livius turned away, shuddering. Lucilla buried her head in her hands.

The raging fire, the screams of the mob increased. A man ran toward the square shouting, "The army! The army is in Rome!"

Inside the forum the mob yelled and turned to where Commodus had mounted a rostrum gesturing, swinging his arms. "Soldiers! Rome is yours!"

Livius stared at the emperor across that sea of humanity, at Xenia's dead body and Ballomar bending over her. He glared around him, found a discarded sword. He ran to it, picked it up. He hefted it a moment, staring at Commodus, and then he plunged into the crowd, fighting his way through it.

XXVII

THE MOB inside the torch-lighted forum seemed to contract, to draw in upon itself as the legionnaires, led by Victorinus, and drunk with gold and wine, streamed in from every avenue.

The drunken soldiers had looted as they advanced. They staggered from the great halls of the *basilicae*, carrying their booty. Much of it was useless to them, but they did not care; all that mattered was that they smash and destroy all that had symbolized authority in a time that was dying, that they themselves were slaying in the spreading civil disorder. Rome would lie like a helpless wino in a gutter in the years to come, battered and robbed and pillaged and raped by all who came upon it, prostrate—but the end was being accomplished here and now by the Romans themselves.

Drunkenly, the soldiers thrust forward, and finding they had reached the square they glared about for anything that could be torn down and smashed.

Victorinus, carrying his sword, leather money bag secured to his girdle, turned in the wild, raging storm of noise. His gaze struck the *tabularium*—the hall of records. He shouted to the soldiers around him, and they followed him, carrying with them a crust of pillaging citizens.

They swarmed up the steps and through the great doors at the hall of records, wrecking, toppling statues, bookshelves, and rushing out of the building with books, scrolls, documents piled high in their arms. The soldiers lurched across the square and hurled the documents on the flaming pyre, watching with raging laughter as the fires spun higher, feeding on the accumulated wisdom of ten centuries.

Back across the square, smoke spiraled from the hall of records, and the huge building was ablaze. Soldiers, carrying torches, ran from the burning hall, moved to the *comitium*.

Running through the mob, pushing his way between them, Livius saw the fires spreading from the *tabularium*. It no longer seemed to matter, all that had meaning inside this sick city was already destroyed. He pulled his gaze from the fires, seeking Commodus.

He saw the emperor standing on the stone rostrum, no longer speaking, but watching the fires, the wreckage of the arches, temples, columns, obelisks that had stood as monuments to Rome's past and its glory. Nothing showed in his face. Reflected fires leaped in his distended eyes.

As if moved by some inner instinct for danger which may have been acutely trained in the gladiator arenas, Commodus turned his head, looking down. He found Livius in the rioting crowd moving towards him inexorably.

Commodus took a backward step, looked about in panic. Suddenly he lunged outward from the rostrum into the crowd, fighting his way through them.

Livius hesitated, Commodus momentarily lost in the confusion and chaos, and then, as if guided by some instinct of the soldier, he pushed his way savagely forward through the crowd.

Commodus, his laurel crown gone, his toga thrown away, crouched, running through the mob, glancing back over his shoulder.

Breathlessly, Commodus burst out of the crowd near the huge statue of the goddess Cybele. He ran up the stone steps behind the goddess, and in a deserted, shadowy corner, toppled against a wall, gasping for air, sighing out in deep relief.

He shivered, hackles rising along his neck, and he realized instinctively that he was not alone in this dark place as he'd thought.

Slowly, he swiveled his head and only managed to stifle an outcry when he saw Livius standing in the deeper shadows waiting for him.

Commodus gave a cry of anguish and heeled around. He bolted into the small doorway, going inside the statue.

He ran to the ladder inside the idol, glanced over his shoulder as he scrambled frantically upward.

Livius ran through the door, stood for a moment on the vaguely lighted base of the idol. He caught the ladder, climbing upward behind Commodus.

Commodus leaped off the ladder on an upper level, caught his balance, turned and slashed out at Livius.

Livius countered the blow with his sword, climbing quickly, pulling himself up on the level with Commodus, a small wooden platform lighted by a single oil lamp.

Their grotesque shadows lunged and parried and advanced and retreated as they fought in the semi-gloom.

Attacking wildly, sobbing for breath, Commodus knocked over the small lamp, spilling the oil and floating wick, dashing the platform into darkness.

They hesitated a moment, unable to see in the sudden blackness. Commodus recovered first, glimpsed the form of Livius and sprang toward it, thrusting with his sword.

Brought close in the darkness, they faced each other. Fearful as he had been as a child wakened in the night, Commodus whimpered, almost forgetting where he was, feeling he was having another evil dream. He could cry out and they would come to him. They never let him be frightened in the dark, or hurt. And the best of all was Livius—no one ever had a better friend than Livius. A few years older, but kindly, understanding, full of laughter and strength. Commodus cried out, in that fleeting fraction of a second making a gesture of recognition, of love, saluting, and a remembrance of his childhood, the good days with Livius.

Then the riotous noises from the square outside the idol, the striking of swords brought it all flooding back to him, with sweat sticky on his body from the heat and terror in the blackness of this dark place.

Commodus panted, whispering, "Whatever I did—was for Rome."

He felt the slash of Livius' sword in the darkness.

Commodus' breathing was harsh, his voice rising. "Rome. For Rome—I even let them—kill my father—" He heard the sharp cry of rage from Livius and his voice sank, almost inaudible. "For Rome . . . for the good of Rome."

Livius advanced upon him. "What kind of Rome could that be, Commodus—that in its name—you—could kill Marcus Aurelius?"

"It was for Rome! For the good of Rome!"

Commodus swung the sword, trying to break the terrible forward striding of the soldier. They did not speak again, only the clash of metal broke the sudden, strange silence. An odd aura of peace seemed to have enveloped them, suspending them from all other sounds; even the rioting outside the huge idol had grown distant, indistinct.

Commodus struck out at Livius, feeling his sword rake a fraction of an inch past the soldier's body. It was not enough. They were in a death combat, and Commodus knew he should have killed Livius before—in that other time—on the stormy plains outside Vindobona. It was too late now; the gods were no longer with him. He was already dead, even their own hoarse panting lacked reality for him, seeming to come from some other source, from a place where he no longer could return.

Commodus felt the chill of sweat, the chill certainty of death. This was a new feeling for him, but he recognized it. He was going to die. Livius was going to kill him and there was no way he could stop it, or delay it.

Commodus shook his head, retreated one step, dropped his sword and opened his arms wide. The weapon clattered to the wooden scaffolding and then fell away in the darkness.

Commodus never heard it strike the concrete base of the idol. Livius, the fury of the battle still on him, did not realize that Commodus had thrown away his sword or that he was coming toward him now with his arms out as if to embrace him.

Livius thrust forward and his sword pierced Commodus' body. Commodus continued to walk slowly forward. He brought his arms up woodenly, embracing Livius, frantically, in the frightened way he had clung to him as a child, asking for reassurance, gazing into Livius' face, begging for forgiveness.

Livius let go of the sword, embracing Commodus. He held him for a moment, hearing the death rattle in the emperor's throat, feeling the way his body trembled. Commodus sagged against him and Livius tried vainly to hold him up, but Commodus was dead.

In the riotous disorder and chaos of the forum, Lucilla frantically fought her way through the crowd as if in a maze. A cry of alarm broke through the violent shouting, and then a silence followed in its wake all the way across the square.

Lucilla hesitated, slowing.

She caught her breath, staring as the lower half of the statue of Cybele opened. People pressed forward around her, surging towards the idol.

Livius, holding the dead body of Commodus in his arms, emerged from the lower half of the statue.

Livius knelt on the concrete platform, placed the body of the emperor before the multitude of upturned faces.

Voices cried out, and other voices joined, chanting in a mournful wail: "Caesar is dead. Caesar is dead."

The cry spread over the square. At first there was a note of agony in the outcry, "Caesar is dead." But as the call reached the far rim of the mob and echoed back, it had a new quality, an insane roar of release, of triumph. "Caesar is dead!"

The mob writhed and whipped about like some mammoth serpent, then broke into thousands and hundreds of thousands of parts, a million serpents spreading out in a new rioting and insane destruction of everything in sight.

Lucilla pushed forward, going past the screaming people toward the statue of the goddess.

Livius was still bowed over Commodus' body when Lucilla came running to him. He stood up, not seeing her at once, standing over the dead Caesar in a churning sea of lawless rioting.

Lucilla closed her hands on his arms, forcing him to face her. He stared at her, his face gray and then he pulled her against him, holding her. The crowd swept past, leaving the forum, looting all the temples and buildings and places of business.

There was quiet about the shadowed base of the huge statue, and Livius held Lucilla as Cornelius, Cleander, led by Lentulus, Victorinus, and drunken legionnaires with a contingent of Praetorian Guards hurried toward him.

Cornelius' face showed his thought process; he was the most powerful man in the world at the moment. Only the Praetorian Guards stood between Rome and total ruin, and he was the commander of the guards, supreme in this new order.

Victorinus stared at Lucilla and Livius coldly, appraisingly, waiting for Livius to accuse him of the treachery he inwardly admitted. But Livius did not speak.

Cornelius gestured toward the flames and destruction. He spoke with the quiet detachment of the professional official. "We'll let them burn a few things—get rid of a lot of outdated buildings and give them a chance to get this violence out of their systems. . . . We can handle them. We'll move in on them and restore total peace in a few hours. We—" He gestured toward Cleander and Victorinus. "We're in charge now."

He waited, but neither Livius nor Lucilla answered.

Cornelius smiled strangely. "We've been talking, we've been looking around for someone we could place on the throne, Livius. Do you understand what we mean? Someone whom the people would readily accept." He nodded. "You would be an acceptable candidate, Gaius Livius. Hero of the Persian Wars. We might even arrange a triumph for you in the next weeks. They would accept you, loved by Marcus Aurelius. We could even say that it was you whom Marcus Aurelius truly wished to succeed him."

Livius gazed at Cornelius, then let his eyes touch Cleander and Victorinus. He felt Lucilla draw closer against him. He said, "And you—what would you want?"

Cornelius shrugged. "For each Praetorian Guard ten thousand dinarii."

Victorinus stepped forward. "For each soldier—an additional five thousand dinarii."

"And for you—for yourselves?" Livius said.

Cleander said, "For us? Only the right to handle all the grain of Rome—"

"No," Livius said. "No, I don't think you'd find me suitable."

"Why not?" Cornelius' face was rigid.

Livius exhaled heavily. "Because my first official act would be to have the three of you crucified."

Victorinus swore and clutched at his sword.

Livius stepped away from Lucilla, bloody sword in hand. Cornelius spoke sharply to Victorinus, and the soldier hesitated, glancing around.

Didius Julianus, out of breath, face flushed with excitement, ran up the steps to them. He stared at Cornelius, Cleander and Victorinus, did not even glance toward the body of Commodus beneath them.

He was panting, barely able to speak. "It's true then? Caesar is dead?"

Cornelius gestured toward the body on the concrete slab. Julianus then gave his old friend one hasty glance, lifted his head quickly, watching Cleander and the Praetorian chief.

Victorinus let his hand slip away from his sword. There were more urgent matters to attend to than the slaying of his former commander—they were auctioning off the crown of Caesar and he wanted his share of the spoils.

Livius, seeing the three leaders were concentrating on Senator Didius Julianus, touched Lucilla's arm. They retreated into the shadows, stood waiting for an opportunity to escape.

Before Julianus could speak, Niger arrived breathlessly, hastened up the steps.

Niger smiled broadly at Cornelius, barely glanced at the body of the dead emperor, but when he saw Julianus he stopped cold. Julianus and Niger glared at each other with hatred in their eyes, whatever had gone between them in the years before forgotten and soured.

Cornelius bowed toward Niger, voice persuasive. "Julianus offers us one million five hundred thousand dinarii for the throne."

Lucilla caught her breath, standing hidden, watching, listening, as the empire was being haggled for. Livius touched her arm, warningly.

Niger was pale. He glanced at Didius Julianus, then said, "I'll offer one million seven hundred and fifty thousand dinarii."

"Two million two hundred thousand dinarii!" Julianus bid.

There was a pause. Niger shifted uncomfortably, and Julianus stared at him, smiling coldly.

Cornelius said, "You'll have to do better than that." He smiled, encouraging them. "Just think. The throne. Emperor of the whole Roman empire. The greatest empire the world has ever known—from Britain to Egypt—from the Euphrates to Spain."

Julianus nodded, voice hoarse. "Three million dinarii."

Niger cried out, "I'll offer—"

"Wait!" Julianus shouted. "I have not completed my bid. Three million dinarii and the grain monopoly."

Niger swung around in a fury. "You do not have that much money. Liar! You lie. You rot! You liar!"

Niger sprang at Julianus, catching him at the throat, choking him. Victorinus and Cornelius stepped between, separating the two senators roughly.

Livius caught Lucilla's arm, drawing her after him into the darkness. As the men raged behind them, they reached the square. They did not look back, went running toward the shadows outside the blazing forum.

XXVIII

LIVIUS WALKED slowly beside Lucilla in the darkness along the road toward the Tiber.

They did not speak. Once in a while Lucilla looked over her shoulder at the glow from the fires inside the walls. The road was littered with debris, and many other people, fleeing from the civil insurrection, passed them running away in the cover of darkness. They did not see any legionnaires; all the soldiers had either deserted, or joined in sacking the city. Up ahead were knots of refugees along the misted banks of the river.

Livius felt a sense of desolation, a depression that would not lift. Lucilla touched his hand, clinging to him, but even the thought that they were together, free and alive, did not revive his hopes. Where would they go—where in the world was there a place for them now? It seemed they had left behind all their hopes in the plundered rubble of the burned city back there. Ahead was only the dark river, and darkness beyond it.

He did not try to fool himself: the world as he and Lucilla knew it was no more, it had gone up in the smoke of the burned city. It was over, ended. How much longer the physical empire existed did not matter; his world ended in fire tonight. How could such an empire, overwhelming in strength and riches, have crumbled like this?

He did not know, there was no simple answer. No one man, no one group of men could be held responsible, no single chain of events had caused its downfall. Hundreds of years from now, Livius thought, historians would still be digging through the ruins of this civilization trying to find the answers. Were there any neat, positive answers? Livius saw none, just as he saw no hope for the western Roman empire ever rising from this collapse. The historians would blame slavery, the way it affected enterprise and self-reliance; even the blight of the Black Death brought to Rome by its conquering armies would be cited as a cause; they would note the stagnation of invention and industry, failures in education, political and military weaknesses, corruption, crippling taxation, apathy on the part of the people burdened by taxes and exploited by their rulers, discontented allies, fears of neighboring states, and self-seeking leaders. Reasons. Reasons. Causes. But nowhere any hope, and no reason to look beyond the black darkness of the river.

However, when Livius reached the banks of the Tiber, he breathed deeply, the air no longer heavy with smoke, and though he was deadly tired, he felt too a surge of strength even though he did not understand it.

Once in a classroom he had studied about the Tiber—the way it flowed, swift, turbulent, clotted with mud brought down from its mountain sources and carried eternally across the plains and the marshes and salt flats out to the sea. The river had been there in antiquity and it would flow into some future he could not even foresee. It belonged to the earth itself, and to the universal things that persisted. The river

would persist, and the earth would, and life. Somehow.
Somehow.

His shoulders sagged, and he stood beside the river, and
felt Lucilla, breathless, at his side.

In the darkness he saw Ballomar, carrying the body of
Xenia, along with other young barbarians who had escaped
the sacrificial fires in the forum, a few women and the
young, blonde Griselda.

Livius shivered. He had saved the child's life one night
in a Marcomanni village. What favor had he done her? He
had saved her from a Roman javelin so she could see Roman
inhumanity and Roman treachery.

Ballomar walked to the brink of the river and placed
Xenia's body gently on the ground. He stood over her, gazing
out across the dark water.

A young chieftain faced north, arms raised above his head.
His voice rose. "Oh great god Wotan! Never again will we
abandon you. Once more will we be your warriors. On the
body of this princess of our people we swear and vow it.
We will avenge you. We will avenge you. We will join with
the Vandals. We will join with all enemies of Rome. We will
not rest until all of Rome is in ashes."

Ballomar did not move. The young chieftain glanced at
the aging leader, at the other younger men. He turned, moving away. Ballomar and several others did not move.

The young chieftain spoke to Griselda. She went to him.
She stared at Ballomar, and for a moment toward the fires
of Rome, a yearning and a terrible loss in her young face.
Then she stepped close within the circle of the young chieftain's arms. She was going with him, Livius saw, back to the
north country where she would forget all Timonides' gentle
teachings at Ravenna. Griselda would not come back here,
but her children would come, and her children's children—
in war bonnets, with painted faces and inbred hatreds.

His arm about Griselda, the young chieftain spoke challengingly to Ballomar: "You will not go back north with us?"

Ballomar shook his head. "No."

"What will you do? Where will you go?"

"Not with you," Ballomar said. "We seek peace."

The young chieftain stared at Ballomar as if the elder had
become contagiously infected with the soul-sickness of the
Roman people. He waited another moment and then strode

away into the darkness, going toward the bridges and the land to the north.

Livius found a crowded boat, going downriver, and with Lucilla he sat in its prow, watching the red sky over the city recede in the darkness. He sighed, feeling that deep melancholy. All they had fought for, all they believed in, lost and forever gone. Yet they had tried. As a soldier he knew even when the battle was lost, the soldier had the sense that he had given his all, and it was no small thing to know you had tried.

In the silence there was only the desolation of a crushing defeat, and yet when he held Lucilla close he felt at peace—for the first time in only the gods knew how many years.

Lucilla cried softly against him. "I can't help crying—yet as long as you love me, there is hope. I remember my father used to talk about a dream of his—the time would come when the sun would not rise—and we would live out our lives like that—in darkness. Is that all there is, Livius? Is that all there is for us?"

Livius drew her closer. The wind across the water was chill. He held her, thinking about Marcus Aurelius, his persistent dream of a world in darkness, and then he remembered the gentle Timonides—and the crude cross about his throat—and the answer he always had for Aurelius when the great man was troubled, apprehensive in the dark. Timonides had said, "The sun always rises—and will always rise . . . and there will be no day without hope, no day when the sun does not rise."

Livius did not speak, but he looked forward, around the next bend in the river, over the nearest hill, or beyond the horizon where the first radiant streaks of a new sun speared light distantly through the darkness.